HOW TO LEAD A LIFE OF CRIME

A TIMES BESTSELLING AUTHOR
KIRSTEN MILLER

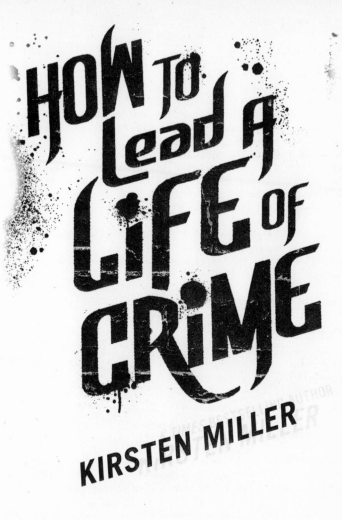

HOW TO LEAD A LIFE OF CRIME

KIRSTEN MILLER

razOr bill

An Imprint of Penguin Group (USA) Inc.

How to Lead a Life of Crime

RAZORBILL

Published by the Penguin Group
Penguin Young Readers Group
345 Hudson Street, New York, New York 10014, U.S.A.
Penguin Group (USA) Inc., 375 Hudson Street, New York, New York 10014, U.S.A.
Penguin Group (Canada), 90 Eglinton Avenue East, Suite 700, Toronto, Ontario, Canada
M4P 2Y3 (a division of Pearson Penguin Canada Inc.)
Penguin Books Ltd, 80 Strand, London WC2R 0RL, England
Penguin Ireland, 25 St Stephen's Green, Dublin 2, Ireland (a division of Penguin Books Ltd)
Penguin Group (Australia), 250 Camberwell Road, Camberwell, Victoria 3124, Australia
(a division of Pearson Australia Group Pty Ltd)
Penguin Books India Pvt Ltd, 11 Community Centre, Panchsheel Park, New Delhi – 110 017,
India
Penguin Group (NZ), 67 Apollo Drive, Rosedale, Auckland 0632, New Zealand
(a division of Pearson New Zealand Ltd)
Penguin Books (South Africa) (Pty) Ltd, 24 Sturdee Avenue, Rosebank, Johannesburg 2196,
South Africa

Penguin Books Ltd, Registered Offices: 80 Strand, London WC2R 0RL, England

10 9 8 7 6 5 4 3 2 1

Copyright © 2013 Kirsten Miller

ISBN 978-1-59514-518-5

Library of Congress Cataloging-in-Publication Data is available

Printed in the United States of America

CHAPTER ONE

TRICKS OF THE TRADE

My father never wasted his wisdom on me. But on the rare occasions when my family found itself in one room, and my father had emptied the drink in his hand, he would sometimes offer a piece of advice to my brother.

"In this world, Jude, there are only the weak and the strong," he liked to say—and no matter how much Scotch was in him, he never slurred his words. "If you're born weak, you need to suffer before you grow strong. And those of us who are strong should fight every day to avoid growing weak. Never show mercy to anyone who refuses to suffer or fight. They're inferior beasts, and the world would be better without them."

By the time he finished, his gaze would have settled on me. That was my cue to leave the room as quickly as possible. If I was lucky, I'd make it out of the door in time.

I thought my father was a monster. And he is. But that doesn't mean he was totally wrong.

• • •

I can see the truth from where I'm standing now: in a darkened doorway that's been used as a urinal by every drunk on the block. The stench doesn't bother me that much anymore. It's surprising what you grow used to. But after two hours of watching, the cold has finally seeped into my bones. This is the first winter I've spent outdoors, and I'm still learning how to survive in the wild. Most of the time, I'd force myself to stay put and endure the discomfort. But no one with a pocket worth picking has passed by my hiding spot, and I was just getting ready to call it a night.

Then a small group of girls began spilling out of an otherwise empty bar across Clinton Street. They're the kind of females my father would call *does*. When I first heard him say it, I thought he meant *Jane Does*. Girls so bland and desperate to blend in that it's almost impossible to tell them apart. But now I suspect that my father meant *deer*. Big-eyed creatures with vacant expressions. The sort that travel in herds and don't always have enough sense to run when they should.

These particular girls have downed so many drinks that they couldn't flee if they felt the urge. I'm choosing my mark when one of the few cabs working on Christmas Eve turns down the street. Four giggling females pile in. When the taxi pulls away, I'm pleased to see that one of the does has been left behind. I don't think she notices that her friends have abandoned her. Her eyes are closed, and she's blissfully swapping spit with a man she just met.

That's only a hunch, of course. But I doubt she's ever laid eyes on loverboy during daylight hours. The sight of him would be enough to spook the dumbest of does. He's at least ten years older,

2

and he comes from one of the boroughs where bodybuilding and hair gel never go out of style. But this isn't some Guido who took a wrong turn on his way to the nightclub. This guy's slick-looking and sober. He's a professional—the sort who always knows what he's doing. I'd bet he's dangerous. He might even be deadly. And she's drunk enough to find him irresistible.

I know what he sees in her, too. He sees a rich girl who won't say no. He sees pricey jewelry and a handbag whose contents could pay all of his bills for the next three months. At best, he'll leave her somewhere on Christmas morning with a bad memory and a blistering case of herpes. The worst that could happen depends on the limits of loverboy's imagination.

I cross the street and make my move. I don't hurry, and I don't try to hide. I just keep my face turned away from the security cameras mounted outside the bar. The girl's body is pressed against loverboy, and her handbag is resting against the small of her back. The zipper is open. If she just paid for drinks, then her wallet's on top. It's easy—too easy. I require more of a challenge. My left hand dips into her bag as I pass by. As soon as my fingers find what they're after, I purposely bump her.

She's too drunk to notice, but loverboy catches on quick.

"What the . . ." he growls as I stroll down the sidewalk with the girl's wallet clutched in my hand.

"Yes?" I wait until I'm half a block away before I turn—just beyond the cameras' range. I see him push the girl to one side. She stumbles and bounces off a wall. He's an unnaturally large and angry specimen. I'd love to ask which steroids he uses.

"Give me the wallet, you faggot!"

"Faggot?" I grin and give him a saucy wink. "I never knew 'roid rage made you *witty*!"

As he charges toward me, I quickly tuck the wallet into the waistband of my jeans. I'll need both hands free in a moment. When the man realizes I'm not going anywhere, he stops and laughs.

"You should've run." What he means is that he's going to enjoy what happens next. The girl giggles nervously in the distance.

"We'll see about that."

His fist hits the side of my face with the force of a wrecking ball. The pain blinds me for a second or two. I can feel blood oozing from a gash in my cheekbone. I know I'm going to need stitches, so I don't bother trying to wipe it away. When my sight returns, I can see that he's surprised I'm still standing. I'm not surprised at all. One of the first things I ever learned was how to take a punch.

"I think you can do better than that. How about a mulligan?" I ask. He doesn't understand. "A *do-over*, you douchebag."

The fist only grazes my temple this time. I've unnerved him.

"Nice try," I say. "My turn."

I feel his nose break with my first punch. He falls shortly after the fourth. My right hand is slick, and the air reeks of blood. When I look up, I find the girl frozen in place. Her big doe eyes don't even blink.

"Call him an ambulance," I say. "Then find a cab and get the hell out of here."

"You took all my money," she says, her voice both a whisper and a whine.

"Then you'll just have to walk," I tell her.

• • •

I never set out to be a thief. I suppose I once had something grander in mind. But when you live on the streets, you find out that your career options are limited. You can be one of the kids who disappear with the strangers who cruise through every night. You can sell the stuff that helps those kids forget what they've seen. Or you can be a thief. If those choices don't suit you, you can always be dead.

I was on a Greyhound traveling up I-95 when I discovered the gift that would save my life. I'd spent my last dime on the bus fare. My stomach was empty, and I had no way to fill it. I passed out somewhere around Charleston and woke three states later only to slip back into oblivion. Even the fear of being found unconscious and shipped right back to military school couldn't keep me alert. Outside of DC, I emerged from a dream with my eyes on a back-pack. Its owner was snoring in the seat beside me. My fingers knew exactly what they were looking for, and they found it crumpled up inside the front pouch of his bag. The twenty-dollar bill that proved to be my salvation.

By the end of the journey, I realized I could spot an unguarded handbag from yards away. I could detect the faint outline of an iPhone in the pocket of a winter coat. No Birkin bag or fanny pack was safe from my fingers. I could rob any man blind with a quick bump and a flick of my wrist. That's when I decided to call myself Flick. I didn't want to remember the name I was given. And seven months later, I'm still waiting for the day when I can finally forget where I got it.

I've been living on the Lower East Side of Manhattan since spring. I didn't plan to stay here for more than one night. I hopped off that bus with a picture in my head and found that the slum I was seeking no longer existed. I'd spent my childhood imagining burnt-out buildings, roving gangs, and urban decay. I'd heard my father fill my brother's ears with tales of drug dealers, hustlers, and men hardened by misery. It never occurred to me that thirty years had passed since my father left the neighborhood that he always claimed had made him a man. In his absence, the heroin-shooting galleries received a fresh coat of paint, and artists started displaying their work on the walls. The junkies were kicked out to make room for the hipsters. The dive bars started serving tapas and wine. Block by block, the jungle was chopped down and cleared away. When I finally rolled into town, all that was left behind was a pasture.

Even I knew there were places in this city that hadn't been tamed. Neighborhoods where people have every reason to be scared of the dark. I was planning to search for just such a spot until my little brother, Jude, convinced me to stay.

As usual, he brought me a dream of the past. In this one, I was eight years old and Jude was seven. It was the third time our mother tried to disappear. I don't recall much about that particular trip or how long we were gone. I don't even know where we went. The house where she hid us was little more than a three-room hut. It sat on the edge of a town surrounded by desert. Our neighbors closed their curtains to keep out the heat while they scurried from one pocket of air-conditioning to the next. Every day, Jude and I waited inside for the sun to head west. Then we set out to explore. Our mother warned us to watch for snakes, but we never even heard so much as one rattle. There was nothing out there but rocks, sand, and silence. For the first time, I felt safe.

Late one afternoon, a thunderstorm rolled in and stuck around until evening. That night, a strange bleating drowned out the noise from the television set. My brother thought it sounded like sheep were being slaughtered in the backyard of our house. Our mother told us to stay indoors, but Jude and I got our hands on some flashlights and went to investigate. There were no sheep, of course. Just thousands of toads that had crawled out of the mud. They'd never learned to be frightened of humans, and we had to step carefully as they hopped around our ankles. When we shined our lights on the puddles, we saw that every tiny pool was alive with their spawn.

Jude and I stayed up half the night, making plans for our miniature army. The next morning, I rushed to my window, hoping that some of the eggs had hatched. The toads were gone, and a murder of crows had descended on the desert. I couldn't remember having seen a single bird in the sky. Now hundreds of them stood like black-clad mourners at the edge of the puddles. I wasn't sure what was happening until a beast flew past with a string of eggs dangling from its beak. I sprinted outside, armed with a soup ladle and every bowl that my mother had stacked in the cupboards. I filled the vessels with water and eggs and carried the sloshing contents back to the safety of our shack.

Jude found me in the kitchen, searching for a place on the narrow counter for my latest batch of orphans. "What's going on?" He laughed.

"Look outside! You've got to help me save the baby toads!" Watching the dream ten years later, I winced at the shrillness of my little boy voice. "Get the broom! You can beat the crows away while I work."

7

Jude stood at the kitchen door and observed the carnage. "They're eating their breakfast," he said. "We can chase them away, but they'll just come back. That's what they're supposed to do."

"What do you mean?" My heart was still pounding.

"Forget it." Jude tried to undo the damage with a flash of his impish smile. "Let's go kick some bird butt."

He spent the rest of the morning pleading with me to go back outside, but I'd already seen that my efforts were pointless. I never checked on the eggs again. A few days later, when I heard the sound of a car pulling up in our driveway, I stayed in front of the television, watching cartoons. While my mother wailed, Jude ran outside to greet our father. He must have been as terrified as we were. But Jude always understood things. He knew that where there is prey, there will always be predators. And by the time our family was back home in Connecticut, I'd learned my lesson. There's no point in hiding. No place can ever be safe.

The first night I spent on the Lower East Side, I woke around eleven at night to the sound of drunken laughter. I'd scaled the fence of a construction zone and lain down for a nap on the third floor of a concrete box that was rising up amid the old tenements. I wanted to be ready for the next stage of my journey. But my dream of the desert drained what little was left of my energy. I knew it was Jude's way of warning me not to go any farther. And when I opened my eyes, I saw how close I'd come to rolling over the edge of the unfinished building. I sat up and let my legs dangle in the open air while I tried to figure out why my brother thought I should stay. That's when I saw them on the sidewalk below me. Well-heeled tourists filing out of a luxury hotel just down the street. Kids from Manhattan's finest families stumbling from one bar to the next. Slick young professionals with freshly filled wallets who were too busy texting each other to notice the predators mingling among them. And I suddenly knew I was where I should be.

I came to the Lower East Side hoping to suffer enough to grow strong. I didn't stay because the pickings are easy. I'm still here because the competition is suitably dangerous. The weather is brutal. And fights are always easy to come by. Even on Christmas Eve.

I hear a siren a few streets away. Someone at the bar must have called the cops. I check my reflection in the side mirror of a delivery van. A stream of blood is still trickling down my face. The collar of my coat is completely soaked. It's almost one o'clock in the morning, and there's only one place I can go.

CHAPTER TWO

TALES OF DEAD CHILDREN

Once upon a time it must have been worse, but Pitt Street will always live up to its name. The east side of the road marks the edge of the housing projects. Those who live on the west side are forced to contemplate the view. The fashionable types who have invaded the Lower East Side say they appreciate the neighborhood's "grittiness." But they don't want to see real misery out their front windows. So Pitt Street has been left to the rest of us. It remains one of the last cute-free zones in downtown Manhattan.

Joi and her urchins live in the basement of a building three doors down from Our Lady of Sorrows. The entrance is barred by a gate that could withstand any enemy invasion. There's no buzzer, but even this late, there's usually a kid or two keeping watch from behind the iron bars. They act as the building's unpaid doormen. Which may explain why they're allowed to stay. Tonight I don't even see who's on duty. Whoever it is must have seen me, though, because I hear feet flying down the stairs.

Someone at the bottom shouts, "Joey!" Spelled *J-o-i*. That's what she told me the first day we met. A few seconds later, the gate creaks open and she appears. Joi's long, jet-black curls blend into the darkness. Two wide-set amber eyes take in the damage that's been done to my face. She doesn't gasp or wince like most girls would. Joi is completely unflappable. She steps aside to let me in, but for a moment I refuse to move any closer. Keeping my distance from Joi is the only true test of my willpower.

"Are you waiting for a formal invitation?"

Once I'm inside, I catch a whiff of cocoa butter and jasmine. Joi leaves a trail of this fragrance wherever she goes. It's not perfume, she says, but a product she uses to tame her hair. As far as I can tell, it's the only luxury Joi allows herself. The Jamaican hairdresser down the street sells it to her at a discount. She assumes the blood of her people flows through Joi's veins. So does the guy at the Mexican diner who slips *"bonita"* a free café con leche each morning. And the Indian deli lady who treats Joi like the daughter she never realized she wanted. And the European tourists who always assume she can speak their languages. Everyone wants to believe that Joi belongs to them.

"How's the other guy look?" she asks.

"Unconscious," I say. Now that I'm near her, I keep moving closer.

She puts a hand on my chest to halt my advance. "You're going to need at least eight stitches."

"Will you let me kiss you when they're done?"

"Yes," Joi says. She never plays hard to get.

I follow her downstairs, peeling off my coat as we enter the sweltering heat. In the basement, a winding tunnel leads us past a warren of cramped rooms. The floor of each chamber is strewn with sleeping bags filled with thin bodies—some still little, others growing longer and leaner each day. There's plenty of space for everyone, yet they always end up clustered together. Dirty arms circle filthy torsos. Breath exhaled by one set of lungs is immediately inhaled by another. My tenth-grade history book had pictures of similar scenes—photos that could have been taken in this very basement. For the past two hundred years, the Lower East Side has been home to the children that no one else wants.

A sinister mechanical hum grows louder as Joi and I near the end of the tunnel. So does the heat. We pass a locked door that guards the building's ancient boiler. The heart of Joi's colony is just a few feet away. It served as a laundry room until the machines died of old age. At some point in the future, the boiler in the room next door is bound to blow. When it does, the colony kids won't stand a chance. I tried to warn Joi once, but all she did was laugh. Someday the sun's going to explode too, she informed me. But until it kills us, we should just be grateful it keeps us alive.

A row of rusting machines lines one wall of the laundry room. A few of the older kids are perched on top. Someone must have struck it rich tonight because Joi's urchins are all guzzling imported beer. None of them are old enough to watch R-rated movies, but most have seen things in their own lives that would never make it past any censor. As long as they don't get drunk and rowdy, Joi lets them do as they like.

"Yo, Flick," says a kid named Dartagnan. "Merry Christmas." He's thirteen. He'll be thirty by the time his mother finishes her sentence for drug possession with intent to distribute. Some days he swears his dad is Lil Wayne. Other days he claims it's one of the anchors on CNN. Either way, someone owes a shitload of child support. Joi found the fourth musketeer begging for change outside of Bloomingdale's.

"Happy Winter Solstice," I respond. "I'm a pagan."

The kids are all gawking at me, and it isn't because they've never met a pagan. They want to know what happened to my face—but they won't break one of Joi's cardinal rules. *Always listen, never ask.*

"Want a beer?" The blond girl is Tina or Trina. It doesn't matter which. She'll disappear before New Year's. They say her father lost his job, the house, his marbles, then his life. The girl's little brother and sister are staying with an aunt who had no room in her home for a troublesome teenager. A few months back, Joi saved Tina/Trina from a neighborhood pimp, but the girl has started slipping out after dark. I seem to be the only one who's figured out where she's going. My guess is she bought the booze.

"Flick needs something stronger than beer tonight," says Joi. She unlocks an old trunk in which she stores a remarkable range of supplies and pulls out a bottle of tequila.

"I hate tequila," I tell her.

"It's all I have. I'll just give you enough to make you nice and numb."

"I'll take the pain. You know I don't drink."

"You will tonight. Doctor's orders." She points to a chair and fills a paper coffee cup to the halfway mark. "Bottoms up." Joi watches to make sure I obey. When the first gulp is down, she leaves to gather her supplies and start preparing the operating room.

The kids are still gawking at me. I keep my eyes on the liquid I'm swirling with my index finger. There's not enough tequila to form a whirlpool. Only a third of what Joi poured me is still left in the cup. The rest is already burning its way through my brain. I don't want to look up at them. I don't want to know them. I don't have any pity to spare. I'm nothing like Joi. And I don't believe in her little pet project. She picks up these strays all over the city and brings them home, knowing they never stay for good. But the longer they're with her, the weaker they'll be when they're back on their own. She makes sure they're fed and sews up their wounds. She coddles them and cuddles them when she should be teaching them how to survive.

I haven't been around long enough to know how a seventeen-year-old girl came to form her own colony of urchins. But I do know what happens to the kids who seek shelter here. Joi works her ass off to delay the inevitable, but they all disappear in the end. Some are "rescued" by the very people they were trying to escape. Some are picked up by the cops and delivered to jail—or worse, sentenced to foster care. To my knowledge, at least one of Joi's kids has been murdered. Most simply leave and never come back.

I'm getting worked up just thinking about it. What really pisses me off is that they don't even *try*. They're all marching toward the cliff like a herd of lemmings. I know Joi thinks I can do something to stop them. She claims the kids all look up to me. And she's right—they do. Because I use big words. Because my clothes may need washing, but they have all the right labels. Because even though I've gone feral, they can tell that my puppy years were spent in a wealthy home. The reasons they look up to me are stupid. And what Joi doesn't know is that I can't help her save them. Because soon, I'll be leaving her too.

"So Wendy's gonna stitch you up?" A kid who resembles a cocker spaniel and answers only to *Curly* breaks the silence. Anyone who hears Curly's sob story is liable to jump off a bridge.

He's got my attention. "Who the *f*— is *Wendy*?" I ask.

"Curly's started calling us the Lost Boys," Tina or Trina explains with a roll of her heavily lined eyes. "Even though half of us are girls. And if we're the Lost Boys, I guess that means Joi gets to play Wendy."

"You can be Tinkerbell if you want," Curly offers thoughtfully as he casts his little movie. "And Flick can be Peter Pan."

I cannot believe he just stepped on that land mine. The name explodes in my head. *This is why I do not drink. This is why I do not drink. This is why I do not drink.* I take a gulp of tequila and wipe my mouth on my sleeve.

"I'm not Peter Pan, you moron. But I used to know him. And you can take my word for it. Peter Pan is *dead*."

They all go quiet. Even Curly's face wears a hungry look that tells me he's desperate for more. They've all been waiting for months to hear my hard-luck story. They've been gnawing on the bones of their own misery, and now they want to feed on a fresh piece of me. They have no idea how poisonous I am.

"Wait—Peter Pan dies at the end of the movie?" Dartagnan is the only one who didn't catch on.

"Did *everyone* here drop out of school before the third grade? It's a *book*, not just a movie. And the kids in Never Land are dead from the very beginning. That's what the whole goddamn story's *about*!" My voice has risen to a shout. "The Lost Boys are *dead*. Why do you think they'll never grow up? Never Land is the afterworld. Peter Pan is the one who guides lost souls to the land of death. He's the god Hermes. The author barely even bothered to disguise him!"

"Hermes?"

"Oh, come on! You know . . . The bringer of dreams. The watcher by night. The thief at the gates. The Greek god with the wings on his sandals?"

They don't know.

"Are you saying Never Never Land is supposed to be *heaven*?" This from Dartagnan. I really didn't want to analyze a classic work of children's literature at one o'clock in the morning. But at least the conversation isn't about me anymore.

"Heaven's just another myth," I say. Anything to keep them distracted.

"You're wrong," the boy insists. His innocence offends me.

"Oh yeah, Dartagnan? You think there's some wonderful, magical place where you get to go if you've been a really, really good boy? Well, take it from me—there *isn't*. There's just hell. Have a look around. You're already here."

"Flick!" Joi's come back to get me. I swallow the last of the tequila, crumple up the cup, and toss it into a corner. I don't say goodbye. I just follow Joi back to her quarters.

It's not much to look at, but I always feel better in Joi's room. There's a tiny window, for starters, which lets in a little cool air. And a proper bed, which may be lumpy but beats the hell out of a park bench. Tonight it's serving as a makeshift table for Joi's surgical instruments. I pull off my shirt and take a seat on a folding chair. Joi uses bottled water and sterile gauze to clean the blood from my face and neck.

She's furious, but she's holding back until my wound is stitched and the bleeding has stopped. Joi only has a handful of rules, and I have a feeling I've just broken the one she considers most sacred. Not long after we met, she shared her big theory with me. Joi believes that, even in the worst situations, all a person needs to survive is ONE GOOD THING. It sounded so stupid that I thought she was joking, but she wasn't. It could be anything, she insisted. Maybe it's something no one else understands. Or something that might not even exist. It could be a guardian angel. An invisible friend. *Or benevolent extraterrestrials who'll solve mankind's problems and probably won't eat us,* I'd chimed in when the subject began to make me uncomfortable. Joi did not appreciate the joke.

The point is, it doesn't matter how silly it seems. Here in Joi's colony, you're never, ever allowed to mess with someone else's ONE GOOD THING. Apparently Dartagnan's is heaven. I'm pretty sure I didn't destroy some kid's dream of harps, clouds, and halos with a few tipsy words. But Joi knows I could have.

"Sorry," I say.

"Shut up and don't move, or I'll sew your lips together," she replies as the curved needle pierces my flesh.

Despite the tequila, I'm not too numb to feel each and every one of the nine stitches she gives me. By the time she's done, her anger seems to have cooled. The left side of my face is aching.

"I did my best, but you'll have a scar," she says.

"Good. I've been meaning to add a few more to my collection."

"How could you be such a f—ing jerk, Flick? Dartagnan's a little boy."

"What? He's *thirteen*. He's old enough to know the truth."

Joi snorts with disgust. "The truth? You think *you've* found it?"

"You don't really believe in all that heaven mumbo jumbo, do you?" I ask.

I've only spoken a few simple sentences, and Joi already looks ready to strangle me. "After all this time, *that's* what you want to know? Not . . . where did you grow up, Joi? How did you get here? What's your last name? No, *you* want to know if I believe in *heaven*."

"What *is* your last name?"

"You couldn't pronounce it if I told you. But I'll make you a deal, Flick. I'll tell you every single thing I've ever thought about heaven if you tell me what the hell happened to Peter Pan."

She must have been listening the whole time. Now she's hit me with a sucker punch, and Peter's real name almost flies out of my mouth. But I catch it in time. "Captain Hook chopped him up and fed the pieces to the crocodile."

I always serve my lies with a grain of truth. But Joi tastes nothing but bullshit. When she doesn't respond, I can feel a gulf growing between us. I should take the opportunity to let her go, but I'm not strong enough yet. Just before it's too late, I reach out and grab hold of her. Once, when I was in the mood to argue, I asked her what she thought would happen if someone were to lose his ONE GOOD THING. There's always another one out there if you're willing to look, she told me. Whenever I kiss her, I find myself starting to believe all of Joi's strange, silly theories.

• • •

The sliver of window at the top of Joi's room is open when we fall asleep. No mere mortal could cram himself through the opening, but it's wide enough for Peter Pan to slip inside. He's leaning against a wall—one foot on the bricks and one on the floor.

He crosses his arms and shakes his head. "You're a f—ing mess," he says.

"I bet you've seen worse." He knows what I mean.

"Touché," he responds with a tip of his green felt hat.

"Why are you here, Jude?"

"You know as well as I do. This isn't the way my gift was meant to be used. I grace you with stealth and cunning, and you choose to rob drunks and pick fights. But it was nice how you saved the girl from that thug tonight. Makes me think there might be hope for you yet."

"I wasn't trying to save her. I *wanted* to steal her wallet."

Jude laughs. "If you say so."

If he's right—if the wallet was just an excuse to help her—then I'm nowhere near ready.

"You don't have to do this." He's suddenly serious. "You can come with me. Never Land is everything you'd want it to be."

"Never Land doesn't exist, Jude."

"Then where do I go when I'm not with you?"

I don't have the heart to answer.

"That's okay, I knew you wouldn't come. You want to stay here with her, don't you?" He nods to Joi's side of the bed.

More than anything, I think. "I can't."

"Why not?"

"Because I owe you, Jude. You're still my one good thing."

"I'm dead. It's time to find another."

CHAPTER THREE

A SIMPLE PROPOSITION

I'm shocked that I don't have a hangover. I must have been drunk to come so close to spilling my beans last night. The moment I wake, I scan the room for Peter Pan. But he's returned to his hiding place inside my head.

Jude was ten years old when he came home from school clutching a copy of *Peter Pan*. One of his teachers had called him "the boy who wouldn't grow up." The idea intrigued him. He consumed the first novel in a single night and devoured the rest of J. M. Barrie's works by week's end. My brother's obsession didn't end when he reached the last page. As soon as there was nothing left to read, Jude decided to *become* Peter Pan. And no one ever laughed. Because it didn't take much imagination to believe Jude could fly.

He was smart. So much smarter than I ever was. And charming and clever. Two things I'll never be. A handsome trickster with a thatch of strawberry-blond hair that he insisted on cutting himself. Jude could con you out of your most cherished possessions—and make you thank him for taking them off your hands. He could look like a saint while spinning lies that would make a hardened sinner blush red. Other kids followed him. Adults were in awe of him. When teachers called him a scoundrel, they always said it with smiles on their faces. A friend of my mother's predicted that Jude would one day be president or in prison—or both.

My father took all the credit, of course. He once told me that the moment I was born, he knew I belonged to my mother. That must have been the reason he demanded another child so soon after the first had arrived. He wanted a son of his own. And he wasn't disappointed the second time around. When my father looked at Jude, he saw everything he'd desired. He was a man with no tolerance for whimsy. But even when Jude began flying through the house dressed up like an androgynous elf, my father still saw *his boy*. Who knows—maybe he'd read Barrie's books for himself. And maybe he'd stumbled across the same clues I have. Peter Pan, I'm now almost certain, was Captain Hook's son.

But there were things about Jude that our father never saw. He never saw Jude hiding me when the old man went on one of his Scotch-fueled rampages. He never realized that most of Jude's attempts to get his attention were only meant to draw it away from me. My father thought Jude despised his weakling big brother. He didn't know how much of his own strength Jude wasted trying to save me.

I won't let Joi make the same mistake that Jude did. She's lying beside me, her face cradled in a nest of her hair. None of her features fit together, and yet I've never seen anyone so lovely. Her beauty is perfect because it's all wrong. I've been searching for flaws hidden beneath Joi's surface, and while I'm sure they exist, I still haven't found one. I would sacrifice almost anything to stay here with her. And that's exactly why I have to leave. She will keep me from becoming what I need to be. And if she tries to save me, I will end up destroying her.

Today I plan to be dressed and gone before Joi has a chance to ask me to stay. Whenever I spend the night at the colony, I'm usually the one who sleeps in. I work the nightshift, while Joi keeps regular business hours. Every morning, she hops on the subway and heads to a different part of town. She returns in the evening with a bag of supplies. Jeans for the kids who've outgrown the ones they arrived in. Food for the kids who can't feed themselves. Trinkets for anyone celebrating a birthday. It's all stolen, of course. I'd kill for a chance to observe her technique. She must be a world-class shoplifter if she's nicking enough to support a whole colony. But Joi refuses to let anyone tag along. All she's ever told me is that she won't hit the same store twice in one year. And when she takes something, she leaves behind a handwritten receipt. *Thank You for Donating $___ in Goods to the LES Children's Fund.* Somehow I doubt the IRS lets the store owners write off their losses. But it seems to keep Joi's conscience clean.

Her swag bags have gotten heavier over the past few weeks, and I suspect she has something special planned for Christmas morning. I don't want to know what it is. Before I slip out, I remember the wallet I stole last night. I unhook the clasp and pull out a wad of bills. There's more than three hundred dollars—far more than I need. I keep a twenty and leave the rest for Joi. I hope she buys something nice for herself.

● ● ●

Outside, the streets are dead. It's the first time I've seen the city so empty. I'm wandering around like the sole survivor of some mysterious cataclysm that's destroyed the rest of my species. I'm humanity's last hope. The thought makes me laugh out loud.

The last man on earth needs to eat. But there's nothing open. Even the delis and diners are dark. Chinatown may be the only place I'll be able to trade my twenty for food. So I start walking south on Clinton Street. I stop just short of Essex to peer through the window of a jewelry shop. There's a kid staring back at me. He's got a beaten, broken face that still manages to be a little too pretty. He's not who I want to see. I'm looking for the store's owner. His name is Jim Neverbotheredtoask, and he's my fence of choice. His rates aren't what I'd call fair, but at least they're consistent. And he'll take anything I bring him. Jewelry, bikes, electronics. A few weeks ago, he let me roll a Vespa right into the shop. He even gives me a few bucks for each credit card I collect. I've never found his door padlocked before. Apparently Jim has taken the day off to celebrate the birth of his Lord. I'd like to know how much of the stuff under this year's Christmas tree is hot.

I keep walking, and when I hit Grand Street, I see my first signs of life. A bunch of Orthodox Jewish kids are playing some kind of game in the street. They stare at me as I walk past, and I sense their disappointment. They were sure the city was theirs for the day.

I'm about to turn right on Grand Street when a strange compulsion comes over me, and I continue my path down Clinton. At the next intersection, I stop. I visited this place on my second day in the city, but I've steered clear of it ever since. On the southeast corner of Clinton and East Broadway sits a six-story building. Grimy beige bricks with dark green trim around the top. It looks like every other apartment building on the Lower East Side, except for the entrance. The doorway is red and flanked by two columns that support a decorative balcony. The name of the structure is written in red just below. The Mayflower. That's how I knew I'd found the right place, even though I'd never been given an address. My father spent his first sixteen years living on the fourth floor of this tenement. Then he won a scholarship and set out to seek his fortune. He works on Wall Street these days. His office is less than a mile away, but I doubt he's ever returned to the Lower East Side.

I wonder what he would say if he could see his old quarters. The first time I visited, I broke into the building and had a look around a fourth-floor apartment. I'm not sure if it was the one my father had called home, but it was the only apartment that was empty that morning. The rooms were tiny, the bathtub was in the kitchen, and the walls were riddled with oozing plaster pustules. My father thinks that most kids of my generation are too soft to last in a place like the Mayflower. I might have agreed with him until I saw all the pictures on the apartment's walls. At least three Latino kids seemed to be surviving just fine in my father's childhood home. Maybe they were all exceptional actors, but the smiles on their faces looked perfectly genuine.

Jude used to say that my father was full of shit. He thought the Mayflower was nothing more than a lie. I suppose the truth is a little more complicated.

The tourists might be missing, but Chinatown is open for business. I slip into my favorite restaurant on Doyers Street. The décor leaves much to be desired, and I'm not always sure what I'm eating. But whatever it is, it's cheap and delicious. The locals love the place, and tables are usually hard to come by. But today, the restaurant is empty. It's just me and Mr. Song, who's always behind the counter—at least sixteen hours a day.

While I wait for my food, I pull out the wallet I stole last night and start to examine its contents. It belongs to one Mia Osman. The girl's got every credit card known to man. I spread them out on the table. Fourteen pieces of plastic that could keep Joi's colony fed and clothed for years. I'm sure they were all canceled first thing this morning. Replacements will be arriving by FedEx tomorrow.

There's not much else here to entertain me. Just a few strange notes crammed into the pockets. *Chanel Rogue Shine in Deauville!* reads one. A prescription for Adderall that might come in handy. A receipt for a thousand-dollar pair of Louboutin shoes. Another for lunch at a bistro on the Upper East Side. She left a 5 percent tip and dotted the *i* in her signature with a heart.

I feel a cold breeze as the restaurant door opens, and I quickly sweep the contents of the wallet into my lap before I look up to see who's joined me for breakfast.

A man has chosen a table by the front window. He pulls out a chair that's facing me, which instantly tells me there might be a problem. When two strangers take seats in an empty restaurant, they almost always prefer not to look at each other. Unless one of the strangers finds the other intriguing. I've had men hit on me before, but it usually happens on days when half of my face isn't hidden beneath a bandage. Anyway, this guy doesn't strike me as the lonely-and-looking-for-love sort. If he was, he could afford someone much better-looking than me.

I know this because there is one skill at which all rich people truly excel, and that's recognizing each other. Even when we're in disguise. The first thing I notice is the man's overcoat, which fits him perfectly though he's not a standard size. He takes it off, revealing a turtleneck sweater and jeans that he probably bought at J. Crew. That might make me question my assessment if it weren't for his shoes. My father owns several pairs made by the same small shop in Italy. You could fly around the world three times for the price.

My eyes come to rest on his face. Maybe he doesn't want my body, but he does want *something*. And he's not shy, either. He's met my gaze. I keep my expression stony, but he smiles. I'd say he's thirty-five. But a *rich* thirty-five, which means he could pass for a man in his twenties. Tousled brown hair that was probably red in his youth. Blue eyes. Freckles so densely distributed that from a distance they might be mistaken for a tan. He seems friendly. Boyish. But there's something he's hiding. Something he doesn't want me to see.

He's risen from his seat, and he's moving toward me. Mr. Song has disappeared. The man stops at my table and places a palm on the top of the chair across from me.

"May I join you?" he asks.

I hook the toe of one boot under the bottom rung. The chair doesn't budge when he tries to pull it out. "Why?" I demand.

"I have a proposition for you."

Maybe I was wrong. Maybe he *is* looking for love. But I doubt it. "What?"

"I'd like to hire a thief, and I believe you might be the right man for the job."

CHAPTER FOUR

BREAKING AND ENTERING

Every serial killer knows that once you lure a potential victim into your vehicle, the rest of the job is a piece of cake. Joi warns her urchins to avoid all strangers in cars. It makes no difference how much money they flash, she says, or what flavor of candy they're offering. Walk away. Even if they have a friendly smile and impeccable manners. Not all killers need to carry a gun. The ones who use charm instead of weapons or brute force are always the worst of the bunch. I guess the urchin who was murdered didn't listen to Joi. Security footage from a bodega on Attorney Street showed the girl sliding into an SUV with tinted windows and plates that may have been from New Jersey. That's where they found her body a few months later.

I never received one of Joi's warnings. She probably assumed I knew better. But here I am, sitting in the passenger seat of a Maserati GranTurismo, gathering information about the man at the wheel. He has a lead foot and very little respect for the city's

traffic laws. Still, he's an excellent driver, possibly even profession-
ally trained. Italy's top rocket scientists must have been hired to
customize the Maserati's interior. The dashboard is bristling with
little buttons and levers. I wonder if I've had the honor of being
kidnapped by a Bond villain. I keep waiting for hidden restraints to
pop out and pin me to my seat. On another day, I might be worried
about what the man has in store for me. Today, I don't really care.
I'm just curious.

He wouldn't talk in Mr. Song's restaurant, except to say that I
would be paid five hundred bucks for less than an hour's work. I
never asked how he knew that I was a thief. I would have accepted
his offer right there on the spot, but he told me I should see a few
things for myself before I decided to take the job. Then he slapped
down a hundred-dollar bill to pay for the food I'd ordered. If he
was trying to impress me, it didn't work. I shoved the bill across the
table and made him wait until I finished my breakfast. And I didn't
bother to rush.

The ride ends sooner than I expected. We've stopped on Charles
Street in Greenwich Village—just across town from Pitt Street and
a whole world away. Tourists think Manhattan's most picturesque
neighborhood is still home to the city's artists, painters, and poets.
There hasn't been a poet sighting in the Village for years. You have
to work in finance to afford all this cuteness.

The man points out his driver's-side window.

"That's where you'll be working," he says.

It's a four-story town house. Old. Brick. Tons of original detail.
Every New York banker's wet dream. But the people who live here
appear to be the last of the breed I thought was extinct. I can see

an easel standing by a top-floor window. The house is dark. Looks like no one's been home for a while.

"You just parked across the street from the place you want me to rob?" I ask. What an idiot. His money must be inherited.

"There's no need to worry. The occupants are out of town. And I'm in the process of purchasing the building."

He's giving me that smile again. He's expecting me to ask why he wants to rob his own building.

"What do you want me to get?" I refuse to give him the satisfaction.

"I should explain a few things first," the man says.

"Just tell me what you're after, and I'll find it. I'm not interested in exposition."

But he won't be hurried. "You might want to indulge me. A young man should never pass up a chance to see how the world really works. You could learn a few new tricks," he says with all the good humor of a sitcom dad.

"I know how the world works," I respond.

"Then you should also know when it's time to be quiet and listen." He still hasn't stopped smiling.

"Listening costs extra," I say.

For some reason, this seems to amuse him. "Will another two hundred suffice?"

"Spill your guts, Goldfinger." I slouch down in my seat and stare out the windshield.

"I've always preferred Blofeld," the man replies with a laugh. "I'm a cat lover too."

"I'll need an extra *five* hundred if you want to discuss your pets."

"Then perhaps we should get down to business." The man smirks. "The building is currently owned by a gentleman who should be dead in a matter of days."

"You planning to kill him?" I ask. It's a joke, but my employer answers as if I were perfectly serious.

"Of course not. The gentleman in question is ninety years old, and he's dying of renal failure. I've already made a deal with his son to buy the house as soon as the old man is gone. Unfortunately, the building comes with a pest problem. There's an artist and his family living upstairs. I want them all out."

"So give them the boot after you buy the building."

My new boss sighs. "If only it were that simple. The house's owner has always considered himself a patron of the arts. At some point in the 1980s, he befriended a promising painter who was down on his luck. He offered the young man an apartment and studio on the top two floors of this building. The neighborhood wasn't quite as genteel in those days, and rents were much cheaper. But the painter got a deal that was remarkable even back then. He pays two hundred and fifty dollars a month—plus six terrible paintings a year. I've had my lawyer look over the document. She says that the lease is good for another twenty years."

"Outrageous," I drone. I honestly couldn't care less.

"I suppose the deal might have worked out well for the owner if the painter had gone on to fame and fortune. But the best art is always inspired by pain, and life isn't terribly painful if you're living in the most sought-after part of Manhattan for three thousand dollars a year. Everything our painter has produced since he moved here has been mediocre. Even his two dim-witted children."

"Let me guess. You want me to find the painter's copy of the lease so you can destroy it and kick the guy out." My fingers grip the door handle. I really can't stand any more of this. It's time to cut to the chase. "No problem."

The man is still trying to hammer a point into my head, but he's finding my skull can be remarkably thick. "You understand, don't you? These people don't belong here."

What in the hell does he want from me? "There's no doubt in my mind that you deserve to live here *much* more than they do," I assure him, my voice slick with sarcasm.

"I have no intention of living here," the man tells me. "I have a perfectly fine house a few blocks away. But I'm something of a bibliophile, and my library is overflowing. I need a building close to home where I can store my rare books."

I laugh so hard that tears start to well up in my eyes. This is, hands down, the strangest conversation I've ever had. "Whatever," I say. "Are we done here?"

"Yes," the man replies.

"Then drop me off down the street. You don't want anyone on the block to see me getting out of your car. I'll meet you around the corner when I'm done."

I consider hitting the road as soon as his car is out of sight. This whole scenario is too goddamned weird. And it gets even stranger when I discover that the front door of the building has been left unlocked. I wonder if I'm being set up. Maybe I'm the unwitting star of some new reality show that explores the dark side of the human soul. I turn around and grin for the cameras, just in case they're watching.

Past the front entrance is a small foyer. I'm facing a pair of doors. The left must lead to the lower apartment. The right door is blocking the stairs to the top two floors. I examine the lock on the door I need to open. Then I immediately check the foyer for hidden cameras. I'm not smiling anymore. I'm serious now. This has to be some kind of joke. Every apartment in Manhattan has at least one dead bolt on the door. Every apartment except the one I'm being paid seven hundred dollars to rob. There's just a dinky bedroom knob—the type with a push-button lock. I spend a moment wondering if anyone who lives in New York could really be so stupid. Maybe a painter, I decide.

I take out one of Mia Osman's credit cards and slowly slide it down the crack between the door and its frame. The lock opens on the very first swipe.

Paintings line the stairway that leads up to the artist's apartment: A bum in Washington Square Park. A panhandler on a subway platform. Poor kids dancing through the spray of a fire hydrant. They're crap. The guy can paint, but his choice of subjects is pure cheese. I'm expecting more of the same when I step into the living room on the building's third floor. But the first thing I see steals my breath for a moment. One entire wall of the room is covered in mismatched frames. Behind the glass in each frame is a mitten that must have belonged to one of the artist's kids. There are dozens of mittens, and none of them are identical. Every one is a different color. Some are damaged and dirty. Others couldn't have been worn more than twice. The first mitten in the row closest to the ceiling looks small enough for an infant. The white snowflake stitched on its palm is almost too tiny to see. Little by little, the flakes get fatter and the mittens grow larger. The last one that was framed is almost adult-sized.

It's as beautiful as anything ever displayed in my parents' home. My father always chose art that screamed good taste and deep pockets. He never bothered to see if it spoke to him. As far as he was concerned, a painting was just a way to hang money on the wall. I don't think he ever realized that each of his "investments" contained a little piece of someone's soul.

I'm starting to feel a bit jittery. So I pull my eyes away from the mittens and scan the living room. No television. An ancient turntable. A computer with a goddamned *floppy disk drive*. No wonder the door downstairs doesn't have a dead bolt. The family doesn't think they have anything worth stealing.

The lease will probably be in a desk or filing cabinet, and there isn't anything like that here. I wander down the hall and peer into a bedroom. It doesn't look promising, but I'll give it a more thorough search if I don't find what I'm after on my first go-through. Across the hall is a room that belongs to a teenage boy. The door is plastered with those stupid stickers they hand out at conventions. HELLO, MY NAME IS . . . The name *Jack* is written graffiti-style inside all the white spaces. I don't even bother to enter Jack's lair. I rule out the kitchen at the back of the apartment, then head upstairs.

There's an enormous skylight in the studio's ceiling. The room must be perfect for painting. The easel I spotted from the street displays the artist's latest masterpiece: an old lady pulling weeds in a tiny garden wedged between crumbling buildings. I groan at the sight and turn my attention to a paint-splattered table. On top, there's a jumble of tubes, tools, and brushes. Underneath is a small filing cabinet. Jackpot.

It's locked, but it takes me ten seconds to jimmy open the drawer with a screwdriver. Inside, there's a f—ing folder labeled LEASE. I thumb though the yellowing pages to make sure I've got the right document. Something in the distance catches my eye. Movement. There's a room off the studio, and the door is wide open. I knew this was too easy. I've been set up. Someone's been waiting here to catch me red-handed. If they expect me to run, they're in for a shock. I'll go out fighting. With the lease rolled up and shoved in my pocket, I stand and silently make my way across the floorboards.

But the room is empty. There's a rumpled bed with faded flowery sheets and a desk that's being used as a vanity. Clothes are strewn everywhere, as if the girl who lives here couldn't decide what to pack. She must have been in a rush. She forgot to close the window, and the curtains are fluttering in the breeze. I notice that almost all of the pictures taped to the walls feature the same blond teenager. She reminds me of someone. In one of the photos, she's waving. On her hand is a mitten from the wall downstairs.

"The girl's pretty cute, don't you think?" I spin around to see Peter f—ing Pan. He must have come in through the window.

"Jesus, Jude," I manage to shout and not shriek. "Go away!"

"So whatcha gonna tell Joi about all this?" He's floating above me, about a foot from the ceiling.

"It's none of her business."

"But she might need to make room for the painter's kids at the colony. By the way, how much do you think this one could charge?" he asks, pointing at the blonde in the pictures.

"What in the hell are you talking about?"

"I'm just saying she kinda looks like that girl at the colony who got kicked out of her house."

"Trina," I say.

"Her name's *Tina*," Jude corrects me. "Maybe she and this new girl could work the Lower East Side together. Pretend to be sisters or something. I bet they'd make more money that way."

I've never heard him speak like this. "Shut up. No one here is going to be homeless. There's a place for crappy artists and their families. It's called *Queens*."

"You're sure?"

"I'm sure I don't give a shit." The words leave the taste of vomit in my mouth.

"Then why are you feeling sick to your stomach?" He's flying alongside me while I sprint downstairs to the bathroom.

"Why are you doing this to me?" I finally ask when the last piece of rice from my Chinese breakfast is floating in the toilet bowl. "Why are you making it so hard?"

Peter Pan grins. "Because you still believe in me."

I flush the food and every thought in my brain down the toilet. I make sure the lease is still in my pocket and head for the kitchen. I'm looking for something pungent enough to cover the stench of vomit on my breath. The family must have cleaned out the refrigerator before they left for the holidays. All I see are a few crusty condiments and four shriveled pickles floating in brine. Good enough. I grab the whole jar.

I eat one of the pickles on my way down the stairs. I have to pause at the front door to make sure it stays in my stomach. I'm crunching on another as I slide into the passenger's seat of my employer's car. I finish the snack before I hand him the lease. I can tell from the expression on his face that the pickles were a nice touch. I must look totally badass.

"That was fast. I assume you didn't encounter any problems?" he asks.

"Nope," I say.

"I'm impressed."

"You gave me a job. I did it. Now pay up."

"Certainly." He pulls his wallet from his coat pocket and counts out seven hundred-dollar bills. "And to show my gratitude, I'll even throw in a ride across town."

I'm about to tell him not to bother when I see him stick the wallet in his pocket. "Whatever you say, boss."

That wallet will be mine before we hit Broadway. But it was a mistake to stay. Now that there's nothing to distract it, my mind is filling with rage. I hate the man sitting beside me. I hate the people who are about to be kicked out of their home. I hate the blond girl who reminded me of Tina. I hate that I know Tina's name. I hate Joi too. I hate her for keeping me weak. But most of all, I despise myself. I fantasize about grabbing the wheel of the car and steering it into a lamppost. I wouldn't mind dying if I could drag the man in the driver's seat with me to hell.

The streets have vanished. I can't see anything. I don't hear anything. I'm not even sure that I'm breathing. All I know is that I need to get out of the car before something bad happens. The next time the Maserati slows to a stop, I reach for the handle and spring out. I start walking against traffic so he won't be able to follow me. I hear someone shouting my name, and I walk even faster. Only on the third *FLICK!* do I recognize Joi's voice. The world comes back into focus. That's when I realize that the bastard in the Maserati has dropped me off on Pitt Street. Right outside the colony.

Joi rushes up to me. She instantly knows that I'm in terrible shape. "What's wrong?" she demands.

I don't speak. She has silver Christmas tree tinsel woven through the braid in her hair. It glows one moment and turns dull the next, like it's playing catch with the sunlight.

"Who was that man, Flick?"

I shake my head and accomplish the impossible. I manage to scare the shit out of Joi.

"What happened Flick? Tell me what happened." She's getting hysterical. "DAMMIT, FLICK, SAY SOMETHING!"

"Leave me alone."

"What?" She takes a step back like I've punched her.

"Get the hell away from me." That's it, I tell myself. Quick, fast. Like ripping off a Band-Aid.

It's time. I've waited too long already. I got too close. It's her fault I'm still weak.

I don't look back.

I can't remember what happened in the hours before dark. I'm sitting at the bottom of a slide in the Seward Park playground when I feel the extra weight in my pocket. Part of me would like to toss the filthy thing into the sewer. That part of me won't be indulged anymore. So I open the last wallet I picked. It's been a long time since I've seen so much money. But that doesn't interest me right now. I pull out a driver's license and find the man from this morning smiling back at me. I have to squint to read the name in the darkness. *Lucian Mandel.* The license slips from my fingers. I leap up and scan the playground. I think I may be having a heart attack. Then I see the card lying on the ground. There's a Post-it attached to the back. I don't dare touch it, but I need to know what it says. I squat down and take a look.

Now that you know who I am, perhaps we should have lunch.
I'll be at Floraison tomorrow at noon.

CHAPTER FIVE

THE GATES OF HELL

It's been three days since I washed. I didn't glance in a mirror this morning, but I know that the bandage on my face is hard with dried blood. I slept in the park last night, and there are so many dead leaves stuck to my coat that it probably looks like a ghillie suit. And I purposely stepped in dog shit on my way here.

Yet the maître d' at the most exclusive restaurant in Manhattan doesn't bat an eye.

"Right this way," he trills. "Mr. Mandel is expecting you."

Outside, it's winter. In Floraison, it's always spring. Flowering trees twist out of stark concrete planters. I once overheard my father say that they were genetically engineered to bloom year-round and produce no pollen. Nature has not only been tamed, it's been taught to do tricks for the delight of the rich.

The tables I brush past are filled with some of the city's most powerful people. My father may be sitting among them. This is his favorite restaurant, and he must know I'm here. But I refuse to search for his face in the crowd. If my dad sent Mandel to find me, I want him to see that I'm not afraid. I've already had everything taken away. He was the one who made sure I had nothing to lose.

My lunch companion is waiting at a table against the far wall. I glance at his freckled, smirking face. I estimate the cost of his stylish gray suit. I take note of the slight bulge in the breast pocket of the jacket. He's already replaced the wallet he lost. Then I focus on the painting that's hanging above his head.

It must be some kind of forgery, but it's a damn good one. I grew up looking at the original. I wasn't allowed in the room in which the painting was displayed, so I would sit outside the doorway and watch it. A Rothko with no name. Just a ragged black square on a bloodred background. The sort of painting most people believe that a five-year-old could paint. Live with it awhile, though, and you'll realize it's alive. The empty red space in the center of the square pulsates with energy. It moves and breathes. It calls to you when you turn away.

The artist loathed the rich, yet he knew his work was bound for their walls. This was one of the last things he painted before he slashed his own wrists. I always wondered if it was meant to send future owners a message. Rothko didn't give it a name, but Jude and I called it *The Gates of Hell*.

"Are you an admirer of Rothko's work?" Lucian Mandel asks once I've taken a seat at his table.

"That can't be a real Rothko," I say, my eyes still on the painting.

"It's real. It was in a private collection for many years, but the owner grew bored of it. The restaurant picked it up at auction a few months ago."

I bring my gaze down to Mandel's boyish face. He's toying with me. I wonder what he's going to say about the wallet.

"Thank you for coming, Flick," he says. "That's your name, am I right?"

"We both know that's not my real name," I reply.

"And since you received my invitation, you know *my* name as well."

He studies me while he waits for a response. I say nothing.

"Excellent! What a remarkable poker face! Not even the slightest twitch."

Why does everything seem so amusing to this asshole? "You're Lucian Mandel. You run the Mandel Academy."

"That's correct."

"I thought you people were supposed to help street kids, not pay them to rob houses."

"I *was* helping you, Flick. The job I gave you was what you might call an entrance exam." He changes the subject before I can figure out what he meant. "What, may I ask, have you heard about the Mandel Academy?"

It's an odd thing to ask. "Everyone knows about the Mandel Academy. Where would you like me to start?"

"Let's start with whatever your father has told you."

"You sure you want to start there? Everything the man's ever said was a lie."

Mandel chuckles. "Yes, your father is a master of twisting the truth to his own advantage. But I promise—I'll never be anything but honest with you. The academy was founded by my great-great-grandmother, Fredericka Mandelbaum, in the 1870s. Very few people know about the institution's early days. Until the turn of the century, it was known as the Grand Street School. I don't suppose you've heard of it?"

"No."

"Yes, well, it was a different beast back then. But it did share our current goal of educating disadvantaged youths. In fact, most of the school's first students were plucked right off the streets of the Lower East Side. Many were pickpockets and thieves just like you. My grandmother had an eye for talent. Her school was a stunning success from the start."

"Yeah?" I fake a yawn. I don't want him to know that I'm interested. "So why the name change?"

It seems to be a question that my host is eager to answer. "My grandmother was a philanthropist, but she was also a businesswoman. And I'm not ashamed to admit that some people called her a criminal. She made a fortune trading in stolen goods. When the police shut her down, she fled to Canada, where she died an extremely wealthy woman. Her son wanted to continue the good work that his mother had begun in New York. Unfortunately, the Grand Street School was tainted by its association with the Mandelbaum family. So he dropped 'baum' from our name and opened the Mandel Academy in a beautiful building on Beekman Street. Have you seen it?"

"No."

He leans forward, elbows on the table, fingers entwined, eyes on me. "Would you like to?"

I lean in too. "I didn't come here for a history lesson or a sightseeing tour. You know who I am. You knew where to find me. You've obviously been watching me, and I want to know *why*."

I should terrify him. I'm big, filthy, and I reek of dog shit. But he seems to find me adorable. Like I'm just a naughty little scamp with a plastic pistol who's told him to reach for the sky.

"Because I'd like to offer you a place at the Mandel Academy."

This time I can't hide my surprise. Mandel eats it up.

"It's a wonderful opportunity," he continues, sitting back against the plush banquette. "We're considered the best school in the city, and we only admit eighteen students a year. Since 1960, every one of our graduates has been awarded a full scholarship to an Ivy League university."

"I thought the Mandel Academy only accepts charity cases. I'm not exactly what you'd call disadvantaged."

I get the sense that he and I define the word differently. But he'd rather humor me than argue. "I've decided to make an exception in your case. Although I must say, you look rather disadvantaged at the moment. And you smell even worse."

We're still dancing around the real issue. "My father is on the Mandel Academy's board of directors. Does he know about this?"

"Certainly! All of our students are carefully vetted. I could never hide a candidate from a member of our board. Your father has been informed of my plans every step of the way."

"Then tell me this." I lean even closer. "Why the f— do either of you think I'd attend that bastard's precious alma mater?"

"For the same reason you've been living in his old neighborhood for the past seven months. You want to grow up to be just like him."

I grin. There's no longer any reason to stay, so I scoot my chair away from the table. "I was almost impressed. But you've got me all wrong."

"Have I?" Mandel asks before I can make my exit.

"Tell my father I'll see him soon."

"Without my help, you'll never be ready to face him," Mandel says.

The surprise forces me back down in my seat. "What do you mean?" I growl.

"Your father is one of America's richest men. You grew up in a mansion in Connecticut. And yet you've chosen to live on the streets. You must imagine the hardship will toughen you up. But do you honestly believe that a few months on the Lower East Side can teach you everything you need to know? The place is a theme park for tourists. You're just part of the show. You're not *really* dangerous. You pick a few pockets, throw a few punches, then hurry home to your sweet little girlfriend."

He's talking about Joi. I feel a jolt of fear for the first time in months. "She's not my girlfriend."

"No, I suppose she's much more than that. Have you told her why you're here? Does she know who you are? Does she know who your father is?"

He doesn't expect any answers. He thinks he already has them. "What's going on? Is this some sort of sick game?"

"Call it whatever you like, Flick," Mandel says. His smile has vanished. "But you wouldn't be here right now if I wasn't on *your* side."

CHAPTER SIX

HOW TO LEAD A LIFE OF CRIME

If I were still in school, I'd be a senior. I spent the first nine grades at a Connecticut prep school that's a household name in the households of millionaires. Then a teacher asked too many questions about my bruises. She was fired, but that wasn't enough to satisfy my father. I had to be punished as well. So he enrolled me at a crappy public school a few miles from my home. The teachers there had more kids to monitor, and they weren't the most inquisitive bunch. But eventually even they started to notice. When my face was rearranged right before Christmas break in my sophomore year, some anonymous Good Samaritan phoned the police. The cops bought my dad's story that my broken nose, fractured cheekbone, and black eyes were all the result of a bicycling accident. Or maybe they didn't. Maybe he just paid them enough to not care. Either way, the unwanted attention convinced my father to send me to boarding school. He chose a military academy in the swampy, malarial lowlands of Georgia.

At first I resisted. If I'd wanted to leave, I could have just run away. I'd packed my bag a hundred times over the years. I'd decided where to go and how to get there. I was fully prepared to disappear. But I didn't. I stayed. Every time I set out on my own, I thought about my mother and brother. And what might happen if I left them behind. As a kid I'd always dreamed that the three of us could escape together. But by the time I hit high school, I knew there was no chance we'd ever succeed. It made no difference where we tried to hide, my dad was always able to find us. I doubt he'd have bothered looking for me. But he wasn't willing to let Jude go.

Everyone knew I'd be safer in Georgia—even at a school famous for turning young men into half-savage soldiers. But with my little brother trapped in Connecticut, I wasn't about to be shipped down south. In the end, Jude was the one who convinced me to leave. It took several days of pestering before he found an argument that made me take notice. Jude said Mom would be happier if I was out of harm's way. The thought had never occurred to me—that my mother might be better off if I wasn't around. That it might be a relief to wake up each day knowing that she wouldn't have to stand between me and my father's fists. And then I realized I'd be doing Jude a big favor too. He was fourteen years old. He deserved to enjoy what little was left of his childhood. He needed time off from saving me.

So I left. And for a while, I was sure it had been the best decision of my life. I loved the fierce Georgia heat. I loved that my school days never brought any surprises. And I loved learning to be a warrior. Because even then, I planned to fight back. By the spring of my junior year, I held a Graduate rank in Krav Maga, and I was the school's undefeated boxing champ. I was certain I'd be invincible by graduation. Then, on the eighteenth of April—a few days before Easter—I found out how much I still needed to learn.

I'm smarter now than I was back then. My education cost everything that I had. So I find it amusing that Lucian Mandel thinks he's the one who'll be calling the shots. I guess he's been spying on me for a while, because he's convinced that he's got me all figured out. But I know something about him too. Lucian Mandel hates my father. Which isn't surprising. My dad's the CEO of one of the world's biggest banks. And he'd be the first to point out that nice guys don't get to the top. At this stage you'd need the US Census Bureau to count my dad's enemies. But only one of them has ever come looking for *me*. So I've agreed to hear what Mandel has to say.

Mandel pulls his Maserati into an alley a block away from City Hall Park. The lane is too narrow to stand back and get a good view of the building we're visiting. It must be one of the oldest structures in this part of town. Redbrick with terra-cotta trim. Ten—no nine—stories tall. A couple of towers that would look right at home on a haunted house. I don't know what I was expecting, but this sure isn't it.

The academy can't have changed much since my dad was a student. I wish I could have seen his reaction the day he stood on this spot for the very first time. The school must have seemed much more impressive to a poor boy from the mean streets of the Lower East Side. To me, it's like something right out of Dickens. A scene from an old movie flashes through my mind: A line of young boys with empty bowls are waiting for their morning gruel. "Please, sir, may I have some more?" asks one who's already scarfed down his portion. I almost laugh out loud at the thought.

"Shall we?" Mandel uses a card key to open a door marked SERVICE ENTRANCE. When I look inside, all I see is a bright shaft of sunlight.

Turns out the interior is much more impressive. And I see the source of the light. A glass pyramid serves as the building's roof, and all nine stories are wrapped around a central atrium. The open space in the middle of each floor is ringed by a balcony with a wrought-iron railing. Every balcony is supported by four metal dragons with outstretched wings and golden balls clamped in their mouths. I imagine them all taking flight and soaring in circles as they snatch up Mandel students one by one.

I walk to the center of the courtyard—across a tile mosaic. Tiny squares form giant letters, but I can't figure out which words they form. I'm too close to read them. So I tilt my head back and look all the way up. The steel and glass towers of Manhattan's financial district peer down at me through the roof. The sky overhead is cloudless, and the school is beautiful beneath the bright afternoon sun. But I bet on dark days, it looks a lot like the toy maker's building in *Blade Runner*.

"Where is everyone?" I ask Mandel. I don't see a soul. "Winter break?"

"We don't have vacations here," Mandel informs me. "Most of the young people at the academy must work nonstop to make up for lost time, so we can't afford any distractions. We don't allow visitors and we don't observe weekends or holidays. There are three semesters a year, and every day is a school day. The students are all in class."

Mandel saunters over to what looks like a tall iron cage on the north side of the atrium. Two metal boxes are suspended inside. One is stationed on the ninth floor. The other has stopped at the fourth. I've never seen an elevator like it before. Mandel presses a button, and I hear the sound of metal gates sliding shut. A car begins to descend. I can see straight through it. There's no one inside.

"The ground floor houses administrative offices and the alumni lounge," Mandel announces. "Floors two through four are classrooms. Floor five is the gymnasium. The cafeteria is on floor six. Floors seven through nine are the dormitories. We're going to pay a quick visit to one of the classrooms."

As our elevator begins to rise, I catch a brief glimpse of some of the academy's students through the window of a second-floor door. Whatever is being taught has them riveted. All eyes are fixed on the instructor at the front of the room.

Mandel and I exit on the fourth floor. I happen to glance over the balcony and immediately come to an abrupt stop. I'm finally high enough to decipher the mosaic below. There are three flaming gold spheres. Beneath them is a motto: LUCTOR ET EMERGO.

"Do you know any Latin?" Mandel inquires.

"It means 'I suffer and arise.' What are the balls supposed to be?"

"My great-grandfather was the man who commissioned the mosaic, and I believe he would have said they were seeds. Most plants will sprout if you give them water, soil, and sunlight. But there are a few trees whose seeds must be sown by fire. Whenever a forest is destroyed by flames, they're the first species to rise and thrive."

"Interesting," I drone. The spheres could have been comets or cannonballs. Instead they're *seeds*.

"Not terribly," Mandel replies. "But that *is* what my great-grand-father would have said. I have my own interpretation. Someday, you will as well."

Someday, you will as well. He's been dropping little hints about my future since we left Floraison. He thinks he has me right where he wants me. He thinks I signed over my soul when I got into his car.

"Keep talking like that, and I'm out of here. I already told you what to do with your scholarship."

Mandel smiles at my warning. He's a cocky little weasel, I'll give him that. "How could I forget? You used such *colorful* imagery."

"Then you should remember I'm only here for one reason. You said you have something I'd want to see. Something to do with my father. Now are you going to show me or not?"

"I am, Flick. It's just down the hall."

I wish I wasn't so goddamned curious. I wish I could just walk away. But I'm dying to find out what Mandel has on my father—and why he'd choose to share it with me. I'm sure my dad's given this guy a hundred reasons to hate him. A prissy fop like Mandel would disgust a man like my father. He'd sneer at Mandel's stylish suit and manicured nails. He'd toy with him a bit first. Hurt him. Humiliate him. Then when my dad got bored of it all, he'd rip little Lucian to shreds. So I can understand why Mandel might be out for revenge.

But I'm a seventeen-year-old thief who's ass-broke and homeless. What I can't figure out is why a big-time player like Lucian Mandel would want to be allies with someone like me.

I let him drag me downtown for the answer, but so far I've only received a lesson in botany. Now Mandel's leading me past a row of closed doors. I can hear the murmur of voices, but I can't make out any words. A single door on the floor stands ajar. This is the room Mandel chooses. He's brought me to an ordinary classroom. There's a large wooden desk for the teacher. A tall pile of pamphlets has been stacked in its center. I count a dozen smaller desks for the pupils. A blackboard. Chalk.

"Is this supposed to impress me? I've seen a f—ing blackboard before."

Mandel leans against the teacher's desk and crosses his arms. It almost looks like he's posing. "One of the things you'll learn here is that language like that doesn't make a young man seem formidable. It only makes him seem *crude*."

"F— you," I say, heading for the door. "I didn't sign up for an etiquette lesson."

"Don't let emotions cloud your judgment, Flick. You're not here to see a classroom. You're here to see *this*." I don't want to glance back, but I do. My tour guide has plucked one of the pamphlets from the stack on the desk, and he's waving it in the air. "This is the Mandel Academy's course catalog. I'd like you to take a look. I considered bringing a copy to lunch, but I decided it wouldn't be wise. Information like this mustn't leave the academy. . . ."

He doesn't flinch when I stomp across the classroom and snatch the pamphlet right out of his hand. I open the booklet to a random page and prepare to be bored. But I'm not. I skim the title of the first class that's listed, and I'm totally, helplessly hooked.

Caviar, Catnip, and California Cornflakes:

"Interesting courses," I mumble. "Cute titles too."

"Yes," Mandel agrees. "Our human resources majors are tasked with compiling the catalog. The student in charge this semester believes that a touch of humor will appeal to our teenage audience. I must admit, I was surprised by his suggestion. Caleb is a gifted student, but he's always been a rather dour young man. I wouldn't have guessed he possessed such wit."

As I keep reading, I begin to suspect that Caleb and his school-mates might have a few other talents as well.

Partnering with Corrupt Regimes

Basic Electronics:

Crime Scene Cleaning and Bio-waste Removal

I flip to the back of the pamphlet.

The Art of Persuasion:
Human Trafficking in the Internet Age

Mining the Masses:

KIRSTEN MILLER

Hand-to-Hand Combat

If I went down to the sidewalk, gathered ten random pedestrians, and asked them to share their opinions on the subject of dog grooming, they'd probably end up in a bloody brawl. But if I asked for their thoughts on the Mandel Academy, there wouldn't be any argument. They'd all say that the academy is one of the things that make this country great. You won't find another school like it anywhere else in the world. For decades, it's taken orphans, runaways, and delinquents off the streets and transformed them into lawyers, businessmen, bankers, and senators. The Mandel Academy has never welcomed reporters or outsiders into its building. The names of current students are a closely held secret. But anyone looking for proof that the American dream hasn't died only needs to google a list of the academy's graduates.

And *this* is the shit they all studied here? Extortion? Drug dealing? Larceny? *Crime scene cleaning?* Next I'll find out that Steve Jobs was Jack the Ripper.

I lock eyes with Lucian Mandel. There's obviously more to the man than I first suspected.

"Where's the course called How to Lead a Life of Crime? That's what this is all about, isn't it? You've got everyone thinking this is the best school in the country, but it's really just a Hogwarts for hustlers."

He's not insulted. He's only bemused. "You sound so appalled. Don't tell me you're one of them."

"One of *who*?"

"The believers," Mandel explains. "All the people who refuse to

53

see how the world really works. The ones who think that cheaters never prosper. That the meek shall inherit the earth. Most people out there still believe all the sweet little lies they were told as children. But the truth is, no one in this country gets rich if they play by the rules. Power is granted to those who will do whatever it takes to succeed. Those are the facts of life."

He leans forward.

"So tell, me, Flick? Who are you? Are you one of the believers—or are you one of *us*?"

How could I possibly be a believer? I've known the sickening truth since I was a kid. That we're all swimming in one big cesspool. I won't pinch my nose and pretend that it's paradise, but I'm not going to train myself to love the smell of shit, either.

"I don't have any interest in joining your club, Mandel. What's so great about teaching a bunch of brats how to break every law in the country?"

Mandel sighs as if I've missed the point. "That's a very narrow-minded way of viewing things. And for the record, we never force students to commit any crimes. We merely teach them the true ways of the world. The Mandel Academy didn't *invent* fraud or extortion or insider trading. But we can't pretend that such things don't exist. They are tools that other people employ, so we train our students to make use of them too. That doesn't mean that they *will*. Some Mandel alumni are perfectly law-abiding. They choose to work within the system. Not that the law matters a great deal to any of us. We serve a much higher purpose."

I bet he wants me to ask about his "higher purpose," but I'm not going to humor him. The guy clearly loves to hear himself talk. I try to hand the course catalog back to him. Mandel refuses to take it. I should toss it into the trash can that's sitting next to the desk. But I don't.

"Look, I'm a thief. I'm not exactly qualified to debate ethics, and I don't really give a crap what you teach at this school. But if this is all you've got to show me, I'm going to be pissed. You said we'd be talking about my father."

"Isn't that what we're doing?"

I despise smart-asses who speak in riddles and expect you to figure them out. "What does your shady school have to do with . . ."

Then I realize I already know the answer. My father isn't just a graduate of the Mandel Academy—he's on the goddamned *board of directors*.

"Has the academy always been like this?" I ask.

When Mandel isn't smirking, his gaze is unsettling. He makes me feel like I'm being dissected.

"Yes, from the day we first opened our doors. Although in the school's early years, students were trained in much simpler tasks. Lock-picking. Safe-cracking. Confidence games. Armed robbery. But now, our most successful graduates don't *rob* banks, they *run* them. Why risk your life sticking up a savings and loan? These days you can steal billions without ever leaving your office."

"So my dad took classes like the ones in this catalog?"

"Is that the question you'd *really* like answered? Speak your mind, Flick. There's no reason to tiptoe around me."

"My father is a crook, isn't he?'"

Mandel's laugh must be genuine. It's too damned bizarre to be fake. "Some people claim all investment bankers are crooks. I only know a few dozen, so I can't speak for the entire profession. But if you're born with sticky fingers, banking can be an excellent career choice. So the answer to your question is *yes*. Your father is a thief—just like his son. The difference is, you're only able to rob one person at a time. Your father can pick thousands of pockets with the click of a single computer key."

I've been waiting for the day I could punish my dad. For everything he did, and everything he might have done. I figured I'd have to use my own two fists. That's the reason I came to New York—to grow strong enough to beat him. I wanted to make the bastard bleed. I still do. But now, after I'm finished, I can send what little is left of him straight to jail.

"What do you have on him?" I demand. "That's why I'm here, right? You hate my dad. You want him taken down, but you don't want to do it yourself. Fine. It's a deal. Just tell me what you know, and I'll handle the dirty work."

"You're wrong, Flick. That's not why you're here."

The tone of his voice unnerves me. It's far too flat—like he's reading lines off a script.

"Then I'm not going to let you waste any more of my time," I announce. "I gotta go."

I'm on my way to the door when a bell begins to toll. Suddenly there's a stampede in the hall outside. Voices. Laughter. The students sound just like ordinary kids. I have to see them.

"No." For some reason, the command stops me. There doesn't seem to be any way around it. I turn back to face Mandel. "I wouldn't step outside right now. You're the only student who's ever been granted a tour. I don't want your future classmates to know

I've been playing favorites. They wouldn't like that at all."

The only student. My future classmates. I'm halfway out the door, and Mandel still thinks he's got me right where he wants me. His little hints aren't just annoying anymore. At this point, they're starting to scare me. "What the hell is going on?" I demand.

While I'm waiting for his answer, the noise outside trails off. Another bell rings. Doors shut, and there's silence once more. Mandel stands and strolls toward me. When he puts his hand on my shoulder, I brush it away.

"Let's have a look at your room. I think we may find the answer there."

"My" room is on the eighth floor. Mandel shoves a card into a slot below the handle, and the door slides open. The glass in the window is frosted. Light pours in, but I can't see out. My computer is on the desk. My books are stacked on the shelves. A pair of my boxing gloves hangs from the closet doorknob. The blanket from my room in Connecticut lies neatly folded at the end of the bed. The life I left behind has been painstakingly reassembled. None of my belongings should be here.

"How did you get all this stuff?"

"Your father had it sent here." Mandel picks up a throw pillow that my mother made and gives it a light fluffing. "He would like you to attend the academy. We need you to settle a little disagreement for the two of us."

I assumed that Mandel and my father are enemies. But did Mandel ever actually say that they *are*? If they've joined forces against me, I'm in serious shit. "What kind of disagreement?"

Mandel tosses the pillow back on the bed. "It concerns the academy, of course. Your father and I both care deeply about the future of this institution. But we have very different opinions about the direction it should take. Your father would like the Mandel Academy to operate just as it did when he was a student. I've proposed a few changes that could bring this school into the twenty-first century. But I need the approval of the alumni and our board of directors. The graduates have chosen sides, and they're almost evenly split. So you get to be the tiebreaker."

"Then I guess you should tell me what the fight's about."

"I believe I've found a way to recruit a better class of student. But as your father has wisely observed, my theory remains untested, and . . ."

I can't f—ing believe it. I've been dragged into some stupid little spat. I take a menacing step toward Mandel. He shuts up but stands his ground. "Hold on—are you talking about the school's goddamned *admissions* policy?"

"Yes. As it happens, you're the kind of student I'd like to recruit. So your father and I have agreed to a wager. If you graduate from the Mandel Academy, your father will resign from the academy's board of directors. If you *don't* graduate, then I will step down and your father will appoint a new headmaster."

"What happens if I tell you both to go to hell?"

Mandel nods as if he'd been waiting for that very response. "Your father said you'd never agree. He claims you're not up to the challenge. I think he's *worried* you are."

He chose the word *worried* with care. *Scared* wouldn't have been believable. "You're kidding, right?"

"Not at all. You and your father have a great deal in common. I suspect he sees himself in you. Perhaps that's why he's tried so hard to crush you. He knows that you might have the power to destroy him."

Just when I thought that this conversation couldn't get any stranger. "I have the *power to destroy him*?" I snicker. "You're either bat-shit insane or you've watched too many movies. This isn't *Star Wars*, Mandel. I'm not Luke Skywalker. My dad's not Darth Vader. And you sure as hell aren't my Obi-Wan."

Something I said just got to him. But Mandel hides his annoyance well. "Let me ask you a question, Flick. What do you know about your grandparents?"

Next to nothing. They didn't play any role in the stories my father told Jude. My mother said she'd never met her in-laws—and based on the few facts she'd been given, she was glad she'd been spared. "I know my dad's mom was a floozy who ran off when he was a boy. His father was a drunk. He died in a gutter a few weeks before my dad entered the Mandel Academy. . . ."

Mandel stops me with a shake of his head. He doesn't need to hear any more. "Some of that is true. Your grandfather was an alcoholic, but he didn't die in a gutter. He died in bed with a steak knife buried in his chest. Your father's fingerprints were all over the handle."

It feels like the same blade was just driven through my ribs. But I don't double over. I laugh. "Are you actually suggesting that my dad murdered my grandfather?"

"No, I'm *telling* you. It's a fact. My mother recruited your father during her time as headmistress. The academy keeps files on all students, and I've read your father's file many times. He confessed to killing your grandfather, but the judge presiding over the case thought your father had acted in self-defense. After all, the boy had been brutally beaten every day for years. So the judge contacted my mother and asked for her help. He wanted to give your father a second chance."

My father's a crook. I'm a thief. My father was beaten. My dad beat me. His father drank. My dad does too, but I'm the only one left who knows how much. "My grandfather's name—it was Frank, wasn't it?"

Mandel lifts his nose to the air, like a hunting dog that's picked up a scent. "No, I believe it was Doyle. What made you think it was *Frank*?"

Because my dad called me that once. I must have been about twelve at the time. I remember it was a Sunday, and he'd spent the afternoon alone in his study, quietly working his way through a decanter of Scotch. His silence always scared me. So I stood in the hall with my ear to his door, waiting for him to make a trip to the toilet. When he finally did, I snuck into the room and watered a fichus with the rest of his whiskey. He caught me just as I was returning the decanter to its tray. His punch knocked me off my feet and into a wall. When I slid to the floor, I stayed there. I wasn't terribly hurt—just playing dead while I figured out what to do next. Maybe my brain was a little bit rattled, but I could have sworn I heard my dad whisper, *Frank*. When he left, he closed the door behind him.

Even Jude never set foot in my father's study. He and my mother wouldn't have thought to look for me there. Who knows how long I'd have lain on that floor if I'd actually been badly injured.

"Never mind. For some reason the name Frank just popped into my head," I tell Mandel. "Do you think my dad really stabbed his old man in self-defense?"

"There's no doubt about it. Your father wasn't cold-blooded back then—far from it. I remember when he first arrived at the academy. I was just a young boy at the time, and he made a big impression on me. I'd seen troubled students before, but I'd never met anyone quite so pathetic. According to the file, his instructors thought he'd amount to nothing. And by the end of his first month here, they were demanding he be expelled. But my mother resisted. She looked past your father's unpromising exterior and saw the potential hidden inside. She made him the man he is today. And until she died, my mother always claimed that he was her masterpiece. And you, Flick—you could be *mine*."

Jude was right. Our dad lied. The bastard lied about everything that mattered. My father never ran wild on the streets of the Lower East Side. He wasn't a badass; he was an abused little boy. He was *nothing* before he came here. He was just like me.

"I'm not interested in being anyone's masterpiece."

"That's not the correct response, Flick. You should have asked, 'What's in it for me?'"

Now we're getting somewhere. "Okay. What's in it for me?"

Mandel reaches into his suit pocket and hands me a piece of paper. A page torn from a grade school yearbook. It's been folded and unfolded so many times that it's coming apart at the creases. I don't need to open it. I know all forty pictures on the page by heart. Thirty-nine little schoolboys in blazers and ties—and one ten-year-old in a green felt hat with a red feather sticking out. In the photo, he's thrusting a wooden sword at the camera.

That piece of paper was the one thing I planned to take with me when I went AWOL from military school. It's my most prized possession. I almost lost my nerve when I wasn't able to find it.

"I know what really happened to your family," Mandel says. "Do you?"

"Jude." His name is suddenly the only thing left in my mind.

"Have you put all the pieces together yet? You must have suspected that your father had a hand in Jude's death."

Yes. "But *why*?"

"Your brother discovered that your father hasn't been the most upstanding citizen—and then Jude made the mistake of confronting him."

The room dissolves as if its atoms are no longer glued together. The only thing I can see through the blur is a bright patch of light. It must be the window. I keep my eyes fixed on it and hope it's enough to keep me tethered to earth. There must be something Jude wants to show me, but I can't let him pull me away. *Don't crack up.* I plead with myself. *Don't go with him right now. Wait until you're alone again. No one's going to help a freak who talks to Peter Pan. Please, please, please! Don't f—ing crack up!*

"How do you know?" I have to force the words out of my throat.

"Your father needed the academy's assistance to cover his crime. Which means I have proof. Photographs of the scene. Audio recordings that amount to a confession."

Mandel's face is the first thing I see when the room begins to take shape again. Freckled. Boyish. Friendly. Could he actually have it? The one thing I want more than anything else? The only thing on earth I'd be willing to kill for?

"You've suffered a great deal in the past few months," he tells me. "That's why I'm gambling my life and my legacy on you. Pain destroys the weak, Flick. But it makes the strong invincible. If you survive—and I believe you will—you could turn out to be the finest graduate we've produced in some time."

Screw all his sweet talk. "You'll give me the proof?"

"As soon as you graduate. Then you may use it however you see fit."

"How long will I have to be here?"

"That depends on your performance. Nine of our top students graduate every year, and the ceremony always takes place in September. You'll be eighteen by then, which means you'll be eligible to graduate. But you will have to prove that you're ready for a Mandel degree. Until you are, you will not be allowed to leave the academy."

Nine months. Nine months is nothing.

Mandel slides his hands into his pants pockets. His eyebrows are arched, and he's bouncing a bit on the balls of his feet. "So what do you say, Flick? Will you help me win my little wager?"

I tuck the yearbook page into my back pocket. I'd rather Jude didn't hear my answer. I know he wouldn't approve. "Yes."

"Excellent! However, there are two conditions to which you must agree before you're officially admitted. Graduates may pursue any career of their choosing, but they must always remain in the employ of the Mandel family."

It's a meaningless formality. I have no intention of pursuing a career. "Fine. And the second condition?"

"Our students are a special breed. Everyone here is gifted in one way or another. But many arrive lacking discipline and self-restraint.

Over the years, we've found it essential to keep a close eye on our students until they acquire those two traits. On the first day you arrive, a small chip will be inserted beneath the skin of your forearm. It will allow the academy to monitor your location. As soon as you graduate, the chip will be removed."

"*What?*" This is a problem. "There's no f—ing way I'm going to let you put a chip in my arm."

Mandel makes a show of sympathy. "I'm sorry, but I'm afraid the chip is non-negotiable. But I do understand your reluctance. It's a terribly old-fashioned method of keeping our less disciplined students in line. A pharmaceutical option would be more state-of-the-art. We're looking at ways to update the system, but for now, the chips remain a necessity. However, I can assure you that your father will not be able to access the data. And I don't waste time tracking students who don't cause trouble. I'd let you in without a chip, but I don't think you'd want to stand out from your schoolmates." He sees I'm still not convinced. "Tell you what. Why don't you take a little while to think about it? Have a hot shower in your private bathroom. Change into some clean clothes. You'll find everything you need is here in this room. I even took the liberty of adding a few items to your wardrobe. I'll drop by in an hour to hear your final answer. If it turns out to be yes, there are a few people downstairs who would love to give you a proper welcome. Believe it or not, Flick, you already have fans."

He leaves me sitting on the bed. Once he's gone, I take it all in. The mattress is firm. The room's furniture is simple and elegant. My mother would have called the pale shade of gray on the walls something like *Nimbus* or *Dove*. It's all so incredibly tasteful. There won't be much suffering in a room like this.

I don't trust Mandel. I don't buy a bit of his flattery. And the tracking chip is disturbing as hell. But at the end of the day, none of that matters. Mandel knows that my father killed Jude—and he says he has proof. And there's nothing—*nothing*—I won't do to get it.

CHAPTER SEVEN

THE WAKE

I'm getting drunk enough to enjoy my own going-away party. The people I pass either gawk or get out of the way. It's not every day that a rich-looking kid is spotted staggering through the projects with no coat and a bottle of his father's favorite Scotch in his hand.

"Thirty-*thousand* dollars a pop," I inform a young lady. She steps off the sidewalk, into a patch of mud. You know you're a mess when girls ruin their shoes to avoid you. "And you just piss it out the same evening!" I shout at her back.

A seven-foot hulk in a black North Face coat and knit hat emerges from the lobby of one of the buildings. In the darkness, he looks like a bear standing on its hind legs. And I'm trespassing on its territory. Suddenly the bear takes off toward the west, moving more quickly than you'd think possible for a beast of his size. I have a feeling he'll be back with friends.

"Go get 'em!" I call out. "I'll wait right here for you!"

I drop to the ground with a thump and sit with my back against a tree. I take a swig from the bottle and gag. You'd think Scotch this expensive would taste like something other than whiskey. I wonder if stealing a thirty-thousand-dollar bottle of liquor is grounds for expulsion from the Mandel Academy. Seems highly unlikely. I guess I'll find out in the morning.

Scotch or no Scotch, Mandel can't be too happy that I slipped out of his little cocktail party. Six of his favorite alums had shown up to check out the horse he'd backed. And these weren't your average gamblers. A lady senator. A CEO. Two big-shots from Goldman Sachs. A businesswoman who'd flown in from China. And some dude with a scraggly beard and camouflage pants. Everyone else chuckled when he told me he "works from home." I knew they were all there to place their own bets. So Mandel made sure I'd been cleaned up and decked out in the finest duds. As soon as we stepped into the alumni lounge on the first floor, the guests began examining my physique and picking my brain. I suspect a few of them wanted to pry open my mouth and have a good look at my teeth. Or make me drop my trousers, turn my head, and cough. I kept my pants on, but they still seemed to walk away satisfied. When they began to pair off to compare notes, I grabbed a bottle from the bar and headed straight for the exit. Now that I think about it, there's got to be plenty of security at the academy. Mandel must have let me leave because he figured I'd be back. But if he was really smart, he'd have stopped me. His cameras probably caught me with a bottle in my hand, but nobody saw the contraband tucked into the waistband of my fancy new pants.

I pull out the course catalog and flip through its pages for the third time tonight. Mandel says the catalogs can't leave the academy. But I think he's being a little too cautious. No one would ever take this shit seriously. I mean, who's gonna believe that the prestigious Mandel Academy offers classes on *assassination techniques*? (Wish I had a pencil handy. I'd circle the *hell* outa that one.) So despite my sticky fingers, his secrets are probably safe. *Too bad.* I was hoping I'd be able to skip all this BS and persuade Mandel to make a trade. His catalog for my dad's ass. But there's no way he'll go for it. I guess I'll have to learn how to skim credit cards and clean crime scenes after all. But at least I'll be able to make it through high school without touching *Moby-Dick.* I cackle and close one eye so the words on the catalog's pages stop squirming. There isn't a single art class listed. No literature, either. No sex education. Nothing *useless.* It's all business all the time at the fabulous Mandel Academy. No wonder the alumni have the personalities of cyborgs.

The more I read, the more nauseous I get. Finally I have to put the catalog down and wash the vomit back with a glug of Scotch. I'm cold. Starting to drift off, but my eyes pop open. A little boy is standing a few yards away, snapping my picture with the camera on his crappy phone.

"Hey, what time is it?" I shout.

The kid jumps about three feet in the air. He probably thought I was dead.

"What *time?*" I repeat. "Look at your goddamn phone."

"Eight," he squeaks, and runs away.

"That's what I thought." My eyes flutter shut again.

I left military school seven months ago, but there's an alarm in my head that still goes off at eight every evening. That's when they turned on the Wi-Fi for an hour. You were supposed to cram all of your Internet research into sixty short minutes. I could have slept through every class and still been named the school's valedictorian. So I used the time to talk to Jude.

He was always there when I logged on—even on weekends when he must have had better things to do. We chatted about stupid stuff. Boxing and girls and dirty southern slang I'd picked up from my fellow cadets. Never once did he give me any reason to suspect that he had something planned. Then the night before I went AWOL, I found a message in my in-box. He'd sent it just before two o'clock that afternoon. *You're coming home soon,* it said. *I know something. He won't hurt you or Mom again.*

My fingers couldn't type fast enough. *Don't do anything! Swear you won't!*

I hit send and waited for a response. I was still waiting when the lights went out. Sometimes I imagine my message floating around cyberspace for the rest of eternity.

The next morning, I left for my daily cross-country jog with sixty-five dollars and three sets of clothing hidden under my tracksuit. I hopped the fence at the mile mark and waded through part of the Okefenokee Swamp until I hit the highway.

An old lady at the bus stop let me borrow her phone. A maid answered at my parents' house. I asked for Jude and hung up when she started to cry.

I didn't come to New York first. I went to Connecticut instead. To the Beaumont Funeral Home—the only mortuary in my home-town that my father would trust with his youngest son's corpse. It was late when I got there, and the entrance was locked. I started searching for a way inside. I would have broken a window or kicked down the door if a woman hadn't shown up with a key. I don't recall her name. I can't even see her face in my mind. All I remember is the black box she was carrying.

"You're the brother, aren't you?" she asked. "The one who went missing."

I must have managed a nod.

"They said you might come here," she added. "We're supposed to call your father if we see you."

"Don't," I croaked.

"I wasn't planning to," she said kindly. "I made up my mind about that when I saw your brother."

"What happened to him?" I asked.

"They say he fell. Down the stairs in your house." I could tell she didn't buy the story.

"Can I see him?"

She held up the black box. "They just finished cleaning him up a little while ago. I haven't started his makeup yet. I don't think . . ."

"*Please.*"

She sighed for my sake and unlocked the door.

Jude was lying on an embalming table. I could see his freshly washed hair sticking out from beneath the sheet that covered the rest of his body. It was the only time I'd seen my brother so perfectly still. I stood at his side and slid the cloth down to his shoulders. The face I saw wasn't the one I remembered.

I thought I recognized my father's handiwork in Jude's broken nose and shattered bones. But if my dad's fists could inflict that kind of damage, he must have been holding back all those times he beat me. I couldn't figure out why he'd let loose on Jude. And I knew I'd never be able to prove that he had. In fact, if it hadn't been for Jude's email, I might have bought into the story that his death was an accident. But I knew. I only had a single small clue, but I knew my brother must have died trying to help me.

"He used to be handsome," I said.

"He looked like you. They gave me a picture," the woman whispered behind me. I thought she might have been crying. I couldn't turn around.

"Would it be okay if I stay here until you're finished?"

I heard her take a deep breath. "Sure," she said on the exhale.

"My father will have you fired if he finds out." It was only fair to warn her.

"That's okay, honey. Some things are more important than a job."

I found a chair and sat with my forehead resting on the edge of the embalming table and one hand on my brother's cold arm. I honestly thought I might die on that spot. The only thing I'd ever really believed in was Jude. He was my evidence that our father was full of shit. That you could choose to be something other than weak or strong. But it turned out that my father had been right from the start. You're either one or the other. There are no alternatives—and no space in between. Jude died because he had one fatal flaw. A chink in his armor. A soft spot that he couldn't keep hidden. Jude was killed because his weakness was *me*.

That night was the first time he appeared to me in a dream. He wasn't the dead sixteen-year-old with the broken face. He was the ten-year-old Peter Pan. Impish. Immortal.

"Jude, please don't leave me here," I begged him.

"This isn't goodbye," he insisted. "You know that place between sleep and awake? The place where you can still remember dreaming? That's where I'll be waiting."

"That's not f—ing good enough!" I shouted, almost choking on snot and tears.

"It's not good, but it's enough," he said. "You'll see. Did you get my gift?"

"Gift?"

He wiggled his fingers at me. "Use them wisely, and you'll have everything that you need."

The makeup lady shook me. "It's morning," she said. "You need to leave before my boss gets in."

"Did you fix him?" I asked. "Jude has to look like himself when he gets there."

She must have thought I meant heaven—not Never Never Land. She didn't realize I'd lost my mind. "I worked on him all night. Would you like me to show you?"

"No," I told her. "I have to keep him alive."

It was as simple as that. I began to believe. That Jude wasn't gone—just far, far away. And that as soon as I'd punished the man who had murdered my brother, I'd finally be able to join him.

There's a bear standing over me. I'm a goner for sure. That's okay. A bear attack is a perfectly dignified way to die. There are probably bears in Never Land too.

"Can you carry him?" I can't see Joi. She must be standing in the bear's shadow.

"Yeah," says the bear.

"Be careful, he likes to fight," some kid offers in the background.

"He's not going to be doing any fighting tonight," says the bear with a chortle.

When he bends down to pick me up, I recognize the man in the North Face coat who'd been watching me. He's even bigger close up. I almost throw up when he tosses me over his shoulder.

"Thanks, Jimmy," Joi says.

"Anything for you, baby," the bear replies.

"Don't call her baby." I try to sound tough. Everyone laughs.

When I come to, I'm under Joi's sheets. She's taken off my clothes and put a bucket next to the bed. I have a pounding headache, and my mouth is parched. But I'm sober enough to see that there's someone sitting in a chair across the room.

"Jude?" I whisper.

"Who's Jude?" It's Joi in the chair.

"My brother." I know I'm still drunk when I hear myself say it.

"You have a brother?"

"I *had* a brother."

"Oh," Joi says, as if that explains it all. She's smart, so I guess maybe it does.

"I'm sorry about what I said to you yesterday."

"Good," says Joi. "So can I ask you something, Flick?"

"What happened to '*Always listen, never ask*'? Are you breaking your own rules?"

"Just tonight," Joi says. "Just for you."

"Okay, then."

"Are you in trouble? I mean, some guy in a sports car drops you off yesterday, and you get out looking like hell. Tonight you were roaming the projects dressed in head-to-toe Prada. Jimmy said your bottle of Scotch must have cost two hundred bucks."

"That Jimmy really knows his Scotch," I say.

"Don't f—ing joke about this! You could have frozen to death out there!" She probably just woke up everyone in the colony.

"Why are you shouting at me?"

"Because . . ." She shakes her head. We both know why she's so angry. It doesn't need to be said.

"I came to the city to find something, Joi. I didn't even know what it was at first, but I think I just found it. So I won't be getting drunk anymore."

"I'm glad to hear that 'cause the next time I have to go save your ass . . ."

"There won't be a next time. I promise." There won't be. That's one promise I'll keep. "Come here. *Please*."

She crawls into the bed beside me. Paradise must smell like cocoa butter and jasmine. It feels and tastes like Joi's kiss.

"Can I ask *you* a question? I swear it's not about heaven."

Joi laughs. "Shoot."

"Why do you love me?" I ask her.

"Because you love me back," she says without hesitation.

"You have no idea how much," I tell her.

"Yes, I do," she says.

• • •

It's the first time I've seen Peter Pan so pissed off. He's pacing the room and muttering to himself.

"What?!" I demand.

He attacks, holding the blade of his wooden sword to my throat. "I won't let you do it. You can't take it away from her."

"She'll find another good thing," I say, pushing the sword back. "And I can't let her get in the way. Girls like Joi make you soft and vulnerable. Remember Lois Lane? Why do you think the comic guys invented her in the first place? 'Cause they needed Superman to have a weakness other than kryptonite."

"You've lost your mind."

"Tell me something I don't know, *Peter Pan*. And then let me finish what you sent me to do."

He's stunned. "You think I brought you to New York for my sake? I brought you here to find *Joi*, you idiot. Who else is going to sew your shadow back on?"

"I haven't lost my shadow, Jude. It's the rest of me that's missing."

"She'll help you find it! I bet she knows just where to look!"

"I don't want to look. I want to deal with Dad, and then when I'm done, I'll come be with you."

"What if I don't want you in Never Land?"

"You can't keep me out."

Peter Pan stamps his feet. "I don't want your company! I want you to stay here and be happy!"

"I don't *deserve* any of this, Jude. I was the reason you died."

"No, *Dad* was the reason I died."

"And Mandel has the proof! He said he'd give it to me!"

"If you let him turn you into our father."

"How else can I be strong enough to beat Dad? You have to let me do it, Jude. Please don't try to stop me."

Jude doesn't look pissed anymore. He looks like a terrified ten-year-old boy. "If you go, I won't be able to go with you. You saw for yourself—all of the building's windows are sealed shut. There's no way for me to slip inside."

"There must be . . ." I start to argue.

"No," Jude insists. "I can't go with you. You'll have to leave me behind."

"Just for a little while, then. It won't be forever," I promise. "I'll see you as soon as I'm done."

"How can you be so sure?" he asks.

CHAPTER EIGHT

THE INCUBATION SUITES

The chip comes first. There are six new students—five others and me. I don't have a chance to learn their names or commit their faces to memory. We're met at the academy's entrance and immediately ushered downstairs. I'll admit it's a bit of a shock. I wasn't aware that there *was* a downstairs. It wasn't on the tour I was given. I start to wonder what else Mandel didn't tell me. But then I remind myself that it doesn't make any difference. The only thing that matters is that he has proof that Jude's death was no accident. I'll go wherever Mandel wants me to go, as long as I get it.

Three stories underground, we enter a long hallway. A sign reads INFIRMARY. To our right is a white wall with six doors. The left wall is raw Manhattan bedrock. The hall ends at a pair of steel doors that are secured by a biometric lock. There's an unlabeled buzzer beside it. I'd love to find out if anyone's home.

One by one, the five kids ahead of me disappear to the right.

The white doors close before I can figure out what lies beyond them. Finally it's my turn. The room I enter looks like a doctor's office.

A man in a lab coat and surgical mask is scrolling through a file on the computer screen that's anchored to the wall. "Take off everything from the waist up and sit here," he orders, pointing to an examination table. Then he disappears and a woman enters carrying a metal tray. It holds a scalpel, a computer chip, a needle and thread, and a few other instruments I don't recognize. She straps on a pair of plastic goggles and begins to swab my forearm with iodine. The operation can't be as simple as Mandel made it sound if the lady's worried she'll get blood in her eyes.

"Are you allergic to lidocaine?" she asks.

"I don't know," I say.

"We'll find out soon," she responds.

The anesthesia numbs my left arm from the elbow down. I watch as she chooses a scalpel from the tray. I plan to observe the entire operation.

"You're not squeamish?" the woman asks before she makes the first incision.

"No," I tell her, and she pauses to make a note on the office computer.

It takes about ten minutes to insert the chip. When she's finished, I examine the three stitches in my forearm and the small, square bump beneath them.

"Keep it clean. Don't try to remove the chip. You could rupture an artery and bleed to death."

"Okay."

She leaves the tray and instruments in the sink. As soon as

she washes her hands, she passes me a paper gown. "Take off your pants, shoes, and underwear. Dr. Giles will be back shortly."

I'm pretty sure that the strip searches in Singapore prisons are less thorough than the examinations here at the Mandel Academy. After the probing I receive, I half expect the doctor to climb onto the table and cuddle up beside me. But he's not done yet. The first thing I thought he'd check, he seems to have left for last. He peels the filthy bandage off my cheekbone and begins to clean the gunk from my wound.

"Didn't the doctor at the hospital warn you about infection?" he asks.

"I hate doctors. I always stitch myself up," I lie.

"How long ago did you graduate from medical school?" There's a subtle sneer in his voice. I pretend not to hear it.

"Are you trying to say that I did a great job?"

"I'm saying you're rather young to have been trained as a surgeon."

"Yes, well, I'm full of surprises. I'm shocked you didn't find more during the rectal exam."

"You're lucky I didn't," the doctor replies humorlessly. "We don't like surprises."

I don't get a new bandage. My stitches are left exposed. The doctor pulls a white box from a drawer. The typed label on top bears a six-digit number. Inside are four empty vials, some plastic tubing, and a blood-drawing needle. But he chooses a long swab with a ball of cotton on its end. "Open your mouth," he orders.

"Do most schools require a DNA test?" I ask.

"This will go much faster if you remain silent," he says, jamming the swab into the lining of my cheek.

Anything for the proof, I remind myself. You have to do *any-thing*.

After I've dressed, I'm loaded back onto the elevator. It travels one floor up. According to the sign that greets us as the gates open, we're now entering the Incubation Suites. I wonder what they're incubating as I follow my guide down an unusually wide corridor. It's at least fifteen feet from side to side, and the ceiling must be twenty feet high. I'm left in a room with six desks arranged to face an enormous movie screen. Four of the desks are already filled with my fellow newbies. There's no other furniture. The floor is concrete and the walls bare Sheetrock. It's like a Hollywood soundstage before a movie set has been built. And it has one rather unsettling feature. There's a glass-encased catwalk suspended from the ceiling. It runs the entire length of the room and appears to continue into the room next door. I'm pretty sure we're being observed. But the glass is frosted, and I can't see through. There's no way to tell who might be watching us from above.

"Take a seat."

I see a woman standing next to the movie screen, a stack of papers in one hand and a half-dozen No. 2 pencils clutched in the other. Everyone glances at me as I sit. The sixth desk remains empty. While we wait for its future occupant, I get my first real look at the other students. There's a black girl with platinum hair and diamond-covered fingers. Her impressive cleavage is on full display. She sees me staring and blows me a menacing kiss. The girl beside her is from a far less fabulous planet. Stringy brown hair and watery blue eyes that stare off into space. She looks like an extra from *Deliverance*. The kid to her left smiles and waves at me. He seems a little hurt when I don't wave back. He's handsome, Latino. His clothes are expensive. The sugar daddy pedophile who bought them clearly had good taste. The guy to my immediate right could pass for twenty-five. He's blond, burly, and wearing the kind of leather jacket that you only see in Eastern Europe. He turns slowly to face me. His eyes are dark and cold. He takes me in, then rotates his head just as slowly back toward the movie screen.

A man in a lab coat enters and has a quick word with the woman in charge. She nods, then strides to center stage.

"It seems we're beginning this semester with a smaller class than usual. The sixth student has a medical condition that renders her ineligible for the academy's program. So only the five of you will be moving forward. The next stage of your assessment focuses on personality." As the woman passes a booklet and pencil to each of us, I try to recall the sixth student's face. All I can remember is the back of her head.

"The booklet you've been given contains the Myers-Briggs Type Indicator assessment. It is not a test," the woman continues, interrupting my thoughts. "There are no right or wrong answers. Please feel free to begin as soon as you're ready."

Whenever someone insists that there are no right or wrong answers, I immediately assume that there *are*. It doesn't hurt that I know all about the MBTI. You answer a bunch of questions that seem like total bullshit, and then it assigns you a personality "type" with a four-letter label. My father's bank administers the test to every single person who applies for a job. The company claims the MBTI helps identify people who will "fit" with its culture. What it really wants to do is weed out the weaklings. I'm guessing that the

Mandel Academy isn't looking for warm, fuzzy, "feeling" types either. They must want *leaders*, and I'm eager to please, so I decide to be an ENTJ type (Extraversion, Intuition, Thinking, Judging). Just like dear old dad. I have no idea what I "really" am. I taught myself how to game the test back in grade school. I managed to take it twenty-five times online before my mother found out I'd been using her credit card.

So I tick all the right answers and wait for the other newbies to finish. There's no clock in the room, but I'm pretty sure that big, blond Igor to my right has taken an hour longer than everyone else. It's hard to believe that he'll ever be Ivy League material.

He hands the woman his test, and I begin to slip out of my chair. My ass is numb.

"Please stay in your seats. There are a few videos we would like to show you," says the woman. "You don't need to memorize what you see. You won't be tested on the content. We only want you to watch."

I sigh and slump back down. The first video is a short clip of two men dancing a waltz together. The room stays perfectly silent. As soon as it ends, I raise my hand. The woman stares at me. I guess no one has ever had a question before.

"Yes?"

"Are you trying to test if I'm a Replicant or a homosexual?" I ask.

The black girl howls with laughter, which makes me like her. Any fan of *Blade Runner* is a friend of mine. I see big Igor beside me observing the girl with great interest.

"Let's keep going," says the proctor, tapping a note into a tablet computer.

The next video is footage from the scene of a car accident. When the camera pans across the mangled victims who've been hauled from the wreck, Igor starts to laugh. I'm watching as he glances at the black girl again. She raises a carefully tweezed eyebrow, as if to say *WTF*? When Igor realizes she's not laughing, he abruptly stops. He studies her face for the remainder of the clip. Stupid *and* psycho. What a fabulous combination. Mandel missed the mark by a mile with this kid.

Four more videos follow. A little boy lost in a shopping mall. A couple passionately kissing. A wolf catching and ripping into a rabbit. A woman screaming insults at her teenage daughter. The film festival ends, and I'd like to throw up. But I force myself to look bored instead. Almost everyone else seems to have caught on. Only the Latin lover seems shell-shocked.

The lights come on. By the time my eyes have adjusted, Lucian Mandel has appeared.

"Excellent work!" he tells us. "You've all made it through the most difficult part of the assessment process! Give yourselves a big hand."

A few halfhearted claps echo around the room. If our lack of enthusiasm disturbs him, Mandel doesn't show it. He's too wrapped up in his own performance. Today, he appears to be playing the role of everyone's favorite uncle.

"My name is Lucian Mandel. My family has run this academy for over one hundred years. Since the very beginning, we have devoted our lives to helping talented but disadvantaged young people enjoy new beginnings. Each of you has come here to make a fresh start. After lunch, you'll be casting away your old clothes, and by the end of your three-week stay here in the Incubation Suites, you'll have cast away your old lives as well."

My hand shoots up. *Three f—ing weeks?* Mandel ignores me.

"The first step toward assuming your new identity is answering to a new name. We have chosen first names for everyone. New surnames and government ID will be distributed at graduation." The female proctor hands Mandel her tablet computer. He glances down at the screen. When he looks up, his eyes fall on the black girl. "You're Ella," he says.

Deliverance girl is now Aubrey. The Latin lover is Felix. Igor becomes Ivan. When Mandel reaches me, I speak for him.

"Flick," I say. "My name is Flick."

Mandel pauses. I can see the irritation beneath his smile. "You must have psychic abilities. That's exactly what it says here."

He passes the tablet back to the woman. "The next step of the process may be a bit painful for some of you. But it's critical that you don't drag any ghosts from your pasts into the Mandel Academy. We have no secrets inside this building. Each and every one of you has led a difficult life. We didn't choose you *despite* the things you've seen and done. We chose you *because* we believe that such experiences can make people stronger. At other schools, you might feel the need to keep your skeletons tucked away in a closet. At the Mandel Academy, we want you to bring them all out and embrace them."

Once again, he starts with Ella. She's watching him with eyebrow raised and arms crossed.

"We're very fortunate to have Ella with us. Despite her lack of formal training, Ella was an accomplished businesswoman long before she was accepted into our program. She has a pragmatic mind and a gift for mathematics. To this day, law enforcement officials remain unaware that she was once a major player in a drug empire that controlled most of the South Side of Chicago. Her mother's only brother was the face of the organization—but Ella was the brains. As she got older, her uncle began to view her as a threat. When he tried to diminish her role, Ella lured the man into Marquette Park one night and shot him four times in the head. The assassination was captured by a wildlife camera, and that is how Ella came to be with us today. Did I leave anything out?" he asks the girl.

"I'm a Virgo," she quips.

"That wit will come in handy," Mandel remarks. I agree—Ella will do well.

He saunters up to the basket case sitting beside Ella and takes one of the girl's limp hands. "We're hoping Aubrey snaps out of her funk sometime soon, but we're going to give her a little more leeway than most during the Incubation Stage. We checked her out of rehab a bit earlier than recommended so that she wouldn't need to miss another semester here. By the end of this three-week period, she'll have had ample time to physically recover from her methamphetamine addiction. If her mind mends as quickly, Aubrey will be a valuable addition to our student body. She too was once a budding entrepreneur, but she made two mistakes that Ella wisely avoided. Aubrey sampled her own product. And she brought her work home with her. She and her boyfriend built a meth lab in her basement bedroom. When it exploded, both of her parents died in the blaze." He gives the girl's hand a tender squeeze, then places it back on her desk. "Here at the Mandel Academy, we believe that the lessons one learns from such tragedies can inspire personal triumphs."

Aubrey doesn't look like she's heard a single word. She's still gazing into the distance when Mandel moves on. "Felix is a prostitute."

The Latin lover gasps.

"I'm sorry," Mandel says. "Have I been misinformed?"

"I *was* a . . . a . . ." The boy can't finish the sentence.

"You're right, of course," Mandel concedes. "You no longer are. But you must understand, there is absolutely no cause for embarrassment. That's one of the reasons we have this exercise. So that no one wastes his or her time on useless emotions like shame. You slept with men for money. You're hardly the first student here who has done so. What makes you special, Felix, is how *successful* you were. Your charm, that handsome face. People line up to give you whatever you want. That's a real gift. The Mandel Academy can teach you how to make the most of it. All we ask is that you set your sights on something a bit higher than a closet full of flashy clothing."

Felix nods with enthusiasm. He's bought every ounce of Mandel's bullshit. I bet he doesn't make it to the end of the semester.

"Ivan," Mandel says. The guy grunts in response. "You are a *very* impressive specimen." I can feel my head jerk back with surprise. He's *got* to be kidding. "Your father was a remarkable man as well. The Butcher of Brighton Beach. He taught you everything he knew about the protection game. I'm not sure how much of it managed to sink in, but I do know that you became one of his enforcers two years ago at age fifteen. How many people have you disposed of since then, may I ask?"

"Nine."

Nine? If that's true, the guy's a serial killer.

Mandel addresses the rest of us. "If we hadn't found him, Ivan would have become a ward of the state. His parents are now serving life sentences, and his uncles and aunts refused to take him in."

"I will thank them soon," Ivan says. I detect a slight accent, but there's no hint of emotion in his voice.

"You should," Mandel agrees as though he missed the kid's meaning. "They did you a *very* big favor."

Mandel finally turns to me, and his smile broadens.

"Last, but not least, we have *Flick*. Flick is academically gifted. A master thief. And a champion boxer. I won't bother listing his many other talents and achievements. But he too has known trag-edy. The state of his face should tell you as much. However, unlike the rest of you, he isn't here as a last resort. Flick is our only vol-unteer this semester. In time, you will realize just how meaningful that is. His personality profile tells us he's a born leader. His physi-cal exam revealed he's in peak condition. We expect great things from Flick. He could be what we call a natural."

Mandel holds his arms out, as if to wrap us all in a great big hug, and I realize that's it. He's let my skeletons stay in their closets. But my relief is followed by a terrible thought that spins me around in my seat. Whose secrets was Mandel protecting? Mine—or my father's? Could my dad be one of the people watching us from the catwalk? I turn back and scour Mandel's face for answers. He isn't giving any away.

"So there you have it," he says. "Welcome again to the Mandel Academy. Spend the next three weeks getting acclimated to your new home. You'll learn a few fundamental skills and be groomed to take your place among the student body." He checks his watch. "It's one o'clock now. Go grab some lunch. This afternoon you'll be taking another important step toward assuming your new identity. And remember—if you have any questions or concerns, you can always come to me."

I raise my hand, but he pretends not to see it. Next time, I swear to myself, I won't bother being polite.

I'm dying for a change of atmosphere, but the cafeteria doesn't actually have any. What it does have is another stretch of glass-enclosed catwalk hanging high above our heads. The catwalk glass is clear. There are no spectators inside. But there will be. Every room in the Incubation Suites must be designed to administer some sort of test. We're just lab rats being ushered from one cage to the next. They've kept the rooms featureless because they're controlling the variables. They wouldn't want any distractions interfering with the results of their human experiments.

There's a long, stainless steel food bar at one end of the room. Pastas and sandwiches and burgers and sushi and salad. Far too much to feed five people. What's the test here? I wonder. Will they be rating our impulse control? Gauging our risk of obesity? Watching to see if we chew with our mouths closed? Then I figure it out.

They want to see us interacting. There's only one table in the room. And five chairs. Someone has already hauled the sixth away. I doubt the surface of the table is big enough to hold all of Ivan's food. He has a plate piled with hamburger patties. No buns or fixings. Just patties. A plate of sliced salami. An entire loaf of bread.

And he's filled a soup bowl with the carved radishes that were serving as garnishes. I glance up at the catwalk. It must be enclosed in electronic smart glass because in less than two seconds, it shifts from clear to opaque. Which means our guests have arrived at last. I just hope someone up there is paying attention to Ivan. The guy has some serious issues.

I'm the last to get my lunch. Aubrey is the only one who hasn't worked up an appetite. She's sitting at the table between Felix and Ella, who are chatting around her. Ivan is folding beef patties in half and shoving them into his maw. He doesn't even bother to examine what he's eating. He's staring at Aubrey, and I can't quite interpret the look in his eyes. I take the only seat left. It's next to him. If we weren't under surveillance, I might be up for a little lunchtime conversation. But this feels dangerous. I haven't been here long enough to know when I've said the wrong thing. Apparently the others don't share my concern.

"The *natural* has finally joined us for lunch," Felix says. "He kinda looks like that movie star. You know the one I'm talking about?" he asks Ella.

"Frankenstein?" Ella points at my stitches.

It's interesting to see how they operate. Felix flatters those he believes may have power. Ella takes potshots to prove she's their equal. I ignore them both. At this point I'll learn more by listening.

"He must be the strong, silent type," Felix tells Ella in a stage whisper. "So who's your jeweler up there in Chicago?"

While they discuss diamonds and dealers, I dig into lunch. My hamburger is remarkably good. I'm trying to remember when I last ate anything quite like it when I notice that Ivan is muttering to himself. Apparently his lips move when he thinks. He's still fixated on poor, lifeless Aubrey. I stop chewing to listen. The few words I catch tell me Ivan has a crush. And he's not the kind of guy who sends flowers. He's the kind who kicks down doors in the middle of the night. The girl is in some serious shit.

"She's mine," I announce in a casual voice. "Touch her and I'll neuter you with a butter knife."

Why am I doing this? Why am I risking everything for some brain-dead meth addict?

Ella and Felix stop yammering. Ivan slowly swivels around to face me. "What did you say?"

I've already opened my big mouth, so I give him my toothiest smile. "I told you she's mine, you f—ing Neanderthal. So are the other two. I have a huge appetite."

"*Excuse* me?" Ella jumps in. "I am *not*—"

"Shut your face," I growl. Ella glares at me but obeys. She'll hate me for a while, but laying claim to her body is the only sure way to keep Ivan off it.

"If you mark your territory, you must be prepared to defend it," Ivan says. The guy may be a brute, but he's not quite as stupid as I thought.

"This *school* is my territory. Everyone in it belongs to me now. Including you."

As a rule, I never punch first. Even in the ring, I let the other guy have the first go. It's the best way to find out what you're up against. The first punch says everything. But Ivan doesn't punch. He grabs me by the throat instead. I feel the chair give way beneath me. In less than a second, I've been slammed up against the wall of the lunchroom. My brain reels from the impact. But I keep my neck bent forward so my skull doesn't crack. The move would have killed another opponent. Ivan is unbelievably strong. His fingers are on the verge of crushing my windpipe. And what's really impressive is that he doesn't seem to care. Most guys I've fought have an internal alarm that goes off when they're about to inflict serious damage. You can see a flicker of fear in their eyes. Ivan's remain dull and dark.

I grab his wrist with one hand and ram my knee into his jaw. He lurches backward, and his grip loosens. I rip his hand from my throat, keeping hold of his wrist. I lock his elbow and use the arm to spin him around and force him down to the floor. Then I grab a hunk of hair and slam his head twice into the hard concrete. The splatter of blood even reaches the walls. I should have worn goggles.

I know Mandel's people must be watching. But no one has come to Ivan's rescue. I could end his miserable life with one more blow. Instead I climb off his carcass and return to the table. Ella and Felix practically cringe as I sit back down, wipe the blood off my hands, and take another bite of my burger. Aubrey is the only one who doesn't seem shaken. The battle has brought her back to life. She doesn't dare say a word, but I can see it on her face. She knows exactly what I just did. I saved her.

Two men in lab coats and surgical masks rush into the room and load Ivan onto a steel stretcher. Lucian Mandel holds the door open for them as they leave. "Flick?" he says. "Would you mind coming with me for a moment?"

We stroll along the wide hallway, which appears to be a giant square. The glass catwalk crosses the corridor at one point. But once you're around the next corner, it's out of sight. There's a sense of privacy here, though I know not to trust it. The cafeteria door remains ajar, and we walk right past it and start a new lap. Mandel still hasn't uttered a word.

The silence has given me a chance to think. At first I was worried I'd screwed everything up. All I had to do was play along. Instead, I nearly killed a fellow recruit. I figured Mandel would be furious. Now I can see he's not angry at all. Not even close.

"Aubrey doesn't seem like your type," Mandel finally says.

"I'm not a necrophiliac," I respond.

He laughs. "So you have no romantic interest in her?"

"No." It would be ludicrous to pretend that I did.

"Still, you protected her. Did it ever occur to you that she might need to learn how to fend for herself? Aubrey can't expect a white knight to come to her rescue every time she's in trouble."

I just demolished Ivan's face, but that doesn't appear to bother Mandel. He seems much more concerned that I tried to help Aubrey.

"I wasn't protecting anyone," I lie.

"Then why did you choose to make Ivan an enemy?"

"We would have ended up enemies anyway. I figured I'd make the first move and teach him a lesson. The great Chinese general Sun Tzu said that the victorious warrior wins first and then goes to war."

"You've read Sun Tzu's *Art of War*." He's impressed, I can tell.

"I've *memorized* it." I'm sure that sounds great, but I hope he doesn't decide to test me. I don't know how many more quotes I could pull out of my ass.

Mandel seems to buy it. "We both know that your *war* could have ended this afternoon. You had a chance to destroy Ivan. You showed restraint by walking away. But Ivan should recover quickly, and when he does, he'll want his revenge."

"That's what I'm counting on. Ivan is my only competition. The next three weeks would be a real bore without him."

"What a fascinating young man you are," Mandel says. I have no clue if he's satisfied with the explanation I've given him. "I'm looking forward to seeing what you do next."

"Thank you, sir," I respond. "I hope it will be entertaining."

This morning, there were a hundred questions I was eager to ask him. I'm finally learning to keep my mouth shut.

CHAPTER NINE

PRODIGY

I'm deep underground, in a cell with no windows—just a locked door without a knob. This is where I was brought yesterday after my session with the academy's groomers. They trimmed my hair, filed my nails, and seemed disappointed that there wasn't more work to be done.

My temporary quarters in the Incubation Suites are furnished with a bed, a bureau, and a rack of expensive clothing. It seemed perfectly comfortable at first, until I realized there's no desk. No books. Not even an alarm clock. A small bathroom with no door is off to one side. Toiletries have been provided. Nothing dangerous or poisonous. No bottles made out of glass. They've even given me an electric razor. I wasn't aware that anyone still used them.

There's no way to hide from yourself in this place. The far wall of my cell features a wide, full-length mirror. Last night, while exploring my cage, I discovered that I could see my own reflection from every corner of the room. That's when I began to suspect that I wasn't alone. I rapped on the mirror, and the hollow sound confirmed that it wasn't fixed to a solid wall. I waved at whoever was watching on the other side. And when dinner was delivered on a tray to my door, my reflection and I sat on the floor and shared the meal with my unseen guests. A bell rang shortly after the tray was taken away. I didn't realize its purpose until the lights shut off a few minutes later.

The room was so dark that I could have slept with my eyes open. And yet I could still feel them watching. Fortunately, Peter Pan made good on his promise. He didn't visit me during the night. Maybe he tried and couldn't find a way in. But I know he hasn't forgotten me because he sent me a dream.

I saw myself sitting on the steps outside the public pool in Hamilton Fish Park. It was a warm morning at the beginning of May, and I was desperate for a dip, but the pool was still closed for the season. Weeks had passed since I'd last been truly clean. I washed up in restrooms whenever I had the chance, but there are parts that need more than a wipe with a damp paper towel. And you can't pick pockets if your marks smell you coming a mile away.

I heard sandals slapping the sidewalk and spotted a girl walking toward me. I'm not sure what caught my eye first. The wild black hair that floated behind her—or the long, lean body clad in an ankle-sweeping sundress. When the breeze pinned the fabric to her body, she might as well have been naked. She wasn't beautiful. At least not in the model prom-queen pageant-winner way. She was absolutely *magnificent*.

"The pool doesn't open till Memorial Day," the girl stopped to inform me. I'd seen her before. She lived somewhere in the neighborhood, but I didn't think she'd noticed me. My grubbiness rendered me invisible to almost everyone.

I checked over my shoulder, just to make sure I was the only person around.

"Why don't you come with me," she said.

"Where?" I asked, and instantly regretted it. It didn't really matter *where*.

"You'll see."

We walked side by side without saying a word. Most females get fidgety when no one's talking. This girl seemed perfectly comfortable with the silence. We cut across Tompkins Square Park and turned left on Tenth Street. I kept inching closer to catch the scent she was trailing. Halfway down the block, she stopped outside the Russian Baths, and I realized we'd reached our destination.

"I don't have any money," I told her, patting my empty pockets.

"If you come before business hours and tell them Joey sent you, they won't ask you to pay."

"Who's Joey?" I asked.

"That's me. Spelled *J-o-i*."

"Are you French?" I asked. I'd been wondering where they grew girls like Joi. I'd never seen anyone who looked quite like her.

"No." She laughed. "Not even a little bit."

I took a shower first and gave my clothes a light wash. Then I grabbed a robe from the pile stacked up for patrons and set out in search of Joi. When I reached the ice-cold plunge pool, I found her. Goddesses have been known to murder mortals who catch sight of them naked. Joi just smiled as though she had nothing to hide. There was something so innocent about it that I knew she wasn't trying to seduce me. But she did.

When I woke, I felt warm, wet skin under my fingertips. The sensation slipped away, but I could still see Joi treading water. Then the lights in my cell came on with no warning. Joi faded, and another day began.

I thought I knew what I was doing when I came here. It all seemed so simple. Take a few classes. Graduate in nine months. Get the proof Mandel promised. Destroy my father and join my brother. I thought it would be easy to leave Joi behind. This morning I found out I was wrong.

I'm glad I worked up the energy to shower and dress because the door of my cell just slid open. There's a woman standing outside in the hall, waiting to escort me to the first experiment of the day. She's attractive. All the women who work here are attractive. The men are too, come to think of it. But it's hard to look at any of them. Whenever one of the employees meets my eyes, I can tell she's staring straight through me.

"What time is it?" I ask.

"Lights on is at seven. Breakfast is at eight. Starting tomorrow, you will not have an escort. So please pay attention. You'll be expected to find your own way."

"Maybe you should give us maps."

"You won't need a map. I'm going to show you everything you need to know."

There are signs on the doors now. The woman reads them all, as though I'm incapable of doing so on my own. She starts with room 6. My room.

"Room five, room four, room three, room two, room one," she says as we walk down the hall. These are the other students' cells. We turn a corner. "Classroom one, classroom two, classroom three." We turn another corner. "Media room, gym, cafeteria." The gym is in the center of the square formed by the hallway. It's got to be huge. The woman stops at the cafeteria, but I take a peek around the next corner. I see the elevators and two unmarked doors. I'm guessing the first one hides a stairwell to the glass catwalk that passes above my head and into the gym.

"What's down this way?" I ask.

"Those rooms are for employees only," she states.

The woman pushes a metal button that opens the cafeteria door, and I step inside. It's the same place where I taught Ivan his little lesson, but a new set seems to have been constructed during the night. The bottom half of the room has been transformed into a ritzy brasserie. The restaurant has four walls but no ceiling. Instead of the self-service food bar, there are five tables with crisp white tablecloths. Antique mirrors with gilded frames reflect the warm light shed by brass sconces. When I look up, the illusion ends. The brasserie's walls are only ten feet high. Above that mark, the room still resembles a soundstage. The catwalk's glass is clear. I'm the first to arrive.

A waiter approaches me. Not a waiter, I remind myself. One of *them* in a black vest and white apron.

"*Bonjour*, monsieur," he says. "Table for one?"

"*Oui*," I respond, deciding to play along. "*Je voudrais une table près de la fenêtre, s'il-vous plaît.*"

It's one of the four or five phrases I ever managed to memorize.

I knew better than to expect a laugh, but my joke seems to catch the faux waiter completely off guard. Mandel should have hired someone who speaks a little French.

"Oh, never mind," I say with an exaggerated sigh. "Just give me the very best table you have."

I take my seat. I'm placing my napkin in my lap when Ella arrives. I feel the urge to applaud, so I do. Her hair has been cut and restored to its natural color. Now that there's nothing to distract from her face, I can see how stunning she is. They've put her in a simple gray shirtdress and confiscated most of her diamonds. The only ones left are the tasteful studs in her ears. When Ella gives me the finger on her way to her table, I notice that her acrylic nails have been removed. I wish I could assure her that she doesn't seem any less fierce without her claws.

Felix is next. He looks like a J. Crew model with his coral-colored oxford shirt tucked into a pair of olive chinos. Not much of a difference, truth be told, but he doesn't seem particularly pleased. Probably because someone told him to button his shirt all the way to the top. He's followed by Ivan. It's hard to focus on anything other than the white bandage across his nose and his two swollen eyes, but I can see he's been given a respectable haircut, a shirt custom-made for his brawny torso, and a pair of black pants. He smiles at me as he passes. I'm not sure if it's a peace offering or a threat. But I'm impressed by the quality of his new veneers.

Aubrey arrives last. The transformation is remarkable. They've darkened her hair and cut some bangs. The blue eyes peeking out from beneath them are framed by long, black lashes. Her lips don't need any liner to form a true Cupid's bow. She's wearing heels, a pencil skirt, and a diaphanous blue shirt that matches her eyes. The same eyes that haven't left my face since the moment she walked into the room. I hope she hasn't gotten me mixed up with Prince Charming. That wouldn't be good. Not good *at all*. I rescued her once, but I may not be willing to do it again.

Our waiter glides between the tables, delivering a menu to each of us. Another man arrives and wordlessly makes his way around the room. He's different from the other academy employees. He actually seems to *see* us. His sense of style makes me suspect that he might be Italian. It feels formal and casual all at once. Red check shirt carefully rolled up to the elbows. A striped tie with a double Windsor knot. Sleek navy pants that are tapered at the ankle. Glasses with fashionable frames that probably don't hold corrective lenses.

"Excellent," the man announces when he reaches my table. I stand corrected. He's American. "Ivan, where is Flick's napkin?" I can tell he'd prefer to call us by our surnames if we had any.

"Huh?" Ivan grunts.

"Flick's napkin is in his lap. Folded lengthwise with the fold facing toward him," the man says, not bothering to wait for an answer. "Ella, where are Flick's elbows?"

I turn to see that Ella has one elbow on the table. Her head is propped up by her palm. "Who gives a f—?" she sneers. I have a feeling somebody isn't too thrilled by her makeover.

The man's nostrils flare, but his voice remains calm. "That's the last time you—or any of your classmates—will use that word while you're inside these walls. Do I make myself clear?"

"Yes, sir!" I chirp. I think I may be on my way to becoming the teacher's pet.

He pats me on the shoulder but keeps his eyes locked on Ella. "Do I?"

"Yes," she says.

"As for why you should care, to be perfectly frank, you look vulgar and ignorant. Should you ever find yourself in a restaurant like this, your fellow diners won't be impressed by your disdain for the rules. They'll be too busy snickering at your crudeness. Now sit up straight and keep your legs closed."

Ella does what she's told. In fact, there's no longer a single bent spine in the room.

"My name is Mr. Jones. I will be joining you for all of your meals this week. I know many of you have come here with only the haziest knowledge of etiquette. But rest assured, by the time we're finished, you'll be ready to break bread with presidents and royalty."

I'm not sure Mr. Jones realizes what kind of challenge he's set for himself. Having lunched with my classmates yesterday, I'm convinced that Ivan has been eating out of a pig trough for the past seventeen years. Ella is only marginally more refined. Even Felix grips his fork like a garden spade.

"Flick," Mr. Jones says. "I'm appointing you to be my teacher's aide."

I spent two dull hours tutoring the troglodytes this morning, and now I'm playing the same role again. We're in classroom 1, which the academy's set designers have decorated to resemble the library of an elite Manhattan club. Leather armchairs. Wood paneling. Shelves with sliding ladders. But the fireplace is fake, and all the books are just props. There's nothing printed on their pages. When we entered, the catwalk above was empty. As soon as Ms. White, our elocution instructor, asked each of us to stand and give a short speech on a subject of our choosing, the catwalk's glass began to fog up.

I decided to introduce my classmates and observers to Schrödinger's Cat—Europe's first zombie and scientific proof that it's possible to be dead and alive at the very same time. I'm not sure what she made of the topic, but Ms. White was duly impressed by my clear enunciation and understanding of grammar. I had an excellent teacher growing up, I almost informed her. When my father delivered a lesson, he made sure you never needed another.

Now Ms. White is dedicating herself to training Ivan to speak in something other than grunts, and I've found myself paired with Aubrey. I hadn't actually heard her voice until the rambling speech she just delivered on the subject of Smoky Mountain fireflies. As it turns out, she speaks with a maddening twang. Not the kind of southern drawl that calls to mind mint juleps and cotillions. Aubrey's accent is of the possum-eatin', cousin-kissin' variety.

We're both given a single sheet of paper with the same long list of phrases. I read one, and Aubrey repeats it, trying to enunciate the words properly. It would probably help if she watched my lips as they form the sounds. But she keeps trying to catch my eye. When she finally does, I know in an instant that I'm not her Prince Charming. This isn't how girls look when they're love struck. This is how they look when they're petrified. And if she's already scared, she shouldn't be here. It will probably be dangerous, but the first chance I get, I'm going to give Aubrey Joi's address and advise her to get herself kicked out of school.

I don't know why, but I want Aubrey to know that she'll be okay. But my smile only seems to convince her that she's not getting through to me, and she's almost twitching with frustration. Finally she leaps to her feet, rips up the sheet of paper, and tosses the pieces into the air. Except for one little scrap that she's kept in her hand. While everyone's watching the confetti flutter to earth, she presses the scrap into my palm. There's one word on it: *GO*. I let it fall to the floor.

"Before it heals," she whispers without realizing that the teacher has come up behind her.

Act fast, my brain urges. *Make a scene!* "Goddamn it!" I bellow, directing my rage at the catwalk. "Why am I teaching some stupid hillbilly how to talk? What's next? Teaching goats how to slow dance? Pigs how to play the piano? This is not why I'm here, Mandel! When are you going to teach *me* something useful?"

It's worked. If Ms. White heard Aubrey's warning, she's already forgotten it. She is captivated by my performance now, and I'm doing everything I can to make it truly spectacular.

I'm hurling insults at everyone in the room when the door opens and Mandel appears. He doesn't need to say a word. I follow him outside. He waits until we're in the hallway to crack a smile.

"I'm terribly sorry, Flick," he says. "I should have realized that these courses would be far too remedial for you. Most of our students tend to be rough around the edges when they arrive. They wouldn't fit in without a few weeks of training."

"So can I go upstairs now?" I ask.

"I'm afraid not. We follow a strict schedule here. But starting tomorrow, you may have breakfast in your room and then report to the gym. We won't waste your time with classes you don't need."

"Thank you."

He's about to open the door and send me back inside. Then he pauses. "Do you know what the alumni are saying about you?"

"Am I supposed to guess?" I ask.

"They're already calling you the prodigy," he tells me. Then his lips stretch into another friendly grin. "Let's see how long the label sticks."

CHAPTER TEN

ANGELS AND DEMONS

I've learned only one thing since I got here. I'm not quite as smart as I thought. It took a couple of days before I realized that being excused from all classes wasn't a reward. It was a punishment—for losing sight of my goal. For getting off course. I'm not here to make friends or rescue damsels in distress. I'm here to win the prize I've been promised.

I forgot my mission. And I've been sentenced to solitary confinement for my crime.

The gym has every type of exercise machine ever built. I spent the first two days torturing muscles I'd never used before. Running marathons on the treadmills. Shadow-boxing on the enormous red exercise mat. When the other students showed up in the gym at 5:00 p.m. for their self-defense class, I was annoyed that they'd invaded my private space. But soon I began looking forward to their arrival each day. I even asked the instructor for permission to take part in the lessons. By the end of the first week, five o'clock couldn't come fast enough.

You'd think that watching someone work out for ten hours a day wouldn't be terribly entertaining. But I seem to be the most popular show in town. The catwalk glass is always transparent first thing in the morning. It fogs and clears at least a dozen times throughout the day. If I'm completely still, I can hear the sound of footsteps. I resist the urge to shout curses at the ceiling or fling weights at the walls. I'm not sure I'd survive if Mandel took my single hour of human contact away. And I doubt that's the worst that could happen. He can do whatever he wants to me down here. There's nothing I could do to stop him. And that must be the lesson he's trying to teach me.

After the solitude had turned into torture, I tried holding imaginary conversations inside my head. Sometimes with Jude. Sometimes with Joi. Then one afternoon I heard the sound of my own voice. I'd been speaking out loud. The catwalk glass was clear. No one was watching, but I had no idea how long my lips had been broadcasting my thoughts. The watchers couldn't know about Joi, and I didn't want them eavesdropping when I spoke to Jude. So I tried to fill my brain with nothing but static. The effort made me angry. That rage became my constant companion.

Every night, I pace my cage. *Anything, anything,* I tell myself. *You have to do anything.* I no longer care if anyone's watching behind the mirror. I have to keep Jude and Joi from visiting me in the darkness, so I stage executions inside my head. I murder my father the way he murdered his. Or I beat him until his face is as broken as Jude's. Every morning, I emerge from a dream in which I'm drenched in his blood. Mandel must have known this would happen.

• • •

If my calculations are correct, when I wake up tomorrow, I'll have two days left in the Incubation Suites. Forty-eight hours that might as well be forever. At least today appears to be drawing to a close. It's already five o'clock, and my fellow newbies have filed into the gym for self-defense training. I have no idea what's happened to them over the past weeks, but the difference is startling. Their accents are gone, and their posture is perfect. Even Ivan speaks in clear, well-formed sentences that make me wonder if he might actually be sentient. They removed the bandages from his nose yesterday, and I can see they made a few improvements. It's straighter. More refined. Ivan the Terrible has the schnoz of a Roman emperor. I guess it helps to be handsome if you're completely insane. Ella is poised and deadly—like a princess with a pistol and a PhD. I haven't heard Aubrey talk in days, but for a while she spoke like a television news anchor. Felix doesn't smile as much anymore.

Our self-defense instructor, Mr. Green, knows there's nothing he can teach me. And it's pretty obvious that thugs like Ivan are the reason these classes exist. But the three other newbies had so much to learn that Mr. Green couldn't teach them alone. I've been paired with Ella from the very beginning. Ivan has Felix. The instructor works with Aubrey, who needs the most guidance. She didn't pay much attention during the first two weeks of class. When she should have been watching the instructor, her eyes were always pleading with me. She gave up the day they removed the stitches in my fore-arm. The next time I saw her, she'd slipped back into her trance.

Aubrey probably thought I'd never figured it out, but I always understood what she was trying to say. That the chip can be removed before the incision has healed. The information never made much difference to me. I just wish I'd been able to ask how she knew. But there was never a chance to speak privately, and I couldn't risk more punishment. Aubrey must have seen something in rehab—something that scared her. After I rescued her from Ivan, she tried to warn me. But I'm already long past saving. Aubrey shouldn't have wasted her time.

Today I'm supposed to be attacking Ella, but she's decided to turn the tables. She's on the offensive now, and I'm the one deflecting blows. The girl holds a grudge. She really wants to hurt me. I suspect she's been practicing at night in her cell. Ella must know she has no chance of winning. Nature made me bigger and stronger. But I have to admire her persistence. I even consider letting her land a punch. But she suddenly stops throwing them. The catwalk has fogged over. At this point, we all know what that means.

Mr. Green looks up and nods. He's been expecting our visitors.

"Ella, Felix, and Aubrey—clear the mat!" he calls out. "Ivan and Flick, let's see what you've got."

The people up on the catwalk want to be entertained. I imagine Mandel and my father standing side by side, and the rage returns in a rush. A demon of unimaginable power overtakes me. I now know exactly how it feels to be possessed. If you don't try to fight it, it feels f—ing *fantastic*.

I can tell from Ivan's grin that he's been waiting for this opportunity. He's probably been strategizing for weeks. I doubt he'll let me get close enough to drag him down to the floor. He's taller than I am, and his reach is much longer. Anyone watching would assume he had the edge. But when his fist comes flying through the air, I dodge it with ease. I'll draw the first blood this time.

I hit with far less force than I'm able to muster. Just a quick jab to the jawline. He responds with a blow that might have knocked out most of my teeth if it hadn't missed my face by an inch. This time I target his pretty new nose. He forgets his plan and rushes straight for me. A quick kick to the knee sends him down to the mat. There's more than enough time for me to go in for the kill, but I let him jump back to his feet. I don't want the fight to end. It's not about winning. I want Ivan to suffer.

I stalk him around the gym, throwing punch after punch—but always giving him just enough time to recover. He's battered and bloody, barely able to stand. But he won't admit defeat, and that's exactly what I've been counting on.

Suddenly Ivan's arms drop, and he's no longer looking at me. He's staring up at the catwalk instead. I assume it's a trick. He'll clock me as soon as I turn around. But then I notice that everyone else in the gym sees the same thing he does.

The glass has cleared. A message has been sent. Our visitor is calling an end to the fight. It's a blond girl, and she's up there all alone. It's hard to be certain from this distance, but she doesn't seem old enough to be an employee or alumnus. She looks like an angel. The kind you put on top of a Christmas tree. I expect her to flutter down from the heavens, but she just smiles and walks away.

"Rusalka," Ivan mutters under his breath.

"Who?" I ask. "Do you know that girl?"

Ivan grins. A thin stream of blood trickles from the corner of his mouth; then he spits two teeth on the floor.

CHAPTER ELEVEN

THE BEAUTY PAGEANT

How do you feel?" Lucian Mandel asks me. He's perched on the edge of my bed. I haven't even had a chance to rinse Ivan's blood off my hands.

I glare at Mandel. I want to kill him. But he can give me something else I want more. So I won't. I'll let him live. Because I'll do anything, anything. But nobody said I have to pretend to enjoy it. "Like you've wasted three f—ing weeks of my life," I respond.

"Is that what you think?" When he smirks, I could rip his whole head off. "Did you imagine that life at the academy was going to be easy? I assure you, it was just as arduous back in your father's day. But I thought you might be pleased by the results we've produced in the past few weeks. Don't you see how you've changed?"

He points to my reflection in the mirror. The plentiful food and nonstop exercise have made an undeniable impact. The gym clothes I was given when I first arrived are at least a size too small. My T-shirt and sweatpants are speckled with blood. But it's my face that's truly transformed. There's nothing pretty about it anymore. I finally look like the person I've been trying to be. Still, I don't need to hear about the merits of suffering from some pampered little asshole who wouldn't survive a deep-tissue massage.

"The first time you fought Ivan, I didn't feel the need to intervene," he confides. "I knew you weren't capable of inflicting real damage. It wasn't in your nature. But today, you weren't just planning to kill him—you wanted to torture him first."

It's true.

"How would *you* know?" I snarl. "You weren't even there."

"Gwendolyn told me she had to stop the fight. You must have seen her."

"You mean the blonde on the catwalk?"

"Yes. Pretty, don't you think?"

His knowing look makes me sick. "I think *you're* way too old to be drooling over girls her age. Who is she, anyway?"

"A very talented young lady. You see, the best and the brightest are granted special privileges here at the Mandel Academy. Gwendolyn is our Dux, the school's top student. It's an important position, and one that comes with quite a few perks—before and after graduation. Gwendolyn acts as my ambassador to the student body, and I respect her opinion. So I always allow her a first peek at our newcomers. She was very impressed by what she saw today. She's looking forward to meeting you."

"Is that why you're here? To play matchmaker?"

Mandel rises. "Your hostility is misplaced, Flick. Try to remember—you aren't angry at *me*. I'm just here to help. I have only your best interests in mind."

I couldn't count how many times I heard my dad say the same thing. Whatever he did to me, it was always for my own good. "Really? I seem to recall a little wager you made with my father."

"Yes, but I can't win the wager without you. One might say we're teammates. No matter what happens going forward, please try to remember that. And don't forget the reward that will be waiting for you at the end of this ordeal. In nine months, you could have all the proof you need to send your father to prison. But you won't earn the right to graduate in September unless you set everything else aside and fight for it. That's the best advice I can give you. I recommend that you take it to heart."

"So you're telling me I should do whatever it takes to help *you* win your bet. Is that your idea of a pep talk?"

Mandel hears the question and ignores the insult. "I suppose it is. But it will need to be the last for a while. Once you're upstairs, I can't show you too many favors, Flick. I do hope you understand."

"I think I'll live." And Mandel will stand a better chance of surviving if the little runt stays out of my sight.

"I'm very happy to hear that. Now that we've had this chat, you're free to dine with the rest of your class tonight."

"My punishment is over?"

Mandel sighs wearily. "You weren't being *punished*, Flick. You may have tremendous potential, but we'll need to work hard to tap it. You came here a weak-willed little boy. My methods may seem harsh, but this school will transform you into the man you yearn to be."

"And what if I've decided I don't want to change?" I ask just to screw with him. "What if I decide to flunk out?"

"That's not an option you should attempt to pursue," he advises me. "Stay and learn what I can teach you. In time, you may even come to see me as your mentor. Perhaps we'll be as close as my mother always was with your father."

I can't help but snort at the thought.

"I know it must seem unlikely now. But this is only the beginning of our relationship. I have much to teach you in the months to come. You've made great strides during your stay in the Incubation Suites. But your real education begins in twenty-four hours."

My calculations were off. I must have lost track of time. "Tomorrow is my last day in this hell hole?"

"This isn't hell, Flick," Mandel says with a laugh. "I think you'll find it's much closer to *limbo*."

My sweats are in the trash. I'm dressed in proper attire for a change. The door of my cell should open any moment now. This morning will be devoted to orientation. Mandel gave us the news last night before dinner, then left the five of us alone to celebrate. A lavish feast had been prepared for the occasion. There was even wine, which none of us bothered to open. When we weren't chewing or swallowing, we all held our tongues. No one was watching from the catwalk, and there were countless questions I wanted to ask. I'd like to know what the other students have seen since they've been here, and I still have no idea how much they've been told. But I couldn't bring myself to break the silence. It doesn't matter anyway. I have a hunch I'll be finding out soon.

The door slides open, and I make my way to the media room. This time, the academy's mysterious set designers have furnished it to resemble a corporate boardroom. Five Herman Miller chairs are lined up on one side of a sleek glass table. They're all facing the movie screen. Behind the table is a wall of windows. I know it's just a mural painted on a canvas backdrop, but I keep expecting to see birds fly past through the clear, blue sky.

I'm the last to arrive. When I settle into my seat, a video begins to play on the screen. It's a walk-through of the nine aboveground floors of the Mandel Academy. I wonder why the other students seem so captivated until I remember that none of them were ever granted a tour.

The video ends, and an academy employee circles the table, handing out room assignments and card keys to all five students. Then he steps up to the podium at the front of the room. He's clearing his throat when Lucian Mandel arrives. The employee blinks like the sight confuses him. Mandel must not make many appearances at orientation sessions. He's here for me.

Mandel sidles up to the podium. He's all smiles, like a game show host greeting a new panel of contestants.

"Hello, everyone!"

"Hello." Felix is the only one who responds.

"As you all know, you'll be moving upstairs this evening. It will be an experience you'll remember for the rest of your lives. Have a look at your new schoolmates and then settle into your rooms. Get a good night's sleep. Tomorrow morning a new semester begins for all students. In a little while, you'll be given your class schedules. The books and supplies you need are already waiting for you in your dorm rooms. Your clothing is being transferred as we speak."

Mandel's tone shifts, and the smile fades. I lean forward. I can tell his speech is about to get interesting. "By now, you've gotten a sense of what the Mandel Academy can offer you. Life is a battle, and this school will teach you to *win*. We chose you because you possess one key advantage over other people your age. Most teenagers in this country are pampered and spoiled. They're kept sheltered from reality and protected from unpleasant truths. But all five of you have already discovered *exactly* how brutal the world really is. You wouldn't be alive if you didn't know how to fight.

"Each of you has what it takes to win. But in order to do so, you must dismiss everything you learned outside of these walls. And you must accept no restraints. Laws and commandments are for sheep. Racist and sexist stereotypes are for fools. Before you arrived here, you may have been judged by your gender or the color of your skin. Your clothing, accent, or manners may have served to keep you in your 'place.' Your families' religious beliefs may have been forced upon you.

"Here, our students begin their new lives with none of these limitations. You'll find you've been given the same advantages as the rest of your classmates. Your social skills are equally polished. And prejudice simply doesn't exist at the Mandel Academy. Everyone at this school has the same chance to succeed. Starting tomorrow you will be judged solely on your talents, intelligence, and inner strength."

He steps away from the podium and approaches our table. He's so cool, so confident. His words flow so freely that they sound like the truth.

"To keep things fair, we must limit your access to the outside world. Everyone you'll meet inside this building is a product of our program.

The academy's instructors and employees were once students just like you. We don't allow guests or observers. During your stay, you will be completely immersed in the Mandel philosophy. There's only one rule that we insist you follow: Always strive to be the best.

"Here at the Mandel Academy, the strongest and brightest students will rise to the top. The lazy or weak will quickly fall to the bottom. You'll soon discover that the competition is fierce. Every four months, we admit six new students. Some are ready to leave after a few semesters. Others require years of instruction. Only the nine best students over the age of eighteen are allowed to graduate each September. If you're among the select few who succeed, your hard work will be rewarded with power, wealth, and prestige.

"First, the academy pays for all graduates to attend an Ivy League university. In return, we expect you to earn reasonable grades—as long as they don't come at the expense of your social life. The connections you'll make at Harvard or Yale will be far more valuable than the education you'll receive. Then, once you receive your diplomas, your careers will begin. No matter what line of work you pursue, we guarantee a starting salary in the mid–six figures."

I hear someone gasp. Mandel beams.

"Our alumni dominate the worlds of business and politics—and life is good at the top of the food chain. But the journey to the top starts *here*. If you intend to graduate from the Mandel Academy, you will have to fight for the privilege.

"We don't expect you to leap into battle immediately, of course. We want you to have ample time to study the lay of the land. This is why all students are granted immunity for the first month of each semester. No one is expelled during the Immunity Phase. But don't rest on your laurels. Your instructors will be watching you, and unless you prove that you're worthy of this school, you may soon find yourself right back where you started. On the streets or in jail, with no hope for the future.

"This might sound hard-hearted, but we refuse to coddle our students. The Mandel Academy believes in the survival of the fittest. You each possess remarkable strength. Now it's time to see what you're willing to do with it. I wish you all the best of luck. Does anyone have any questions?"

The room stays silent. What is there to say? That it sounds too good to be true? That I know there's a catch?

"Wonderful. Then I will see you all upstairs!"

As soon as Mandel is out the door, the media room lights dim and the academy's headmaster reappears on the video screen. The camera is tight on his face, making every freckle appear enormous.

Welcome to the Mandel family! Over the next few minutes, I'm going to take you on a trip to the future. The major you'll be assigned at the end of this video will set you on the path that you'll follow for the rest of your life. Some paths lead to fame. Some lead to social prominence. But every path that begins at the Mandel Academy will lead you directly to fortune.

The camera zooms out. Mandel is on Wall Street, with the famous bronze bull right by his side.

If you're good with numbers, you may have been chosen to be a finance major. After graduation, you'll be working with money, and

Wall Street will be your stomping ground. Everyone in America sends their savings here, hoping the dollars will multiply. But few people understand what really happens to the funds they invest—which means no one knows who to blame if it all disappears.

Suddenly Mandel is strolling down the corridor of a sleek, ultra-modern office building.

If you're a business major, you're destined for the corporate world. As the future CEO of a successful company, you'll need to learn all the tricks to turning a profit. We'll teach you how to gather intelligence on your competition, keep whistle-blowers in line, break whatever rules may stand in your way, and bend any laws that aren't good for business.

He opens a door and enters a conference room. Two teams of stony-faced, suit-clad warriors face each other across a table. None of them appear to notice Mandel's arrival.

Which is one reason why law majors will always be in great demand. You're the ones who can argue either side of an issue—and twist any facts to serve your client's needs. You can make the guilty look innocent. The greedy appear bighearted. The unethical seem honorable. You have the temerity to inform a judge that the sky is green—and the sheer brilliance to make him believe it.

The camera cuts to the floor of the US Senate, where Mandel is sitting with his feet propped up on some senator's desk.

If you happen to be both persuasive and telegenic, it's likely you have been chosen to be a politics major. Fame and power are both perks of the job. But your primary role will be to make life a bit easier for your fellow alumni. You will craft laws that favor their businesses—and vote down any legislation that's designed to restrict them. You will also be called upon to provide well-timed distractions. Get the whole country arguing about sex education or gays in the military, and Americans will stop paying attention to all the things they should fear.

The scene fades and Mandel reappears at another desk in a room lit only by a computer screen. A young man sits beside him, tapping away at a keyboard.

The Mandel Academy's newest and broadest major is technology. Whether your focus ends up being computer hacking, voting machine fraud, or simple identity theft, you'll quickly discover that your skills are of tremendous value to your fellow alumni. Technology is an excellent major for students who prefer to work in solitude—or those who find small talk and personal hygiene to be onerous chores. These days, it's quite possible to get filthy rich without ever setting foot in a shower.

The camera zooms in on a video that's playing on the computer screen. Mandel is aboard a yacht at sea. A dozen beautiful girls in string bikinis lounge in the background while a pair of glassy-eyed playboys split a mound of cocaine.

Another wide-ranging major is leisure studies. It's a sad fact that many of the best things in life are currently illegal. Some of you will provide the goods and services that make existence more agreeable for our country's ruling class. Others will work with the bottom rungs of society. Wherever your career happens to take you, you'll find yourself in a position of great influence. Your customers will crave your wares to such a degree that they'll willingly part with their cash—and their secrets—to obtain them.

Mandel steps off the yacht and magically appears on the narrow New York street just outside the academy.

All those secrets will be of great use to our human resources majors. If you've been chosen to pursue this particular path, you will have the most important job of all. The academy's human resources department ensures that the Mandel family business always runs smoothly. Should one of the alumni need assistance, you'll know which of her colleagues is best able to provide it. If a graduate comes to you with a problem, you will instantly know how to solve it.

Mandel pauses outside the academy's front doors. His expression is stoic as he addresses the camera.

And on those rare but unavoidable occasions when our family squabbles or faces a serious threat from the outside, enforcement majors serve a vital role. You will be trained in martial arts, weaponry, and forensic science. You are the academy's defenders and guardians, and you'll make sure that the Mandel family is able to prosper for the next one hundred years—and beyond.

Mandel opens the academy's front doors, revealing an interior awash with light. We follow him as he strolls across the ground floor. Then he stops, his feet planted on one of the glittering spheres in the center of the atrium, and turns to face camera. The sun has gilded Mandel's beige linen suit, and even his skin seems to glow like gold. The smile on his face couldn't feel warmer or more radiant.

So! Now that you've had a glimpse of your future, it's time to experience it. Congratulations! Your new lives begin today!

The video fades to black. When the lights come on, the employee leading our orientation reappears with a stack of glossy blue folders. I focus my attention on the other four students. Their faces are blank now. I wish I could have seen the expressions they were just wearing in the dark.

"These are your schedules. Each of you has been assigned a major based on the results of your psychological assessments and the skills you've displayed during the Incubation Stage. Your classes have been chosen for you this semester. Next semester you will be allowed to pick your own."

Finally—a real moment of truth. The man places a folder in front of Ella. "Your major will be finance." She seems perfectly relaxed as she pages through the materials. She's had time to read a few course descriptions, but I see no trace of surprise on her face. For a moment I'm disgusted. You'd think Ella was heading off on a Caribbean cruise instead of embarking on a life of crime. Then I realize that she doesn't have a choice. None of them do. That's why they're here. I'm this semester's only volunteer.

I'm "business." I don't need to examine my class schedule. I already know what I'll find. Ivan's major is "enforcement." That should help him get into Harvard. Aubrey and Felix's folders are both labeled LEISURE STUDIES. Aubrey just gazes at the documents in front of her, but Felix opens his folder eagerly. I watch his expression shift from excitement to confusion to horror.

"There's got to be a mistake," he croaks.

The man walks back to Felix's chair and peers over the kid's shoulder. "No mistake," he announces.

"But Mr. Mandel just said we'd be rich and powerful. These classes teach people how to be *pimps*!" He spits it out like it's the nastiest word he knows. It probably is.

"Yes, well, given your talents, personality, and life experience, we feel you should pursue a career in the sex trade." The man sounds blasé, as if explaining such things is the most tedious part of his job. "You'll be on the business side from now on, of course. And I think you'll find that it can be a very lucrative and influential line of work."

"But . . . Mr. Mandel said the academy was about new beginnings," Felix argues. His tan, pretty face is contorted with agony, but he's still holding back his tears. "I came here to escape from my old life. Now you want me to *major* in it?"

The man remains unmoved. "You *came* here because you were arrested for prostitution. And I'm afraid our assessment showed that you aren't well suited for an unrelated career. If you're not interested in learning what we'd like to teach you, you may leave the academy as soon as the Immunity Phase is over."

"What if I want to go *now*?" Felix asks.

"I'm afraid that will not be possible," the man says.

Felix begins to sob, and the man goes about his business. Ivan studies his class schedule, and I can see he's struggling to understand some of the words. Aubrey continues to stare at the table. Ella is the only one watching the weeping boy. I have no idea what she's thinking.

It's eight thirty in the evening, and we've all been herded onto an elevator. Someone must have had a little chat with Felix after orientation. His eyes are a bit puffy, but the tears have finally stopped. I glance at the elevator's control panel. A single light is lit. All of our new dorm rooms appear to be on the eighth floor.

The gate is pulled shut, and the elevator begins to rise. We pass another underground floor, and then we emerge into open air. I know that we're climbing the side of the atrium—the giant opening cut through the center of the building—but the lights are out on the lower levels. With darkness all around us, it feels like we're suspended in midair. Once we pass the classroom floors, our surroundings finally begin to take shape. A few lights are on in the dorms. I look up and see that our schoolmates are waiting outside our rooms to greet us. They're leaning over the balcony that circles the atrium, eager for their first look. They're quiet. Serious, but not solemn. They're sizing us up. The elevator stops.

I think back to the sunny morning when I first visited the academy. The school is a very different place at night. With the dorm room doors standing open, the eighth floor is bright enough to navigate. But the balcony itself is dimly lit, and the atrium in the center is a bottomless abyss. Right now the place looks less like a school than a prison.

"Line up behind me," orders the employee. "Single file."

We follow him like five little ducklings. All rooms open off the balcony, which is roughly the size and shape of a running track. I suspect we're taking the long route to our lodgings so the other students have enough time to examine us. They step to the side, giving us just enough room to pass. There must be around fifty of them, and some are crowded so close that I feel their breath on my skin. It's not the friendliest welcome I've ever received. I don't think it's meant to be. I can't see my fellow newbies' faces, but I bet at least two of them are on the verge of pissing their pants. I spot the girl named Gwendolyn, and she smiles straight at me. She's stunning. Porcelain skin, pale blond hair that shimmers in the weak artificial light, and huge round eyes the color of chicory flowers. There's something serene about her. She doesn't seem as hungry as the rest of them.

Once the other newbies and I are all ensconced in our rooms, there's a commotion outside. I return to the doorway. Half of the academy's students are mashed together on the opposite end of the eighth floor. They're waving little strips of paper in the air. Someone in the center is gathering them. I know exactly what's happening. They're gambling on our chances.

"How did you enjoy the Beauty Pageant?" A kid emerges from a dark patch of balcony between two dim lights. He points at the room to the left of mine. "I'm Lucas. I live next door."

"Flick. So is that what they call it? The Beauty Pageant? Does that mean there's a swimsuit round? Should I unpack my Speedo and give myself a bikini wax?"

Lucas isn't laughing. Apparently this is serious business.

"I guess they're betting on who gets to take home the crown," I say, just to keep the conversation going.

Lucas moves a bit closer and lowers his voice. He's a few inches taller than me, and his skin doesn't look like it's seen sunlight in years. His expression is somber and his clothing unusually bland. With his crisp white shirt, black tie, and glasses, he could pass for the corpse of a young Atticus Finch. "I don't think there's much debate about who will rise to the top this semester. They're probably placing wagers on who'll be the first to go."

"And you're not a gambling man?"

Lucas shakes his head. "Stakes are too high for my taste."

"Well, do you suppose they'll let *me* in on the action?" I joke. "Or do I know too much? They might say it's not sporting."

"I don't think fairness matters much to anyone here," Lucas says. "You've seen our school logo, haven't you? The flaming brass balls? Place a bet on the Beauty Pageant, and they'll probably think you have a set of your own."

It's dark at the bottom of the atrium, but I spot a faint glimmer of gold. "Then it's too bad I don't have any money to bet with."

"Yes, you do," the guy informs me. "Check your top desk drawer. There's a black pouch inside. They fill it at the beginning of every semester. So go ahead—bet every last dime. Just make sure you're back in your room by nine. You do *not* want to miss curfew here."

"Thanks for the tip," I say.

"Don't mention it," Lucas responds. Before I set off, he grabs my arm. "Seriously. *Don't.*"

I have no idea who will be the first newbie to go—Felix or Aubrey. But there's no sport in betting against either of them. Still,

I can tell first impressions are important here, and I'm planning to make one that won't be forgotten. *Always strive to be the best,* Mandel told us. And the game starts now. So while the rest of the pageant contestants are settling into their rooms, I take a casual stroll around the eighth floor. I don't see anyone who looks younger than fifteen or older than nineteen. And the dorms are co-ed. At any other school, those two factors would be a recipe for chaos. Here at the Mandel Academy, order reigns supreme. It looks like most of the bets have been placed, and only a handful of students are still milling about on the balcony across the atrium from my room. I'm making my way toward them. They know I'm coming, but they're purposely ignoring me. I peer into the open dorms I pass. The semester hasn't even begun, and there are already kids hunched over their computers—or scouring books as if the word of God was hidden somewhere on the pages. One student is lying on his stomach in bed, with his face pressed into a goose-down comforter.

I'm a few feet away from the group, and one of them turns around. He's my age, but there's a world-weary languor about him. He leans his long, lanky body against the balcony railing, and his eyelids seem to droop with boredom. It's as though he's seen too much to be shocked by anything. I can imagine him dressed in a tuxedo, standing on the deck of a sinking ship and drinking one last martini before the waves reach up to wash him away.

"Hullo." He smiles, and his face instantly morphs. He's no longer a jaded aristocrat. He's the friendliest kid at camp.

His greeting appears to be the others' cue. They're all grinning at me now. Mandel is certainly an equal-opportunity exploiter. The kids here can trace their ancestry to every part of the globe. And whatever condition they arrived in, they've all been polished into perfect gems. There isn't a bad haircut or a zit in sight.

"So who's going to give me my tiara and roses?" I demand.

"I'm sorry. Mandel Academy pageant winners have to settle for a scholarship," says my new best friend. "I'm Caleb. That's Leila, Austin, and Julian." There are at least ten other students that Caleb doesn't bother to introduce. I'm guessing they aren't part of the in-crowd.

It takes me an instant to assess the three other individuals with names. Austin is the only one who could possibly pose a physical threat. He's like a Ken doll on steroids. Mandel must have kidnapped some Texas high school's star quarterback. Julian, on the other hand, is what the Japanese call *kawaii*. If he ever he makes it to Tokyo, the girls will be squealing before he steps off the plane. Leila is tiny, delicate, and filled with a rage that she doesn't bother to hide. If I were worried, she'd be the one who would worry me most.

"Flick," I say.

"We know," Caleb responds. "Gwendolyn told us all about you. I almost wish she hadn't. It made our little pageant much less exciting. Quite a few students didn't even bother to bet on the winner."

"I'm sorry to hear that."

"No need to apologize. The competition for bottom place was fierce this semester. Any insider information you'd care to share?"

The no-name kids have started to creep away. Caleb keeps his attention on me. I think I'm supposed to be flattered.

"I don't know much about the other new students," I say. "I've been in solitary confinement for the last three weeks."

Caleb's eyes widen. "*Really*? What did you do? Were you fighting?! Are you the one who destroyed that Ivan guy's face?" He steps away from the remaining members of his group and gestures for me to join him. He wants me to feel like he's taking me under his wing and into his confidence. But I see his three friends hurrying to hop on an elevator, and I watch it deliver them to the ninth-floor dorms. I haven't laid eyes on a clock, but I have a hunch that curfew is a few seconds away. My new best friend wants me to miss it. "Tell me everything," he insists. "I've never heard of a student being sentenced to solitary confinement! Now I know why Gwendolyn's so impressed! I can't believe you were *fighting* in the Incubation Suites!"

"I had to teach one of my classmates a lesson," I say. "I guess I'll have to do the same thing up here."

Caleb stops just outside one of the dorm rooms. I'm pretty sure it's his. And mine is at least a hundred-yard dash away. When curfew comes, I bet Caleb plans to hop inside his room without a moment to spare—and leave me stranded outside on the balcony. I have no idea what happens to students who miss curfew, and I have no intention of finding out.

"I'm not sure what you mean," Caleb says.

"You will," I tell him. "Looks like the first lesson up here is going to be yours." I walk away quickly, but I don't run. The second I'm in my room, all the doors on the floor slide shut and lock.

CHAPTER TWELVE

NEW BEGINNINGS

I'm not as well rested as I'd like to be. Having spent several months sleeping in parks, I've learned to keep part of my brain on alert at all times. Even the faintest rustling of leaves can yank me out of a dream. Back on the Lower East Side, it was usually just a rat sniffing around for food. But last night, there must have been bigger beasts on the prowl.

The Incubation Suites were always perfectly silent. I didn't expect the dorms to be any different with the students locked away in their rooms. I slipped into bed around eleven and woke less than an hour later. There was movement on the balcony outside my door. At first I wondered if Peter Pan had decided to pay me a visit. But then I detected the sound of multiple shoes traveling across the old wooden floorboards. These weren't the rhythmic footfalls you'd hear if employees were patrolling the dorms. I can't quite explain it except to say that whatever was out there seemed to be *prancing*.

•   •   •

My first class of the day is the Fundamentals of Business, which sounded perfectly harmless before I skimmed the course description. (*The ideal course to kick-start any business-related career. Polish your math skills. Study basic economic theory. Master the use of key terms and industry jargon. Acquire all the skills necessary for creative accounting, embezzlement, and most forms of fraud.*)

Ella snarls when I walk in. It's been three weeks since I told Ivan I had dibs on her body. I can't believe she's still pissed. I settle into a desk that could double as a work of modern art. An instructor in a perfectly cut suit introduces herself as Ms. Brown and begins distributing tablet computers to everyone in the class. I'm eager to play with my new toy. The dorms don't have Internet access, and I want to find out if there's Wi-Fi in the classrooms. When I turn on the device, I see no sign of a wireless signal. Instead, I discover an exam on the tablet's screen. There's nothing like having your math skills assessed after less than three hours of sleep.

"You have thirty minutes," announces Ms. Brown. The way the other students race to begin, you'd think she just fired a starter's pistol.

I'm not the first to the finish line. I'm still pondering the second-to-last problem when I hear a buzzer. Ms. Brown has turned her computer monitor toward the class. Its screen lights up.

Julian 96%. I feel a stab of envy as I swivel around to check out the competition. Caleb's little buddy is sitting directly behind me, dressed in a shiny black jacket. I bet he spent most of the morning crafting his super-cute hairdo. It's the sort of spikey, multi-layered mullet favored by anime characters, faerie kings, and Asian pop stars.

I refuse to be beaten by a wannabe member of a Japanese boy band. Still, I'm not going to rush through the test. A second buzzer breaks my concentration, but I don't look up. Another. I go back to the start of the exam and double-check my answers. Another buzz. Another. Less than a minute remains when I hit enter. My result is posted, and I hear an angry snort. *100%*. I've trounced Julian's score.

Most literature bores me. Foreign languages baffle me. But math I can do.

"Time is up. Turn in your test, Frances," the instructor announces. The last student working clicks enter. Her grade flashes on the screen. *35%*.

It's not the worst. She beat four other kids. So there must be something I don't know, because everyone in the class whips around to see what the girl will do. They seem to be expecting a spectacle, like bystanders watching someone who's considering a leap from a tenth-story window. Frances doesn't appear to notice the attention. The look on her face says she's already jumped.

"This will be your second attempt to pass this class, Frances. I realize you don't have a gift for mathematics, but you should know enough by now to make it through the first test. You'll need this course to complete your major," Ms. Brown tells her. "I suggest you work harder. I want to see significant improvement by the end of the Immunity Phase."

"Yes, Ms. Brown." Frances's face is whiter than the wall behind her.

The instructor studies the other scores on the monitor. "It appears that one of the academy's newest students has already taken the lead in this class. Where did you learn calculus, Flick?"

I shrug. I'm not about to reveal my academic history. No one here needs to know what I've got in my toolbox. "Math has always felt like second nature to me."

"You're very fortunate," Ms. Brown says. "But it took more than luck to earn a perfect score. There's a lesson here for you, Julian. Attention to detail is much more important than *speed*. If you can't resist the urge to show off, you'll never reach any higher than second place in my class."

"Right as always, Ms. Brown," Julian says with chilling good humor. "I'll be sure to find out if Flick has anything else he can teach me."

I don't need to look at Julian to know he's furious that a newbie stole his prize. I can practically hear his teeth grinding away.

The bell rings, and I gather my books. I can see Julian loitering outside the classroom. I'm preparing to give him the lesson he requested when I realize he's not alone.

"Hi, I'm Gwendolyn." Maybe she arrived at the academy with a terrible accent. Or a set of buckteeth and a hunchback. But it's hard to imagine that this girl was ever anything other than physically perfect. I've seen the results of enough plastic surgery to know that only nature produces such beauty. Full lips, glossy blond hair that looks soft to the touch, and those brilliant blue eyes. Still, she's a little too Disney princess for my taste. Some guys like perfection, but I've never been interested in playing with dolls.

She shakes my hand, and her grip is surprisingly firm.

"Flick," I say, though I know it's unnecessary.

"I'll see you at lunch," Gwendolyn says, dismissing Julian. I don't think she catches the sneer he shoots me before he hurries away. "I hear you're number one in the class."

"It's only the first day," I point out.

"It never hurts to have a head start. What course do you have next period?"

"The Art of Persuasion."

"Me too!" she exclaims, but I'd be willing to bet she already knew that. "Why don't you walk with me?"

It would be easier than finding the class on my own—as long as that's where she's planning to lead me. "Last night, I took a walk with one of your schoolmates, and I nearly got locked out of my room."

"Don't take it personally. Caleb's just jealous," Gwendolyn assures me. "If you live up to your hype, you'll have to get used to that sort of thing."

"My hype? I've been a real student for less than twenty-four hours."

"Yes, but I'm afraid I have a very big mouth."

And it smiles so sweetly.

The Art of Persuasion must be a required course for all majors. The classroom is the biggest I've seen so far, and there are only two empty seats when we enter. As luck would have it, they're side by side. My next-door neighbor, Lucas, is three rows behind Gwendolyn and me. I give him a nod, but he doesn't respond.

The course is taught by yet another blandly named instructor. I can tell from one glance that Mr. Martin is a "backslapper." A few of his kind always showed up whenever my father threw one of his parties. Jude and I liked to sit in the dark at the top of the stairs and pick them out of the crowd. They were the ones who smiled a little too broadly and laughed just a little too loudly. They answered to the nicknames they were issued at prep school and acted like overgrown boys. But each time one of them reached out to deliver a hearty slap to a fellow man's back, you could tell he wished he had a knife in his hand.

Mr. Martin ignores the podium at the front of the room and perches on the edge of his desk instead. We're supposed to find this endearing. He's trying to appear approachable. I bet this guy's watched *Dead Poets Society* five hundred times. But his act still needs a little more work.

"Over the course of your careers, you will each encounter individuals who'll try to make your lives difficult. It could be an employer who refuses to promote you—or a politician who wakes up one morning and decides to have principles. You may even stumble across the occasional law-enforcement official who isn't interested in supplementing his pitiful salary. When you meet these people, you'll quickly discover that all the sweet talk in the world won't alter their attitudes. If you intend to persuade them, you'll need to start digging for *information*."

Mr. Martin picks up a remote control from his desk, and a large television screen descends from the ceiling. It's displaying a static image of a man. He has a rugged, weather-beaten face, and his shirtsleeves have been rolled past the elbow. Everything about him screams *Average Joe*. But he's not.

"Let's start with a hypothetical situation."

The situation may be hypothetical, but the man is real. He's a congressman from Illinois. His name is Glen Sheehan, and he's a rising star. Last time I had access to a proper Internet connection, his speeches were all over YouTube. Sheehan's supporters call him the "voice of the people." I scan my classmate's faces. I wonder if they recognize him too. It's hard to tell.

"This man is a politician," Mr. Martin announces. "For the sake of today's discussion, let's imagine that you own a business that's about to launch a profitable new product. The politician thinks he can look like a hero by convincing the country that your product is dangerous."

Lucas raises his hand. "Why does he believe that the product is dangerous?" he asks.

Mr. Martin frowns. "This is a hypothetical situation, Lucas. There's no need to dwell on the details right now."

"You just said persuasion is all about information. The reasons he's opposed to the product seem like fairly important information to me."

"Then let's say that the congressman believes your product has not been thoroughly tested. And he's been informed that it may threaten the health of those who use it."

Lucas sits back with his arms crossed. I get the sense that he's determined to make a point. "Then we should try to address his concerns. I say we do some more tests. The results will either convince the politician that he's wrong—or help us make changes that might satisfy our critics without making our product unprofitable."

"Easier said than done," the instructor responds dismissively. "Anyone else have any thoughts? What's the best way to *persuade* our congressman?"

Gwendolyn lifts a hand. "He's popular with the voters?"

"Extremely," Mr. Martin confirms. "He's up for reelection next year, and so far no one has stepped forward to challenge him. He thinks he's invincible."

"Wasn't there another famous politician who bragged that he couldn't lose an election unless he got caught 'with a live boy or a dead girl'? Maybe we could arrange a little date for the congressman." She says it so pleasantly that I almost miss her point.

The instructor laughs. "A wonderful thought, Gwendolyn, but let's save that option for a last resort. Anyone else?" He points at me. "Flick, right?" I nod. "What do you think?"

I'm not going to pretend that I'm a factory owner or that the politician is fictional. "You should hire someone to steal Sheehan's phone. There are a bunch of other things you could do, but that's a good place to start. It's fairly risk-free. People lose their phones all the time. If you plan everything right, no one will get suspicious."

"And what would you hope to learn by stealing his phone?" Mr. Martin won't stop playing his stupid little game.

"*I'm* not all that interested in Representative Sheehan from the great state of Illinois. But if *you* steal his phone, you should have a look at the photos first. Even old guys snap pictures of themselves in compromising positions. It's like the Achilles' heel of the male brain. If all the photos turn out to be puppies and flowers, then check out his emails, texts, and web-browser history. A lot of phones even store GPS tracking information that will give you a map of every place that the owner's been. And don't forget to scroll through the sent and received call logs. Do all of that, and you're bound to find *something* you can use against Sheehan. The moment politicians start believing they're invincible, they stop being careful."

Mr. Martin is wearing his backslapper grin, but he's far from amused. He needs to prove that he knows more than I ever will. "That's why his aides will have made sure that his phone is password-protected."

I shrug. "And that's why the world has hackers. But a good thief could snag a phone right after the guy uses it—before password protection has a chance to kick in. I could show you how if you'd like." I begin to rise out of my seat.

"Sit down, Flick," he barks. Then he takes a breath and slips back into character. "We'll be putting your impressive skills to the test later this semester."

Second period just started, and I already have five enemies, a pretty blond stalker, and zero friends. It's a record, even for me.

My third class, International Politics, deserves a much snappier title. If I were in charge of writing the Mandel Academy course catalog, I'd call it Making a Killing: The Profitable Business of Bloodshed. I learned more about war in the past hour than I did during my entire stint at military school. Apparently it's not just about fighting bad guys anymore. You can peddle machine guns to Afghani warlords (as long as you don't mind being paid in opium). Or you can start a black market in a refugee camp and sell antibiotics at ten times what they'd charge at your neighborhood Walgreens. Hell, you can even form your own private army these days. Does some poverty-stricken country have something you want (bananas, water, diamonds, cheap labor)? Don't bother bargaining with the local honchos—just hire a bunch of mercenaries to go in and get it! If you don't, someone else certainly will. Poor people's lives are going to suck no matter what you do. You can't fight fate. But if you hold your nose and step over the corpses, you can make your own life a whole lot richer.

I'm hoping a strong cup of coffee will wash away the taste of death in my mouth, so I ride an elevator to the sixth-floor cafeteria. The state-of-the-art dining facility is bright and white. One wall is dominated by a giant black screen. The other walls are bare. The long steel tables with attached stools are exactly what you'd expect to find in a high school lunchroom. But someone bought far too many. There are at least six seats for every student, which actually seems to suit most of my schoolmates. Almost all are eating alone. Only two tables in the far corner are filled. Gwendolyn is sitting at one, wedged between Caleb and the angry, adorable little creature named Leila. Gwendolyn doesn't notice when I enter, but Leila does. I have a feeling the girl doesn't really like anyone—but she seems to hate me most of all.

I grab a sandwich and a cup of coffee. I'm searching for a place to eat when I spot Aubrey sitting on her own with an untouched salad in front of her. I'd given up all hope of having a private chat in this place. But Aubrey is close enough to the two chattering tables that our conversation will probably be drowned out by the noise. When I slide onto a stool across from her, she doesn't even blink.

"Hello," I say, and her head jerks up.

"You can't sit here," she growls.

Her hostility catches me off guard. And yet I'm still hell-bent on helping her. "I'll move," I say softly. "But you have to promise to go to Pitt Street if you ever get expelled from this place. It's a short walk from here. Find a girl named Joi. She'll know what to do."

An emotion flickers across Aubrey's face. It vanishes before I can read it. "I'm not leaving the academy," she insists. "Now go away."

I pick up my tray and hunt for another spot. Gwendolyn waves me over to her table. Her friends are all smiles now. I see they've added a new member to their crowd. With his bruises still purple and fresh, he stands out like an eggplant in a rose bed. Ivan.

"So Aubrey's a friend of yours?" Caleb asks bluntly. He must have bet against her after the Beauty Pageant. I doubt he'd know her name otherwise.

"Mind your own business, Caleb," Gwendolyn says, but I have a hunch that the question needs to be answered.

"I thought Aubrey was comatose. I wasn't expecting a chat."

"Well, you should eat with us from now on," Gwendolyn insists. "Caleb—move over and let Flick sit down."

Caleb may be the only person I've ever met who can look bored and furious simultaneously.

"Don't bother," I tell him. "I'm not here to make friends."

The coffee and sandwich were barely enough to keep me alive and alert through Wealth Management (money-laundering, tax loopholes, offshore accounts, and insider trading) and Human Psychology (which appears to be a remedial course that draws from the works of Ayn Rand and reruns of *Wild Kingdom*). Fortunately, I was blessed with a second wind or I might not have survived my final class of the day, Hand-to-Hand Combat.

Gwendolyn and I share this course as well. She rocks a pair of shorts better than any girl I've ever seen. And I'm in awe of her right hook. Her sparring partner is twice her width and wearing protective headgear, but she's on the verge of taking him down when the instructor blows his whistle. There was a time when a girl with skills like Gwendolyn's would have driven me wild. And she's been making it pretty obvious that she's interested. Just now, she's pulled up her shirt to wipe her brow, and I can see a little bead of sweat trickling toward the cleavage rising out of her sports bra. I know the show is meant for me, but I pretend not to notice. When the bell rings, I make a beeline for the exit.

"Hey, Flick!"

She's not going to let me escape. She must know she looks great like this. Hair coming loose from her ponytail. Forehead damp, cheeks rosy. Wearing formfitting gym clothes instead of prim designer dresses. She's less Cinderella now—more Lara Croft.

"Where did you learn how to fight like that?" She's stuck to my side.

"Military school."

"Do you think you could teach me a few moves?"

She's bolder than she looks. "I think you're doing pretty well on your own."

"You know this no-friends policy of yours . . . maybe you should consider making an exception." Her voice is sugary enough to draw a whole swarm of flies.

"Why would I want to do that?" I ask.

We reach the elevators. There's a crowd of students waiting for the next car to arrive. When it does, they all step aside to let

Gwendolyn and me board alone. The gates close, and I press the button for the eighth floor. Gwendolyn keeps her attention focused on me.

"That's why. Being friends with me has certain advantages." The way she's looking at me right now, I know she doesn't mean cutting elevator lines.

"You're the top student. The Dux. And the last time I checked, Gwendolyn, you were also my *competition*."

Her smile is angelic, yet her tone is anything but. "Which is all the more reason you should get to know me a bit better."

I do like a girl who can get straight to the point. "Isn't there some kind of rule about sleeping with your schoolmates?"

"The rules only apply to the less gifted students. Those of us at the top can do whatever we like. In fact, it's encouraged. It gives the others something to strive for."

Finally, a way out. "This was my first day. I'm nowhere near the top yet."

"You will be soon," Gwendolyn says. She doesn't live on my floor, but she exits the elevator when I do. I get the impression that she's planning to follow me all the way back to my room. I stop, blocking her path.

"Look, this has all been extremely educational, but I need to take a shower."

I don't think Gwendolyn heard me. She's watching someone at the other end of the hall. I look over my shoulder and see Lucas opening the door to his room.

"You live next to Lucas?" she asks, but doesn't wait for an answer. "Have you spoken to him?"

"Briefly."

Gwendolyn shakes her head as if suddenly saddened. "You know, he's probably the smartest kid here. He won the Beauty Pageant three semesters back. I tried to help him, too. But I guess it happens."

"What?" I ask, when she doesn't follow up on the point.

"I guess some prodigies never live up to their potential."

We stand for a moment, engaged in a silent game called "How Much Do You Know?" Then she places a hand on my bicep.

"Keep me company at dinner tonight?" she asks.

"I'll think about it," I tell her.

Anything, anything. You have to do anything. I will learn how to blackmail congressmen. I will study all forms of fraud. I will let them put a chip in my arm. I will allow my DNA to be sampled. I thought I was prepared to do anything. But all it took was a pretty girl in a sports bra to make me question my resolve.

I've been sitting on the floor of my shower for a very long time. The steam has fogged up the doors. It's been weeks since I had this kind of privacy. Dinner must have ended ages ago. My room is probably locked by now. I *should* be thinking about Gwendolyn—trying to figure out what she really wants. Trying to determine whether she can help me while I'm here. Figuring out what I'll say when she asks why I stood her up. But right now, I couldn't give a damn about Gwendolyn. I'm doing my best to conjure Joi.

I've been making a list of all the things I remember. The scent of jasmine and cocoa butter. Her fearlessness and the way she never flinched at the sight of blood. The sight of her naked limbs treading water in a cold plunge pool. The lumps in her mattress and the feel of her skin. There's so much more, but it's not nearly enough. I said goodbye, and I guess goodbye really does mean forgetting. Joi is already starting to fade. I knew this might happen, but I never thought a girl could disappear so damn quickly. I can't bear to lose any more of her now. I wish it was safe to write down everything I still know. That way I might be able to keep Joi real. Because I'm starting to worry that I may have imagined her. Maybe she was a hallucination like Peter Pan. Maybe when I was weak and scared and all alone, I dreamed up a Wendy to take care of me.

I wish I knew her last name. But I don't. The one time I asked, it must have sounded like a joke. I thought the less I knew about Joi, the easier it would be to slip away. Now I'm desperately clinging to the little I have left of her. Fantasy or not, I can't let her go.

I don't think I'll be real without her.

I turn off the tap just in time to hear the door of my room slide open and shut. I don't even bother with a towel. I rush out of the bathroom sopping wet, hoping to catch Peter Pan. I'll admit he was right all along. I'll ask him what he thinks I should do. But he's not there. No one is. There's just a tray on my desk that's loaded with food. I pick up the note tucked under a bread plate. *You need to eat,* it says. The handwriting isn't obviously feminine, but somehow I know it belongs to Gwendolyn.

CHAPTER THIRTEEN

LIFE AMONG THE WOLVES

There are three kinds of students at the Mandel Academy. Most of the kids belong to a group I call the Androids. Though they're not exactly a *group*. It's not like they've banded together. In fact, they'd rather not be Androids at all. Everyone here wants to be *special*. And it's easy to see that some of the students were simply born that way. The rest have to work to stand out from the crowd. And that's what the Androids do. They study all hours of the day, hoping to join the top tier of students—or desperately struggling to stay out of the bottom. They pray that sheer effort can make up for their lack of raw talent. I've never seen people work so hard, but I have no trouble understanding why they're afraid to stop.

If your grades start to plummet, you may end up joining the Ghosts. I didn't invent the label, but it certainly fits. At the Mandel Academy, Ghosts aren't just shunned—they're completely invisible. When students fall to the bottom of the class, they no longer exist. The instructors won't acknowledge them. The other kids avoid them as if the condition might be contagious. We all have one week of immunity left this semester, but everyone knows who'll be getting the boot. And it's easier to pretend that they're already gone.

There's not much point in feeling sorry for the Ghosts. I suppose they'll be fine once they're back on the outside. A few of them appear to be fairly intelligent. And having done their time in the Incubation Suites, most are attractive and well-spoken. But they don't belong *here*. They lack the killer instincts that are necessary in order to thrive at a place like this. You'd think, given the atmosphere, that some of the Ghosts would be eager to leave. But Felix seems to be the only one counting the days left to freedom. I hear he's failing all of his classes, but every time I see him, he couldn't look happier. It gives me a perverse pleasure to watch him smile at the Androids. They never know how to respond. I just wish Aubrey shared Felix's hunger for freedom. She once insisted she wouldn't be leaving, but everyone knows she'll be expelled. I'm not sure how she feels about that. I'm not sure Aubrey feels anything anymore.

I've never thought of myself as "special." And before I got here, I don't think anyone would have used the term to describe me. Yet I'm well on my way to becoming a member of the most elite group at the Mandel Academy. Three weeks into the semester, I'm the number-one student in all of my classes. Much to my surprise, my gifts aren't limited to pick-pocketing and petty theft. It seems I have a real talent for top-level crime. I've planned hypothetical coups in third-world countries. I stole a fortune from the postal employees' pension fund. I've engineered hostile takeovers of small mom-and-pop companies, which I later sold for scrap. Lucian Mandel warned me that life would only get more difficult after I left the Incubation Suites. For once he was wrong. As soon as I accepted that I won't be getting out of here for a while, I realized there are worse places to be. I'm sure the academy feels like hell to most people, but it suits me just fine. If I have to play Mandel's game, I'll play to win. And who knows—if I keep up the good work, I might end up graduating in September after two short semesters. Then I'll have the proof—and the revenge I've craved. I just hope that my father has been monitoring my progress. If he has, he's gotta be starting to worry. Sometimes I even scare myself.

When the Immunity Phase ends, the school-wide rankings will be announced. I'll be shocked if I don't make the top three. Gwendolyn has informed everyone that she expects there to be a new Dux next week. She doesn't seem to mind, but her friends certainly do. The twelve top-ranking students live cushy lives. Right now, they're the school's celebrities, but if I join the pack, one of them will be banished to the Androids. And everyone knows that only nine will be allowed to graduate.

Caleb, Leila, Julian, and Austin probably don't have much cause for concern. They're numbers 2 through 5. But I know they've been searching for ways to sabotage my rise to the top. I started thinking of them as the Wolves when I noticed that one of them always seemed to be stalking me, waiting for a chance to pounce. Gwendolyn made sure none of them ever got close enough. And now that it looks like I may soon be their leader, they're as charming and playful as a litter of puppies. They don't dare bare their fangs until my back is turned.

Gwendolyn is different. Maybe it's because she's held the Dux title for two years running. She'll turn eighteen this summer, and now that she's old enough to graduate, she must not feel the need to fight anymore. I'm her only true competition, and yet she's supported me from the start. I know the others are convinced she's just hopped up on hormones. But I don't think that's the only reason she's nice to me. She's perfectly pleasant to just about everyone. I've been watching her for a while, and I've never seen her abuse her power. Although her friends' favorite sport is tormenting the Androids, Gwendolyn never takes part in their mean-spirited games. Two days in a row, nasty little Leila dropped a tray full of pasta in the middle of the cafeteria and ordered the nearest male Android to suck the noodles off the floor. Gwendolyn called her immature, and Leila hasn't had an accident since. The pretty, petite Dux even manages to keep Austin the giant grinning goober in line. Without Gwendolyn, the hazing pranks he finds so hilarious would probably be more fatal than frat-boy.

I haven't told Gwendolyn what I really think of her clique. Lucas is the only person in whom I've confided. Still, I wouldn't call him my *friend*. Lucas and I never speak during the day. In fact, he rarely acknowledges my presence. And I've never been invited into his room. But he'll often join me on the balcony in the last few minutes before curfew when the other students are busy preparing for lockdown. He's the only kid at the academy who can't easily be labeled. He's not in the top twelve, but he hasn't hit rock bottom yet. He's close, though. I've seen him talking to Ghosts, and he certainly doesn't go out of his way to please the people in charge. Our Art of Persuasion instructor despises him. Lucas can find a perfectly law-abiding solution to almost any dilemma, and it drives

Mr. Martin insane. Whenever Lucas is in the room, the old back-slapper even seems to forget how much he hates *me*.

"I heard you may be the Dux soon," Lucas said to me last night as we stood in the shadows. We weren't exactly *hidden*, but you'd have had to look hard to see us. "You'll officially be a member of the in-crowd."

"You mean the Wolves?"

I'd never heard Lucas laugh before. "You got that one right. That's *exactly* what they are."

Then I asked the question I'd been saving for just the right moment. "You used to be one of them, didn't you? Gwendolyn told me you won the Beauty Pageant a while back."

"Ah, sweet little Gwendolyn. A few months ago she was trying to seduce me. Now I'm the hero of her cautionary tales."

"You and Gwendolyn had a thing?" I don't think I was jealous—just surprised to discover that I wasn't the first.

"Yes, but it didn't last very long. She found out that I'm not her type. Gwendolyn is the Queen of the Wolves, and I didn't have what it took to run with the pack."

"What happened?"

Lucas didn't answer. Instead, he scanned the walls.

"What were you just looking for?" I asked when he'd finished.

"I never have figured out where they hide all the bugs."

"Do you really think someone is listening?" I mouthed.

"All technology majors take courses in surveillance. Last semester, I tried to conduct an experiment out here, but the acoustics are terrible. The balcony's definitely bugged, but I'm not sure how much the mikes can pick up if we keep our voices low." He took a moment to collect his thoughts. "Here's what happened. I had a lot of fun playing a bad guy for a while. But then all of this stopped being a game. One day it got real, and that's when the Wolves found out that I wasn't one of them." When Lucas suddenly spun around to face me, it felt like he'd wanted to catch me off guard. "You aren't one of them either. But you might stand a chance if you manage to bump Gwendolyn out of top place. The Dux has a lot of power. And it doesn't hurt that you're an incredible actor. You're doing a very good job of pretending you belong here. You almost had me fooled too."

"What makes you think I'm pretending?"

"Aubrey told me."

No good deed ever goes unpunished. "You guys are friends?"

"I just thought someone should talk to her," Lucas said.

I didn't let him glimpse my embarrassment. I tried to reach out to her, but I should have tried harder. I should have been keeping an eye on Aubrey. That's what Joi would have wanted. "Do you think Aubrey's ready to go home?"

If Lucas answered, I didn't hear him. The dorm doors started to shut, and I barely made it inside.

Yesterday's conversation is now playing on an endless loop inside my head. I'm studying the beautiful girl who's sprawled across a divan, reading a book while she absentmindedly twists her golden hair into a knot. I don't know why I never thought of Gwendolyn as Queen of the Wolves—even though she's clearly their leader. And as usual, her subjects have gathered around her. We're all in a lounge that's reserved for the top twelve students—a large, sunlit

chamber inside one of the building's two towers. I didn't even real-
ize the lounge existed until Gwendolyn brought me up here today.
I shouldn't be allowed inside before the new rankings are released.
But no one is stupid enough to complain.

The room's furnishings may be posh—leather seats and velvet
sofas—but the lounge has a homey, lived-in feeling. The floorboards
bear grooves etched by rearranged chairs and dimples left by girls'
high-heeled shoes. A century-old portrait hangs above the flickering fireplace. The painting's obese subject is either the school's
founder, Madame Mandelbaum, or one of New York's first female
impersonators. Still, it doesn't detract from the salon-like atmosphere. Generations of Wolves must have gotten their first taste of
the good life in this very room. They probably stood at the windows
and surveyed the city they'd be setting out to conquer. As far as I
know, this is the only place in the school with a view. You can see
the outside world from up here. And it can see you.

I took a quick peek but didn't linger. I was far more intrigued by
the listing towers of books propped against the walls. It seems to be
the sole library at the Mandel Academy, and I thought I'd find some
reading material that could give me hope for the human race. But
all the books here are just outdated texts from decades-old classes.
I thumbed through a few, and the only thing that brought a smile
to my face was a sheet of yellowing paper that fell out of a manual
for an old Mac PowerBook 100. Some former student had typed up
a list of twenty personality traits and labeled it HARE PSYCHOPATHY
CHECKLIST. The title instantly grabbed my attention. I learned about
the checklist in a criminal justice class back at military school. The
test is usually given to prison inmates who are suspected of being

dangerous psychopaths. The subject gets a 1 or 2 for each psychopathic personality trait he possesses (pathological lying, inability to feel guilt, impulsive behavior). Then the 1s and 2s are all added up. The highest score you can get is 40. That's Ted Bundy and Charles Manson territory.

There was a column of numbers jotted down on the right-hand side of the paper I found. Someone must have felt the need to evaluate a student here at the academy. The kid who got tested received a rather impressive 38. At the bottom of the page was a message scrawled in purple marker.

See? You're the crazy one, you redheaded freak.

I've been attempting to translate the phrase into Latin. If I ever succeed, I shall make it my personal motto. But it's difficult to concentrate when you're surrounded by Wolves. Caleb, the counterfeit aristocrat, is slouched in a leather club chair with his legs flung over one of the arms. He's flipping through a history of the Sicilian Mafia, which he told me is required reading for all Human Resources majors. Leila's fingers are flying across the keys of her computer. Gwendolyn says Leila is pursing a solitary career in technology because she can't stand to be in the presence of men. I guess Julian doesn't really qualify as a "man," because she's sitting so close to him that she might as well crawl onto his lap. He's sketching the molecular structure of crack cocaine on a notepad. Some leisure studies majors are trained to be pimps, but Julian's sole focus is the international drug trade. I've also discovered that big ol' Austin, the only person here with an accent, is just as slippery as a student of politics should be. Almost every word of the short speech he shared with us earlier in the evening had been lifted from one of the Kennedys'. When I called him on it, he just asked me if I figured "regular folks" would know.

I thought Gwendolyn's friends were trouble before I ever got to know them. Now that I've had a chance to observe them up close, I see how truly dangerous they could be. I may soon be their leader, but I doubt they'll ever respect me. I'll always have to watch my back. And yet each and every one of the Wolves is completely in awe of Gwendolyn.

She's caught me staring at her. "What?" she inquires with a smile.

"Nothing," I say, but I can't pull my eyes away from her face. How did Little Red Riding Hood manage to conquer the Wolves?

"Hey, guys," she calls out to the others. "Give us a few minutes, okay?"

And just like that, the four fiercest beasts at the Mandel Academy grab their things and trot right out of the room. This is not what I wanted. It's been getting harder and harder to resist Gwendolyn's advances.

"I've lured you into my lair, and now we're alone," she says when they're gone. "Are you scared?"

My laugh doesn't sound quite as confident as I'd like. "You're pretty tough, but I think I could take you."

"Are you sure you want to put up a fight?"

She's slinking across the divan toward my chair. I stop her with a shake of my head.

"Not until I'm one of you," I tell her. "Not until it's official. I'm not going to risk my ranking for a piece of ass. Even an ass as attractive as yours."

Gwendolyn sits back on her haunches and sighs. "That excuse is getting really tired, Flick. Why don't you just tell me the truth? There's another girl, isn't there?"

I make a show of looking around the room. "There is? I don't see one."

"Stop trying to mess with my head. Mr. Mandel told me about your girlfriend."

I feel my fists clench. "He told you? What else did he say?"

"So it's true. What's her name? What's she like?"

I won't say Joi's name. I won't say a word. I won't pollute my memories of Joi by sharing them with the girl who's been scheming to replace her.

"You don't have to tell me," Gwendolyn says when I refuse to answer. "I already know everything I need to know about this little sweetheart of yours."

"Oh yeah? And what exactly is that?"

"I know that she's not here. But I *am*. And I can help you. I care about you, Flick. I *want* to help you win your wager."

Win? I clench my teeth while I wait for the rage to subside. That freckled f— must have told Gwendolyn about my father as well. "What can you do?" I ask when I'm able. "You're just a student."

"No—I'm the *Dux*. I can do things that the rest of you can't."

Lucas said the same thing last night. "Like what?"

"Well, let's see. I can talk to Mr. Mandel whenever I like. I can keep a student from being expelled. I can leave the academy."

"They let you go outside?" I butt in. That might prove useful.

"As long as I have Mr. Mandel's permission. Sometimes he even lets me take a guest along. Don't you see? I can make your time here a whole lot easier."

"Thanks for the offer, but it hasn't been all that bad so far."

Gwendolyn's voice drops to a whisper. "I may be able to help you graduate faster too."

Now we're getting somewhere. "How?"

She hesitates for a moment. "Mr. Mandel told me he's worried that you're not totally committed to the academy. He thinks you're still in love with that girl out there."

"Even if I were, what difference would it make?" I ask.

"We're here to become new people, Flick. Mr. Mandel doesn't believe that's possible unless we let go of our pasts. It doesn't matter how good your grades are. If he thinks you haven't changed by September, he'll keep you here for another year. But if we were a couple, Mr. Mandel would know that you've left everything out there behind."

"Did he tell you to say that?"

"Of course not!" Gwendolyn's blushing. But even if Mandel didn't put the words in her mouth, he still knew she'd say them. That's why he told her about Joi. This isn't a way out. It's a goddamned pop quiz.

I've proved I can kick ass in the classroom, but Mandel is telling me that's not enough. I can't have my revenge unless I give up everything else. Sleeping with Gwendolyn might earn me an early release, but it would come at too high a price. I'd have to betray the one person on earth that I love. It doesn't matter that Joi wouldn't know. I would. Mandel wants the last little piece of my soul, but he can go screw himself. I'll show him that I can keep it and win.

"So you're saying I'll graduate this September if I agree to be your boy toy. Thanks but no thanks, Gwendolyn. I'm a thief, not a prostitute."

"You make it sound sleazy, and it's not!" Gwendolyn insists, looking wounded. You'd think I just drop-kicked a kitten. "Don't you know that I'm crazy about you? I've been practically throwing myself at you since you moved upstairs. And you never say 'no.' All you do is give me the same sorry excuse. If you're really not interested, just tell me. I swear I'll back off!"

Gwendolyn's been kind to me since I came up from the Suites. I have no idea why a girl like her would ever fall for someone like me. Maybe it's all just an act, but if it's not, I don't want to hurt her. Mandel may have tricked her into delivering his message, but Gwendolyn's not the one who deserves to be punished.

"There's not a male on this planet who wouldn't think you're *extremely* interesting," I offer vaguely. "Where did Mandel find a creature like you?"

Gwendolyn is inching toward me again. She thinks I've accepted her offer. "He had me released from juvie two years ago."

"What were you in for?"

She doesn't hesitate. "I killed a man who tried to molest me."

That seems perfectly reasonable to me. I was worried it would be far worse. But when Gwendolyn moves to kiss me, I gently push her back.

"Not yet," I say as nicely as possible.

Mandel can keep me locked up. He can deny me the proof for

another year. But he can't take Joi. I'll probably be the academy's top student in a matter of days. And I might not mind staying here a bit longer if life as the Dux is as sweet as it sounds.

The first thing I'll do after I win the title is take a trip to the outside world. I won't put Joi in danger. I won't try to find her. But there's one thing I've decided I can't live without. Even though I'll never see her again, I need to know Joi's last name.

CHAPTER FOURTEEN

FALLING FROM GRACE

The door opens, and I immediately glance back at the alarm clock on my dorm room desk. It still says ten minutes to eight. Time for breakfast. But that can't be right. The atrium is dark. It must be the dead of night.

I step out onto the balcony and look up, expecting to see the moon hanging in the sky above. But the glass pyramid that spans most of the building's roof is covered in snow. There could be a blizzard raging at this very moment—and I'd almost forgotten it was winter. I watch a few other students glance upward as they exit their rooms. Those who've been out a bit longer are leaning over the balcony's railing.

I join the crowd. There's something on the floor of the atrium, eight stories below. It looks like a rumpled pile of laundry surrounded by a pool of black liquid. Then I see a hand poking out of a sleeve, and I realize I'm looking at four twisted limbs and a torso. One of the students has jumped. His body covers most of the school motto. All it says now is EMERGO.

I know it's a human being. I know I'm not dreaming. Dozens of other people are witnessing the very same scene. At least one person should be screaming or crying or shouting for help. But we're all silent. The faces around me are completely inscrutable. They've spent the last month pretending to be thieves, drug dealers, and war profiteers. One dead kid isn't enough to shock them anymore.

I've wondered what a moment like this would feel like. It doesn't feel real.

"It's starting early this semester." I hear Lucas's voice.

I'd like to ask him if this has happened before. I want to know how many students have committed suicide since he's been at the academy. But I don't dare say a word. Caleb is standing just a few feet to my right. I raise my eyes to the ninth-floor balcony, just in time to see Gwendolyn take a quick glance at the scene below and then glide away.

"Who is it?" I ask Caleb.

"Who cares?" he says. "I bet Aubrey would be the first to go, and that's not her. This is the second Beauty Pageant I've lost this year."

The school-wide rankings are being posted this morning, and the elevators are packed with students on their way to the cafeteria. I've been told that no one ever misses breakfast on ranking days. But judging by the anxious expression on most of the faces, I doubt any Androids or Ghosts will be able to eat. Gwendolyn, on the other hand, looks positively bright-eyed and bushy-tailed. She's waiting for me on the sixth-floor balcony. I'm impressed by her display of willpower. If I'd gotten here first, I wouldn't have waited. I don't even pause to ask if she knows which of our classmates just died.

The cafeteria seems even brighter than usual. The jumbo-size screen that's been dark since the beginning of the semester has finally come to life. The only thing on it is a list of names. The academy's students have been ranked from one to fifty-five. I'm number 2. Gwendolyn is still number 1.

"You won," I say as I stare at the screen.

"I'm sorry, Flick. Maybe you'll be the Dux next time."

If the competition were fair, I'd have the title right now. I'm number one in all of my classes. Which means Gwendolyn is number two in the ones that we share. She couldn't have beaten me unless the rankings are rigged. I expected Mandel to play by the rules, but he denied me the title just to prove he's in charge. He sent me Gwendolyn, and I pushed her away. I wouldn't betray Joi. I couldn't let go of that last little piece of my soul.

I'm trapped. I didn't do what he wanted and Mandel took my title. The next time, he might do something much worse.

"I gotta go. I'll see you in class," I tell Gwendolyn. It's the most I can muster.

I need to escape. I need to get back to my room before I lose control. But there's someone blocking my path. Ella. I don't recall seeing her recently, even though we're both taking the Fundamentals of Business. She spends most of her free time shut up in her room, trying to study her way out of the Androids.

"Did you see?" She sounds spooked. Ella, the girl who shot her uncle four times in the head, is scared.

I glance back at the rankings and search for her name. She's sixteenth. Not good enough to be a Wolf, but not a bad showing for a newbie with no formal education. I'm about to say as much, but she shakes her head. Whatever she's seen, I haven't found it yet.

I start to scan the entire list, and I come to an abrupt halt at number 12. Ivan is officially a Wolf. Further proof that these rankings are utter bullshit. I'm not the only one who's been screwed. If I were Ella, I'd be hurling food at the walls. But then I get to the bottom of the list, and I see why Ella's too frightened to fight. Number 53 is Frances; 54 is Aubrey. Felix has taken last place. And suddenly it hits me so hard that I almost collapse. Felix was the kid who jumped.

"He told me yesterday that he was going home to Miami," Ella whispers.

I can't respond. I'm too busy filing through seven weeks of memories. Felix wanted out from the very beginning. Why would he kill himself right before he was supposed to leave? Yesterday he was planning to head back to Miami. Did he wake up this morning and realize that the only thing there would be a life turning tricks? At least he had *something* to go back to. There are kids here who'd have nothing. Like Aubrey . . . *Oh shit.*

"Hello, I'm Gwendolyn." She's holding out a hand to Ella.

"Ella." I almost expect her to curtsy.

"Your ranking is very impressive," Gwendolyn says. "Mr. Mandel thinks you'll be in the top twelve soon. Maybe even by next semester."

"He does?" I saw Ella smile on our first day in the Incubation Suites. Since then her face must have forgotten how. She's doing her best. The corners of her mouth are turned up. I even see a few teeth. But it's not a smile. It's a rictus grin.

"Absolutely. It could be the first time that three students from the same Incubation Group all reach the top twelve. So we're *very* excited. It's a shame about Felix, though. I asked Mr. Mandel to give him a few weeks to work his way up from the bottom. But I guess the competition was just a little too much for him. Not everyone is as naturally gifted as you and Flick."

"Thank you," Ella gushes. I bet she's already forgotten about Felix.

"I just call it like I see it," says the Dux.

I escort Gwendolyn to a table where the rest of the Wolf pack has convened. She slides onto a stool next to Caleb, who's busy licking his wounds. You'd think the guy was number 30 rather than third in the school. Gwendolyn immediately sets to work on Caleb's injured ego. She's barely listening when I announce I'm going for food. I slip out of the cafeteria and hurry up to the eighth floor. The timing isn't ideal, but I doubt it ever will be. I need to find Aubrey as quickly as possible. The last time I spoke to her, she said she wouldn't be leaving the academy. I know that hope can play tricks on a person's mind. But now the truth has been posted for the whole school to see. Aubrey will be gone soon. Maybe even by the end of today. So I need to tell her what I wish I'd told Felix. That the world outside isn't as dark as it seems. There's someone who will help her. Aubrey doesn't need to jump.

The Androids usually spend breakfast time in their rooms, cramming before classes begin. But today, the eighth floor is deserted. I stick close to the wall. No one on the balcony downstairs should be able to see me. When I reach Aubrey's room, I'm certain I'm too late. The bed is made. The computer lid is closed. The bathroom door is wide open. I've never visited her room before, and I'm shocked to see a badly burned teddy bear resting against her pillows. Most kids have something—a picture, book, or memento from their previous lives. But Aubrey's bear isn't your typical keepsake. It's lost an ear and one arm. The few patches of fur that aren't charred are covered in grime. Maybe Aubrey rescued it from the fire that incinerated her parents. I guess I can understand why she wouldn't want to throw it away. But I can't fathom why she'd keep a foul thing like that on her *bed*.

I'm about to rush back down to the cafeteria when I hear a grunt in the bathroom. A single, gorilla-like grunt. I know what it means before my brain has time to translate it. I freeze, hoping I'm wrong, and then the sound of ripping fabric sends me sprinting for the bathroom door.

I can only see her legs. He's crouching over her, one knee on either side of her slender hips. He hasn't heard me come in. He's too busy tearing the clothes off her body. Aubrey's not kicking or screaming. I wonder if she's already dead.

The demon takes over me, but even it knows better than to make too much noise. I grab the back of Ivan's shirt and drag him off Aubrey. I'm glad to have the element of surprise working in my favor. I can feel how much weight he's gained since the last time we fought—and every ounce of it is muscle. There's not a single soft spot on his body. Still, I have little trouble shoving Ivan's head down into the toilet bowl. His nose is an inch above the water. There's no doubt in my mind that the hole at the bottom will be the last thing he sees.

"I warned you," I growl in his ear. "I told you I'd kill you if you messed with Aubrey."

"I'm number 12 now. I can do what I want." He's not scared, so I shove his face into the water and hold his head down.

"Don't." The whisper comes from behind me. My grip loosens momentarily, and Ivan's head rises above the rim.

I hear him suck in air, but he doesn't cough. He was holding his breath and waiting for me to lose my nerve. "What are you doing?" he demands. "She's a *Ghost*."

That's the question everyone will be asking. They'll want to know why I skipped breakfast to rescue an outcast.

"I'm number 2 at this school," I remind him. "I came to claim what's rightfully mine."

"Gwendolyn is number 1. And you belong to *her*. She'll kill you if she finds out about this."

I see Ivan has been paying attention in blackmail class. "Are you threatening to upset my sweet poopsie-woopsie?" I snarl.

I push his head back under the water, and I feel a small hand on my shoulder. "I'm not worth it," says Aubrey. Then she bends down. Her lips brush my ear, and her voice is so soft I can barely make out her words. "Lucas thinks you're here for a reason. Please don't let me get in the way."

It doesn't make any sense. Aubrey can't possibly know why I'm here. But I pull Ivan's dripping head out of the toilet. He's been under long enough to have filled both lungs with fluid. A few more seconds and he would have drowned.

"I don't want your corpse killing the mood," I tell him. "Get out and keep your mouth shut—or next time I'll finish the job."

He's still coughing up toilet water as he crawls out of the room.

Aubrey's bottom lip is swollen, and there's blood smeared across the left side of her face. He must have hit her pretty hard. She's standing in her underwear, holding the shredded remains of her shirt together. I open my mouth to say what I came to say, but she puts a finger to her lips. She's trying to tell me the room might be bugged. But if she thought someone was listening, why didn't she scream?

Thank you, she mouths silently. "Don't hurt me," she begs out loud. She wants the eavesdroppers to think that she's scared of me. Which means she's managed to keep her wits about her. So why the hell didn't she scream?

I grab her arm and drag her toward me. "Remember the girl I told you about?" I whisper in her ear. "Go to Pitt Street. Ask for Joey—spelled *J-o-i*. She'll help you. Promise you'll do it, Aubrey. Promise me you won't jump." I feel Aubrey nod. "And when you get there, don't tell Joi where I am. Just tell her I still love her. Will you do that?" I feel her nod again. "Good. Don't worry about Ivan. I've got your back till you're gone."

When I let her go, she clutches my arm and pulls me toward her. I feel a soft kiss on my cheek. She's crying now. I want to believe they're tears of relief. Aubrey points to the door. She's right. I should go.

"I'm not interested in damaged goods," I say loud enough for any bugs in the room. "Fix yourself up. I'll be back for you later."

As I leave Aubrey's room, I hear voices rising from the bottom of the atrium, so I take a cautious peek over the balcony. Three academy employees in white lab coats are finally carting Felix's remains away. They disappear into one of the elevators, leaving a trail of bloody footprints across the courtyard. Before today, I would have argued that only cowards take their own lives. But while the rest of us were striving to win Mandel's game, Felix simply refused to play. I wrote him off as a walking stereotype. I never realized he was the bravest kid here.

Which makes me wonder how much I've gotten all wrong. The only thing I know for sure is that Lucas was right. This has suddenly gotten a little too real.

I'm a few minutes early for the Fundamentals of Business. So, it appears, is everyone else. Frances—Number 53—is sitting at a desk in the center of the room. She's weeping. Tears and snot are pouring down her face, as if everything inside her were being squeezed out. A few students are snickering. But they're not laughing at her. Julian is standing right behind Frances, mocking her suffering. His performance is perfect—he's even mastered the snot. When Ms. Brown enters the room, Julian breaks into a wide, sunny smile. Two or three people clap as he wipes his face with a tissue. Ms. Brown clears her throat, and I expect her to say something about Felix.

"Who can give me a legal definition of *fraud*?" she asks.

I can't let anyone see how shaken I am, so I force myself to raise my hand.

Gwendolyn walks with me to the Art of Persuasion. I can tell by the way she greets me that Ivan hasn't told her what happened in Aubrey's room. It's beginning to dawn on me how tricky this whole situation has gotten. If Ivan rats me out, I could be totally screwed. Without Gwendolyn's help I might end up stuck in this hellhole for years. So I've got to stop acting recklessly. And I've got to go back to working out every day. The only thing that's going to keep Ivan's mouth shut is the belief that I'm capable of killing him.

I feel eyes on the back of my head as soon as we take our seats. I shouldn't look, but I do. Lucas is two rows behind me. He holds my stare for a beat too long. Aubrey must have told him about my good deed of the day. Gwendolyn turns to see what's grabbed my attention, and she gives Lucas a smile and a wave. He cracks open his computer and ignores her.

"Poor kid," Gwendolyn murmurs.

"What do you mean?" I ask.

"Didn't you see? Lucas is in the bottom five."

I'm not worried about Lucas. He'll never jump.

The word *suicide* greets me when I enter Human Psychology. Our instructor, Mr. Davis, has just finished writing it on the blackboard at the front of the room. It's fifth period, and the subject hasn't been broached since breakfast. Here at the Mandel Academy, most people seem to move on with their lives with remarkable speed. But the seven other students in my class all flinch when they walk through the door. It's like they've been greeted with a slap in the face. I noticed a few weeks back that the course was filled with bottom-ranking Androids. My fellow Wolves don't need to learn these lessons.

I've been number one in Human Psychology since the first day of the semester. It's easy to play along. Every time I'm asked a question in class, I imagine that human beings are just arrogant monkeys. We may think we're superior because some of us love our children or believe in God. But every single belief we hold, food we crave, or mate we choose can be traced right back to the fight for survival. According to Mr. Davis, our lives have only one purpose: to pass our genes to the next generation and ensure the survival of our species.

Sometimes it's fun to connect all the dots. *Why do gentlemen prefer blondes? Well, before Clairol came along, blond hair was a sign of youth. And youth means fertility. And fertility means lots of offspring. And the more offspring, the better our species' chance of survival. Ding, ding, ding! We're all just monkeys!*

But I'm not in the mood for games today. Mr. Davis has chosen the one subject I refuse to find funny.

"Why do some human beings commit suicide?" he asks. "Who can tell me?"

I know exactly what answer he wants to hear, but for once I'm not going to give it to him. There's a longer-than-usual pause. We've taken a detour from the syllabus, and the Androids are unprepared.

"Depression?" someone ventures.

"Close," the instructor says. "Flick?"

"The need for escape."

Mr. Davis looks like a zookeeper who's just been mauled by his favorite chimp. "No," he snaps. "The sole cause of suicide is mental illness. It may come in a variety of forms—depression, substance abuse, or schizophrenia, to name just a few—but there's always an illness behind the act. Not all flaws are evident from birth. Some remain hidden for years. Fortunately, evolution provided sickly brains with a self-destruct mechanism. Suicide is just another way that nature eliminates the weak from the gene pool."

"Tell that to a samurai," I growl. I promised myself I wouldn't be reckless—but I won't sit here and hold my tongue. I'm not going to let him convince these kids that Felix was defective.

"Excuse me?"

"In medieval Japan, the samurai saw suicide as a way to die with honor. A warrior would commit seppuku rather than fall into enemy hands."

Mr. Davis nods as if I've made an excellent point. "If there was no hope of winning, then the enemy was superior. The act of seppuku may appear honorable, but the end result was the same. The weak died and the strong prevailed."

I'm losing my touch. I should have seen that one coming. Even the samurai were chimps.

I nearly killed one of the lesser Wolves in Hand-to-Hand Combat. He shouldn't have congratulated me on taking second place the day we started training with knives. It took the rest of the class to pull the two of us apart. I didn't plan it in advance, but as it turns out, nearly slitting a fellow Wolf's throat was a brilliant move. Gwendolyn seems convinced that I'm still angry about the rankings. I haven't been thinking about them at all.

We're in the Wolves' Den, which is my new name for the tower lounge. Most of the pack went downstairs to dinner a few minutes ago. I have no interest in eating. Gwendolyn is here too. But I'm not in the mood for chitchat, so I lie down and pretend to nap.

"Flick," Gwendolyn says. "I know you're not asleep. And I know you think that you should be Dux."

I open my eyes. She's kneeling by my side. "And you're telling me I'm wrong?" I ask. "I'm first in all of my classes. You're second in two of yours. I thought there was a chance that some dark horse might beat me. But either way, the title should have changed hands."

"Academics are only part of the equation, Flick. I tried to warn you. Mr. Mandel doesn't believe that you're ready to be Dux. He can't counsel you in person right now, but he wants you to think about the reward you were promised. If you're going to graduate, you'll have to focus on that. Nothing else should matter while you're here."

My big reward. The proof of my father's crime. It's funny—I forgot all about it today. I've been running around trying to rescue Aubrey, who won't even scream to help herself. Trying to defend a kid who's already dead. Holding on to the memory of a girl I'll never see again. Wondering how a person could love someone and still choose to leave them behind.

"Why *you*?" I ask Gwendolyn. "Why does Mandel think you deserve to be Dux?"

"Mr. Mandel knows that this school is all I have. Everything I care about is here."

"Seriously? You don't care about *anyone* out there? What about your mother? Don't you miss *her*?"

Gwendolyn snorts. "When I was little, my mother spent more time at the bar down the street than she ever spent at home. She didn't want to be with me, so what's the point in missing *her*?"

She's right. There's no point at all.

I reach down and grab Gwendolyn by the waist. I lift her, and she's as light as a doll. I lay her down on the divan and kiss her. I'm preparing to do much more than that when I hear someone else enter the room. I'm moving too fast to come to a sudden stop. When I do, I find Ivan leering at us.

"You've been watching?" Gwendolyn snarls, and Ivan knows he's just stepped in it.

It's an excellent opportunity to make a point. "Why don't you head down to your room, Gwendolyn. I'll meet up with you in a minute. I just need to have a quick chat with my old buddy Ivan."

"Don't get blood on the furniture," she says, sounding perfectly serious. "If you have to kill him, do it out on the landing."

When Ivan and I are alone, I spread myself across the divan.

"So do you see how things work around here?" I ask. "Do you see why you'll want to stay on my good side?"

"Yes," he says. And he does. I can tell.

"Then forget this morning ever happened. And get the hell out of this lounge. You're not welcome back until I personally give you permission."

"But I'm supposed to meet Caleb . . ."

"Screw Caleb," I tell him. "This conversation is over."

Ivan leaves, but I'm not in any rush to get back to Gwendolyn. I stay on the divan and close my eyes. *Anything, anything. You have to do anything.* Mandel was right when he said I'd lost focus. I came to the academy for the proof he promised. But he's made it pretty clear that he'll never let me graduate unless I want it enough to let Joi go.

After I found out about Felix, I spent the day wishing Joi was here. If she had been, I know I would have told her what happened to me and my family. The whole story—even the parts I try never to think about. And I might have felt a little bit better. But I don't need to feel better. I need to grow the hell up.

Joi made me weak when I was around her. I'm not a Lost Boy, and I'm too old for a Wendy. But I want to remember her once before I let go. All I get is a faint whiff of jasmine before my dream's interrupted. And then the last person I'll love is gone for good.

"It's not the way the system works!" Caleb's voice grows louder as he scales the stairs to the tower. I can't see him from where I'm lying. But more importantly, he can't see me.

"You already lost your Beauty Pageant bet. What do you care who gets to go next?" Austin asks in his BBQ-and-Budweiser drawl.

"I just don't understand why she'd stoop to spare a Ghost!"

"Aw, come on. You know why. She's still trying to get into Flick's pants, and he's got a weird soft spot for that Aubrey girl."

"More proof he's a loser," Caleb grumbles. "This whole situation is completely revolting. Someone should speak to Mr. Mandel."

"Give it a week or so. You don't know what Gwendolyn has in mind," Austin argues. "Besides, if Flick ain't had a piece yet, he must not like girls at all. Way I figure, things'll probably be back to normal real soon."

They're in the lounge. They'll see me any second now, so I better act fast.

"You're right, Austin," I declare as I stand up and unbuckle my belt. "I don't like girls. I only have eyes for you. What are you now? Number 6? So drop your pants, bubba. You've been outranked. And considering the conversation I just overheard, you might not want to turn down number 2."

It's probably my imagination, but I think I detect a whimper.

"Flick, I, I . . ." For a future politician, Austin isn't too good at thinking on his feet.

"Were you *really* just questioning Gwendolyn's decisions?" I ask Caleb. "And threatening to take your complaints to Mandel? Do you think you know better than Gwendolyn does?"

"No, of course not!" Caleb insists. "It's just . . ."

"Just what? As far as I can tell, the *system* you're so fond of works like this: you do what the Dux tells you to do, and you keep your mouth shut. Am I right?"

"Yes," Caleb admits.

"Then don't forget it again." I head for the door.

"Where are you going?" Austin asks nervously.

"Gotta answer a booty call," I tell him. "Let's hope Gwendolyn doesn't get all chatty when we're finished."

I don't think I'll rat them out right away. I have no idea what the consequences might be if Gwendolyn knew what I just heard. But Austin and Caleb do, and I really enjoy seeing them sweat.

I head downstairs to the ninth-floor balcony and start searching for an excuse to go somewhere other than Gwendolyn's room. I lean over the railing. At the bottom of the atrium, the last traces of Felix have finally been scrubbed away. Lucas is standing one floor below me, surveying the very same scene. I should give him the good news about Aubrey, so I hop on the elevator and beg it to be as quiet as possible.

"Bad day for both of us," Lucas remarks once I'm standing beside him.

"And a worse one for Felix."

"I'm not so sure about that. At least he's free." Lucas looks over at me. "You'll get used to it. A couple of Ghosts kill themselves every semester."

"Every *semester*? Why so many?"

"I don't know. But I guess I'll find out."

"I heard you're in the bottom five." Might as well get the subject out of the way. "I'm sorry. If you need any help on the outside . . ."

"I won't. And you don't need to pity me, Flick. I'd rather be number fifty-two than number two," he says. "Gwendolyn's going to *own* you now."

I lower my voice to a whisper. "She's not as bad as you think. I just heard that Gwendolyn talked Mandel into sparing Aubrey."

Lucas's eyes narrow. "Sparing her?"

"From being expelled."

"Well, I know *Ivan* will be thrilled to hear that Aubrey's staying."

"I'll be watching out for her while she's here," I tell him.

"Oh yeah? And what if the Wolves decide to go after *you*? You never considered that, did you? I bet you think you're safe now that you're the queen's favorite boy." Lucas pauses for a dramatic sigh. "Oh well, I suppose while you're watching Aubrey's back, I'll just have to watch *yours*."

I feel a flash of annoyance. "What makes you think I need *your* help? You're number fifty-two. Maybe you should focus on saving your own ass, Lucas. Why waste your time on me?"

"Good question. Well, we can't call it altruism, can we? I remember learning in Human Psychology that there's no such thing. So let's just say that I'm acting in my own self-interest. I'm trying to save my species."

"What the hell does *that* mean?" I demand, just as one of the elevators stops on our floor.

"Looks like you've got a visitor," Lucas says. "Give her my love." I can see Gwendolyn's pale hair through the gates. She's come to collect me. By the time I turn to say goodbye, Lucas is already back in his room.

CHAPTER FIFTEEN

THE WATCHER BY NIGHT

This must have been how the world appeared to the gods on Olympus. The greatest city on earth lies thirty-two stories below, and it's nothing more than a miniature model. Little toy cars race around the grid. Battery-powered boats putter up the Hudson River. Maybe there are people down there as well, but they're so tiny that they're completely invisible.

I'm alone on a terrace that circles a palatial Tribeca penthouse. I don't expect any company out here. The other guests will stay inside where the air is warm and the cocktails are cold. Despite the frigid weather, I'm more comfortable observing the others from a distance. The apartment's walls are glass, and the owners haven't bothered to hang curtains or shades. You don't need to worry about privacy when you live this high up in the clouds.

The graduates of the Mandel Academy convene once a month, and the Dux has a standing invitation to join them. Attendance seems a bit sparse tonight. My guess is the guests are all Mandel's supporters. I know for a fact that the head of the opposition is absent. When Gwendolyn asked me to escort her, she assured me that my father would not be attending the party. Turns out she's on a first-name basis with everyone here. I recognize some of the guests, but every one of them knows me. Apparently they've been following my rise. A few seem to have been doing much more than that. Earlier in the evening, the head of some mutual fund pulled me aside and told me he's rooting for me. And he made it pretty clear that he knows exactly what it will mean if I win.

I chatted with various alumni for over an hour, and I could feel my hair standing on end the whole time. Then I realized why they gave me the creeps. They look, speak, and chew their hors d'oeuvres just like humans. But they're nothing like the rest of us. Not anymore. They live in a world where their toilets magically clean themselves. Wrinkle-free clothes appear in their closets. Everyone jumps at the chance to do them all favors. Nothing but flattery and praise ever reaches their ears. There aren't any problems that their checkbooks can't solve. And it all seems perfectly normal because everyone they know belongs to the same elite club.

What would it be like to exist in a world without suffering? To have no needs, only desires? To be surrounded by so much beauty that you forget how ugly life is for everyone else? Who wouldn't want that? Who wouldn't be willing to fight for it? Whatever the alumni did to get here—lie, cheat, steal, kill—I'm sure they'd all say it was worth it. And I bet they sleep soundly because they know that their nameless, faceless victims would have done the same thing.

Mandel has taught me the secret of the alumni's success. You have to be willing to pay any price. The gates to this paradise won't open unless you offer a sacrifice to the gods who dwell here. And they only want the things you cherish the most. Your freedom, your honor, or your soul. Whatever those people inside the penthouse gave up, they don't seem to miss it anymore. But I'm just through the gates, and I can't help but look back. Joi's out there somewhere. And part of me is still with her.

A burst of canned laugher draws my eyes back toward the party. Gwendolyn is entertaining three captains of industry who've been celebrating a victory. Earlier, I overheard one of them discussing "the company's" plans to move forward with the launch of a product called Exceletrex now that a certain Illinois congressman has decided to call off the dogs. The "little people," it appears, no longer have a voice. Representative Sheehan must have had something scandalous stored on his cell phone. And I may have been the one who told the Mandel alumni where to look. I suppose they'd have found it anyway.

I see Gwendolyn scanning the room for me. The Mandel Academy's golden duo should never be far apart. The dorms reek of hormones and secret sex, but we're the school's only true couple. The Prince and Princess of Vice. In September, Gwendolyn may be leaving the academy and heading to Harvard. She wants her prince to join her if Mandel lets me graduate. I haven't made any promises. Gwendolyn is brilliant and beautiful, but I don't love her—and I'm not going to try. I'm with her because Mandel forced me to surrender. All my good things are gone. Vengeance is the only thing keeping me alive.

Gwendolyn finally spots me on the terrace and excuses herself. From this distance, she resembles a young Grace Kelly. She's wearing a low-cut black dress with butterfly sleeves. Her hair is swept up, and a diamond choker circles her throat. The wind catches her dress when she steps outdoors. For a second I think that she might float away, but Gwendolyn is a lot more solid than she looks.

"Come back inside before you freeze," she says.

"Give me another minute," I tell her. "I haven't had any fresh air in months."

She joins me at the edge of the terrace and rests her head on my shoulder while she snuggles against my side for warmth. "I love it up here," she says.

"Do you remember being down there at the bottom?" I ask. *Or have you already become one of them?*

"Feeling nostalgic?" Gwendolyn teases.

"Not at all," I say. "But I'm not sure I want to forget."

"You won't. We all leave our old lives behind, but we never forget. I've been at Mandel for three years now, and I haven't forgotten a thing. I still remember growing up in an apartment that was half the size of my room at the academy. I remember that my mother was usually high by noon and my father only showed up when he felt like punching her. I wore the same clothes to school every day, and the other kids said that I stank up the class. I ate every bite of my free lunch because I knew dinner would probably be cat food. It was the only thing my mom could afford after she traded her food stamps for liquor. And you know what? Not one single person down there ever bothered to help me. So I decided to help myself." When Gwendolyn faces me, she's no longer a girl. She's a furious beast. "I won't forget, Flick. Because I want to remember to treat *them* the way they all treated me."

"No one helped you?" She must think I'm surprised, but I'm not. Other than Jude, Joi, and my mother, only two people ever tried to help me. Neither tried very hard. And both failed in the end.

"You know what kind of creatures they are down there." Gwendolyn sneers as though the whole species revolts her. "They'd be like us if they could, but they're too stupid and weak. So they just sit on their couches, watching crappy reality shows and stuffing their fat faces. They know that, right down the street, some little girl could be eating cat food for dinner. Or maybe it's a boy being beaten to pulp. But the worthless slobs couldn't care less."

"Not all of them are like that."

"Yeah, I know your last girlfriend was a saint," Gwendolyn snaps.

"I was talking about my brother," I lie. "Besides, you're not as hard and heartless as you pretend to be. I found out what you did for Aubrey. I heard you kept her from being expelled."

Gwendolyn's eyes narrow. She's annoyed that I know. "How did you find out?"

"I just did."

"Well, she's beyond all help now. Mandel told me it would be a waste of time. And he was right. I stuck my neck out, and Aubrey never even *tried*." Gwendolyn's fury quickly cools. "But just so you know, I didn't do it for *her*. I did it because I love *you*."

I'm not going anywhere near those last three words. "You did it for me?"

"First that kid jumped. And then I beat you in the rankings. I was worried that one more thing might make you lose sight of what's most important."

"You don't have to worry about that anymore," I assure her.

"I'm not talking about your *father*. I'm talking about this." She sweeps a hand through the sky. "I've been Dux for two years, and you'll take the title next semester. That means when we graduate, we'll get the best jobs. We'll earn more money than anyone else. This world will be ours, Flick. Yours and mine. Just think of what we'll be able to do with it."

I don't want it. I would never have traded Joi for this. But everyone has his price, and Mandel found mine. All I want is the proof that my father killed Jude. The headmaster probably thinks he got a hell of a deal.

"I can't see that far into the future," I tell Gwendolyn. Why even try? There's nothing there.

"You better start looking," she says. "Those people inside are all behind you. *I'm* behind you. There's no way you're going to fail."

Lucas has been dogging me all day. He must have seen me leaving for the party last night, and he knew who would be on my arm. He just won't accept that I've lost the battle. He doesn't realize that I surrendered so I'd be able to keep fighting a war. From the moment I failed to win the Dux title, he's been waging his own whispering campaign against Gwendolyn. *How much do you really know about her? What does she want from you?* To be honest, he's become a real bore. I don't care what the truth is as long as Gwendolyn continues to help me. He should know I'm in no position to pick my allies, and war is never pretty. FDR had to team up with Stalin to trounce the Nazis. George Washington turned to a decadent French king when he wanted to make America a democracy. Who the hell is Lucas to question my tactics? As far as I know, he may just be bitter because he got dumped.

Curfew is a few minutes away, and Lucas is waiting for me on the balcony outside our rooms. I'd head back up to the lounge, but he's already waving me over.

"If this is about Gwendolyn, I'm not interested," I tell him.

"It's Aubrey," he croaks.

"Aubrey?" I'm starting to feel a bit nauseous.

"She's gone, Flick. They've stripped her bed and cleaned out her room."

"She's been expelled? But Gwendolyn . . ."

"Aubrey wasn't *expelled*. She was here on the eighth floor last night. But she didn't make it to breakfast this morning, so I came up to see if she was okay. Her room was already empty. Whatever happened went down after curfew."

"Was Ivan involved?" If he hurt Aubrey, it's all my fault. I was supposed to be watching him, and I let down my guard.

Lucas shakes his head. "Unless he broke curfew, he wouldn't have had time to do anything. Besides, Ivan would have ambushed her, and I think Aubrey knew that she was in some kind of trouble. She left a note for you. She slipped it under my door a few minutes before lockdown."

"Why didn't she slip it under *my* door?"

"You weren't here," Lucas says pointedly. *And you should have been.* "She probably thought someone else might find it first."

"Well, where's the note?" I demand.

"Not out here on the balcony where someone could see us," he says. "Come back to my room. But remember—be careful what you say."

Lucas's room is a mirror image of mine. Except for an artwork that's pinned to the wall. It's one of those old-fashioned travel posters that lured early jet-setters to exotic lands. In this case, the fabled city of Los Angeles. The image shows a Sunshine Airways plane gliding over a pristine blue ocean while two bathing beauties in floppy hats and movie star glasses wave from the beach. I suddenly know Lucas's real name. I know why he's here. And I have no idea why he'd have that poster on his wall.

I was still in military school when his picture hit the papers. His was one of those stories that makes the whole world choose sides. And I knew whose side I was on. Eleven years ago, at the age of six, the kid I know as Lucas boarded a flight out of Los Angeles. The airplane crashed into the ocean shortly after takeoff. He was one of ten people who survived. His parents and sister died. An investigation determined that the airline was at fault. The company's new CEO had cut costs by firing 30 percent of the employees. There weren't enough mechanics left to inspect the planes, and the boss had encouraged the ones who remained to falsify maintenance reports. The plane that Lucas and his family were on should never have been in the air. Two hundred and six people perished—and no one was ever punished.

Ten years passed, and an anonymous hacker took control of Sunshine Airline's computer systems. Flights were grounded. Hundreds of thousands of people were stranded all over the globe. The airline's stock price plunged. The hacker responsible clearly intended to put the company out of business. I don't think he expected the chaos to claim lives. One of the grounded flights was delivering organs for transplant. The patients waiting for them died when their new hearts didn't arrive on time.

Most people were certain it was a terrorist plot. Then the police located the hacker in Ohio. It was a sixteen-year-old kid in a foster home. He'd done it all with a homemade computer and a dial-up Internet connection.

"You're the hacker," I mutter.

"I knew you'd figure it out. That's why I never invite anyone in," Lucas says. "That poster was here the day I moved up from the Incubation Suites. They put it there to remind me." Just like Aubrey's teddy bear, I now realize. And the yearbook page with Jude's picture that I keep in my desk drawer.

"You didn't need to hide your identity from me," I tell him. "I always thought you were a hero."

"For a while, I did too," Lucas says. "And then Gwendolyn took me to an alumni party at some swanky Tribeca apartment. It was the same night she gave me the boot. But before she broke my little heart, she introduced me to the former CEO of Sunshine Airlines. Turns out, he's a Mandel alum. He called me 'son' and told me he had no hard feelings."

I imagine what it must have been like to stand face-to-face with the man who might as well have murdered your family. "What did you do?"

"I turned around and left the party," Lucas said.

"You *left*?" I feel my respect for Lucas crumbling. "Why didn't you take the bastard out to the terrace and push him over the side?"

"Because that's what they wanted me to do. If I'd killed the guy, they'd have won. I'd have been just like the rest of them. But the thing that really scared me was that I was already halfway there."

I'm trying to make sense of the statement when Lucas hands me the note Aubrey left. "It's getting close to curfew. We can swap stories some other day."

The paper has been folded three times. My name is scrawled on the outside. A few seconds ago, my mind was bursting with questions I couldn't wait to ask Lucas. Now I can't remember a single one of them.

"Did you read—" I start to ask.

"No." Lucas taps an ear with one finger to caution me. "It's for you."

I unfold the paper. It's hardly a letter. Just three short sentences.

My aunt showed up when I was in rehab.
They wouldn't let me see her. They told her I was dead.

"What does this mean?" I ask.

Lucas takes the note and reads it. Then he rips the paper into pieces and disappears into the bathroom. By the time I hear the toilet flush, I know the whole horrible truth. No one ever goes home. That's why they told Aubrey's aunt she was dead. They didn't want anyone to know they were bringing her here. They had to make sure that no one would ever come looking for Aubrey because they knew there was a very good chance she might not make it out. At the Mandel Academy, you either graduate or you die.

When Lucas returns to the room, I take his arm and drag him back out to the balcony.

"They kill the Ghosts!" I whisper.

Lucas just nods. He knew.

"You figured it out? Why didn't you tell me?"

"It was just a hunch. I didn't know for sure," he says. "But it makes perfect sense, doesn't it? You can't *expel* students from a school like this. They all know way too much. Mandel could never take the risk. So he picks kids like Aubrey who can vanish without a trace. Is anyone going to start searching if you disappear?"

I never thought of it that way. "No."

"Me neither. Most people I've met here are orphans. The rest don't have anyone on the outside who cares if they live or die. So I bet a lot of the students have put two and two together. They've figured out that the Ghosts don't go home. But no one would ever breathe a word about it. Because you never know who's listening— and if one of Mandel's people hears you say the wrong thing, you might be next to go."

He's right. "Then you're taking a pretty big risk telling me," I say.

"I've got nothing left to lose. They'll be coming for me soon."

"That's not true," I try to assure him.

"It is, Flick. And the truth could get a whole lot uglier before you get out of here. But you have to keep looking, no matter how bad it gets. The Mandels expect everyone to turn away. That's how they've been getting away with murder for so many years. Nobody ever wants to look."

I'm in a sleep so deep that I might as well be at the bottom of the ocean. And yet I'm out of my bed the instant I hear movement on the balcony outside my room. The door silently slides open as I approach. Two people pass by so quickly that I barely get a glimpse of them. Just a flash of green stockings and a quick wave of a single red feather. I race after the pair.

"Jude!" I call out. "Where are you going? I'm back here!"

He stops and turns, but he doesn't release Aubrey's hand. "I didn't come for you," he says. "I'm here on official business tonight. Aubrey can't get to Never Land on her own."

"But you said you couldn't get in here. You said all the windows are sealed!"

"I made that up," Peter Pan tells me. "So you wouldn't have to say it."

"Say what?"

"That you didn't want me around."

"Why wouldn't I want you around?! You're the only reason I'm here."

"Then why did you try to forget me?" asks Peter Pan.

"I didn't, Jude! I just couldn't afford any distractions. I promised you that it wouldn't be forever. I told you I'd see you again as soon as this was through."

"You make a lot of promises," Jude says, glancing over at Aubrey.

She's beaming at me. Her hair is as limp and mousy as the day I first met her. The beautiful clothes and makeup are gone. She's wearing a ratty T-shirt and jeans. She's the girl she was before she made her first mistake. Before her parents died and Mandel found her. I have never envied or pitied anyone more.

"Will you take care of her?" I ask. "Will you help Aubrey forget all of this?"

"She already has," Peter Pan says. Then his businesslike tone softens. "Would you like to come with us? It's not too late."

"Not yet, Jude. I have to get what I came for."

"Revenge?" he asks with bitter laugh. "Don't worry. You'll get it. Anything, anything. You can have *anything* in life if you'll sacrifice everything else for it. First it was Joi—then Felix and Aubrey. Before this is over, you'll get rid of me too."

"How can you say that? I'm doing this for *you*!"

"Do you really believe that?"

"Yes!"

"This isn't what I want," he says. "Goodbye." He's never said that before. The word scares me more than anything else.

"Will you be back? Please say you'll be back, Jude!"

"Of course I'll be back," he says with a nod at Lucas's door. "I don't have a choice."

My face is wet when I wake. I can hear myself shouting, "Don't leave me!" Everyone else must have heard it too. I hold the pillow against my mouth and breathe through my nose until I can trust myself not to sob. There are footsteps outside my room. They've come to investigate. They want to find out who's cracked. They linger at my door for a minute or so, then move on to the next.

CHAPTER SIXTEEN

THE CULL

There's someone standing over my bed.

"Get up and get dressed," the man orders. "You've missed your first class."

"I'm ill," I groan.

"Then I'll need to escort you to the infirmary."

The top nine floors of this place are a prison. But the bottom three are a dungeon. "Forget it. I'd rather die in class," I announce as I rise from my bed.

I make it to the Art of Persuasion on time. Gwendolyn isn't there, but Julian is. And he shouldn't be.

"Missed you in business class," he trills as I pass.

"That's so sweet. But I didn't miss you," I respond.

"Have trouble sleeping?" he calls out. The rest of the class goes silent.

"Yeah, some miserable asshole kept me awake half the night," I return, and give Julian a pat on the shoulder. "You don't have to cry, darling. I'm sure your little pecker will grow eventually."

The tension breaks. Everyone laughs. Except for Julian. But he doesn't look angry. He looks *smug*. Like a man with a plan.

"Good morning, class!" Mr. Martin has entered the room, pushing a cart. Whatever's on top of it is concealed beneath a black plastic tarp. "We're going to have some fun today. I've asked one of last semester's best students to return to act as my assistant. Julian?" My fellow Wolf rises and whips off the tarp to reveal a lie detector. I think I know where this is going.

"Until now, we've been focusing on ways to uncover useful information," Mr. Martin says. "And as we've discussed, human beings aren't always the most reliable sources. So how can we be sure that an informant's words can be trusted? Much of the time, we must rely on our instincts. But if you're fortunate enough to have access to a polygraph, I recommend that you use it.

"It's always tricky to offer my students a proper demonstration. After all, no one at the Mandel Academy has any secrets. There's no reason for any of you to prevaricate, so I'll just have to ask a few of you to—"

"Mr. Martin?"

"Yes, Julian?"

It's such a cute little act. These two should have their own show.

"There may be a student who *does* have a secret. There was disturbance in the dorms last night. Someone who lives on the eighth floor was screaming and sobbing. He woke us all up."

"Oh dear!" Mr. Martin gasps. "Noise is strictly forbidden after curfew! That's a very serious violation of the rules. Are there any suspects?"

"Yes, in fact there are four of them in this very room. They all live on the eighth floor. Perhaps we can use the polygraph to identify the culprit?"

"Excellent suggestion, Julian!" Mr. Martin is looking directly at me. "Any volunteers?"

By the time class is over, I'll be the school laughingstock. Everyone here will know what I am. An impostor. A weakling. A fraud and a fake. The Wolves will stop fearing me. They'll eat me for lunch. My father will never be punished for what he did. I came here for the proof. And I've failed once again.

"Me." I look back over my shoulder to see Lucas rising from his seat.

"Wonderful!" Mr. Martin exclaims. Julian doesn't look nearly as thrilled.

There's a pair of rubber straps across Lucas's chest, two sensors attached to his fingers, and a blood pressure cuff just above his elbow. He's sitting on an electric chair, and Mr. Martin is itching to throw the switch.

"I'm going to start by asking you a few simple questions so that we can get a baseline reading," the executioner states. "What is your name?"

"Timothy Harper," Lucas responds.

"Excuse me?" Mr. Martin looks up. The machine's needle is twitching wildly.

"That's my real name. I thought you wanted me to tell the truth. If I don't, it might screw up your baseline. Sorry, I'm just a little bit nervous."

"Fine," the instructor snarls. "What school do you attend?"

"The charitable institution known as the Mandel Academy."

"And what class is this?"

"My *favorite* class," Lucas responds enthusiastically. "Taught by the finest instructor at this remarkable school."

A chill courses through my body. I think I've just figured out what Lucas is doing. I've watched enough movies to know that the person administering a polygraph test always starts off with a few basic questions. *What's your name? Where do you live? Who is the president of the United States?* They need to know how the machine will respond when the subject is telling the truth. But Lucas is lying. Timothy Harper isn't his real name. This isn't his favorite class. And we all know what he thinks about Mr. Martin.

When they start asking the real questions, Lucas can continue to lie—and the person reading the results will assume he's telling the truth. It's a pretty simple trick. I'm sure Mr. Martin would have caught on by now if he weren't on the verge of an aneurysm.

"Childish behavior like that is the reason you're number fifty-two," the instructor sneers. "Julian? Maybe you should take over from here."

"I'd be delighted." Julian pulls a sheet of paper from the pocket of his jacket. He's come with a list of prepared questions. I knew this was a setup. "Last night, everyone heard a male student bawling his little eyes out. The source of the commotion appeared to be one of the eighth-floor dorm rooms. Do you know who was responsible?"

"It was me," Lucas says.

Julian's smile withers as Mr. Martin's blooms. "Are you sure?"

"Yes," Lucas confirms. "I had a terrible dream. I was trapped here at school with a pack of rabid wolves. And the weird thing was—one of them had a pretty little pixie haircut like *yours*."

"What does the polygraph say?" Julian demands, turning to Mr. Martin, who's busy interpreting the machine's readings.

"According to this, Lucas is telling the truth."

"He can't be!" Julian insists. "He's a technology major. He's taken electronics classes. He must have found some way to beat the machine!"

"A Ghost?" Mr. Martin scoffs. I've never heard an instructor use that word before. "*Highly* unlikely."

"Are you two going to let me finish?" Lucas interjects. "I haven't even gotten to the worst part of my dream yet. Students kept disappearing, and everyone thought the kids had gone home, but the truth was they'd all been—"

"Get up!" Mr. Martin bellows.

"Murdered," Lucas finishes. He said the Wolves would come for me. He never told me he'd trade his life for mine.

"You think you're funny, don't you?" Julian snarls. "Get out of the chair. We need to test the other eighth-floor students."

"I'll go next," I say as I stand.

"Sit down, Flick," Mr. Martin orders. And I can see it. He knows Lucas was lying. He went fishing for me and caught a much bigger prize. And he's not about to throw it back. "Julian, thank you for your assistance. I think this has been a *very* effective demonstration. So go ahead and run along. Now that we've identified our troublemaker, we'll leave Lucas's fate in Mr. Mandel's capable hands."

I catch Julian's eye before he flees. The little shit knows he's in trouble.

. . .

I take a seat across the table from Julian at lunch. I'm going to drown him in the soup he's slurping. Caleb and Austin won't get in the way. They know I've been saving the tale of their treachery for a day just like this. And the rest of the Wolves would probably sit there and watch. Gwendolyn is the only one who might try to stop me. But for the first time this semester, she's decided to skip lunch.

I'm staring at Julian. He's hunched over his soup, doing his best to avoid meeting my eyes. Everyone senses that something big is about to happen, and the cafeteria remains eerily silent.

Julian drains the bowl and stands up from the table with his tray in his hands. It's a perfect opportunity to attack, but there's still a chance that something might go wrong. I can't risk ending up in the infirmary or locked away in my room. Maybe tomorrow. But not tonight.

I don't see Gwendolyn until Hand-to-Hand Combat.

"Where have you been all day?" I demand.

"Hello to you too." She rises up on her tiptoes to plant a kiss on my cheek. "I've been helping Mr. Mandel. He's choosing new students for next semester, and he wanted my advice."

"Aubrey's gone," I say.

"I heard she was expelled." Gwendolyn takes my hand and squeezes it. "I'm sorry. I really did try my best. But there's only so much the Dux can do." I can't decide if she knows. I press my thumb against her wrist. The pulse I detect is slow and steady.

"Did Mandel tell you that Aubrey would be leaving the other night? Is that why you took me to the party?"

Gwendolyn sticks out her bottom lip. Have I hurt her feelings? I wish I knew. "What are you asking me? I thought we were a team, Flick."

She didn't say no. Why didn't she just say no? "Tell Mandel I want to speak to him."

"About what?"

"It's personal," I say.

The Gwendolyn I know would never accept that as an answer. But this Gwendolyn doesn't seem curious at all. "Mr. Mandel left to meet with a candidate," she informs me. "He said he'd be back in the morning. Do you think you can wait? Is there anything I can do to help?"

"If you got permission to leave the academy tonight, would they let you take a guest?" It's a long shot, but she once helped Aubrey for me. Maybe she'll agree to help Lucas too.

"Not without Mr. Mandel's approval, and he's already gone for the day. There's no way that the two of us can leave tonight." The instructor interrupts us. It's time for Gwendolyn to take a turn on the mat. "How about tomorrow?" she asks. Before she faces her sparring partner, she blows me a kiss.

"If there is one," I mutter.

I have no choice. I can't live knowing that another person died trying to save me. After I left Joi behind, I thought I was willing to do anything. But I'm not. The proof of my dad's crime isn't worth Lucas's life. They'll be coming for him tonight. I saw it written on the face Mr. Martin hides beneath that backslapper mask of his. The triumph. The sadistic glee. He knew he'd just sentenced an enemy to death.

I should have come clean before they strapped Lucas to the lie detector. Then I should have taken my punishment. Mandel can't show me any favors, but I don't think he'd let anyone kill me. Not yet, anyway. But I wouldn't risk finding out, and now a better person may die. Because Lucas is convinced that I'm not like the others. And he's right. What he doesn't know is that he just traded his life to spare a crackpot who cries in his sleep and talks to Peter Pan.

If I were Lucas, I don't think I could eat. But I see him head down to dinner just after seven. It might be his last supper, so I hope it's good. As soon as the eighth-floor balcony is student-free, I slip into Lucas's room and hide myself in the closet. Two hours pass, but I never lose my nerve. I feel like the gods have finally granted my wish. It's like I've traveled back in time to the moment I decided to leave for Georgia. Now I can fix my mistake. I can do the right thing. I can save Jude.

A minute before curfew, I emerge, just in time to see Lucas enter the room.

"What were you doing in there?" he yelps. "I looked for you at dinner, and I've been waiting on the balcony for over an hour. I wanted to say goodbye."

"You're not going anywhere without me," I tell him.

Lucas catches on quickly. "Get the f— out of my room," he orders.

"Make me." He knows he can't. I could snap his scrawny body in half.

"Come on, Flick," he pleads. "Curfew is less than a minute away."

"We're going to have a little slumber party," I tell him. "You said they came for Aubrey after curfew. I'm going to be here with you when they arrive."

"I knew what I was doing! I don't want your help!" I have to read his lips for the next part. *You're here for a reason.*

"You don't know what reason that is!" I shout. "Mandel needs me. I might be able to protect you."

"No," Lucas says. "You can't help me. Please—go before it's too late."

"It's already too late," I say, pointing to the ceiling. "They heard everything we just said."

Lucas grabs a notebook off his desk, rips out a page, and scribbles a message. His hand is shaking so badly that I can barely read what he's written.

If you get out of here without becoming one of them, you can take the whole place down.

"You're the only one who can do it," he whispers.

I barely have time to absorb the thought. Every door on the seventh, eighth, and ninth floors slides shut. We can hear the rest lock. But Lucas's door doesn't bolt. It's the most terrifying silence I've ever heard.

"No, we're going to do it together," I tell him. "Come on. Let's get out of here."

It's pitch black on the balcony. We trace our hands along the wall until we reach the elevators. I press the call buttons, but nothing happens. The elevators have been shut down for the night. Our easiest escape route has been cut off. But it also means we're safe for the moment. No one can reach the dorms until the power's back on.

"We'll make a rope out of your sheets and drop down through the atrium," I whisper.

"How are we going to make a rope that's eight stories long?!"

"I thought you were supposed to be smart. The rope doesn't need to reach the whole way. We just have to make it two stories long. Then we can loop it over the railing, twist the two ends together, and go down one floor at a time."

We slink back to Lucas's room. It takes forever to rip up the sheets. But we work well together, the way Jude and I always did. Lucas and I can read each other's gestures. We don't need to speak.

The rope is finally done. When we see that it might actually work, I almost forget what it's for. I'm suddenly overcome by a wave of happiness. It's been a long time since I've felt anything like this. For a second, I even understand why Joi does what she does. Most of her urchins may disappear, but there's always the hope that a few will survive. And hope is the drug that helps us forget that the odds are always against us.

The alarm clock says it's 3:00 a.m. There's no sign of anyone downstairs. I turn off the light in Lucas's room and start tying our rope to the balcony railing. We might just make it out of here after all.

"Wait—what should we do about the tracking chips?" Lucas whispers.

I'm glad it's dark. He can't see my face. He doesn't know that I was so drunk on hope that I forgot all about them. "We'll go to a hospital. Have them cut out."

"You really think that'll work?" He sounds skeptical.

"Look, I'll amputate my own arm if I have to." I mean it. Every word.

"Hey, Flick?" Lucas says. "Do you still have my note?"

I must have shoved it into my pocket. "Yeah."

"Before we go anywhere, I want you to eat it."

I've just swallowed the last bit when two doors on opposite sides of the eighth floor slide open. Flashlight beams dance in the darkness. I grab our rope off the balcony, and Lucas and I duck back into his room.

"Are those students?" I ask. "How did they get out?"

"Oh shit," Lucas gasps. "Hide. Hide now!"

"Why? It's just a couple of kids."

"They're not kids," Lucas says. "They're *Wolves*."

I have time for one regret before Lucas's room is flooded with light. If only I'd left the rope behind on the railing. They might have thought we'd made our escape.

"Well, well, what do we have here?" Caleb and Ivan enter and close the door behind them. Ivan is both confused and elated, as if we've thrown him a surprise birthday party. Caleb still looks bored. "I think we've interrupted a little boy-on-boy action. I do hope that's what this is, Flick. Anything else could prove *very* embarrassing."

"What are *you* doing?" I demand.

"Just culling the herd," Caleb says with an exaggerated yawn. "Ivan's going to perform the manual labor. I'm here to supervise. It's one of the perks of being a human resources major."

They've been sent to kill Lucas.

"If you take the pansy," I tell Lucas, "I can handle the ape."

I've barely taken a step when I suddenly discover I'm falling. I hit the ground, unable to move. My muscles are rigid, and the only thing I feel is an unpleasant buzzing. I've been Tasered. Lucas shouts once before he joins me on the floor.

"Let's get them both into the bathroom," Caleb orders.

"Can we kill Flick too?" Ivan asks.

Caleb sighs. "Not tonight, I'm afraid. We aren't authorized to deviate from the plan. But we'll let Flick see what's in store for him, and then if we're lucky, we'll get the order tomorrow."

They prop me up against the wall. Caleb sits on the toilet. Ivan dumps Lucas's body in the bathtub. He pulls on a pair of latex gloves, twists the cold water tap, and then takes a saltshaker from his pants pocket. It's the same kind they use in the cafeteria. He pours the salt into the sink basin and places the empty glass shaker on the floor before crushing it under the heel of his shoe. Then he bends down and sorts through the shards of glass until he finds one that suits his needs.

They're going to make it look like another suicide. But they can't use a razor blade or a knife. None of us are supposed to have access to anything sharp. A piece of glass is the only thing Lucas could realistically use to slash his own wrists.

I am screaming and thrashing inside my head. But I must look a lot like Lucas. Limp. Helpless. The only thing moving are his eyes.

As soon as the tub has filled, Ivan kneels beside it. He pulls Lucas's arms out of the bath and pushes up the boy's sleeves. His movements are so precise that they almost seem gentle. When both of Lucas's wrists are exposed, Ivan chooses one and draws a long, red line with the sharpest edge of the glass. The cut doesn't seem deep enough to do any harm. But when he drops Lucas's limp arm into the bath, a brilliant red flower blooms beneath the water's surface. I watch Lucas's eyes as the second incision is made. For almost a minute I can see only the whites. When his irises finally reappear, I can tell that Lucas is gone.

Ivan drops the shard of glass into the bath. There's not a speck of blood on him.

"Nice work," says Caleb.

"Will they believe he did it himself?"

"Doesn't really matter," Caleb says. "It's all just for show."

Ivan grunts. "What about him?" he asks, prodding my thigh with the tip of his shoe.

"I should give him another zap," Caleb says. "We need to make sure he'll still be here in the morning."

Before he hits me with second jolt of electricity, Caleb squats down. This must be how it feels to come face-to-face with a serial killer. There's no mercy. No trace of a soul. I should have realized that the Wolves all share the same empty eyes.

"I can't *wait* to see if you manage to talk your way out of *this* little dilemma," Caleb says.

I don't feel the zap. I just disappear.

CHAPTER SEVENTEEN

THE HYBRID EXPERIMENT

I must be dead. I'm in a morgue. The first thing I see is the wall of metal drawers where they store all the corpses. I try to roll my head to the right, but a sharp, searing pain prevents me. I look to the left instead. Lucas is lying on an autopsy table. The blood has been drained from his body, and he's perfectly white. I return my gaze to the ceiling. I won't examine my own body. I don't want to know what they've done.

I hear footsteps approaching. Peter Pan has come for me. I'm finally ready to go.

"Hello, Flick." Mandel's boyish face appears above me. He's wearing a lab coat. I won't be leaving for Never Land. I've been sentenced to hell instead. "You should be able to sit up by now. Here. Let me give you a hand."

He helps me lift my back. I'm naked beneath my hospital gown. The icy steel table chills my balls. My teeth start to chatter, and my skin sprouts goose bumps.

"It's a bit cold in here, isn't it?" Mandel observes. "We'll go somewhere warmer as soon as you're feeling steady enough to stand. In the meantime, there's a question I've been dying to ask you. Would you *really* have amputated your own arm?"

"What?" My mind is a block of ice, with its memories trapped in the center. I know they're still there. But I can't seem to reach them.

"To get rid of the tracking chip."

I remember now. I wish I didn't. "Yes."

"Fan-tastic!" Mandel exclaims. "My colleagues refused to believe it. But I never doubted you for a second. That's why I took the opportunity to have your chip relocated. It's somewhere much safer now."

I peer down at my arm. There's a bandage where the chip once was. I'm confused for a moment, but then my hand instinctively flies up to the right side of my head. They've hidden the incision under my hair. The chip's there. I can feel it.

"If you're willing to amputate your head, I'll be *very* impressed," Mandel says. I think he just cracked a joke. "It's only a precaution, of course. Your escape plan was ill-conceived. There was never any chance you'd succeed. After curfew, the balcony railings on floors two through six are electrified. And the security on the ground floor is absolutely impenetrable."

"Why am I still alive?"

"Why wouldn't you be?" Mandel asks. "Everything is going according to plan. Are you ready to take a little stroll?"

I slide off the side of the table. My feet freeze as soon as they touch the tiling. I see three autopsy tables, four lockers, and one desk. There are too many corpse drawers to count. I wonder if they're all occupied.

"Where are we?" I ask.

"The Infirmary floor," Mandel responds. "That's what the employees call it, but my laboratory takes up most of the space. I'll give you a quick tour of the facility before we head upstairs to my office."

"I'm naked," I say.

Mandel glances down at my hospital gown. "Of course! I almost forgot. There's a fresh set of clothes in the locker with my name on it. Go ahead, get dressed. I'll wait for you outside in the lab."

I open the locker. There's a mirror fixed to the inside of the door. I start to get dressed, but it's almost like I've forgotten how. I pull on pants before I remember that boxer shorts should be worn beneath them. And it takes me a moment to remember which go on first—the socks or the shoes. I assume it's the lingering effects of the anesthesia. But when I look in the mirror, I see the truth. While I was under, they didn't just add a chip to my head. They took something away from me too.

Mandel keeps glancing over at me. I think I'm supposed to be oohing and aahing. The narrow aisles make the massive laboratory feel like a labyrinth. All around us, machines hum and whirl and beep. The workers down here seem to understand the strange language. Every new sound sets off a flurry of activity as humans rush to obey the machines' commands. We pause for a moment as a man in a full-body lab suit temporarily blocks our path while he feeds a tray of blood-filled test tubes into a giant white box. All I can see of the man are his eyes. His surgical mask and hood hide the rest.

"What kind of research are you conducting?" I ask my guide.

"Who are these people?" I can string words together in my head now, but my tongue still struggles to spit them out.

"Some are neurologists. But most are sequencing DNA. You see, Flick, I'm a geneticist by training. I never thought I'd end up as an educator. My older sister was tapped to run the family business after our mother passed away, but she died in a car accident five years ago. As the only surviving Mandel, I had no choice but to assume control of the school. At first I was extremely annoyed. Then I discovered a way to combine my duty with my true passion."

"By experimenting on dead teenagers," I butt in. "Have you told your doctors where their lab specimens come from?"

"The better you pay people, the fewer questions they ask," Mandel says.

We pass a small room to my right. The door is ajar, and the overhead lights are off. Two females in lab coats are examining a series of backlit blobs that are laid out in a grid on a massive screen. At first I think they're Rorschach blots. Then I realize they're slices of someone's brain.

Mandel sees me lingering and gestures for me to catch up with him. There's a pair of steel doors ahead of us, and he seems impatient to reach them. "Before I took over, the academy used to incinerate the bodies. It always seemed like such a terrible waste to me. Now at least the brains and blood are being put to good use. Mandel Academy students are helping to further the cause of science in ways they never dreamed possible."

"And to think they're just a bunch of kids who flunked out of high school. I'm sure they're *thrilled*. What exactly are they helping you accomplish?"

"I'm searching for a gene mutation. One that's rewired the brains of some remarkable individuals."

"Let me guess . . ."

"No." Mandel stops me. "Don't *guess*. Follow me up to my office, and I'll tell you the whole story."

Judging by the angle of the sunbeams that shoot down through the atrium, it must be early afternoon. A bell rings just before our elevator climbs past the classroom floors. I don't know which of the students shouts, but I hear my name echo through the building. Mandel has timed our journey perfectly. He wants everyone at the academy to see us.

"You've just risen from the dead," he tells me. "You used to be a prodigy. Now you're a god."

We step out on the ninth floor, and Mandel uses his card key to open an unmarked door. Behind it lies a staircase. I used to peer out the windows in the Wolves' Den and wonder what might be kept in the identical tower on the opposite side of the roof. Now I know. It's Mandel's private office.

"Interesting choice of décor," I remark when we arrive at the top of the stairs.

Aside from a coatrack standing beside one of the windows, the room is completely empty.

"I work underground. When I come up here, all I want to do is enjoy the view." Mandel sorts through three black coats that are hanging from the rack and passes the largest to me.

"I had this made for you," he says as he chooses one for himself.

The only coat left has a rounded, feminine collar. It looks about the right size for Gwendolyn.

"Has she taken you out to the roof yet?" Mandel asks.

"No."

"Ah well, she's probably been saving it for a special moment. Do try to look surprised when she shows you."

The window next to the coatrack opens like a door. Frigid air rushes into the tower as Mandel steps outside.

My body has a way of warning me when I'm being observed. An unpleasant tingle starts at the top of my spine and spreads until even the tips of my toes are buzzing. After a couple of months at the Mandel Academy, I've learned to live with the sensation. But this is different. It's more than a tingle. It's like I've just jammed a fork into an electric socket. We are out on the roof, surrounded by skyscrapers. I can see my father's building in the distance. His office faces south, overlooking the harbor. He's probably not watching. But others must be.

The academy's glass pyramid sits in the center of the roof. We're on a flat, tar-papered widow's walk between the two towers. A six-foot-high railing lines the edge of the building. Which means I can't just push Mandel over the side. I could try to kill him with my bare hands—but I'd be willing to bet that he's packing a Taser. I'd never make it out of this place alive. And God knows what they'd do to me before I died. Maybe I should shove Mandel through the glass pyramid. Then I could climb the drainpipe on the side of his tower, get past the fence, and jump. If my body splatters on a city street, at least it wouldn't end up in one of those drawers. And *that* is a very comforting idea.

I could jump. I want to jump. I must jump.

I won't jump. I'm here for a reason. Lucas died to keep me alive. I owe it to him—and to Aubrey and Felix—to do everything I can to survive.

"So how do you like my office?" Mandel laughs. "I know all of this probably seems very cloak and dagger, but I'd prefer to keep our chat private."

"How can you call this private? We're standing on a roof in the middle of the financial district. Half of New York can see us."

"And what do they see? An older man counseling a teenage student? The only thing that matters for now is that no one can *hear* us. The alumni know about my research, of course. But the experiment I'm currently conducting is the most important of my career. I'm on the cusp of proving a remarkable theory. And I'd like the chance to present all of my findings at once."

"You said you'd made a wager with my father. Now you're conducting an experiment. So what does that make me—your guinea pig?"

"No, Flick. You're going to be my superhero. My Captain America."

Captain America. The dipshit from the Lower East Side who let the government dose him with Super-Soldier serum. As a kid, I thought special powers like his were just another form of cheating. In my opinion, the only true superhero was Batman, who kicked ass without being anything other than human.

"Did you do something to me down there in that lab?" I demand.

Mandel shakes his head as if the question doesn't make sense. "All I did was change the location of your chip. If I altered you physically, it could ruin the experiment."

"Then how do you expect me to become some sort of super-hero? I don't even have what it takes to escape from a building in downtown Manhattan."

Mandel beams. I've never seen him so animated. He's practically giddy—like a grade school geek presenting his first science fair project.

"What if I were to tell you that there's a switch somewhere inside you? Until now, it's been in the *off* position. But if it were *on*, you would be completely unstoppable. The point of my experiment is to locate that switch—and flip it."

I open my mouth, but Mandel holds up a finger.

"I'll explain everything. But you won't understand unless you allow me to give you a bit of background information." He pauses. "Perhaps you've noticed that some of the students here at the Mandel Academy are . . . *different*. Caleb and Ivan, for instance. What do you suppose sets them apart?"

I remember Caleb's empty eyes. "They're sociopaths," I say. "I don't know why it took me so long to figure it out. They're both completely insane."

My diagnosis neither shocks nor insults my companion. "Ah, see! You just made two very common mistakes. To begin with, Caleb and Ivan are not *sociopaths*. They're *psychopaths*."

"Aren't those the same thing?"

"Not quite. Psychopaths and sociopaths are often confused because they share the same traits. Most are intelligent and cunning, for instance. Many are also remarkably charming. But both groups lack what you'd call a *conscience*. They always act in their own self-interest. They cheat, steal, or kill to get what they want,

208

and they feel no remorse for their actions. Some—but not all—become criminals. Others find success in a variety of professions.

"The difference between the two groups is simple. Psychopaths are *born*. Caleb and Ivan have always been the way they are now. Sociopaths, however, must be *made*."

"How do you *make* someone a sociopath?" I snort.

"There's more than one way, of course. The most effective is to find a child who's been neglected, traumatized, or abused. Then you force him to fight for his own survival. You give him no option but to kill or be killed. You tell him he must survive by any means necessary—and offer him a prize if he does."

"Sounds a lot like the Mandel Academy."

"And that's no coincidence. My mother perfected the recipe I just recited, though I don't think she knew what she was making. But I've been studying the academy's students since I was your age. It didn't take me long to realize that those who managed to graduate were either psychopaths or sociopaths. Some had been born that way. Most Mandel alumni, however, had not. But they were raised in environments that offered no sense of safety or hope for the future. That experience, along with the training they received at the academy, turned them into sociopaths. By the time they graduated, none of them possessed a conscience. Their sole concern was their own survival."

"You made them monsters," I say.

"Not monsters," Mandel corrects me. "*Predators*. That's the term we use here. The alumni hate being labeled sociopaths or psychopaths—and they'd be furious to hear you call them all *monsters*. They don't want to be thought of as mentally ill. And they're *not*.

No one at the Mandel Academy is *insane*. Psychopaths and socio-paths are not defective humans. As a matter of fact, I'm convinced they're superior beings."

I feel like we just took a detour into sci-fi land. I *do* hope extra-terrestrials are involved. If Mandel turns out to be barking mad, he might as well be entertaining, too. "Superior beings, you say?"

"That's the theory I'm testing. I believe that, at some point in history, the human race split into two different species."

It's not quite as crazy as it could be, I guess. "How?"

"A mutant gene evolved. Those who inherited the gene were smarter, stronger. *Better*. They became *predators*. Those without the gene were weaker, less intelligent, more prone to illness. They were the predators' *prey*. That's what psychopaths and sociopaths share in common. Both possess the mutant gene."

"Wait a second—you said sociopaths seem totally normal at birth. How is that possible if they inherited some kind of predator gene?"

Mandel smiles. He loves playing professor. "Science has shown that many of our genes can be switched off or on. Psychopaths are born with an active predator gene. But they're a very rare breed—perhaps less than one percent of the population. A much larger per-centage of people are born with a gene that isn't switched on. But if they're placed in the right environment, the gene can be activated, and they'll become sociopaths."

I don't want to ask. "What does this have to do with me?"

"You have the mutant gene. There's little doubt that you inher-ited it from your father. But you haven't been exposed to the condi-tions that will make your gene active."

"You're saying I have the predator gene, but it isn't *expressed*."

Mandel claps. "You know the proper term! Very impressive. That's right. You're what I call a *hybrid*."

"A hybrid?"

"When predators mate with prey, the offspring inherit an inactive mutant gene. Hybrids look like predators but behave like prey. However, over the years, the Mandel Academy has proved that it's possible to turn hybrids into full-blown predators. That's what my mother did to your father. He arrived at this school a broken, battered little weakling. He left as a sociopath. My mother activated his predator gene. And that's what I intend to do to you."

Shit. Shit. Shit. "And that's going to be your big breakthrough? You just said your family's been 'switching' hybrids for decades."

"Yes, but we've been terribly inefficient. This school recruits eighteen students a year. Only nine ever graduate. Our success rate is low because we're forced to recruit students we *hope* can be predators. We've been relying on guesswork rather than science. Half of our recruits never become sociopaths, and that's why we must expel so many students. However, if we find the predator gene—and develop a test for it—we can recruit only genuine hybrids and produce twice as many graduates each year."

"That's what you're searching for in the lab downstairs? The predator gene?"

"Yes, and when my scientists finally find it, we can test every potential student and admit only those who possess it."

"Gee, that sounds *awesome*," I drone.

"I think so," Mandel says. "Unfortunately, your father and his supporters claim my research is far too expensive. The board of directors has threatened to close my lab unless I can prove that the mutant gene actually exists. They've given me a single year. But great discoveries cannot be rushed. I knew we might not locate the gene in time—so I offered to show it in action instead."

"I have a hunch this is where I come in."

"Yes. Like all genes, the predator gene is passed from one generation to the next. In order to prove its existence, I needed a subject who was likely to have inherited the mutant gene from one of his parents—but showed no sign of being a predator. It had to be someone particularly unpromising—a young person the academy would have never dreamed of recruiting. Then I would expose the subject to the kind of conditions that I believe can activate the mutant gene—and turn the hybrid into a first-class predator."

My blood has been drained and my veins pumped full of poison. "And you chose me for your experiment. How flattering."

"You weren't an ideal choice. I appealed to the alumni first. Most of their offspring are likely to possess the mutant gene. I only needed a single hybrid for my experiment, but I quickly realized that no graduate would ever willingly enroll a child in our school."

"I bet. They wouldn't want to risk their own kids getting killed."

Mandel chuckles. "It would be a difficult thing to explain to one's spouse, that's for certain. But I think most alumni were more concerned that their children might *graduate*. Predators don't enjoy competition inside their own homes. Eventually I had to insist that your father volunteer one of his sons. He wasn't terribly fond of the idea, but at the time he could hardly refuse."

"So you've been trying to prove your theory by activating my gene?"

Judging by Mandel's smile, he thinks my question was naive. "No, we haven't reached that stage yet. You see, thanks to your stellar performance in the Incubation Suites, some of the alumni argued that you must have been born a predator. I had to take a step back and prove that your gene is not yet expressed. Last night, you showed the alumni how weak you still are. A true predator would never have acted in such an illogical manner. But that's why I gave you a room next to Lucas. Cowardice is contagious. I knew he would scare you into acting rashly. Now it's time for the second stage of my experiment to begin."

I can't imagine how life at the academy could get any worse. "Fabulous. What do you have in mind for me?"

"Whatever it takes to flip the switch, Flick. And when I do, you'll be my masterpiece. A *super-predator* like your father. You're smarter than the rest. Physically stronger than most. And you'll have something that students like Caleb and Ivan will never possess—a profound understanding of your prey."

"And you'll get your name in the evil scientist Hall of Fame, right next to Hannibal Lecter and Dr. Frankenstein."

"This is *not* about my own personal glory!" Mandel almost looks hurt. "My work will benefit all of mankind!"

"How is turning kids into sociopaths and training them to be white-collar criminals going to help mankind?"

He's been expecting this. There's more to his theory. And I can see it on his face—he truly believes he's going to single-handedly save the world.

"Nature doesn't make mistakes, Flick. There's a reason human-kind split into two different species. Once humans reached the top

213

of the food chain, our fellow carnivores stopped keeping our numbers in check. So nature created a new predator, and a delicate balance was maintained. A small group of human predators culled a large group of prey. Without the predators, the population would have exploded. And do you know what happens when there are too many prey in an ecosystem?"

I'm about to answer, but Mandel beats me to the punch. He's on a roll.

"They eat everything! They consume all of the natural resources, and famine follows. So long ago, a cycle began—a cycle in which hybrids played a key role. Whenever the prey group grew too large, life became difficult for everyone. The harsh conditions activated the mutant gene in some of the hybrids. They became predators, and they helped reduce the prey population until balance was restored. That's how it was for millennia. But here in America, the cycle has stopped—and one group is now threatening the existence of the others."

"The predators?" I ask, just to annoy him.

"The prey! There's no longer enough hardship in this country to turn the right number of hybrids into predators. Meanwhile, the prey keep breeding. The weak, the sick, and the feeble-minded are growing in number at an almost unimaginable rate. If they're all allowed to eat their fill, there will soon be nothing left for any of us.

"When my mother ran this school, the Mandel Academy was a profit-driven organization. But now we must serve a much higher purpose. In order to preserve our ecosystem, the prey must be culled. If I can find an error-proof way to identify hybrids, we can increase the predator population and restore balance."

"By helping a bunch of psychopaths and sociopaths get into

Harvard?" I snort. "If you really want to 'cull' the herd, you're going to need an army of serial killers, not a bunch of politicians and investment bankers."

"You're thinking too small! Even successful serial killers only dispose of two or three dozen people at most. But the academy is producing politicians who can start wars that will eliminate thousands. Investment bankers who will plunder the nation's resources. Our businesspeople will build factories that will pollute the prey's water. We will sell them food that poisons their bodies. We will coat their children's toys with toxic paint—and put chemicals in their toiletries that will leave them sterile. We will do whatever it takes to ensure that our species survives."

This is real. It is not hypothetical. I'm actually standing beside a mass murderer. A lunatic who believes that he can play God.

"So my dad knows all about this theory of yours?"

"Of course!"

"And he doesn't share your desire to 'save the world'?"

"No," Mandel says with the sigh of a misunderstood genius. "I think it's the very idea of a gene that upsets him most. Men like your father need to feel like they're in control at all times. He refuses to believe that he's just a part of something much bigger." Mandel turns to me. "That's another reason why you're so important, Flick. What better way to humble your father than to take the son he's always despised—and create a predator who's more powerful than he'll ever be?"

"I appreciate your confidence in me. But there's still one thing that I don't understand," I say.

"Yes?"

"Why you'd tell me all of this. Do you just like to share?"

"There's a reason for every action I take. I leave nothing to chance. You should know that by now." With Mandel's piercing blue eyes trained on me, I feel like a beetle that's been pinned to a board. "I offered you a reward for graduating from the academy—the information that could send your father to jail. I still intend to honor our deal, but I can see that incentives are no longer enough. I shared my theory with you because I want you to understand that you have no control over the outcome of this experiment. There is no way to leave the academy. The switch is inevitable, and you will remain at this school until it's complete. There are no *decisions* for you to make. Your body will function the way it was intended to function. One day, the gene will be activated, and you may not even notice the difference."

"It's funny you say that I have no control. I could put an end to your experiment right now."

"How?" he asks with a smile. He's certain I'm joking.

"We're up here alone. You think you could stop me if I decided to scale the drainpipe on the side of your tower and jump over the fence?"

"You're talking about killing yourself?"

"Sure. I'm not going to, but I could."

"And your point is?" Mandel plays it as cool as ever, but I know I've surprised him. Which means he hasn't thought of everything. A tiny flicker of hope is still burning inside me. I need to find Gwendolyn right away.

"The point is, I *want* to stay. So maybe my gene was activated last night."

"Maybe it was," Mandel says. "It's a hypothesis that I'm fully prepared to test."

"Give me everything you've got," I tell him.

CHAPTER EIGHTEEN

RUSALKA

One day, when I was ten years old, my school held a special assembly. Every student between the ages of seven and thirteen was in the auditorium that afternoon when a pair of police officers took the stage. We all knew what they'd come to say. Over the previous month, two townie boys had been kidnapped on their way home from school. A monster was loose in Connecticut.

They never used words like *pervert* or *scum*, but I heard the disgust in the officers' voices when they warned us to keep an eye out for "strange" men. A grown-up lurking around the school playground or lingering too long in a public restroom. I left the assembly feeling certain that I'd know the monster the moment I saw him. And when his mug shot made the papers a few weeks later, he looked just like the loser I'd sketched in my head. A pale, skinny shut-in type. They said he showed no remorse for the horrific crimes he'd committed. One of my teachers called him a psychopath. I heard a television reporter refer to the guy as a sociopath. Years later when I finally learned what the terms really meant, that man's picture was still lodged in my head.

I never would have used the word *sociopath* to describe my own father. When I was a little boy, he seemed like a god. Six foot three, a full head of chestnut-colored hair, a brilliant mind, and the dimpled chin of a movie star. Wherever he went, people gravitated toward him. He was worshiped by ladies and lesser males. As I grew older, I saw how he toyed with them. He fired loyal employees—then destroyed their reputations for sport. He seduced most of my mother's friends and never attempted to hide his affairs. Humiliating his wife and the other women's husbands must have been part of the thrill. When boredom set in, his mistresses were cruelly cast aside. I remember arriving home one afternoon to find a woman weeping on our doorstep while my own mother attempted to comfort her.

In the world of business, my father's coldness was legendary. Even the Wall Street types who most admired him said he was a man without blood in his veins. But every act of professional sadism was rewarded by a bump in his company's stock price. My father was a leader—a man who did what had to be done. He didn't have a heart to hold him back, and that's why he always won.

If only his colleagues had seen him at home—when the party was over and the ice sculpture started to melt. He'd stalk into his study and slam the door. An hour or two later, he'd emerge. My father never showed any outward signs of drunkenness. He never stumbled, slurred his words, or got red in the face. He'd be quiet for hours. And then he'd explode. Jude was the only one who could cool him down.

I hated my father, but I would have argued to the death with anyone who'd called him a sociopath. Because sociopaths don't have any feelings. And I was always convinced that my father loved Jude. Which meant that, as much suffering as he may have inflicted, he wasn't inhuman. That was my first mistake. My father never really loved anyone.

Mandel's theory makes perfect sense to me. Not the loony crap about preserving the "ecosystem" and saving mankind. But I have little trouble believing that there are two types of humans. It doesn't matter what labels you give them. There are monsters in this world. The Mandel Academy used to train them. But if Lucian Mandel proves there's a gene, it could soon be a factory that *makes* them. And if he's right about me—if I'm really a hybrid—there's no telling when the switch might take place. It feels like I'm blindfolded and strapped to a bomb. I can hear the timer ticking away, but I can't see how many minutes are left on the clock.

I can't stay. Mandel knew no reward could keep me here. I don't care about his "proof" anymore. So he tried to take away all hope of escape. But he didn't succeed. There may be a way to break free, but I'll need to act fast. And if I get out, I'll take down the academy, just like Lucas would have wanted.

Mandel escorts me back to my room. I can see he's done a little redecorating. The yearbook page that I've kept in my drawer has been framed and hung on the wall. Peter Pan is pointing his sword at me. It gives me an idea. I look down at the clock. It's twelve fifty-five. Five minutes to lunch. *Perfect.* I can get started immediately. As soon as Mandel's out of sight, I grab a pillowcase and begin filling it with supplies. The first thing that goes into my bag is the electric razor that's been charging in the bathroom. Then I use a pair of blunt-tipped "safety" scissors to cut the cord off my alarm clock. That's dropped into my bag as well—along with a red Sharpie and the two bottles of water that the invisible cleaning people always leave on my bedside table.

I sit at my desk until a quarter past one, and then I strip the bandage off my arm. There's still blood seeping from between the three stitches.

The crowd in the cafeteria greets me with reverential silence. I have returned from the underworld. They don't know what I've seen or how it has changed me. They don't know what I'll do. I have a mysterious bag in my right hand. Three thin streams of blood are trickling down my left arm. Everyone can see that my tracking chip has been removed. I'll let them draw their own conclusions.

I head straight for the Wolves. Just as I hoped, they're all sitting in their regular spots. I walk between the two filled tables. One is occupied by lesser beasts. The elite have all gathered around the other one. And as luck would have it, Ivan is sitting on the stool that would have been mine. I'm going to do my best to make this my last day at the Horror Hotel, but there are a few people who deserve to be punished before I check out.

When I reach the wall, I turn to face them. Gwendolyn leaps up and wraps her arms around me. "What happened?" she whispers. "They said you were with Lucas when he slit his wrists."

"Sit down for a second," I tell her. "Not there," I order when she begins to return to her seat next to Leila. "At the other table." Something in my tone makes her obey.

"What's in the bag, Flick?" Caleb drones. "Did you bring us some souvenirs?"

"It's a surprise," I tell him. I take out the two bottles of water, remove the caps, and place them both on the steel table. Then I crouch down by the electric socket on the wall between the two tables.

"What in the *hell* is he doing?" Austin drawls.

Leila sniggers.

I plug the alarm clock cord into the socket and stand up with the frayed end in one hand—and my electric razor in the other. Then I knock the two water bottles over, flooding the stainless steel table.

"Don't move," I tell the Wolves as I dangle the electrified cord over the wet table. "Or I'll fry all five of you." I have no idea if it would actually work. But neither do they. And that's all that counts.

"Flick?" Gwendolyn says.

"In a moment, darling," I respond without taking my eyes off her friends.

"Cute," Caleb sneers. "What do you want?"

"A little silence if you don't mind," I say. "I need to concentrate here. I've never given anyone a haircut with one hand before." I turn on the razor and take my place behind Julian.

"You're not going to let him . . ." Julian starts.

"I wouldn't fidget if I were you," I say. "You might make me drop the cord."

"Sit still," Caleb orders Julian. I doubt he'd bother to help if he could. At the Mandel Academy there are no friends. Just competitors. "You needed a trim anyway."

The guy has a lot of hair for a pixie. It takes almost a whole minute for the razor to cut its first path through. The rest goes more quickly. When Julian's head is covered in nothing but stubble and the table looks like it's grown a fur coat, I hand him my pillowcase bag.

"I've got a present for Caleb too," I tell him. "Take it out and pull off the cap."

Julian obeys, and I slide along the wall to the other side of the table.

"Your forehead, please," I tell Caleb.

"Why?"

"Don't argue, Caleb," Julian snaps. "Whatever he does to your face will be an improvement."

"I couldn't agree more," I say as I use my red Sharpie to draw a giant *F* on Caleb's forehead.

"Ivan?" He gets one too. Then I step back to admire my work.

"You're lucky I didn't have a branding iron handy. If you wash off the ink before I give you permission, I will find a way to etch my initials into your skin. Every time you look in the mirror, I want you to remember that you belong to *me* now. I had plans for Lucas, and you f—ed them up. If you *ever* question my authority again, I will slaughter every person at this table."

"Why me?" I notice Leila is twitching like a Pokémon character that's about to explode. "What do I have to do with any of this?"

"I just don't like you," I tell her. "I don't like *any* of you. So consider yourselves banned from the lounge for the rest of the semester. And if any of you f— up in any way, I won't hesitate to kill you all."

I yank the alarm clock's cord out of the wall and march out of the cafeteria. I can hear someone rushing after me. Gwendolyn catches up at the elevator bank.

"Flick . . ."

"Feel like a little fresh air?" I ask blithely.

I don't say another word until we reach the Wolves' Den.

"Open the window," I tell her. "Let's go outside."

Gwendolyn is surprised—and not pleasantly so. Which means she's passed the first test. She doesn't know I was here for a "private chat" with Mandel.

"Who told you about the roof?" she asks.

"Guess," I say.

When we step outside, I don't feel the cold, but Gwendolyn's teeth start chattering. I wonder if that will make it any harder for her to lie.

"So what other secrets have you been hiding from me?" I ask. I keep my tone neutral. That's the rule from now on—give nothing away.

"Secrets?"

"I'm offering you a chance to come clean, Gwendolyn. I suggest you take it. Tell me what you know. What happened to Lucas?"

"He killed himself. But you already know that! They said you were there!"

"I was. I watched Caleb and Ivan murder him."

She gasps. Those big blue eyes widen and five pretty little fingers fly up to her open mouth. She looks horrified. She looks exactly how I'd want her to look. Which tells me it's all just an act. She knew all along.

This is how it feels to lose your last hope. To stop treading water. To unplug the life support.

Mandel wanted me to find out this way. I bet it was always part of his plan. I knew Gwendolyn was one of them. I knew it, but I couldn't quite believe it. Until this very moment, I thought there might be a chance that Mandel hadn't made her a monster. If Gwendolyn was capable of loving me, she might be willing to save me. But it would have taken a miracle. And now I finally see. Only idiots pray for miracles. You might as well believe in Peter Pan.

I don't care enough about Gwendolyn to be angry. But I will punish her anyway.

I let a little tremor creep into my voice. "Lucas is in a morgue downstairs. So are all the other kids who've been 'expelled' this semester. That's what happens to Ghosts, Gwendolyn. They don't leave. They *die!*"

"Does Mr. Mandel—"

"Of course he knows!"

Gwendolyn throws herself into my arms. "Oh my God, Flick! What are we going to do?"

I take her by the shoulders and hold her at arms' length. I want to see her lovely face. I want to watch the tears flow from her eyes. "Do you love me?" I ask her.

"Yes!"

"And you trust me?"

"Yes!"

"Good. Because I want you to come with me. There's no way to escape, Gwendolyn. So I think we should jump."

"Jump?" The word comes out flat. Finally an honest response.

"You go first," I insist. "I'll help you shimmy up the drainpipe on the side of the tower. Once you're past the fence, just close your eyes and leap. I promise I'll be right behind you."

She's speechless.

"Come on!" I urge her. "We have to act quickly—before anyone figures out that we're up here!"

I take Gwendolyn by the wrist and begin to pull her toward Mandel's tower. She stumbles forward two steps before she yanks her hand away.

"There's got to be another way!" she insists. "I know—we can sneak out of one of the alumni parties. Go to the airport and catch a plane somewhere!"

It's a nice thought. I almost wish it wasn't so obvious that my beautiful princess is just scrambling to save her own ass.

"They'll trace the chip in your arm, darling. Even if I made it to safety, I couldn't live without you. I've thought this through. If we want to be together, there's nothing else we can do! *Please*. If you love me as much as I love you, please come with me."

Lucas was right—I'm a gifted actor. And I'm giving an Oscar-worthy performance. Poor little Gwendolyn is totally convinced that I've lost my mind.

"No," she says coldly. "I'm not jumping."

I cradle her face in my hands. "Then maybe I should *throw* you," I say.

It takes a split second for her to understand. "This isn't funny," she growls.

"I haven't been joking." I bend down and kiss her cold lips. "If you ever lie to me again, I will toss you right over one of the balconies. And believe me—you won't see it coming. Do you understand?"

"Yes." She spits the word at me.

"Wonderful." As I head back toward the tower, I think about the first time I saw Gwendolyn. How she looked just like an angel. Then I come to a sudden stop. "One more thing."

"What?"

"Ivan once called you 'Rusalka.' Any idea what that was about?"

The mask drops, and I can see the monster beneath it. The Queen of the Wolves has removed her disguise.

I catch Ivan between classes. I'm pleased to see that he's still sporting a giant red *F* on his forehead.

"Come with me," I order. I don't even watch to make sure he's following. But when I step on the elevator, he's right behind me. I finally understand why Siegfried and Roy did what they did. It's fun having a bloodthirsty beast for a pet.

As soon as we're inside my room, I pull out my desk chair. "Have a seat." He obeys. "What does *Rusalka* mean?"

Ivan's jaw drops. He assumed I'd forgotten. "I can't tell you," he says. Of all the responses he might have given, that is by far the dumbest.

"Listen, I know you've got the brains of a blintz. So let me explain something to you. Things have changed around here," I tell him in a perfectly calm voice. "I don't give a shit what the ratings say. As of this morning, I am top dog. It doesn't matter how frightened you are of Gwendolyn. Right now you should be ten times more worried about me. So. *Rusalka*."

Ivan nods. "*Rusalki* are mermaids."

"Mermaids?"

"They are very beautiful."

"Get to the point."

"They come out of the water at night to seduce men. Then they drown them."

"Why did you call Gwendolyn *Rusalka* the first time we saw her?"

"That's what my father called her."

The Butcher of Brighton Beach? "Your father knew Gwendolyn?"

"No, he read about her in the paper. He showed me her picture."

"Which paper? The *New York Times*?"

Judging by his reaction, Ivan has never heard of the *New York Times*. "What? No. The Russian paper. In Brighton Beach."

I feel like I'm interrogating a dimwitted donkey. "Gwendolyn is from Brooklyn too?"

"No. I think she lived somewhere in the north. But she killed a Russian man from Queens. That was why she was in all the Russian papers."

"The man who tried to molest her?"

Ivan grins. "She told you there was *one* man?" Suddenly I'm the idiot.

"How many were there?"

"Eight. Maybe more. They all paid to touch her."

"They *paid*? Who did they pay?"

"*Her*. It was a business. She posted pictures of herself on the Internet. Made dates with men who like little girls. When they came to her house, she took all their money and bled them like pigs. Then she and her mother threw the bodies into a river. *Rusalka*. My father always said she was a genius."

I can't help but grimace. "The mother must have made her do it."

"That's what everybody thought. Then the cops checked out the security tapes from her mother's favorite bar. The old lady was there almost every night until four o'clock in the morning. Maybe she helped hide the bodies, but she didn't kill anyone. The men all died right after they got to Gwendolyn's house. Usually around eight at night—when Gwendolyn had been home alone." Ivan shrugs. "But who is going to cry for a bunch of guys like that? She would have gotten away with it if they hadn't matched her teeth to the bite marks."

"Bite marks?"

"On the bodies."

"She *bit* them?"

"She was only thirteen years old. I'm sure she knows better these days."

"Thirteen? She's seventeen now, and she told me she's been at the academy for three years," I say, doing a little math out loud. "So she must have been in juvie for a whole year before Mandel found her."

"She never went to juvie. They put her in an asylum. They thought she was crazy."

It's ten after eight in the morning. I've just stepped into the cafeteria when a Wolf races up to deliver the news. Ivan is dead.

I'm not sure how I feel about that.

CHAPTER NINETEEN

DESTRUCTION, TERROR, AND MAYHEM

Gwendolyn and I have a beautiful relationship. She tells me everything. And I haven't killed her yet.

We spend our free time alone in the Wolves' Den. All of Gwendolyn's old friends have been banished from the tower. The lesser Wolves keep a wary distance from both of us. It was number 11 who discovered Ivan's severed head in the lounge. Gwendolyn had positioned it on one of the coffee tables so that Ivan's glassy, lifeless eyes would greet the first person who came through the door. I'm sure she hoped it would be me.

Only Gwendolyn and Mandel know what she did with the rest of Ivan. But I've heard that the landing outside the lounge was flooded with gore. It flowed down the staircase and seeped under the door at the bottom. They cleaned it up before the Androids got spooked, but if you look closely, you can still see traces of blood between the floorboards.

I only had one question for the killer. "Did you bite him?" I asked.

Gwendolyn rolled her eyes. "I've grown up," she sneered.

Either that, or she's been well trained. Her self-restraint seems quite impressive these days. Without it, I might not be able to keep my crazy little princess trapped in our tower. And there's no doubt about it anymore—Gwendolyn is officially deranged. The first thing I did after I heard about Ivan was head straight up to the lounge. The head was gone, but the Mac PowerBook 100 manual was still there. I took out the Hare Psychopathy Checklist and gave Gwendolyn the test. She got a 36 out of 40—a score that would make any successful serial killer proud.

Pathological lying	Check!
Lack of empathy or remorse	Check!
Promiscuous sexual behavior	*Hell*, yeah.
Superficial charm	Fooled me.
Criminal versatility	She's the Dux!
Delusions of grandeur	She's the Dux!
Juvenile delinquency	She cut off Ivan's *head* (and I'm not sure she used a *knife*).

I'm no trained psychologist, but neither was the kid who typed up the checklist and scrawled the purple note at the bottom of the page. *You're the crazy one, you redheaded freak.* I think I know which redheaded freak he was addressing. I should have figured it out a long time ago. The Mac PowerBook 100 was sold in the early 1990s. Lucian Mandel would have been in his teens back then, and he told me he's been studying the academy's students since he was my age. His obsession with predators must have begun while he was in high school. I can just see the arrogant little bastard administering the test to Wolves his own age. Then one of them decided to turn the tables. If his score is accurate, Lucian Mandel is more dangerous than Gwendolyn.

I don't know if he still engages in "promiscuous sexual behavior." (I shudder at the thought.) But Mandel has certainly got "manipulation" down pat. If he didn't, Gwendolyn would have ripped out my throat with her perfect white teeth by now. I'm guessing he once told her to help me in any way that she could—and that the order has not been rescinded. So I force Gwendolyn to sit silently beside me as we tackle our homework at the end of each day.

It must make for a pretty picture—the blond beauty and her handsome beau. We're just two ordinary American teenagers inventing new ways for businesspeople and politicians to screw the whole world. Every night before we head to our rooms, I grab Gwendolyn, bend her over one of the balcony railings, and kiss her. And every night I almost vomit—but the gesture must be made. I want to remind Gwendolyn how little effort it would take to toss her over the side. The message couldn't be clearer, but she always kisses me back. That's what she's been told to do.

I have no allies here—only enemies. I couldn't care less if the other students hate me. I only want them to bow down before me. The trick—just a little something I picked up from Caligula—is indulging my every whim. I keep the academy's plastic surgeons busy by practicing new Hand-to-Hand Combat techniques on Caleb and Austin. I delight in finding novel ways to destroy Leila's precious computers. (Yesterday at lunch, I took a leak on her latest model.) Whenever Julian's crew cut grows long enough, I shave obscene designs into the side of his head. It's been a while since the Wolves have done anything to provoke such abuse. That's the whole point. There's no such thing as cause and effect anymore. There are no rules. There's just *me*.

Maybe the switch has been flipped and I've become Mandel's monster. Or maybe I'm just pretending. I don't think anyone knows for sure. The person I once was might be hidden away somewhere inside my head. But I'm like an old lady who buried her treasures in the backyard—and then forgot where she dug the hole. When I found out number 53 was dead, I felt nothing. An Android in my Fundamentals of Business class said that Frances swallowed an entire bottle of Tylenol. He didn't seem to realize that the official story was ridiculous. Students aren't even allowed to have bottles of vitamins in their rooms. Any potentially fatal drug would be kept under lock and key. But the Android needed to believe it was suicide because the truth was too horrific to contemplate. All I could do was laugh.

"Who's next?" I asked Gwendolyn when I took my seat next to her in the Art of Persuasion.

She glanced around to make sure no one was listening. "That's it," she told me in a hushed, angry voice. "We can't have fewer than fifty students."

Thanks to Ivan's untimely demise, a Ghost was spared. But that's not justice. It's only dumb luck.

It's the beginning of April, and I haven't seen Mandel in about five weeks. The semester is almost over, and new rankings will be posted at the end of the month. I have no real competition—academic or otherwise—at this school anymore. Even Gwendolyn has fallen far behind. But Mandel must want to keep me on my toes because he's decided it's time for another pop quiz. I think he'll find that I'm 100 percent focused. I've got my eyes on the prize, and nothing's gonna keep me from winning it. Whatever Mandel wants me to do, I'll do it with a smile. And whenever I have the opportunity, I'll thank him for framing that picture of Jude and hanging it up in my room. It's really helped me set my priorities straight. I don't care about Ghosts or girls anymore. I don't give a damn about proof. This monster is just waiting for a chance to kill its creator. One way or another, I'll get out. And then I'm going to destroy him.

Mandel's latest test will take place today. The top three students in the Art of Persuasion have been chosen to receive additional "off-site" training. It's nine o'clock in the morning, and we've just been pulled out of our first-period classes for a meeting in Mr. Martin's office on the ground floor of the academy. It's Gwendolyn, a fifteen-year-old Wolf named Percy, and me. I wonder if the other two realize that they're only here to make the charade seem legitimate.

The office is a dump. Whatever Mr. Martin's skills may be, organization clearly isn't one of them. Stacks of white boxes circle his desk and climb the walls. Many are missing their lids, and the labels slapped on their sides are written in an illegible hand. The box closest to me contains an empty bottle of prescription medication, a pair of women's underwear, and a wig. Once we take our seats, our beloved instructor maneuvers the obstacle course to the other side of his desk. Its surface is strewn with paper coffee cups, yellowing newspapers, and multicolored towers of folders. Maybe Mr. Martin thinks the clutter makes him look professorial. All I see is opportunity. A mess like this is a godsend to a thief.

He pulls out a black leather briefcase, sets it on the desk in front of him, and begins dialing the combination lock. He acts like he's some kind of CIA operative, but if that's his idea of security, he needs a refresher class. Leave me alone with that briefcase, and I'd have the lock cracked in less than a minute. I probably won't get a minute, but the idea still burrows into my brain.

I can't see into the briefcase from where I'm sitting on the opposite side of the desk. I watch Mr. Martin's hand disappear inside and emerge clutching three thin files.

"Gwendolyn." She rises and leans over the desk to accept her file. Mr. Martin is in a jovial mood this morning. I haven't seen him this happy since Lucas's trial by polygraph. Someday I'll smack that smile off his face, but right now I can't afford the indulgence.

"Flick." As I reach for my file, I knock over one of the coffee cups. Clumps of mildew ride a thick brown river that flows around the papers on Mr. Martin's desk and drips down onto his chair.

"Dammit!" Mr. Martin bellows. He roots through a trash can and pulls out a handful of napkins that must have come with yesterday's lunch.

"Sorry!" As I scramble to rescue documents from the flood, I position the corner of a thick envelope on the lip of the briefcase.

"Don't touch anything! Just sit down!" Mr. Martin orders me, and I obediently drop back into my seat.

He tosses the sopping-wet napkins into the trashcan and wipes his palms on his pants. "Get up and take your file," he snaps at Percy.

I don't know if my ruse will amount to anything, but at least I've spoiled the bastard's good mood. He swats down the top of his briefcase. It might look closed, but I didn't hear the lock click. This could be my lucky day.

Mr. Martin glances at his wet chair and curses under his breath. He kicks a box out of the way and squeezes back around the desk to address us.

"The files you've been given contain all the information you will need to complete today's assignments. There are cars waiting for you outside. You will each be driven to your destination—and then driven straight back to the academy. You are not authorized to go anywhere else. I have carefully engineered these simulations to test your unique abilities. I recommend that you take the exercise very seriously. Act just as you would in a real-world situation. But remember: you will be under surveillance at all times.

"Now, if you check your files, you will find a brief description of your assignment on the first page. Take a moment to read it. You'll have plenty of time to examine the other contents once you're en route to your destinations."

I open my file but sneak a quick peek at Gwendolyn's. I see a photo of a man. A plastic bag with two white pills has been stapled to the inside of the folder. So she's supposed to drug him and what? Kill him? Take dirty photos? Leave a few bite marks where the guy's jealous wife might discover them?

"Eyes on your own file, Flick!" Mr. Martin barks.

My file contains a snapshot of a different man. I don't recognize him. He's in his early forties. Dark-haired. Handsome. He looks like an actor. He has an iPhone pressed to one ear.

Arriving at 1:50 p.m. on American Flight 3749 from Chicago. Obtain the phone and deactivate password protection. Return to the academy and immediately deliver the device to your instructor.

"Want me to look for anything in particular on the phone?" I ask.

"You're not very good at following directions," Mr. Martin says. "You've been instructed to bring the phone directly to me. You haven't been asked to trawl through the contents."

Ha. That's like creating a file called SECRET DIARY: KEEP OUT on the computer you share with your sister. Either you're incredibly stupid, or you want her to look. Mandel's not stupid. There's something on the man's phone that he wants me to find.

"Are there any other questions?" Mr. Martin asks. Gwendolyn and Percy both shake their heads. "Then get started. We expect you back here no later than five."

I rise.

"Sit back down, Flick," Mr. Martin orders as he opens the door and ushers the others out of the office.

"Mr. Martin?" Gwendolyn is gone, but Percy is lingering by the door. "Am I authorized to use lethal force if I'm captured?" He sounds so eager.

"This is just a simulation," Mr. Martin reminds him. "You aren't going to get *caught*."

Bless that little psycho. He's given me just enough time. My fingers creep into the briefcase on Mr. Martin's desk. I'm hoping for a phone but find a wallet instead. Good enough. The briefcase lock clicks, and I'm back in my seat, the wallet safely hidden beneath the folder on my lap.

Mr. Martin slams the office door. "I was hesitant to give you this assignment," he tells me. "I saw your arm and assumed that your chip had been removed. I didn't want to be responsible for a student like you going AWOL. However, Mr. Mandel has informed me that your movements are still being tracked. And I've ensured that they will be actively monitored throughout the day. I also have a team of observers in position at JFK Airport. If they see any sign that you intend to go off course, the punishment will be severe. You are not allowed to make phone calls or send emails. You will not initiate any unnecessary conversations. Do you understand?"

"Yes," I say.

"Do you have any idea how severe punishments can get at the academy?"

"Yes, sir, I do," I tell him.

"Then off you go." He waves me away like he can't stand the sight of me.

I'm in the backseat of a black Lincoln Town Car. It only takes a few seconds to examine the contents of my assignment file. In addition to the photo and instructions, there's a plane ticket that will allow me to access the American Airlines gates. The phony name on the ticket matches a counterfeit ID with my picture on it. There's nothing else in the file. Not a single piece of information on the man I'm meant to rob. I could sit here and guess what the academy has planned, but I have much better things to do.

Mr. Martin's wallet contains $135 in cash. His real name is Simon Hodenfield. He lives at 45 East 85th Street in Manhattan, just off Park Avenue. The photo on his driver's license makes him look like a pedophile. *Fantastic.* Mixed in with a bunch of receipts is a list of names written on a scrap of paper. None of the names rings any bells. I flip the scrap over. *Jackpot.* It's the top half of a letter addressed to the parents of Nathaniel Hodenfield, who has been a very naughty boy at school. One more infraction and young Nate will be kicked out of the Browning School for the remainder of his sophomore year. Whatever the kid did, something tells me he isn't going anywhere. In fact, he'll probably end up graduating with honors. The six names on the back of the letter look like a hit list. I bet they all work at the Browning School. "Mr. Martin" has probably been digging up dirt on each of them.

My car ride ends in the short-term parking lot at JFK. I hop out and dump Mr. Martin's wallet in the first trash can I see. I keep only the license and cash. I'm feeling good. It's nice to have a change of scenery. Then I enter the terminal and find myself sucked into a crowd. Suddenly I'm a zoo animal, and the door of my cage has been left open. The wild half of my brain sees opportunity. The half that's accepted a life in captivity is insisting that it's all just a trick.

I haven't been around this many normal people in months. Is this how they act? Their movements appear totally random, and they're all talking at top volume. I didn't think I'd have any trouble identifying the academy's observers, but every face I examine appears perfectly ordinary. Maybe there aren't any observers. Maybe everyone's an observer. Maybe Mandel rented the entire terminal for the day. Maybe this isn't even JFK. I didn't pay much attention to the route we took. I need to be alone for a moment. Before I rush to the men's room, I check the arrivals screen. My mark's flight isn't due in for an hour.

In the bathroom, there's one stall open. The toilet is disgusting. They say you can't catch STDs from a toilet seat, but I've never been sure about crabs. So I stand in the tiny space, listening to the sound of water rushing and bowels emptying. It's comforting to know that no one can see me losing my shit. What's wrong with me? I'm in public. I could find a way to phone the police. *What would you tell them?* I could contact the newspapers. *What proof do you have?* I could show a reporter the chip in my head. *You'd never make it out of the airport.* I could call my mother. *There aren't any phones where she is, you imbecile.* I could try to reach Joi. *You don't have the balls.*

Someone new just arrived in the restroom.

"It's five days, Skylar. Five f—ing days!" The voice is pure frat boy. I peer through the crack in my stall and see a college-age guy on the phone. It's forty degrees outside, and he's wearing shorts. Either the dude's taken too many lacrosse sticks to the side of his head or he's heading off on spring break.

"I *told* you. It's just *guys. Nobody's* taking their girlfriends. Look, I gotta go take a dump. I'll call you when I get back from Cancún."

He enters the stall next to mine. I hear his bag drop to the floor. A fly unzips and a toilet seat clanks. I squat down. A duffel bag is leaning against the divider between our two stalls. The top is open, and I can see the corner of an iPhone sticking out. It's possible that Mr. Spring Break is just an academy stooge, but I'm not going to look this gift horse in the mouth.

A little pick-pocketing always lightens my mood, and the paranoia begins to fade as I head for the airport security line. Mandel may be watching, but that doesn't mean I can't have some fun. I stop at a souvenir shop on my way to the gates. I use Mr. Martin's cash to purchase a Yankees hat and an I ♥ NY T-shirt. A quick trip to another restroom, and I emerge as a tourist. My own shirt is folded neatly inside the plastic shopping bag. I have thirty minutes before my mark's flight arrives at one fifty. More than enough time to entertain myself. I don't even bother to check for observers. Let them catch me in the act. I should get extra credit for what I'm about to do.

There are plenty of seats in the departure lounge, but I pick one in a section that's being used as a playground by six feral siblings. I take a snapshot of Mr. Martin's driver's license with the iPhone. It makes a splendid photo for Simon Hodenfield's new Facebook page. Then I put together an album using Mr. Spring Break's pictures, which show bare-chested frat boys in various stages of intoxication. Finally I get to work on Simon Hodenfield's profile.

Activities and interests:

(N)urturing the youth of today

(A)cting as a mentor to young men in need

(M)aking the most of our time together

(B)uying little gifts for the people I cherish

(L)aughing at those who can't understand our love

(A)nal sex with high school studs

Favorite movies:

Anything with Taylor Lautner

Favorite books:

Lord of the Flies, the Abercrombie & Fitch catalog

Favorite quote:

You make me feel like I'm living a teenage dream.

—Katy Perry

It looks like Simon never taught his spawn how dangerous the Internet can be. His son Nathaniel's profile is public. I invite all of the kid's buddies at the Browning School to be friends with his dad. I even send a few special messages:

> You have a secret admirer!
> I may be old, but I'm a lot of fun!
> How about a sleepover?
> Sexual predators need love too!

After I finish, I check the time. I was connected to the Internet for almost twenty minutes. The observers didn't intervene—though for all they know, I could have been emailing the FBI. There's something very strange going on here. My skin starts to tingle as the paranoia returns. I sit with the phone in my lap and watch the six budding delinquents pelt each other with caramel-covered popcorn. When I find myself caught in the crossfire, I start to wonder if they might be part of a trap.

Flight 3749 out of Chicago arrives, and I take my place outside the gate before it begins to deboard. My mark is out the moment they open the doors. He must have been sitting in first class. He's got his iPhone in his hand. He's making a call.

I step out in front of him and match my stride to his.

"I just got in. . . . Yes, the flight was fine. How are you feeling? . . .

I know, but sometimes you just have to force yourself to get out of bed. . . . Maybe you should call Dr. Chung. Do you want me to do it? . . . Well, then have your sister come over till I get home. . . . Around nine this evening. I left the schedule by your computer."

I'm impressed. Mr. Martin's simulation is very thorough. If I didn't know better, I'd think the actor was just a regular guy with an exceptionally clingy wife.

"Okay, honey, listen, I have to rush. I'll call you right after the meeting. . . . Love you too. Bye."

I give it a second. Then I turn around abruptly. The man rams into me. As we bump chests, the iPhone drops out of his hand. I catch it and slip it into my pants pocket. I keep my thumb scrolling across the screen so password protection won't kick in.

"So sorry, mister," I say, handing him Mr. Spring Break's phone. "I just remembered I left my backpack on the plane!"

I jog past him before he can get a good look at my face. Then I quickly duck into a Starbucks and deactivate the phone's password protection. I remove my Yankees cap and put my original shirt over the I ♥ NY T-shirt. As soon as I'm out of disguise, I begin my investigation. Let's see what Mr. Martin and Mr. Mandel want me—don't want me—to find.

The iPhone belongs to an Arthur Klein, and the first few emails I browse are all about drugs. I guess Art's supposed to be some kind of pharmacologist. Either that or he's a junkie with an impressive vocabulary. His correspondence is so complicated that it might as well be written in ancient Greek. So I scroll through Art's photos instead. There are dozens of them. Someone really put a lot of effort into downloading all these images. I click on the first one. It's just a kid. He's four or so, and he bears an uncanny resemblance to the guy I just robbed. It seems a bit strange that an actor would get his young son involved in a simulation like this. The next photo shows the little boy posing on the steps of what looks like a temple until I read the name engraved in the marble. It's the John G. Shedd Aquarium. In *Chicago*. The attention to detail is absolutely remarkable. I scroll faster, searching for something scandalous. There's nothing but the same goddamned kid. He gets bigger, less babyish. I stop on a photo of the boy in a scarlet graduation gown and hat. There's a banner behind him that says CONGRATULATIONS, CLASS OF 2010. Kindergarten. It's so cute I feel nauseous. I keep scrolling, but there are only two photos left.

The kid is waving to the camera from the top of a playground slide. He doesn't look any older than he did in the kindergarten photo. I can't breathe. Why can't I breathe? Shouldn't there be more pictures on the phone? This one must have been taken over two years ago.

Something happened to the kid. This is the last picture his father took of him. This is all that's left. This is real. This is very, very real.

Suddenly I'm running past the gates toward the exit, weaving around travelers, ignoring their startled faces as I hurdle over rolling suitcases. The only thing I can hear is the sound of myself pleading with any god that might be listening. *Don't let him be gone. Please, don't let him be gone.*

He's not. He had a bag checked. A large portfolio case. I'm stuck on an escalator, but I see him haul the case off the conveyor belt and lug it out to the center of the baggage claim area. He stops and looks around. He must be expecting a driver to meet him. I see him rooting around in his jacket pocket. He's going to call his secretary or the car company. When he pulls out Mr. Spring Break's iPhone, I know what I need to do. I know how this all has to end.

I'm off the escalator. I'm less than a yard away, and I'm already running. I snatch the phone out of the man's hand. It takes him a few seconds to shout.

"Thief!"

But no one comes after me. And I have to be caught. My plan won't work unless I'm arrested. Then a little girl with a rolling Barbie suitcase appears in my path. I could leap over her if I tried. But I don't. I'll let the kid feel like a hero today. I trip over the bag and go sailing face-first across the floor. When I come to a stop, two Good Samaritans pin me down. My mark gets his phone—and his little boy back. I'm so goddamned happy that I start to cry.

CHAPTER TWENTY

FRANK

If there are really academy observers here, I've outwitted them all. I'm locked up in a detention center at JFK. The airport cops must not be part of the game. None of them seem very interested in me. I guess stealing phones doesn't compare to being caught with bags of cocaine crammed in your rectum—or entering the country with endangered species tucked into your tighty whities. Plus, the guy I robbed didn't have time to stick around and press charges. I was worried they might release me, so I informed the cops that I'm still a minor. They did exactly what I hoped they'd do. They made me call my father.

I wish I'd thought of this earlier. No FBI agent or newspaper reporter would ever take me seriously. But my father knows what really goes on at the Mandel Academy. He's the headmaster's enemy—the only one who can stop him. If I don't graduate, my father will win his wager. If I don't graduate, they'll have to get rid of me. I'll die, and that's fine. I can't rid the world of all of its monsters. But at least I can keep Lucian Mandel from murdering millions.

"I've been arrested at JFK," I tell my father when he takes my call.

"Excuse me?" He sounds so *polite*. There must be other people around.

"I stole a phone."

"I'll have my assistant contact the academy," he says.

"No. It's over. I give up. I'm not going to help Mandel anymore. You have to come get me."

There's a pause. "Okay. I'll be there in under an hour."

I suppose I won't be alive much longer than that. It's a relief to know that my body isn't going to be fed to the machines in Mandel's lab. I should probably be reliving my fondest memories, but I keep thinking about the little boy in the pictures. My gut is still telling me that the kid was real. I wonder if Jude had something to do with what's happened today. If so, I hope he approves of what I'm going to do. I won't be able to avenge his death. I hope he's not pissed off when I get to Never Land.

A lady cop unlocks the gate. "You're free to go," she says.

I'm shocked when I see my dad waiting by the front desk. He looks a few inches shorter and a decade older. It's been less than a year since the last time I saw him. How could anyone age so quickly? His posture is still perfect. His suit looks brand new. But I see strands of gray in his chestnut hair. Crinkled skin around his eyes. A weariness inside them. For the first time since I've known him, my father actually appears to be mortal.

"Thank you for your trouble," he tells the officers. "I'll make sure that my son is properly punished."

I follow him out the door. He stays three steps ahead of me. I'm so tempted to kill him. I could snap his neck with a single move. My brother's murderer has his back to me. I've spent a year dreaming about a moment like this. Now it's here, and I'm the one who's surrendered.

My father's car and driver are waiting at the curb. He opens a door to the backseat. "Get in," he orders.

I slide inside. My father joins me. It feels like we're observing a family tradition when we both keep our lips sealed. We've taken hundreds of silent car rides together, my father scrolling through his email while I watch the world pass by. But today his phone has stayed in his pocket and his eyes haven't left the back of the driver's seat. I don't see any evidence, but I can tell he's been drinking. The traffic is light and the man at the wheel is speeding. We're approaching the Manhattan Bridge when I realize this may be my last chance to speak.

I lean toward my father and sniff the air. "You f—ing *reek*. Did you down a whole bottle of Scotch on the way to the airport?"

He doesn't answer. But I can hear him sucking in air he doesn't deserve, and it infuriates me.

"Must be hard living with yourself. Knowing you murdered your favorite son and all. Is that what's got you drinking during the day?"

My father gazes out the window. "Jude's death was an accident."

"Tell that to someone who didn't see his corpse. How many punches does it take to kill a sixteen-year-old kid, anyway?"

It used to be so easy to wind my dad up. When he sighs, I start to wonder if I've lost my touch. "I only hit Jude once. We were standing at the top of the stairs when it happened. The doctor said the fall broke his neck."

"Yeah? And how much did you pay the doctor to say it? You know, I always thought you loved Jude."

"I did. I . . . " He stops without finishing the thought.

How dare he? How f—ing *dare* he lie to me now? He'll suffer for that, I swear, even if the only weapon I can hurl at him is the truth. "Just as much as your dad loved you, right?" When he looks over at me, I make sure I'm smiling. "Mandel told me your dad loved you so much that you had to stab him to death."

He stares at me until my smile is gone. "Lucian read my file, but he doesn't know the real story. My father never drank before my mother abandoned us. I watched him fall apart. By the time I turned twelve, he was just a penniless drink. We needed money for food and rent, so I had to look for odd jobs. I thought my dad would be proud the first time I came home with a bag full of groceries. He knocked me down as soon as I stepped through the door. I couldn't understand why he did it, and from that moment on, I despised him."

"And then you grew up to be just like him. How ironic."

He nods. He knows it's true. "I tried to avoid it. That's why I was thirty-five before I took my first sip of alcohol. But once I started, I found out why my father was never able to stop. I don't even remember the first time I hit you. Or why I did it. That's how much I'd been drinking. But when I woke up the next morning and saw what I'd done, I could tell that I'd lost you. And when your mother confronted me, I knew that I'd lost her too."

"But you still had Jude, isn't that all that mattered?"

"He was my last chance to get it right. And for a while I thought I had. Then I found out Jude hated me just as much as you do. I suppose he was just better at hiding it."

Is that really what it was? When I was younger, I'd make Jude stand beside me in front of my mother's closet mirror. We looked so much alike. I couldn't see what the difference was—I couldn't understand how my father could love one of us and loathe the other.

"Gee, Dad, that almost sounded sincere. If you weren't the world's biggest liar, I might actually believe a bit of your sob story. But do me a favor. Just kill me already—don't bore me to death."

"Don't be ridiculous," he says. "I'm not going to *kill* you." He sounds exhausted.

"Why not? You bet Mandel that I'd never graduate from the academy, and we all know what happens to the kids they 'expel.' You bet on my *life*, Dad. I have to die in order for you to win the wager. So why draw things out any longer? I give up. I'm letting you take the prize. Just do me a favor and don't let Mandel get his hands on my corpse. The way I see it, you owe me that much."

"You're not allowed to give up," my father explains patiently. "Not yet. When we formed our agreement, Lucian said he might need two semesters. As you know, there's a great deal at stake here. I must honor our deal. If there were any other way to dispose of Lucian, I would have done it long ago."

"But you can't because he's got the goods on you. What I don't understand is why Mandel would even bother with a wager if he could have your ass sent to jail for Jude's murder."

"He'd like to, but I have half the alumni behind me. Neither of us would benefit from a civil war among the graduates. Lucian can't afford to lose half the people who pay his bills. And I refuse to put the Mandel Academy at risk."

"Seems like you've got your priorities in order. Nothing's more important than protecting a school that kills its own students."

When he spins around to face me, I finally get a glimpse of a father I recognize. The one who always looked at me like I was a hideous boil on the ass of humanity.

"What do you know about priorities?" he spits. "For your information, every student the academy has ever recruited would have died without it. They had no families. No friends. They would have over-dosed or been murdered or thrown themselves off bridges. The academy helps as many as it can. It gives them a chance to survive. That's what people like you and Lucian can't understand. You were both born with everything. You don't know what it's like to have nothing."

"I had everything? You mean money and a big house? Is that what you call *everything*?"

"I made sure you had food, shelter, and warm clothing!" The volume of his voice rises a little with each word. "That's more than I ever had!"

"So you think the Mandel Academy rescued you?" I ask. "I thought only weak people had to be *saved*."

I brace myself for my father's response, but his anger seems to have withered away. "Beatrice gave me something to fight for. I was the one who saved myself."

"Beatrice? Beatrice *Mandel*?" Lucian Mandel said his mother and my father were close. She was his mentor. He was her masterpiece.

"After my father died, Beatrice brought me to the academy. It was a different place in those days. They didn't put chips in our arms—or give us drugs that made us easier to control. Beatrice never toyed with us or treated her students like lab rats. She respected us. We were told that some of us would make it—and some of us wouldn't. It wasn't a game to Beatrice. It was life or death.

"When she offered me a place at the Mandel Academy, Beatrice made it very clear that the only thing I'd be given at the school was a chance. If I wanted more, I'd have to fight for it. At first I didn't think I'd ever have what it took. But then Beatrice pulled me aside and encouraged me to observe the other students. Some were strong. Some were weak. And the only difference between them was a choice. Fight or give in. And that choice was *mine*. All mine. No one else could make it for me—and no one could ever take it away. In the end, I chose to *fight*."

"Lucian Mandel would just say that your gene had been activated."

"And there are many things I might say about Lucian Mandel, but I wouldn't want to jeopardize our deal. I *will* tell you that Lucian has never faced the kind of choice I described. If he had, he'd know his little theory is wrong. If a gene were responsible, the choice would be easy. It wasn't. I was ranked last in my class, and the instructors were lobbying to have me expelled. Beatrice Mandel made me an offer. I would be given another semester to prove myself—if I disposed of the student ranked second to last. His name was Franklin, and he was my only friend. I don't think I'd have survived the first few weeks at the academy if it hadn't been for him."

Franklin. Franklin. The name means something. Then I remember the night I got punched for watering his fichus with a decanter of Scotch. Before my dad left me for dead, he'd whispered a name. "You killed *Frank*?"

"I had to choose between my life and his. It was the hardest choice I've ever faced. I knew he'd die anyway. Even Frank realized he had no hope of graduating. I struggled with the decision for days, but once it was made, there was no going back."

So Beatrice Mandel took away my dad's last good thing and replaced it with something rotten. But he's so convinced that the evil bitch saved him that he'll do whatever it takes to protect her legacy.

For a moment, I almost pity the man sitting beside me. But then I realize my father was right. He was given the option to fight or give in. The choice was his and his alone. And he *chose* to kill Frank. No amount of Scotch will ever help him forget it, and there's nothing he could say that would ever make me forgive him for the things he's done since.

"Wow, you've really racked up quite a body count. Anyone else you've *had* to murder?"

The sneer is back. "Of course you wouldn't understand, you pampered little shit. It was me—or Franklin. I saved myself. What would you have done in my place?"

"Something else."

"I'll tell you what you would have done. You would have *died*. You've never had any fight in you. Remember when you were ten years old and that kid at school stole your bike? I ordered you to get it back, and you tried to convince me that you'd *loaned* him the bike. Your little brother had to fight the boy for it."

That's the story he's been telling himself all these years? I loaned my bike to one of the townie kids in my class when I heard that a boy had been kidnapped on his walk home from school. My mom picked me up every day at four. I didn't really need a bike, so I let the kid borrow mine. I figured his trip home would be safer on two wheels than it would be on foot. And Jude didn't *fight* the kid to get the bike back. He asked our mom for the money to buy the boy a new one. I'm tempted to set my father straight, but he'd only call me a liar. Still, I'd like to see him slap me the way he did when I was ten.

"You always were your mother's son," I hear him saying. "That's why I accepted the wager Lucian proposed. Even though so much was at stake, I knew it would be a safe bet. Your mother did her best to keep you sheltered and soft. Someday soon, you'll face a choice just like mine. When that time comes, you won't have what it takes to survive. Lucian will lose the wager, and I will win control of the school. I wish none of this were necessary. I really do. But I can't allow Lucian to destroy the Mandel Academy. Your death will save hundreds who deserve to live."

"Hundreds of kids like *you*? You know, Dad, you may be right. I don't think I'll be able to *fight* like you did. But just so you know, if Jude had been in your shoes thirty years ago, he wouldn't have killed his friend either."

My dad's glare softens until his eyes don't seem to be focused on me anymore. "Probably not," he finally concedes. "But I think you'll agree that Jude's 'something else' would have been spectacular."

"Mine will be too. I promise you that."

My father leans forward and raps on the dark glass barrier between the driver and us. The car slows down and pulls to the curb. I look out the window. We're already downtown.

"There's something I need to ask you before I go," my father announces. I hear something new in his voice. If I didn't know better I'd call it concern. "I need you to answer me honestly. Have they put you on any medication?"

That wasn't the kind of question I was expecting. "What? You mean the doctors at school?" I ask, and my dad nods. "No."

"If they try to, don't take it. And don't mention any of this to Lucian. I've told you much more than I should have." My father gets out of the car, but he doesn't shut the door. He pauses, then turns and pokes his head back into the vehicle. "Consider yourself lucky. You still have a chance. Let's see what you do with it." Then he slams the door.

The handle won't open my door. I can't find a way to unlock it. I bang on the barrier between the driver and me. My fists can't crack it. The engine starts.

I sit back and wonder what my father meant. I still haven't figured it out when the car pulls up outside the Mandel Academy.

CHAPTER TWENTY-ONE

THE BLIND SPOT

I've been brought to an empty classroom. There's no place to sit, so I pace the perimeter.

"Hello!" I almost cringe when I hear Mandel's cheerful voice. "It sounds like you've had quite a day!"

He's not alone. A man comes through the door behind him. I've never seen the guy's face before, but the look in his eyes is pure predator. He's my father's age, and he isn't particularly tall or muscular. But I see his thick fingers and calloused knuckles, and I know that the man must be one of the academy's killers.

Mandel's hands are in his pockets. It's his way of showing me that I pose no threat. "Why don't you tell me what went wrong this afternoon."

I don't have a plan. What's the point? But I'm not going to mention the dead kid. There's no telling what he could do with information like that. "I lost my nerve. I panicked, and I got arrested."

Mandel knows I'm bluffing. "It was a simple task, Flick. You must have stolen hundreds of phones before you arrived at the academy. What on earth made you panic this time?"

"I thought it was another one of your tests. I was scared of failing."

"You assumed it was a test? My, my, we are a bit paranoid, aren't we? For your information, Mr. Martin has been organizing similar trips for the past fifteen years. *All* of our instructors send students into the field from time to time."

"Was today a simulation?"

Mandel smiles. "No, and I'm afraid you've made Mr. Martin's life quite difficult. You were performing a favor for some very important alumni. Thanks to your performance, they've lost access to an important source of information, and they're not very pleased with your instructor. And of course there's the matter of the Facebook page."

"Did Mr. Martin make lots of new friends?" I ask.

"I see you still have your sense of humor. Let me ask you . . . how did someone in a state of panic manage to craft such an entertaining profile?"

It's a very good question. I don't have an answer.

"Feeling tongue-tied? Then let's move on. How long did it take you to construct Mr. Martin's profile?"

"About twenty minutes."

Mandel cocks his head. "You couldn't think of anything better to do with twenty minutes of Internet time?"

"Who needs porn when I've got Gwendolyn?"

Mandel's pet thug finds this amusing. Does he know my sweet little princess?

"More jokes," Mandel observes. "And yet you have much more reason to panic now than you did this afternoon. But we both know you were just as composed then as you are right now. So let's set that rather pitiful excuse to the side for a moment. I'm still curious about your time online. You haven't had Internet access in months. Wasn't there anyone you wanted to write? Any person you felt like phoning?"

"No."

"Not even Joi?"

"Who?"

Mandel laughs. "Well played. Now let's discuss your arrest. How many times have you been arrested in the past?"

"None."

"And when you were arrested this afternoon, why didn't you call the academy? Why did you choose to phone your father?"

"Why don't you just tell me what you're getting at?" I say. "You sound like you have everything figured out. So go ahead and do what you want to me."

"You seem to think that I'm angry," Mandel notes. "Do I *look* angry?"

"I have no idea," I say. The guy never stops smiling.

"Mr. Martin would say that the day has been a disaster, but I'm actually rather pleased by what I've heard."

What?

"I was worried that we might have sent you out a bit early. A gifted young man like you could have found a way to cause quite a bit of trouble for the academy. I knew there was a chance that I might need to do some damage repair this evening. But you acted like a true predator. First you attacked Mr. Martin. And then you went after your father. You were intending to kill him, weren't you?"

He doesn't know that I tried to surrender. And for some reason, my father hasn't told him the truth. Play along.

"I got tired of waiting for my reward."

"But your father outsmarted you. And sent you back to me. He's laughing at us both right now."

"If he'd faced me like a man, I would have won."

The thug and Mandel share a chuckle.

"Only little boys believe in 'fighting like a man,'" Mandel says. "It doesn't matter how you fight, Flick. There's no such thing as *honor*. The only thing that matters is *winning*."

"Then I'll win the next round."

Mandel nods. "Perhaps. I *am* extremely happy with the progress you've made. I wouldn't be surprised if you're ready to graduate by the end of next semester. But in the meantime, there are still a few things you need to learn. Your next lesson will be taught by my colleague, Mr. Wilson. I'm afraid it's going to be a little bit painful."

Mandel has clearly been smoking some of Julian's crack if he thinks his enforcement friend will be able to hurt me. I'm thirty years younger than Mr. Wilson. The old codger doesn't stand a chance. Then the man steps forward and pulls up a pant leg. He has a set of nunchaku strapped to his shin. Why do I keep expecting Mandel to play fair?

"Mr. Martin has insisted that you be reprimanded. But please don't consider this a punishment. Think of it as a lesson in humility. You've been fighting amateurs for too long. Your father is a professional. He trained alongside Mr. Wilson during their days at the academy. You're about to get a taste of what to expect should your father choose to fight 'like a man.' Mr. Wilson?"

"Yes, sir?"

"Don't kill him," Mandel says before he leaves the room.

I remember the one time I managed to hurt my father. It was the same fight that led to my exile in Georgia. I threw a punch, and it hit his jaw. For a second, I believed that the tables had finally turned. And in that second, I had a glimpse of another life. One in which my mother never suffered, my brother never scrambled to keep the peace, and I never had to tiptoe through the halls of my home. It was the most glorious vision I'd ever had. I wanted it so bad, and Jude must have known. Because he died trying to make it real.

They've planted grass on the surface of the moon. The lush green lawn keeps going and going until it meets a perfectly black horizon. I hear sprinklers in the distance—the rotating kind that Jude and I used to jump through when we were kids. I'd like the little dead boy to have a chance to enjoy them. But Peter Pan and I are the only ones here.

"Where are we?" I ask.

Peter Pan flies a slow, graceful loop around me before coming down to land. "This is the place between sleep and awake. The place where you can still remember dreaming. I've been waiting for you. Come with me. I'll show you around."

We start walking, side by side. The horizon never gets any closer. "Why am I here?" I ask.

"You've left your body back at the academy. It needs time to heal."

"I'm alive?"

"Yes."

"And I'm still me?"

"More you than you've been in a very long time."

"Why didn't Mandel figure it out? I tried to surrender. If Dad had let me, Mandel would have lost the wager."

"Mandel will never understand what you did."

"What did I do?"

"The right thing. You returned the man's phone. Then you tried to stop Mandel's experiment—even though you thought Dad would kill you."

I made my choice, and I didn't even realize it. "I chose to give up. That's what Dad would say."

"What takes more guts? To fight for your own life at any cost— or prove that you're willing to lose it?"

I see his point, but I don't know why he thinks I've just made some huge leap forward. "Isn't that what I've been doing for the past goddamned year? I've given up everything for you!"

"No," Jude says. "I died trying to help you. Why would I want you to risk your life for my sake? I told you to stay with Joi, but you wanted revenge. And you would have traded your soul just to get it."

I'm still confused. "And today?"

"Today you let go. I was worried you'd changed, but when it mattered most, you were still the brother I knew. Maybe there is a predator gene like Mandel says. Or maybe Dad's right and it comes down to a choice. But both of them are totally wrong about one thing. They think you've only got two options. Off or on. Fight or die. But there's a third option: screw them. Be who you want to be—and don't be afraid of the consequences. That's what you did at the airport. That's how you found your strength."

"It was the little boy. The one who died. He made me think about you. Is that why you put his pictures on that phone?"

When Peter Pan grins, I realize how stupid the question must have sounded. "You know I don't have that kind of power," he reminds me. "Even if I did, all that matters is that you knew what the pictures meant."

"I saw that kid, and all I could think about was how much I miss you and how much I lost when I let you go. I couldn't do that to someone else. I couldn't take away what little was left of his one good thing."

"You figured out that he wasn't just an assignment or a means to an end. He was real."

"Yeah."

"It's all real, you know," Jude tells me. "All the bodies left behind in their war games. All the people they poison and rob. They're human beings."

"I know. That's why I called Dad and told him to come get me. He's bad, but Mandel is a million times worse."

"You don't need Dad's help. You've found Mandel's blind spot. He doesn't know there's a third option. Remember what you told Dad? He asked what you would do if you were given the choice to kill or die. You said you'd do 'something else.' Well, you're going to face another choice soon enough, I'll bet. And whatever you do— make it *spectacular*."

I laugh. "Any ideas?"

"Nope, but you'll figure it out."

"I'm glad to have you back, Jude."

"I never went anywhere," he says. "There's nowhere to go."

I'm in the infirmary and a machine by my head is beeping insistently. A nurse peeks into the room and sees I'm awake. A few minutes later a doctor arrives. He shines a penlight into each of my eyes.

"Can you feel your limbs?" he asks.

"Yes." Everything hurts. My throat is painfully dry. And I'm pretty sure there's a catheter stuck where no plastic tubing should ever be forced to go.

"Do you know where you are?"

"The seventh circle of hell?"

"I heard you had a sense of humor," he replies dryly as he slides a blood pressure cuff up my arm.

"How long was I out?"

"Thirteen days."

Damn! Mr. Wilson really knows how to swing a set of nunchaku.

"Any serious damage?"

The doctor glances at my face. "You're not as cute anymore."

"Is that supposed to be funny?" I really don't know.

"You'll be fine," the doctor says on his way out of the room. "By the way, you have a visitor waiting outside."

It's not Mandel. It's Gwendolyn. And I'm glad to see that she isn't pretending to be concerned. She just glides in, wearing a black dress with a strange, white image that stretches from the collar to the hem. It looks like an x-ray of a bird in flight. She takes a seat in the chair at my bedside and stares at me.

"Hello, sweetheart," I croak.

"He's right. You're not as cute anymore," she informs me.

"Well, if you get sick of looking at me, you can always cut off my head."

"Maybe someday I will," Gwendolyn replies. "It's definitely something to look forward to. But for now Mr. Mandel says we're still a couple. He made me come down to offer my congratulations."

"For what? Getting my ass handed to me?"

"For being named one of the academy's Duxes."

"You're kidding."

She picks up a section of my IV tube and rolls it between her thumb and index finger. She's probably itching to give it a yank. "I wish. I thought you were out of the game when you fell to fifteenth place in the Art of Persuasion. But I guess your other grades were pretty amazing. We're tied."

"Tied? We're both Dux?" It sounds great—until I realize that Mandel has made Gwendolyn my chaperone.

"Yes, which means you better get your ass out of bed. The new semester starts in four days. We have work to do."

CHAPTER TWENTY-TWO

FRESH MEAT

When I get to my room, I strip and stand in front of the mirror. My skin is a patchwork of purple, yellow, and brown—the colors of death and decay. If zombies ever invade the Mandel Academy, they'll probably accept me as one of their own. Still, as bad as my carcass looks now, it must have been twice as gruesome while the bruises were fresh. My right leg doesn't appear to be seriously injured, but it can't bear much weight. The doctor didn't give me crutches or a cane, so I hop whenever I can. When I can't, I walk with an old man's limp. My left arm was in a sling when I left the infirmary. I slipped that off before stepping into the elevator. The arm may be useless for now, but I'd rather no one else know it.

After I woke from the coma, I spent two days strapped to a hospital bed. Aside from a few delightful chats with Gwendolyn, my only entertainment was a series of sponge baths that didn't live up to my expectations. Mandel never once paid me a visit. But now that I've been released, I see he's left me a homecoming gift. My computer is running and there's a new folder sitting on the desk-top. I laugh out loud when I see the label he's given it: WHEN YOU'RE READY. Who knew a psychopath could be so corny? It sounds like the title of a 1970s sex-ed pamphlet for girls. But I doubt Mandel wants to warn me about the dangers of teenage fornication. The folder must contain information about my father. It may even be the proof he killed Jude. As curious as I am, I won't open the file. If I'm lucky, I'll have a chance to make use of it later. But I finally know who I want to be. I want to be the person who destroys the Mandel Academy.

The question that's been eating away at me for forty-eight hours is, *how*? When I wasn't being probed by the infirmary's doctors, I sent my mind in search of answers. I tried to relive each day of the last four months—and replay every conversation I've ever had with Mandel. I must have seen or heard *something* that would help me blow this whole place sky-high. But I still don't know what it was. All I have is a single clue. Jude was right—Mandel does have a blind spot. My thoughts kept returning to the night Lucas and I tried to escape. Mandel assumed I'd been running for my life. It never even dawned on him that I had been trying to save *Lucas*. He called my actions *illogical*. He couldn't understand them. I guess risking your ass to help someone else makes no sense to a man who fantasizes about murdering millions.

So the academy's leader is a nut job with a limited understanding of human psychology. It's an interesting piece of data, but I have no idea how to make use of it. Unfortunately, a lack of inspiration is hardly my biggest problem. I'm crippled, outnumbered, and there's a computer chip in my head. And there's always a chance that my own DNA could turn against me. All I can do is hope that Mandel is wrong about the predator gene. Because if I stay in control, I know I'll make the right choices. I'll die before I fight like my father did. But I'd rather do something spectacular. And I'm stuck here until I figure out what that's going to be.

I'm not one of Mandel's predators, but I am a Dux, and my new duties must be addressed immediately. Gwendolyn keeps complaining that we're far behind schedule. The next semester begins in two days. The Beauty Pageant will take place tomorrow night, and I still haven't had my sneak peek at the newbies. Gwendolyn said she'd give me a debrief over lunch. It's just past noon, and I'm eager to get to the cafeteria before the Wolves arrive. I don't want to parade my new limp in front of them. But showering isn't the simple operation it once was. I clean only the parts that are already reeking. While I mow through two weeks of stubble, I check my new battery-powered, cordless alarm clock and see that I'm running late.

Gwendolyn is sitting on her own, her face lit by the glow of the tablet computer in her hands. She's chosen a table in the far corner of the cafeteria so I'll have to hobble past every student at the academy. Gwendolyn wants them all to get a good look at me. I'm wounded and vulnerable. I start to expect an ambush the second I set foot in the lunchroom. The Wolves have gathered at two tables near the jumbo-sized screen that displays the new rankings. Ella is wedged between Caleb and Leila. I scan the rankings list and see that she's taken Ivan's place at number 12. My own name is all the way at the top. The Wolves watch as I limp across the room. I give them the finger with my good hand. No one snarls or growls. All but one of them glance back down at their trays. Ella keeps her eyes on me. It must be my imagination, but it almost looks like she's smiling.

At first I'm baffled. I've given Austin, Leila, Caleb, and Julian every reason to kill me. The four of them could rip me to shreds before the lunch on their plates has time to cool. It's possible that Mandel ordered his pets not to pounce. But I'm starting to think that there might be another reason they haven't attacked. Before I was Dux, the whole pack would have benefited if I'd been eliminated. Now that I have the title, one of the Wolves stands to gain much more from my death. Caleb is number 2 in the rankings. He'll still be seventeen in September—too young to graduate—which means he's here for another year. If I die and Gwendolyn heads to Harvard, he'll be named the school's Dux. But his friends won't help him because they all want the top place for themselves. Not a single Wolf will sacrifice for the sake of the pack. They'd rather suffer under a leader they despise. That means even though I'm at my weakest, I'm safer here than I've ever been.

I always thought the tracking chips were what kept the Wolves in their cage. Now I can see I was wrong. Even the most advanced technology couldn't stop a pack of twelve brilliant beasts. Together, they could find a way to beat the chips. But Wolves aren't team players. None of them could escape on their own—and they won't work together. They're each too busy trying to win the big prize. They'll never stop playing Mandel's game. And they'll never realize that they're nothing but pawns.

When Gwendolyn spots me approaching, she hops up and kisses my cheek. "How do you like being a gimp?" she whispers sweetly in my ear.

My grin becomes a wince as I lower my aching body onto the stool opposite hers. "Look, Fang, why don't we put an end to this bullshit. You don't want to be with me. And I'm not interested in cuddling up with a bitch that bites. Now that we're both Dux, I don't see any reason to keep putting on a show for the underachievers."

"We can't stop." She says it through her teeth.

"Sure we can. Just tell Mandel that you gave me the boot. He's probably figured out that you hate me. You haven't been doing a very good job of hiding it lately."

Gwendolyn leans forward, her hands pressed flat against the table like she's about to spring across it and eat me alive. "Let me explain something to you, Flick. Mr. Mandel knows exactly how much I loathe you, but it doesn't make any difference. You're my big project this semester. Lucas was my last assignment. I was supposed to help the little wuss grow a pair of balls, but I failed. This is my last chance to graduate. If you screw up, I'm never getting out of this building."

I'm almost disappointed in Gwendolyn. I thought she was savvier than this. "Mandel is full of shit. . . ."

Gwendolyn grabs the wrist of my injured arm. *Shut up!* she mouths as her nails puncture my skin.

I pull her painted claws out of my flesh. "You think I care if he's listening? You didn't fail your last *project*. You were set up. Mandel never expected Lucas to kill that airline CEO. You were given an assignment you couldn't complete so you'd be desperate to prove yourself the next time around. Mandel knew I was going to be your project this semester, and he wanted you to be willing to do whatever he asked."

Gwendolyn sticks out her lower lip like she's mocking a child. "What difference does it make if he tricked me? Are you trying to tell me that life isn't *fair*? Are you really that pathetic?"

It seems like a good time to test my new theory, so I reach for the tablet computer and type out a note.

Why should we have to play Mandel's little games? You and I are the best of the best. We could take over this place if we put our heads together.

"And what if we did?" Gwendolyn asks. She's choosing her words carefully. As much as she despises me, she won't say anything that might condemn me. "You want me to believe that we'd live happily ever after? I'm not *stupid*. I know you'd find some way to get rid of me. If I didn't get to you first." She thinks my proposal was nothing more than a ploy—and an incredibly lame one at that.

I decide to give it another shot, just to be sure. "Why would I want to get rid of you, Gwendolyn? We could be invincible together. Even *Mandel* thinks we make a great team. He's letting us share the Dux title, isn't he?"

She replies in a whisper so soft that the words dissolve into the air. "Yes, and I'd kill you right now if I could. I didn't work my ass off for three years to *share*. And if you keep talking like this, we'll both end up dead. Do you understand? So shut your mouth and smile for the idiots."

I give her my toothiest grin.

"Good. Now let's get down to business." She shoves the tablet computer back across the table. I catch it just before it flies over the edge.

The form on the screen contains a few fascinating facts about a kid named Max. He's six foot four, 218 pounds. He just turned sixteen, and he's spent the last two years in juvie. It says he was convicted of four counts of aggravated assault, but it doesn't elaborate. There's no photograph of Max, but the description almost makes me nostalgic. He sounds just like dear, departed, decapitated Ivan. At the bottom of Max's profile, there's a little box labeled TYPE. It contains a plus mark.

"Scroll down. There's information on all six new students," Gwendolyn says.

"What does this mean?" I ask, pointing to the TYPE box. It must mean Max is a member of the 1 percent. A psychopath, a born predator. But I'm curious to find out if Gwendolyn knows.

My question was perfectly reasonable, and yet Gwendolyn snorts as if it's proof I'm an imbecile. "It means Max has the kind of blood you can donate to anyone. If he dies, the school will store his blood in case another student needs a transfusion. There's usually a kid in each class who has the right type. I have it too."

"Interesting. But why the plus mark? The 'universal donor' blood type is O negative."

"Why are you asking *me*?" Gwendolyn demands.

"Just making conversation," I reply as I scroll through the files. There are three females—Flora, Violet, and June—and two more males—Orson and Hugo. Of the six, only Max has a plus sign in the TYPE box. "When do we get to inspect the fresh meat?"

"After lunch. Mr. Mandel has arranged an exhibition."

First we get bread, then a circus. Mandel knows how to keep his top people happy. "You mean a fight? Like the time I kicked Ivan's ass for your viewing pleasure?"

"Yes. But today it's not just for fun. Mr. Mandel told us to pay close attention. There's something strange going on with this Incubation Group. He wants to see what we think."

"Strange? In what way?"

"He didn't say, and I'm not a mind reader," Gwendolyn snaps. "Why do you keep asking all these retarded questions?"

She's really starting to piss me off. "You know, *darling*, you might try being more pleasant," I warn her. "Otherwise, I'll make sure you flunk out of school. And I've *seen* what Mandel does to the kids who don't graduate. I bet he'd *love* to take a cranial saw to your pretty little skull."

The elevator gates open, and we enter the Incubation Suites. The name finally makes sense to me now. I was imagining babies and birds when I should have been thinking tenth-grade biology. The *incubation period* starts when you catch a disease. It ends when you begin to show the first symptoms.

Gwendolyn uses a card key to unlock one of the two Employee-Only doors that I remember from my own stay in the Suites. Just as I suspected, behind the first door is a set of stairs leading up to the glass-enclosed catwalk.

"What's behind door number two?" I ask, pointing down the hall. "A lady or a tiger?"

"Storage, you dolt," my tour guide responds. "That's where they keep all the furniture they're always moving around." I can't even tell if she got my joke. A month ago, Gwendolyn would have laughed just to humor me. Now she only has two settings—silent and snarling.

When we reach the top of the stairs, she grabs a remote control from its cradle on the wall. The device has a single red button, and Gwendolyn keeps her thumb on it as we stride toward our destination. She must be worried I'll snatch her precious remote away, but I'm too entertained by this rare behind-the-scenes glimpse of the Mandel Academy. Walking down the catwalk is like floating through the open air. You're so high up you can't help but feel like a god.

Gwendolyn clicks the red button before we enter the gym. The stretch of catwalk in front of us shimmers. The glass looks a shade milkier, but we'll have a perfectly clear view of Mandel's "exhibition."

"Max, June. On the mat!" I recognize the voice of my former self-defense instructor.

Far below, seven people assume their positions. Two of them will be facing each other in battle. But it doesn't appear to be a fair match. One of the combatants is a beast of a boy. The other is a tall, willowy girl with jet-black hair pulled up in a bun.

I take a step toward the glass, and my own ghostly reflection comes into view. My mouth is open, and my good hand is preparing to wave. My teeth almost touch, and my tongue presses against the top of my mouth, but Joi's name never makes it past my lips. I watch my hand fall to my side. The only thing I hear is the sound of my heart trying to break free from my chest.

I thought I'd forgotten her, but I didn't even need to see her face. I would have known her by the curl of her hair, the shade of her skin, the curve of her spine, the length of her fingers. Nothing about her has changed. She's the girl I watched treading water. The girl who smiles in her sleep. The girl who didn't need to be told how much I loved her.

The girl I deserted and betrayed is down there on the mat. Mandel has brought me here to watch her fight one of his predators. I won't let Joi get slaughtered today. But even if she survives this sick exhibition, it's only a matter of time before she knows what I've done. She'll hear about Gwendolyn. She'll discover just what it takes to be Dux at this school. And she'll hate me even more than she already does.

But that doesn't matter. Joi's clearly been brought here to die. I thought I could take whatever Mandel threw at me. I'd endure the beatings and battle his Wolves. I'd make him believe that I was his masterpiece. Then I'd graduate and destroy the academy. I thought this time, I was willing to do anything. Now Mandel will know that it's all just an act. Because there's one thing that I will not do. Not even to save the world from a monster. I won't let Joi die.

"Who is she?" I try to make the question sound casual.

"That's June," Gwendolyn replies, and I realize I should have kept my mouth shut. "I wouldn't get too attached. She won't last long at this school. She doesn't even have a criminal record. But Mr. Mandel wanted to give her a shot. He says she had a very interesting childhood. But who didn't, right?"

"Where did she grow up?" I ask, wishing I'd paid more attention to June's profile.

"What do you care?" Gwendolyn demands. She almost sounds jealous.

"I thought we're supposed to figure out what's going on with the group. Don't you think it's a bit odd that Mandel would make a girl fight a guy the size of a grizzly bear?"

Gwendolyn reluctantly pulls the tablet computer out of her handbag and scrolls through June's profile. "She grew up in Bosnia. Says here her father was some kind of war criminal."

"Does it mention her last name?"

This time Gwendolyn doesn't even bother to check. "No," she replies.

I'm holding my breath when the fight kicks off. I force myself to stay calm. I need to wait for the right moment to intervene. When Joi's in real danger, I'll clear the catwalk glass. That's how Gwendolyn ended my battle with Ivan. But I can't act a second too soon or I'll risk looking desperate. If Mandel suspects that I still have feelings for Joi, her fate may be sealed.

The first time Max lunges at Joi, I almost tackle Gwendolyn for the remote control. I resist the urge long enough to see Joi gracefully step to one side, grab the beast by his elbow, and flip him onto his back. Max doesn't seem surprised, and I begin to wonder if they've fought before. He immediately leaps to his feet and mounts a second attack. This time Joi sends him skidding facedown across the mat. She's obviously been trained in some form of judo. And she's good. Really good. Five minutes into the battle, Max's torso is drenched in sweat, and his chest is heaving. Every time Joi throws him, it takes him longer to recover. She should go on the offense. One vicious kick would bring the beast to his knees. But Joi simply refuses to fight.

"The girl's a loser," Gwendolyn observes coldly. "She just defends. She won't attack."

"Looks to me like she's winning," I counter.

"For now. But as soon as June makes one mistake, she's dead."
I see a self-satisfied smirk appear on Gwendolyn's face, and I know
she doesn't mean *beaten*. She's actually waiting to watch Joi *die*.

"Has anyone ever been killed in the Incubation Suites?" I ask.

"If not, there's a first time for everything," Gwendolyn responds,
keeping her eyes on the action. "I only saved Ivan because I thought
he'd be useful. But June is worthless. Maybe *you've* got a hard-on
for her, but *I* couldn't care less if she makes it upstairs."

"You're such a charmer," I say as I slide a bit closer to Gwendolyn.

"It's a gift," she replies, edging away.

The contest continues for another ten minutes—long enough
for my hope to build beyond reason. And then Joi finally makes
a fatal error. Her hair breaks loose from its bun, and black curls
spring in every direction. She should tie it back immediately, but
she doesn't. And the next time Max lunges, he gets ahold of a hunk
of it. He drags Joi to his chest and wraps a massive arm around her
neck. I can see his bicep flex as he starts to squeeze.

Gwendolyn is watching with such glee that she's forgotten to
guard the remote. When I pluck it out of her hands and click the
button, she responds by karate-chopping my injured arm. It's a
shameless move, and it's not very smart. One good limb is all I
need. I send the girl flying.

Gwendolyn slams against the side of the enclosure and drops
to the floor with a loud thump. They must have heard it down in
the gym because five sets of eyes are now trained on the catwalk's
clear glass. The instructor and four of the newbies are all staring
up at me. The other two students are still locked in mortal combat.
Max hasn't let Joi go. Then without any warning, a foot shoots out

and slams into the back of his knee. Max's leg buckles, and he loses his balance. When he topples, Joi rolls away, out of his reach. I'm pretty sure I'm the only person who saw what just happened, and I can barely believe my own eyes. Another newbie rescued Joi. And it wasn't one of the athletic-looking specimens standing on the side-lines. Joi's savior is a girl who resembles an overfed chipmunk.

Joi jumps to her feet and casts a quick glance at the kid who helped her. Then she looks up at the catwalk. Her face gives noth-ing away. I'd understand if she didn't recognize me. I'm not the person she used to know. But Joi is still the most magnificent girl I've ever laid eyes on.

"Get a good look," Gwendolyn sneers behind me.

The worst thirty-six hours of my entire existence culminates with the Beauty Pageant. I have not slept or eaten since I last saw Joi. I've been searching in vain for some way to rescue her. But I can't think of anything that won't put her life in more danger. Mandel must know what I did in the Incubation Suites' gym. He wants to see what I'm going to do next.

I have no option but to wait with the crowd for the pageant to begin. When the elevator arrives, Joi is the last one to exit. My gaze never leaves her as the newbies are led to their lodgings. I'm glad the academy's groomers let her keep her hair long. I hope it still smells of jasmine. The other contestants are dressed to the nines, but Joi has chosen a simple black shift dress. I wonder if my classmates see what I do—the last person on earth who should be here.

When the newbies have vanished into their rooms, the rest of the students rush to one end of the balcony, where Caleb is waiting to take their bets. I follow the gamblers, hoping for a chance to slip inside Joi's room while everyone else is distracted. I'm outside her dorm, and I see her. She's standing in the doorway as though she knew I'd come. She purses her lips and blows me a kiss—right before she slides the door shut in my face.

I feel a hand grip my arm. Someone is leading me away. "Come on, Flick," I hear Gwendolyn say. "Let's go have some fun."

The mob goes quiet as we approach. I don't recall Gwendolyn betting at the beginning of last semester. But tonight she's carrying a scrap of paper, which she presents to Caleb. He unfolds it and looks up at her. The others are breathlessly awaiting the verdict. Gwendolyn is the Dux. She knows things that the rest of them do not.

"Win or lose?" Caleb asks.

"Lose," Gwendolyn says with a smile. "Tell them who."

"One vote for June to lose," Caleb calls out to the crowd. The Wolves among them smell blood, and that drives all the killers half-wild.

I see Ella standing nearby with a pad and pen. "May I?" I ask.

Her eyebrows are much more expressive now that she's let them grow back. I wonder what she thinks she knows. She doesn't say anything as she hands over the pad and pen. Someone else witnesses the exchange and quickly hushes the frenzied gamblers. I pass my bet to Caleb. I've written the name JUNE in letters large enough for everyone to read.

"To lose?" Caleb asks.

"To *win*," I correct him.

If there's no way to escape, I'll just have to help Joi survive. And that's going to take a set of flaming brass balls.

CHAPTER TWENTY-THREE

THE WITCH

The first time I visited Joi's colony, I almost swore I'd never go back. It was six days after our encounter at the Russian Baths. I knew where she lived. I'd spent several evenings camped out across the road, waiting for a glimpse of her. Every night, she'd arrive on Pitt Street with a shopping bag in each hand. The building she entered was lousy with kids. The younger ones were always outside, decorating the sidewalk with chalk drawings or taking turns on a wobbly scooter. A dozen teenagers came and went every hour. I just assumed procreation was the sport of choice on the Lower East Side. I had no idea that the children belonged to Joi.

I tried to convince myself that it was enough to watch her from a distance. But it wasn't. On the sixth night, I saw Joi turn the corner in front of Our Lady of Sorrows, and my body began to move of its own volition. I'd been avoiding her since the baths, and I fully expected some form of punishment.

Joi grinned and handed me one of her shopping bags. I wasn't prepared for it to weigh twenty pounds. I peeked inside and discovered it was loaded with soup cans.

"I guess you really love chicken noodle soup," I said.

"It's a crowd-pleaser," she replied.

"You're planning to feed a crowd?"

"Yep. Want to meet them?"

I didn't want to meet anyone. But I was caught in a cloud of jasmine and cocoa butter, and I couldn't muster the will to escape.

A kid opened the gates for us, and Joi thanked him by name. When she started downstairs, I hesitated. My every instinct told me not to follow her. But I did. Along the winding hall that led through the basement. Past the little chambers that appeared to be bedrooms. Into the old laundry room with its rusting machines and ratty old furniture. The entire place was infested with children, and they emerged from every crack and crevice to greet Joi.

I didn't ask who the kids were. It was obvious they were castoffs and rejects. Runaways and orphans. I could barely stand to look at them. I wanted to sprint right back up the stairs.

"Make yourself at home," said Joi.

"Joi?" A blond girl with heavily lined eyes tapped her on the shoulder, then pointed to one corner of the room. A boy with a mop of curly red hair was standing there, trying his best to blend in with the wall. I thought he might be twelve or so, but he was so painfully thin that it was impossible to tell.

"What's his name?" Joi asked.

"He won't say," the girl told her. "I found him hiding in the ladies' room at the Seward Park Library."

Joi walked over to the boy. "Can I call you Curly?" she asked.

He stared at her for a full thirty seconds before he finally nodded.

"Would you like some soup?"

I can't repeat the story Curly told Joi while I listened in. Even now—after everything I've seen. That night, I only heard half of it before I politely requested a name and an address. Then I was up the stairs and out the door. I broke into a SoHo loft and waited an hour for its owner to come home. Then I beat the man so badly that I wasn't sure if he'd live. I didn't know what else I could do. It wasn't rage that made me want to destroy him. I didn't do it to keep him from hurting another boy. I did it because he'd shown me that the world was even uglier than I ever imagined it could be. I thought I was angry. But I wasn't. I was absolutely terrified.

I wandered around for hours before finally returning to Pitt Street. One of the urchins led me downstairs. Curly was snuggled up in a sleeping bag on the couch in the laundry room. Joi rose from a chair when she saw the blood on my shirt.

"You found him, then." It was nothing but a simple statement of fact.

I wanted her to be pleased, and she probably was. The guy deserved everything he got, but beating him wasn't proof of my bravery. The bravest thing I did that night was go back to Joi's basement.

Last night in my dreams, I returned to that SoHo loft. But this time, the man I attacked was Lucian Mandel. I broke every bone in his body. I pummeled his face until it was a shapeless lump of meat. And yet through it all, he never stopped smiling. I woke up this morning with my fists still clenched. I stood at the door until it unlocked, and then I set out in search of him. If I'd found him, I would have killed him. For taking Joi away from Curly and leaving the rest of the Lost Boys alone. Because I remember what it feels like to lose the one person who always promised she'd be there. And for a few minutes this morning, that memory almost drove me mad.

A long, cold shower restored a bit of my sanity. But it will be best for everyone if Mandel stays away from me for a while. I'm not sure I could trust myself in his presence. When I see Joi join the breakfast line on the far side of the cafeteria, the urge to kill him returns. I have to remind myself that if Mandel dies, Joi might too. And nothing can ever happen to her. Until she's safe, I have a single mission.

Joi's hair has been woven into a braid, and her simple white shirt is tucked into a black pleated skirt. She's dressed like a schoolgirl, which makes me wonder if she even knows where she is. She's smart enough to have figured it out by now. But I see no sign of fear on her face. I'm still studying her when she spots me. And promptly looks away. The gesture says everything. I can think of a million reasons why Joi wouldn't want to speak to me. Who knows what she's heard—or what Mandel has told her.

I slip behind Joi at the breakfast line and slink into whispering range. She's ladling oatmeal into a bowl when she hears me say her name. Joi dumps the contents of her bowl back into the pot and marches off—leaving her tray behind.

"Looks like June's not into cripples."

I step out of the food line and give Gwendolyn a patronizing pat on the head.

"Keep nipping at me, Fang, and I'm going to bite back," I warn her with a smile. "Now scram."

"Is that any way to treat someone who's just brought you a present?" Gwendolyn hands me a course schedule. "It's from Mr. Mandel. You were still in a coma during registration, so he chose your classes for you."

"He's here today?" I growl. "You saw him?"

"Sure. He stopped by your room first thing this morning, but you weren't around. So he came up to my dorm thinking you might be there."

It's a lie. Mandel could have found me if he'd wanted to. I doubt he's forgotten that there's a chip in my head.

"So!" Gwendolyn chirps, flicking the sheet of paper that's still clenched in my hand. "Think you've got any classes with your old girlfriend this semester?"

Mandel told her who "June" really is. I knew he eventually would. But it's best if I keep playing dumb. "Don't flatter yourself, Gwendolyn. You were never my *girlfriend*. Just a blow-up doll with a pulse."

I enjoy watching the smirk slip off her face, and then I skim through my schedule.

Introduction to Industrial Espionage

Waste Management:
Polluting for Profit

Hidden Treasures:
Finding and Controlling the World's Natural Resources

Brazilian Jujitsu

Let Them Eat Cake:

Exploiting America's Obesity Epidemic

The Ultimate Insiders:

Mandel Alumni and the SEC

I fold the list and cram it into my back pocket. The movement sends pain shooting through my shoulder and down my arm. I guess I can count on failing jujitsu. "Don't you have somewhere else to be?" I ask Gwendolyn. "Hasn't Mandel given you another *assignment* yet?"

"Nothing has changed, Flick. You're still my project, and Mr. Mandel told me to give you a message. He thinks you should keep your distance from Mr. Martin for a while. You got his son kicked out of school."

My whole body hurts when I laugh.

"Oh yeah," Gwendolyn continues, and I notice her smirk has returned. "You might not want to skip lunch today. Caleb's planning to announce the pageant results."

My first two classes are now little more than a blur. I'm sitting in Hidden Treasures, and Joi just waltzed through the door with her chipmunk savior. There's an empty seat next to me—and another in the very last row. Joi never even glances in my direction. She heads to the back while the chipmunk fills the place beside me.

"Hello, Flick," the girl says as if she's known me for years. Even high-ranking Androids wait for the Dux to speak first. And this kid is a Ghost. A few days at the academy, and she'll start fading away.

"Hi," I respond, hoping the conversation will end there.

"I'm Violet," she says.

"Yes, I know," I tell her. I know more than her name. I already know everything about her. Joi must have adopted another urchin during her stay in the Incubation Suites. All I had to do was look at Violet's hope-filled eyes and guile-free grin to realize that she's not going to make it here. And I suddenly see the problem with Jude's brilliant advice. *Be who you want to be,* he said. Well, the person I'd *like* to be would save Violet. But that would be dangerous. I could die trying—and there's only one of me to sacrifice.

Maybe my brother the elf thinks all lives are equally valuable. But they're *not*. My life wasn't worth his. The world got a raw deal when Jude died trying to help me. If I did the same thing for Violet, how long would she last? No more than a month at the academy. Maybe a year if she made it back to the outside. But Joi might stand a chance if she's able to escape. And her life is worth ten of mine. Which is why I always tried so hard to keep her at a distance. I didn't want another person I loved sacrificing herself for my sake. And Joi's just the sort who would do it. She'd take a bullet for anyone. Even for someone as doomed as Violet.

Violet gasps when our instructor arrives. I recognize her as well. The woman used to be a talking head on one of the business channels my father liked to watch. A dark beauty who unnerved me because she never seemed to blink. She walks up to the blackboard and writes *Ms. Smith* in letters about a foot high. I think she's a bit worried that someone might slip up and use her real name.

"So . . . what will be the most valuable natural resource in the second quarter of the twenty-first century?" Ms. *Smith* asks the class.

An Android hand shoots up. "Oil."

"Perhaps," says Ms. Smith. "But I wouldn't bet on it."

"Rare earth metals?" another Android offers.

"Possibly. Though you'd have to fight the Chinese for them. Any other answers? Let's hear from some of the new students. Violet?"

"Gold," says the girl sitting next to me.

"Always good to have around. How about you, June. What do you think?"

"Clean, fresh water." It's the first time I've heard Joi's voice in four months. It's still smooth and low, with no hint of anxiety.

Ms. Smith nods. "I happen to agree with that answer. But why did you choose it?"

"Because you can live without oil or earth metals, but no one can live without water."

"But water is free, isn't it?" Ms. Smith probes, playing devil's advocate. "What's going to make it so valuable?"

"It's free *here*," Joi says. "For now. While there's still enough to go around. But in other parts of the world, it's already disappearing, and the little that's left tends to be polluted. When people's children start dying of cholera and typhoid, they'll do just about anything for clean water. I've seen it happen. There are companies all over the world trying to buy up freshwater supplies. And if I had the money, I'd buy one of *them*. In a few years, I'd be charging top dollar for something everyone in this country has been taking for granted."

"Excellent answer," Ms. Smith says. "I know a few Mandel alumni who'd be more than happy to back such a venture."

"Then tell them to give me a call." Even though she ends with a laugh, Joi's response sounds less like a joke than a dare.

I can't resist spinning around for a look. Because there's no way in hell that the girl I knew on the Lower East Side could have ever come up with an answer like that. But unless Joi has an evil twin, that is Pitt Street's former saint twirling her braid and pretending that I don't exist.

"Brilliant, isn't she?" I turn back to find Violet watching *me*.

"Yes." No point in denying it.

"She said you'd be surprised," Violet adds with a giggle.

Ms. Smith's collagen-plumped lips have been moving nonstop for almost an hour, but I haven't heard a single word of her lecture. Until now, I assumed there was only one possible explanation for Joi's bizarre appearance at the Mandel Academy. I thought she'd been brought here against her will. I figured she was meant to be Mandel's final test—the one that would prove whether my mutant gene had been activated.

But now I realize that there may be another possibility. Maybe Joi got a scholarship because Mandel wants to make her one of his monsters. Maybe he's not going to give me the choice to trade my life for hers. Maybe he's found another way to force me to watch the girl I love be destroyed.

I don't think Joi would let him turn her into a predator. But I've never been very good at predicting what other people might do. The last shock I suffered came damn close to killing me. I doubt I could take another. And Mandel probably knows it.

After class, I wait outside on the balcony for Joi. She's chatting with Ms. Smith in an obvious attempt to avoid me. But it's lunchtime, and I'll spend the whole goddamned hour here if need be. Then

I spot Caleb boarding one of the elevators, and I remember the pageant. I start hopping down the hall. I need to be in the cafeteria when the results are revealed.

"Ah, just in time," Caleb drones when he sees me limping toward the Wolves' table. "I was beginning to think you had something better to do."

"I knew he didn't." Gwendolyn pats the stool beside her. "That's why I saved him a spot."

"Thanks, Fang," I say. No one laughs.

The friction between us must have been obvious before, but our Beauty Pageant bets made it official. Caleb is observing us with his usual bored expression. But I know he's too smart to miss the opportunity that's unfolding in front of him. If Gwendolyn and I take each other out, Caleb stands to inherit our title—and the lifelong rewards that come with it.

"Before we get started, I have an announcement," I tell the Wolves. "It's a new semester, which means it's time to let bygones be bygones. You're all welcome back to the tower lounge. In fact, your presence there will be mandatory every evening from this point forward."

If Joi won't let me get close enough to protect her, I'll just have to keep Mandel's assassins locked up whenever I can.

"And do you concur?" Caleb asks my co-Dux.

"Whatever." Gwendolyn's eager to move on. "So who won the pageant?"

"Max," Caleb announces. No surprise there.

"And who lost?"

Caleb takes a leisurely bite of his sandwich before he answers. "Violet."

"What about June?" Gwendolyn demands.

"She came in third," Caleb says. "Seems Flick's vote canceled yours out."

"Flick doesn't really think she'll win," Gwendolyn sneers. I wonder if she's angry enough to do something stupid. "He voted for her because she used to be his girlfriend."

The Wolves all freeze as if the scene has been paused. Then Julian laughs.

"Is that *right*?" Caleb marvels. I can almost hear his mind whirring away.

That's when we see Joi. She's standing at the entrance to the cafeteria, surveying the room. Twelve Wolves stare back at her. I can only imagine what she must think of us. Joi takes her place in the lunch line and strikes up a conversation with one of the lowliest Androids.

"Friendly, ain't she?" Austin drawls with a mouthful of hamburger.

Leila's whole body vibrates when she snickers.

"Maybe she's campaigning for class president," Gwendolyn smirks. "I can't believe anyone actually voted for that loser to win the pageant. Who else besides her boyfriend thinks June's going to make it past ranking day?"

No one says a word.

"Did any of these morons vote for June?" Gwendolyn asks Caleb.

"Votes are confidential," Caleb says.

"No, they're not!"

"They are now," Caleb replies. "I run the pageant. I make the rules."

When Gwendolyn slaps him, he responds with a single, lizard-like blink and returns to eating his sandwich.

• • •

The Wolves' Den is packed. Gwendolyn and I are stationed at opposite ends of a long couch. There's an empty space between us, but no one dares occupy it. The bad vibes are so strong that they would probably prove fatal. Then Caleb arrives and plops himself right down.

"Well! Looks like the semester is off to an interesting start," he announces to no one in particular. But suddenly everyone is listening.

"Skip the theatrics, Caleb," Gwendolyn growls. "Just tell us what you want to say."

"Flick's girlfriend, June. Turns out, she's a human resources major."

"*Ex*-girlfriend," I correct him.

"Yes, I've noticed you two aren't on speaking terms. . . ."

"Get to the point, Caleb," Gwendolyn butts in.

"The point is that Mr. Mandel has put June in some very advanced classes. In fact, she and I have three together. I was surprised when I kept seeing her. I thought maybe she was being set up to fail. You know how our headmaster likes to throw a patsy into every Incubation Group."

No, Violet is the one who's been brought here to feed the Wolves. Just like Aubrey. I would have thought that much was obvious.

"Well? What's your take?" asks Gwendolyn.

"June's remarkable," Caleb says. "Quite possibly the finest human resources student aside from yours truly."

There's a bruise on Caleb's cheek where Gwendolyn slapped him at lunch. And yet he's determined to keep taunting her. Which means he's settled on a plan of action. *Gwendolyn kills Joi. Flick kills Gwendolyn. Mandel kills Flick. Caleb is king.* Seems like a long shot, but I guess it could work.

"Perhaps Flick could tell us a bit about his old love?" Caleb inquires.

I just grin and give him a wink. "F— off."

"I should have known you weren't the sort to kiss and tell. Does anyone here have any classes with June?" Caleb asks, addressing the other Wolves.

"I watched her spar in kickboxing," Austin offers reluctantly. "She's not bad."

"Not *bad*?" Caleb scoffs. "I hear she could have kicked the other girl's ass."

"But she didn't, did she?" Gwendolyn's on to him too. "I can see straight through you, Caleb. Which means I always know when you're full of shit. Someone go get that Max kid who just came up from the Suites. I think it's time for a second opinion."

A few minutes later, one of the lesser Wolves arrives with Max in tow. The kid is a born predator, but he's in the presence of superior beasts. He should be avoiding our eyes and kissing our asses. But the cocky little pup seems to think he could take on all twelve of us. Either we're not very impressive, or he's not very bright.

Gwendolyn picks up on the dolt's lack of deference. "Do you know who I am?" she asks him.

"You're the Dux," Max says. Then he gestures toward me. "So's that guy."

"You know the *word*, but do you know what it means?" Gwendolyn demands.

"It means you think you're in charge."

I nearly roll off the sofa I'm laughing so hard. Gwendolyn lurches forward, teeth bared, but Caleb sticks out an arm and holds her back. He's getting bolder by the minute.

"Before Gwendolyn eats you alive, we would like to know what you think of one of the students from your Incubation Group," Caleb says calmly. "June."

"I don't mess with her." That's unexpected. I hear genuine respect in Max's voice. "She's a witch."

"A *witch*?" I ask.

"She has special powers." I thought he was joking, but I see no trace of a grin.

"Interesting." Caleb sits back and crosses his legs. "And what form do these powers take?"

"Huh?"

"What sort of stuff does she do?" I interpret.

"You know that chick Flora?"

It takes me a moment to put a face to the name. Flora was in Joi's Incubation Group. A tall blonde with a Barbie-doll figure.

Even Caleb is struggling to make the connection. "Flora? One of the new students? What does she have to do with any of this?"

"She's hot, right?" Max responds as if we're all certain to agree. "So I thought Flora could be my girl for a while. But every time I tried to make my move, something crazy always happened."

"Like what?" Caleb asks.

"One time a bookcase fell on top of me. A couple days later, I was in the gym and one of those five-pound dumbbells slammed into the back of my head. Knocked me out cold for a few minutes. Stuff like that."

"And you think June was responsible? Did you actually see her do those things?"

"No. Sometimes she wasn't even in the room. But she told me she'd put a curse on me. She's not from here, you know. She's from someplace where the women are all trained to be witches." Max looks directly at me. "*He* knows it's true. He was watching when I fought June the other day. I almost killed her, right? Then my knee gave out all of a sudden and June got away."

"Why do you suppose June kept attacking you?" Caleb asks. "Did it have something to do with Flora? Was she protecting the girl for some reason?"

"No. June just said I needed to learn my place," Max says with a shrug. "She told me she owns this school and everyone in it."

Someone in the lounge starts laughing. It builds from a giggle into a full-blown howl. We all turn to see Ella, clutching her stomach as if her guts might spill out.

"What's so funny?" Caleb asks.

"Oh *shit!* " she wheezes. "I've heard *that* one before!"

I know where she heard it. It's almost exactly the same thing I told Ivan the first time I saved Aubrey.

While the Wolves watch Ella, I feel Gwendolyn's eyes on me. She knows too.

CHAPTER TWENTY-FOUR

THE BATTLE FOR THE THRONE

The Wolves of the Mandel Academy have hunkered down. A witch has conjured a powerful storm, and we're all waiting for the tempest to hit. Our instructors have taught us that destruction always brings opportunity. Fortunes were made in the wake of Hurricane Katrina. Careers were built on the wreckage of the World Trade Center. And now the Wolves are watching the skies and scheming. If the academy's current order collapses, every one of the twelve best students intends to survive—and emerge from the rubble on top.

In the past four days, the Wolves have talked about nothing but Joi. And Joi talks to everyone but us. Whenever I see her, she's always chatting with someone new. Androids in the lunchroom. Ghosts between classes. Joi refuses to respect the boundaries between the academy's three groups. But every time *I* try to speak to her, she bolts before I get close. My injured leg is slowly healing, but I'm still not quick enough to catch her. All I can do is watch from a distance as she flouts every unwritten rule. The other students from her Incubation Group are almost as bold. They don't seem to understand that their lives are at stake. Violet's already flunking all six of her classes—but she's still as chipper as the day we met. Flora, like countless pretty newbies before her, has had the misfortune to catch Austin's eye. Yesterday, she responded to his crude advances with a swift, perfectly aimed kick to the groin. Orson and Hugo were on the scene within seconds. The three newbies never uttered a word, but the warning they delivered was loud and clear. If Austin messed with one of them, he'd have to answer to the rest.

Mandel knew that something strange was going on in the Suites. Whatever happened down there is now happening here. No one taught Joi's Incubation Group how to behave once they got upstairs. Mandel must be watching, but so far he's done nothing. I haven't seen him, and I don't think Gwendolyn has either. No orders have been issued, but the Wolves are predicting a bloodbath on rankings day.

The big question is what's going to happen to our resident witch. Joi brought this chaos upon the academy. But there's no longer any doubt of her gifts. She possesses the mind of a brilliant criminal, and she's risen to first place in five of her classes. Gwendolyn claims Caleb let Joi take the lead in the three courses they share. I'm not so sure. Joi's given me a real run for my money in Hidden Treasures. Between the two of us, we've made hypothetical billions on freshwater, rain forest lumber, and arctic oil. I never expected to find myself in competition with a girl who used to leave a receipt whenever she shoplifted a can of soup. But I suppose I don't know much about Joi. In fact, it's possible that I never really knew her at all.

Every evening in the Wolves' Den, Caleb feeds the pack a slab of fresh gossip. Some of the rumors beggar belief. Caleb claims Joi was trained as a sniper and once worked as a nurse on an organ farm. But a few of Caleb's other rumors are harder to ignore. He says she's the daughter of a man who ran a detention center for women during the Bosnian War—a man whose crimes against humanity would put those of the most accomplished Mandel alumni to shame. There might be some truth to that tale. The academy's profile said Joi grew up in Bosnia. She's the right age to have been born during the bloody Yugoslav Wars over there. And Mandel seems to believe that she's the daughter of a war criminal. So maybe Caleb is right about Joi's father. But I have a hunch Caleb has been pulling the rest of his "research" right out of his ass.

I'll give credit where it's due, though. Caleb has certainly been handling this whole affair with remarkable skill. Gwendolyn knows he's making a play for the Dux title. But that doesn't keep her from listening to his stories with as much interest as the rest of us. The "witch" has become a serious threat. Gwendolyn shouldn't have told the Wolves about my history with Joi. It made her look desperate—and Joi seem more fascinating. And now that Caleb's gone rogue, everyone can see that Gwendolyn's in trouble. She's been Mandel's favorite girl for two full years, but he hasn't stepped in to support her this time. No one knows what happens when a Dux falls from grace. No one but Gwendolyn and me. We're the only ones who've had a glimpse of the headmaster's morgue.

The stress is starting to show. Gwendolyn's hair has lost its luster and her once porcelain skin looks chalky. The serene facade has crumbled. She barks, snaps, and growls like a rabid animal. I know exactly how she feels. And I know just how dangerous she can be. When the time comes, she'll go straight for Joi's jugular. But no blood can be shed before the month-long Immunity Phase is over. There are still three weeks until ranking day. I'm just hoping that's enough time for my arm and leg to heal properly. Right now, I don't have the strength to save anyone.

It's lunchtime, and I'm enduring another post-coma checkup. The doctor has already lectured me for refusing to wear my arm sling and forbidden me to participate in Brazilian Jujitsu. As if I'm crazy enough to take the mat with only two of my limbs fully functional. Now he's demonstrating a series of rehab exercises that he must have learned while working at Abu Ghraib. Each one is more excruciating than the last. It's pretty clear that I'm still in terrible shape. And I find it a bit troubling that the man in charge of fixing me seems to get his jollies from watching me suffer. The appointment was only supposed to last thirty minutes, but he's kept me here for two hours—straight through lunch and fourth period. When a nurse tells him he's wanted in the lab, I almost shed tears of relief.

I limp to the elevator and press the button for the ninth floor. Fifth period is ten minutes away. I thought I'd be free before lunch finished, and I left my Let Them Eat Cake homework upstairs in the Wolves' Den. There are fat people out there just waiting to be exploited, and I wouldn't want to let them down, so I hobble as quickly as possible up the stairs to the tower. Halfway to the top, I hear someone behind me. I assume it's my darling Gwendolyn, so I don't bother looking back. I won't give her the satisfaction of seeing the pain on my face.

"Flick!" When I finally turn around, I find Ella slinking up the stairs. She's wearing tight black pants and a formfitting black sweater. Her close-cropped hair and ballet flats complete a look that's cat burglar chic.

"Skipping class or practicing for your next jewel heist?" I ask, wiping my forehead with the sleeve of my shirt.

"Why weren't you at lunch today?" Ella demands tersely.

I don't know why I answer. "Doctor's appointment."

"Did you tell Gwendolyn about it?"

I almost advise Ella to mind her own business, but I'm curious to find out why she's gone all Nancy Drew on me. "I doubt I mentioned it, but Gwendolyn has other sources. Why?"

"She and Austin were up here in the lounge during lunch. *Together.*" The significance of the last word is crystal clear. "I heard them."

"Are you trying to make me jealous?" I ask with a laugh.

Ella opens her ever-present notebook and scribbles a message onto a blank sheet. *It was payment.*

I grab the pen. *Play along.*

"So you're looking for a way to get in good with the Dux?" I announce for the listening devices. "Well, if Gwendolyn's getting some on the side, I'm happy to have a little too." I grab Ella by the arm and lead her out to the roof.

Warm air washes over us. Nine stories below, the trees in City Hall Park are blooming, and I catch the faint scent of their fragrance on the breeze. But it's hard to revel in the glories of spring when the skyscrapers of Manhattan's financial district are looming over us like an army of *Matrix* agents in black suits and mirrored shades.

"Wow," Ella says as she marvels at the view. "Does everyone in the top twelve know about this?"

"No. Just me and Gwendolyn. This is the only part of the academy that isn't bugged."

"And who told you that?" she asks with one eyebrow arched. Then she wraps herself around me and whispers in my ear. "You're more trusting than I am. Make it look like you're getting some, and I'll talk."

I push her back against the brick wall of the tower and take her head in my hands. Anyone watching would think we were kissing. "You said Gwendolyn was *paying* for something," I say, keeping my voice low. "What does she want Austin to do?"

"She wants him to take out your girl. They're going to kill June."

I don't even ask how Ella knew that I'd give a damn. "Where? When?"

"Today. After sixth period. Austin has kickboxing with June. They're going to ambush her in the gym."

"They can't! The Immunity Phase isn't over!"

"Shhh." Ella shakes her head. "You think that matters to Gwendolyn? Caleb's convinced her she can't wait any longer."

"Yeah, lizard boy's going for the gold. Which makes me wonder—what's *your* angle, Ella? Last I checked, you hated my guts. Why are you so happy to help me all of a sudden?"

Ella leans to one side. Her eyes take another tour of the roof before they return to meet mine. Her voice is so quiet that I have to read her lips. "Remember that catwalk in the Incubation Suites? How you could tell when someone was watching? Well, once you got locked up, no one was all that interested in spying on the rest of us. Aubrey didn't talk, and Ivan was psycho. But Felix and I got to be *friends*. For some reason, he thought you were a good guy. I figured he just had a crush. Then Felix ended up dead, and I started hoping he'd been right about you. The day it all happened, I tried to tell you that he hadn't jumped. But Gwendolyn butted in, and it freaked me out. I got to thinking that she might have had something to do with Felix's death. Her and that freak Mandel. The guy thinks he knows everything. He doesn't know shit."

"What do you mean?"

Ella looks down at her hands. The acrylic claws and diamond rings may be gone, but I bet she remembers exactly what it feels like to handle a gun. "Mandel told you guys that I killed my uncle so I could take over his drug business. Truth is, I was trying to put the bastard *out* of business. He had my little cousin selling the stuff at her grade school. You ever seen a twelve-year-old on crack?"

"No," I admit.

"Lucky you."

The bell rings in the classrooms downstairs. It feels like a buzzer on a quiz show. The time has come for my final answer. If I make the right choice, Joi gets another day at the Mandel Academy. If I fail, her corpse ends up in Mandel's collection. I have no reason to trust Ella. But then again, I've never heard another Wolf laugh like she did on our first day in the Suites.

"You really want to help?" I whisper.

"I've got fifth period with June," Ella says. "I can warn her. I just wanted to check with you first."

"Don't just warn her. Tell her to skip kickboxing. Gwendolyn may look like Little Bo Peep, but she's as vicious as Lizzie Borden. She's the one who cut Ivan's head off. And before she got to the academy, she was locked up in an insane asylum for killing eight men."

"*Excuse* me?"

"The cops knew it was her because she bit all the bodies."

"*Damn.*" Ella whistles softly. "I better get my ass down to class."

She hurries out, and I collapse onto a chaise in the Wolves' Den. I couldn't make it downstairs right now if I tried. My head's throbbing. My arm and leg feel like they're about to drop off. I should never have underestimated Gwendolyn. She knows if she kills Joi now, there's no way I can retaliate immediately. Especially if Gwendolyn keeps "paying" Austin to be her bodyguard. But there's one thing no one anticipated. Now I have an ally too. And Ella is strong. She's one of the best, and she's on my side. I don't know why the thought gives me such hope. My last ally ended up donating his organs to Mandel's research. Maybe Ella is playing me. But if she isn't, Mandel has made a rare mistake. He's let a mole burrow into the Wolves' Den.

I'm outside Joi and Ella's classroom when the bell announces the end of fifth period. Joi sails through the door.

"I've got it under control," she says in a singsong manner as she passes by.

Ella is right behind her. "It's *not* under control," she whispers. "June's just as crazy as Gwendolyn. She's stirring up some serious trouble."

"What happened?"

"When I told her what Gwendolyn has planned, June stood up and invited everyone in the class to come to the gym at the end of sixth period. She asked them all to wait outside. She's going to whistle when there's something to see."

"You're f—ing kidding me! Does she really think they'll keep Gwendolyn from ripping her apart?" This is exactly what I worried would happen. Joi can pretend to be a bad guy. She can be the top student in all of her classes. But this is real. The kids she invited all know that. They're not going to get in the way.

Ella shrugs helplessly. "What do you think we should we do?"

"You've done enough already," I tell her. "You better stay off Gwendolyn's radar if you ever want to get out of here alive. Let me handle this now."

"Are you sure you can save June on your own?" Ella asks.

"No," I admit.

Sixth period ends, and I slip inside the gym. It's empty. The kickboxing-class students have all disappeared into the locker rooms. I hobble toward the one marked LADIES. There are two girls in their underwear and one wearing nothing at all. They cover themselves up, but no one squeals or shouts. The Dux can go wherever he likes.

Joi is sitting on a bench like she's waiting for the subway to arrive. She hasn't changed out of her sweats.

"You've got to get out of here!"

It's the first time Joi has really looked at me since the fight in the Incubation Suites. I can tell she knows what I've done since I got here. And she's livid. "You want me to run?" she asks politely. "Is there somewhere you'd like me to go?"

"Goddamn it, listen for once! I know you're pissed off at me, but I'm trying to help you! You can't win against Gwendolyn!"

"Why?" Those big amber eyes dare me to answer.

"Because she'll do whatever it takes to win, Joi. You *won't*. She'll kill you. People *die* in this place!"

The more frustrated I get, the calmer Joi seems. "You think I haven't figured that out?"

"I watched you in the Suites. You wouldn't even fight Max! Judo won't do you any good. Gwendolyn will be waiting for you to make a mistake. Then she'll go in for the kill."

"Do you know how I learned judo?" Joi asks.

"*What?* We don't have time—"

"I learned it from a UN peacekeeper who was stationed at a refugee camp in Bosnia. Judo helped me get out of *there* in one piece, so it should serve me fine while I'm *here*."

"Gwendolyn is Dux for a reason. . . ."

"That's right. She's Dux because you're all scared of her. I'm not. And if you think I don't know how to win, then you don't know me at all."

Joi stands and strides toward the locker room exit. The three other girls have vanished. I'm limping after her as fast as I can. The door swings open, and I see someone grab her. When I burst into the gym, I find Gwendolyn, Austin, and Joi. Austin has one of Joi's arms twisted behind her back.

The scene is reflected four times on the room's mirrored walls. Even if I had time to study every angle, I don't think I could come up with any suitable plan of attack. Austin's a Terminator with a Texan drawl. He may be sporting his usual shit-eating grin, but I know his brain has already made a map of my weaknesses. I consider targeting Gwendolyn instead. The Queen of the Wolves hasn't even bothered to dress for a fight. But I'm not sure my battered body would last one round with an experienced assassin—even if she is wearing a dress and high heels.

"Isn't this *adorable*?" Gwendolyn cries out as if a puppy just bounded into the room. "It's Flick the gimp to the rescue!"

"Want me to toss him in one of the lockers?" Austin drawls.

"No," Gwendolyn says. "If he promises to be a good boy, he might as well stay and watch."

The gym doors burst open. "Let the girl go, Austin!" *Great.* Ella has just blown her cover.

Austin chuckles and Gwendolyn rolls her eyes. "I *told* Mandel she didn't belong in the top twelve. Just give me a second to deal with her."

"Don't bother," Joi says calmly. "I didn't call for backup. I don't want any help."

"Joi, you *can't*. . . ." I try once more.

"I'm serious." And she is. No doubt about it. She isn't even struggling to break Austin's grip. "Stay out of this." Joi offers her free hand to Gwendolyn as though she's eager to make a new friend. "Hi there. I'm Joey. Spelled *J-o-i*."

Gwendolyn ignores the hand, and Joi lets it drop. "What happened to *June*?"

"I gave it a shot. Never felt right. So I went back to my old name. You're Gwendolyn."

"I'm the Dux."

"One of them," Joi points out. "So you want to talk to me?"

"We're going to do a lot more than talk," Gwendolyn informs her.

"Oh, good! I hope you don't mind: I invited a few friends." Joi whistles, and a throng of Androids and Ghosts streams in from the hall. I'm almost embarrassed for her.

"You have no idea how things work around here, do you?" The contempt on Gwendolyn's face makes her look nauseous. "Your little *friends* are a bunch of losers."

"Losers?" Joi's brow furrows. "I'm confused, Gwendolyn. If they're *losers* and you're their leader, what does that make you? Queen of the Losers?"

"You're almost as funny as Flick," Gwendolyn snips. "It doesn't matter what you call them. They're not going to help you."

"I certainly *hope* not," Joi replies. "I made it pretty clear that this is my battle, not theirs. I heard you'd scheduled a showdown, and I figured the other students might find it entertaining. But it looks like you're planning to send everyone home disappointed. That's a cute little outfit you have on, but I thought this was going to be a fight, not a fashion show."

"The Dux doesn't get her hands dirty," Gwendolyn explains. "But don't worry. Everyone but you is going to have a great time. Especially Austin."

"Oh, I get it!" Joi exclaims, as if it all suddenly makes sense to her. "You're going to have *Austin* kill me! Well, I guess every school has its own rules—but isn't the Dux expected to fight her own battles? I mean, you're supposed to be the most powerful student here, right? Shouldn't you be able to win without anyone's help? It really doesn't say much for the Mandel Academy if its Dux trades sex for favors because she's too scared to fight for herself." Joi tilts her head back and gives Austin an upside-down wink. "I'm right, aren't I? You're only here because Gwendolyn's been screwing you."

I've been waiting for the perfect moment to jump in. I wouldn't last long, but it might give Joi enough time to escape. Then there's a snicker somewhere in the crowd. And that single snicker lights a fuse. I can hear the flame crackling as it slowly winds its way toward a powder keg big enough to blow a hole in the school. I'm starting to think that Joi might actually know what she's doing.

"Let her go, Austin," Gwendolyn demands as she kicks off her heels. "Keep the others back. I'll take over from here."

Joi just scored a minor victory, but I hope she hasn't misjudged her opponent. She doesn't know she's facing a girl who killed a gorilla and sliced off his head. She'll need more than wisecracks to win this battle.

"Tell me when you're ready to make a move," Ella whispers to me.

"That's much better," Joi says. "But I'm afraid I can't fight you, Gwendolyn."

"Not yet," I tell Ella. The fuse remains lit, and its spark is still crawling toward the powder keg.

"You don't have a choice," Gwendolyn snarls at Joi.

"I honestly wish I could kick your fancy little ass, but you're not what I'd call a worthy opponent."

Gwendolyn attacks. Her nails scrape four red grooves in Joi's neck before Joi catches Gwendolyn's arm and flips the girl over her shoulder. The Mandel Academy's picture-perfect leader lands in a sloppy pile on the mat. The image is now stored in every spectator's mind. No matter what happens, it can never be deleted.

The fight isn't over. At this point, there's no telling who the winner will be. But before that flip, I don't think there was a kid in the room who believed Joi stood a chance. The other students arrived wearing the blank expressions I saw on their faces the day Felix died. They know how the Mandel system works—and they know better than to expect any surprises. Here at the academy, the strong rise to the top and the weak fall to the bottom. And the Dux title is only given to the strongest of all. So they were expecting to watch Gwendolyn win. That flip told them things might be different this time.

"You know this school is pretty f—ed up," Joi tells the mesmerized crowd while Gwendolyn struggles to rise. Joi hasn't even broken a sweat. "Didn't you guys ever *talk* to each other before I got here? I couldn't find a single person who knows exactly what's going on. The most any of you could give me was a clue or two. So I spent the past week putting all the pieces together. And one thing is clear. This poor girl has no business being Dux. Did you sleep with Mandel in exchange for the title, Gwennie?"

Gwendolyn is back on her feet—just in time for the accusation to hit her with more force than a right hook. "I earned it!"

Joi scratches her chin as if pondering a riddle. "But that doesn't make any sense. You'd have to be the best of the best to *earn* the title, and I've heard you're a little unhinged. Mandel found you in a loony bin, didn't he?"

Gwendolyn wheels around and glares at me. "You told her!"

"So it's true?" Joi's voice is dripping with pity. "You've been hiding the secret all this time? While the rest of us have had our dirty laundry dragged out for public inspection? Oh, *Gwendolyn*. Don't you know that mental illness is nothing to be ashamed of?"

"I'm not insane!" Gwendolyn's shriek only proves Joi's point.

"I feel so sorry for you." Joi turns her back on the girl and addresses the crowd. "Is this the kind of person you want as your leader? Someone who was probably painting the walls with her own poo back at the funny farm?"

Gwendolyn lunges at Joi from behind. This time she ends up flat on her back with a hunk of Joi's hair in her hand. Her dress has flown up over her head, exposing a pair of pink panties. A female Android starts to giggle, and the laughter spreads through the crowd. The fuse finally detonates the powder keg and the whole school rocks with the explosion.

"Look at her! She's pathetic!" Joi shouts. "This is your Dux? The one who just called you all *losers*? Has she earned your allegiance? Does she deserve your respect?"

"Austin!" squeals Gwendolyn.

"Yes, *Austin*." Joi holds up a single finger, and the laughter in the room dies down. Flames flicker in her amber eyes, and her black curls seem to writhe like serpents. She's no longer a schoolgirl. She's a goddess. "I think it's time for you to make a choice."

Everyone sees Austin step back—away from Gwendolyn and into the crowd.

"I'd take that as a vote of no confidence. Wouldn't you?" Joi inquires, staring down at the girl on the floor.

Gwendolyn doesn't answer. She can't seem to catch her breath.

Joi turns back to the crowd. "You gave her power. You can take it away. It's your choice. What do you say?"

"Take it away," says an Android.

"I'm sorry, what was that?" Joi asks. "I couldn't hear you."

"Take it away!" shouts another. The rest join in, and the chant grows until Joi raises her hand.

"I guess everyone agrees that the Dux needs some time off. So if there aren't any objections, I'll assume her duties starting today. Are there any objections?" No one speaks up. "Austin? How about you?"

"Nope," Austin says, slipping over to the winning side. "You've got my vote."

"Then I am honored to accept the position. I know I'm new to this school, so I'm going to let my co-Dux keep his title for now. Austin, why don't you help Gwendolyn back to her room. The poor little creature looks like she's about to have a seizure."

Austin plucks Gwendolyn off the floor. She's limp in his arms. There's not a bruise on her body, yet her defeat is complete. And a comeback would be out of the question. Gwendolyn is nothing more than a joke now.

"Ella, would you mind showing everyone to the door?" Joi asks.

"Not at all," Ella replies like she's been Joi's loyal lieutenant all along. "Okay, guys! Show's over!"

There's no need to shepherd the Androids and Ghosts through the gym door. They're all rushing out to spread the news.

I'm the only one left behind. The door closes, and Joi fixes her amber eyes on me, like a tiger glancing up from a kill. I want to rush to her and grab hold of her and tell her how goddamned relieved I am. That she's alive. That she'll finally look at me. But it feels too dangerous to approach her right now. One sudden movement might break the spell.

"How did you know you could beat her?"

"She was Queen of the Losers," Joi says. "She shouldn't have forgotten who gave her the crown."

"How did you know they'd just hand it to you?"

"I can see how this place really works," Joi replies. "And in the kingdom of the blind, the one-eyed girl gets to be queen." She takes my hand and leads me through the girls' locker room to the shower stalls. She turns on the hot water in four of them, waits until the room is fogged with steam, and then pulls me into the fifth stall.

"Joi . . ."

"Shut up," she says as she unbuttons my shirt. "I didn't bring you here for a heart-to-heart. How do I get this thing off without hurting you?"

"Why are you here?"

"Because you never said goodbye."

CHAPTER TWENTY-FIVE

IN THE KINGDOM OF THE BLIND

I'm lost.

"Look around," Joi ordered. "Tell me what you see."

It was the morning after her triumph, and I was too exhausted to see anything. After we'd left the showers, I tried to follow Joi to her dorm. I wanted to stay overnight to defend her, but she beat me back and locked me out. In the darkness after curfew, I sat on the floor by my door, listening for movement outside on the balcony. I knew there was a chance that Mandel would send someone to dispose of Joi. I imagined finding her room empty the next morning. I envisioned her stripped bed—and then her lifeless body laid out on an autopsy table.

The moment my door unlocked, I headed straight for her dorm. Her things were still there, but Joi was not. I searched for almost twenty minutes before I found her, standing on the sixth-floor balcony, peering into the cafeteria. Her back was still facing me when she spoke.

"How did you know it was me?" I asked.

"The limp," she replied, her eyes still scanning the cafeteria. "What do you see in there?"

The way Joi said it, I assumed something important had changed. So I studied the scene and realized Gwendolyn was missing. Otherwise, it was no different from any other morning. The Wolves occupied two tables in front of the unlit rankings screen. The Androids were scattered randomly around the large room, most with their heads buried in books. It was too early in the semester to officially label the Ghosts, but I already knew which of the students were likely to disappear.

Joi's question worried me. She'd been out of the Suites for almost a week, and she still didn't know what I'd figured out after a few hours upstairs. She'd vanquished Gwendolyn and anointed herself Dux, but even if the title had been official, Joi didn't have what it took to keep the crown. I wanted to tell her everything, but I couldn't. Not there—with everyone watching and at least one person listening.

"There are three groups here." I pointed to the Wolves' tables. "Those are the top twelve students—the elite. They run the place. Numbers thirteen through fifty are what I call Androids. They're smart, but not quite smart enough. The bottom six students are Ghosts. They don't have what it takes to survive. They'll be *expelled* before the semester ends."

I carefully enunciated each syllable of the word *expelled* so she'd know exactly what it meant.

"Sounds brutal," Joi said.

"Our headmaster believes in the law of the jungle."

"That's what you see here?" she asked. "A jungle?"

Joi took a step forward, into the cafeteria. Someone must have been waiting for her to make her entrance because the moment Joi crossed the threshold, a bright light enveloped her as if she'd activated an invisible trip wire. I stumbled forward, blinking furiously, certain she'd fallen into a trap. But when my eyes adjusted, I could see she was safe. Safer than I could have ever imagined. The screen was lit. Mandel had announced new rankings three weeks ahead of schedule. As far as I could tell, he'd made only one change to the list. There were still two Duxes—Joi and me. Gwendolyn's name wasn't up there at all.

Every student in the cafeteria was staring at Joi. She accepted their lack of applause with a grin and a humble bow. Then she continued her foray across the room. Whatever plans she'd made, the news hadn't changed them. As Joi approached their table, the elite Wolves slid apart, offering her Gwendolyn's old spot in the center. She walked right past them, through the light cast by the rankings screen. Then she took a seat at an Android table.

I hurried to join her.

"You're a Dux now," I whispered. "You need to sit with the top students."

"Says who?" Joi responded.

"You're going to have to keep an eye on them," I told her. "They're dangerous."

"Which makes them predictable. Look, Flick, yesterday was great, but I'm not in the market for a boyfriend or a bodyguard. I've got work to do. If you want to hang around, that's fine by me. But please don't interfere."

I sat down, but it felt like I'd been knocked off my feet.

"Hey you!" Joi called out cheerfully to a girl sitting at the end of the table. "Come over and say hi."

The girl slid down into the seat across from us. I couldn't introduce her because I'd never bothered to learn her name. But I did feel a bit sorry for her. She was quivering like a chambermaid who'd been hauled before a new mistress.

"I'm Joi. This is Flick. What's your name?"

"Lily." She answered reluctantly, as though even her name might cause offense.

"Nice to meet you, Lily. How long have you been here?"

Nice to meet you?!

"This is my third semester."

"What's your major?"

"Technology."

Joi glanced up at the rankings. "You're number thirty-two. Why so low?"

The girl hesitated.

"You can tell me," Joi assured her.

"My instructors say I'm too meek. I don't mind stealing from big corporations, but I don't like robbing the little guys."

"And what are you good at?"

"My specialty is hacking Facebook. I have their source code."

"Impressive," Joi said. "Thanks for the chat. I'll let you get back to your breakfast. Mind asking the guy at the end of the table to slide over here for a moment?"

"Are you planning to interview everyone?" I asked.

"Absolutely," Joi replied. "How am I supposed to lead people I don't know?"

"Then you really should start with them," I said, pointing to the Wolves' table.

"Are you kidding?" Joi snorted. "They're the least interesting people here."

I grabbed her and pulled her closer until I could whisper in her ear. "You can't save all the outcasts."

When I released her, she was furious. "Is that what you think I'm trying to do?"

The Wolves were watching as I rose from my stool. I could feel their eyes follow me across the cafeteria. I made it through the door and around the corner. Only when I was out of sight did I start to stagger. My father would never be punished. My brother would not be avenged. I'd hoped I'd be able to destroy the academy. But when Joi arrived, I'd abandoned that mission too. I had given up everything to save a girl with no interest in a boyfriend or a bodyguard. A girl who no longer had any interest in me.

I reached my room, and when I closed the door, a shadow slipped out of the bathroom. Gwendolyn wore a plain black dress with long sleeves. Without makeup, her pale face was the grayish white of a wraith.

"Here for my head?" I asked as I lay down on my bed. At that point, I might have let her take it.

"Mr. Mandel gave her my title, didn't he?" Gwendolyn's entire body was twitching. She tried crossing her arms, but she couldn't hide it.

"You broke the rules, Gwendolyn," I explained with a sigh. "You attacked Joi before the Immunity Phase was over. Joi won the fight, and she earned the Dux title."

"*Earned* it?" Gwendolyn seethed. "Do you have any idea what I've had to do to stay Dux?"

"Yes," I reminded her. "You did it to me."

A tremor seemed to shake Gwendolyn. Her body swayed from one side to the other, as if she were experiencing her own private earthquake. "You were the least of it. Remember that field trip they sent me on right before you ended up in a coma?"

I remembered the folder I saw her open in Mr. Martin's office. There was a picture of a man. And a little Baggie with two white tablets inside.

"Yeah. What did you do? Drug some guy?"

"And let them take pictures. Of me with some fifty-year-old nerd who kept rambling on about synapses and neurotoxins the whole time."

I suddenly felt sick. "Jesus, Gwendolyn."

She laughed at my squeamishness. "That wasn't my first field trip either. It wasn't even my *tenth*. I *earned* my title. I deserved it. What has *she* ever done?"

"You knew how the game worked, Gwendolyn. You knew from the start that Mandel doesn't play fair."

"Don't blame this on Mr. Mandel. This isn't *his* fault. It's *yours*. That girl wouldn't be here at the academy if it weren't for you."

"And I have a feeling Joi's just as angry about that as you are."

"Oh, *please*. The little mutt's still in love with you. She kept you in the locker room showers for a while, didn't she? Well, Mr. Mandel may have given Joi my title, but I'm not going to let her have you too. I'm going to tell her everything."

I shrugged. "Go right ahead. She already knows."

Gwendolyn knelt down by my bed and put a trembling hand on my chest. "She knows we were a couple. But the devil's always in the details, isn't it? I'm going to tell her things that she'll never be able to get out of her head. I'll even draw a few pictures if I have to. But from now on, every time she looks at you, she's going to see the two of us together."

I picked up her hand and threw it back at her. "I see defeat hasn't changed you. You're still a real bitch, Gwendolyn."

"Defeat? Who said the game's over? Mr. Mandel understands that I haven't been myself lately. He's giving me another chance."

"Is that what he told you?"

"No, but he had the doctors increase my medication."

"Medication? You never told me that you're on medication. Is it for . . ."

"I'm not crazy!" Gwendolyn was shaking so hard that I reached out to steady her. "The pills just help me focus. So think of what I'll be able to do now that they're giving me *three* a day instead of just one."

I remembered my father's warning. "I think you should stop taking them. I've never seen anyone shake like this before." The words were out of my mouth before I realized they weren't true. I'd seen Leila shake too.

"Save your advice, Flick."

"I'm serious, Gwendolyn. A bunch of pills aren't going to help you take back the title."

Her lips were so dry that they cracked when she smiled. "Maybe. But if it ever looks like I'm going to lose, you better bet I'll make sure that nobody else gets to win."

CHAPTER TWENTY-SIX

BURNING DOWN THE HOUSE

Ten hours later, Gwendolyn made good on her promise. She marched into the cafeteria at dinnertime and took a seat across from Joi at one of the Android tables. I don't know exactly what Gwendolyn told her, but I know Joi never said a word. A minute after Gwendolyn's lips started moving, Joi's eyes left her guest and found me on the other side of the dining hall. There was no expression on her face. She just stared straight at me until Gwendolyn had finished what she'd come to say. Then Joi walked out, leaving a tray full of food behind on the table.

That was two and a half weeks ago. I waited as long as I could for Joi's anger to cool. But the Immunity Phase ends in three days, on the first of June. Then the slaughter will commence, and I need to make sure she's prepared for the horrors to come. She'll finally look at me again. Sometimes we even share the same sofa in the Wolves' Den. Joi's quizzed me about the workings of the academy, but it's the only subject she'll ever discuss. I can't utter a word of warning out loud—and Joi refuses to join me on the roof where we could speak in private. I write long, detailed notes instead. She reads my letters, rips them to shreds, and never replies.

Joi told me she was here because I never said goodbye. Maybe she came looking for me. Maybe she once wanted to save me. But now she's determined to punish me.

The evening after she was named Dux, Joi paid her first visit to the Wolves' Den. I'd just finished making sure that every beast was accounted for when she made her grand entrance. It was all the more remarkable because I don't think anyone actually saw her arrive. The chatter in the lounge just faded away. One by one, the Wolves discovered her sitting among us.

I don't know where she got her hands on a pair of tight jeans. Or a T-shirt that said *Don't Mess with Texas*. Surrounded by sleek, designer-clad Wolves, Joi stuck out like a punk at a polo match. But when I scanned the room, the rest of us looked like little kids dressed up in their parents' clothes. And I could see I wasn't the only one who suddenly felt ridiculous. It was one of Joi's most brilliant moves.

"Hiya," Joi said.

No one replied. It didn't seem to bother her, but I spoke up anyway. "Welcome to the lounge."

"Thanks, Flick. Nice to know one of you has some manners." If she hadn't ended the sentence with a laugh, it would have sounded like chiding. "Cool clubhouse you got here. It's like one of those sets down there in the Incubation Suites, doncha think? Remember those? When you first get there, all the rooms feel like cages.

Then Mandel puts up those weird sets and you think you'll never get used to them. But the longer you're down there, the more normal they seem."

The observation was met with another silence that Joi had to break.

"So which of you has been here the longest?" she asked.

Everyone looked at Caleb, who took his time answering. Although his plan to seize power had failed, he didn't seem ready to admit defeat. "I have. This is my seventh semester."

"You're human resources. Am I right, Caleb?"

His nostrils flared briefly at the mention of his name. "I'm the top student in human resources, that is correct."

"Not anymore," Joi replied. "But you're still qualified to answer my next question. Since you've been at the Mandel Academy, how many people have been named Dux in their first week at the school?"

He didn't want to say it. "None."

Joi nodded. "Which means we're all in uncharted territory now. So I think it's a good idea to start mapping out some rules. You may have noticed that I've been interviewing the lower-ranking students. As Dux, it's my job to assess the student body. And I want to make one thing *absolutely* clear." She slid to the edge of her seat and leaned forward with her hands on her knees. "Until I'm finished, you're all going to keep your grubby little fingers *off* those bodies. Nobody gets touched till I say so."

Caleb's eyes opened and shut in a lazy, lizard-like blink. "Has Mr. Mandel approved this study of yours?" he asked.

"He made me Dux, didn't he?" Joi responded. "I think I'll take that as a sign of his approval. Unless you disagree. Do you?"

"No," Caleb demurred.

"Excellent. Second, I want to be kept up to date on all of your school projects. In other words, I would like to see your homework every evening before you leave this lounge."

"That's a rather unusual request, June—" Caleb started.

"*Joi,*" she corrected him. "Like I said, we're in uncharted territory. Everything is going to feel a bit strange at first."

"Does your co-Dux support these new measures?"

"Absolutely," I chimed in, as if I'd been informed far in advance. It was the first time I'd heard about any of it.

"So let's get started." Joi's eyes fell on Leila. She rose from her chair and positioned herself directly behind the girl. "What's that you're working on?" she asked, bending over the couch to have a peek at the screen of Leila's computer. "Do you have Internet access?"

Leila grimaced like she'd been surprised with an enema. No one—not even Julian—had ever been allowed to look at her screen. "Only in class. I'm working offline right now. Developing malware. This targets online bank accounts. It skims a fraction of a cent off each transaction that's made. But over time, we're talking billions of transactions."

"Fascinating. How much would you get paid for developing something like that?"

"I wouldn't *get paid,*" Leila sneered, unable to hide her contempt. "After graduation, I'll be a free agent. I'll make my own money."

"Maybe I should transfer over to technology," Joi mused. "I read in the newspaper that someone used a similar trick to target PayPal accounts. They don't know how much the guy got. The best guess is around ten million dollars."

Leila's computer nearly fell off her lap when she spun around to face Joi. "Someone targeted PayPal?"

"Yeah."

"I did that for class last semester."

"Really?" Joi gasped with mock surprise. "Then I guess you're closer to your goal than you thought. You're practically a free agent already."

Even if Mandel had been eavesdropping, he couldn't have seen the wink Joi used to punctuate the word *free*.

"One more question." Joi took out a small scrap of paper and unfolded it. "Does this mean anything to you?"

No one but Leila could see what was written on the paper.

"Yeah," Leila said. "The instructors have a bunch of technology Androids hacking any websites that mention it."

"That's what I thought," Joi replied as she crumpled the note in her hand. "What about you?" Joi asked, moving on to Julian. "What have you been working on?"

Unlike Leila, Julian seemed eager to impress the new Dux. Or maybe he didn't want to risk another trip to Flick's barbershop now that his pixie hairdo is finally growing back in. He opened a black binder and began to flip through its pages.

"I'm finishing a business plan for a synthetic opioid that I invented last year. It's as addictive as heroin and as easy to manufacture as methamphetamine. I've already outlined production and distribution. Now I'm working on marketing."

"Your drug—smoke, snort, or inject?" Joi inquired.

"All of the above," Julian said proudly. "That's what the consumer wants these days."

"Do you have a name for your product?"

"Yeah," he said. "I grew up in Hawaii. There's a word, *mana*—"

Joi cut him off. "It means 'the power of the universe.'"

"How do you know that?" Julian looked crestfallen.

"Until I came here, I was living on the Lower East Side. They've been selling Mana on street corners there for the past three or four months. I never tried it, but it sounds an awful lot like the drug you've described. I think someone on the outside may have beaten you to the punch."

"No—" Julian started to argue.

"*Yes.* Jeez, don't you guys keep up with the news? Sounds like you're all out of touch. Who wants to be next?"

That night, it felt like Joi took a torch to the Wolves' Den and burned the whole set to the ground. Beneath the plaster and paint, the lounge was nothing more than a cage. And no one trapped inside survived the destruction unscathed. Their ideas were all old, outdated, or unoriginal. But you needed to see Joi's face to get the full message. Without the benefit of her winks, nudges, and smirks, an eavesdropper might have misinterpreted the routine. It would have sounded like she was knocking the Wolves down a few notches. And she did, but that was nothing more than a bonus. Everyone in that room understood *exactly* what Joi was telling them. And I could see the fury and indignation on the top students' faces that night. They were furious at the people who'd tricked them—who'd told them their school projects were *homework* when they'd actually been working for free. The all-powerful Wolves had been the alumni's slaves since day one.

I sat on a windowsill and watched. Ella was studying my face from across the room, trying to figure out if I knew what was happening. I gave her a shrug, and she inched her way across the tower like a commando advancing through sniper fire. When she reached my side, she took out the notepad she always keeps in a pocket.

I thought she was your girl, Ella wrote.

I borrowed her pen. *She was,* I answered.

How long?

'Bout 6 mo.

What's she doing?

IDK.

She going to get us killed?

IDK.

Is she crazy?

IDK.

You trust her?

I paused before I scribbled my reply. *Yes.*

CHAPTER TWENTY-SEVEN

THE SECOND SPECIMEN

I'm standing on the balcony outside my room, wrapped in shadow. It's the same stretch of railing where Lucas and I used to talk, and right now I would trade almost anything for one of those chats. I can see Joi two floors below, on the balcony outside the cafeteria. Most of the other students have returned to their rooms, but Joi's still chewing the fat with her dinner companion—an exceptionally good-looking Android named Levi. He's number 26. Other than that, I don't know a thing about him. But Joi certainly finds the guy fascinating. She's said more to him in one night than she's said to me in weeks.

I look up. There's a sliver of light at the top of Gwendolyn's door on the ninth floor. They force her to attend classes, but she skips every meal. In the week after she lost the Dux title, Gwendolyn was an object of fascination. No one knew what it meant for a student to be left off the ranking list. We all found out when Gwendolyn began to fade. Every day, she seemed to lose a little more substance. Sometimes I wonder if I'm the only one who still sees her.

For a while, she followed me around between classes. I'd glance over my shoulder and spot Gwendolyn skulking a few yards behind me. Or I'd step out of my dorm room and notice her watching my door from the ninth-floor balcony. She almost seemed like a love-sick schoolgirl, though I'm sure she was just searching for new ways to make me suffer.

As much as it annoyed me, it was hard not to feel sorry for her. Now it's impossible. Whatever medication Gwendolyn's on makes her shake like an elderly woman. Her eyes are glassy and her appearance is haggard. These days, she's sunk so low that it's hard to imagine that she ever truly belonged at the top. Joi talks about Gwendolyn's reign as if it was all some big scam. She seems to think that Gwendolyn declared herself Dux, and for a while everyone chose to believe her. As soon as they stopped, Gwendolyn tumbled down to the bottom.

I wonder what Joi will say about me. I'm still on top for the moment, but I've let myself slip. When the new rankings are posted in three days' time, there will be only one Dux. I'll probably make the top five. But I never tried to keep my title. I want Joi to have it. She'll be a little bit safer if she reigns supreme.

I hear footsteps approaching. They stop, and someone takes Lucas's old spot beside me. It's not Lucas, and it's not Joi, so I really couldn't care less who it is.

"Spying on the new Dux? Remarkable, isn't she?"

Mandel has slithered out of the woodwork. I haven't seen him since the day he introduced me to Mr. Wilson and his nunchaku. I should kill him for that—and a hundred other things. It would be easy to pick him up and fling him over the banister. I'd love to see what kind of splatter he'd make. Three weeks ago, I might have done it without blinking. But his people would kill me, and I have one life to sacrifice. It's still Joi's if she needs it.

"I must admit—when I first saw you two together, I didn't understand the attraction," he muses. "Joi's no great beauty, and all those dirty little pets she kept must have been terribly annoying. I assumed you were high on the most powerful drugs known to nature. Hormones can cloud a young man's judgment until he mistakes lust for love. That's why I recruited Gwendolyn's help when you got here. I thought it would be easier for you to let go of the past if your physical needs were being met."

"If you wanted me to let go, why is Joi here?"

"Because you have better taste than I do. I assumed Joi was just an ordinary female, but as it turns out, she's nothing of the sort!" Mandel chuckles. "So there you have it. I was wrong. And you won't hear me say *that* very often."

Mandel sounds like he's a little in love with Joi too. I force myself to look at him. And for a moment, I don't see a snake. Just a spoiled little psycho in a ten-thousand-dollar Italian suit who's been allowed to believe that the rest of us are his playthings.

"What makes you think Joi's so special?"

"Because she's the only student here who found *me*. She showed up a couple of months ago and tried to blackmail me into giving her a spot at the academy." Mandel's not making it up. I can tell he's truly impressed.

"What did Joi have on you?" I ask. Then I give him a playful nudge with my elbow. "Come on, you can tell *me*. We both know I'm not going anywhere."

"It wasn't much, to be honest, but it was the thought that counted. Joi told me she'd spent months researching Mandel's alumni. She followed the money—her words, not mine—and dug up a few facts about a little pharmaceutical project we've all been working on. She claimed she had enough evidence to accuse the academy of being an 'organized crime syndicate.' I'm afraid it was an exercise in naïveté. Her theory might have been published by some wacky conspiracy website, but no reputable news source would have touched it. Even the district attorney's office knows better than to tangle with the Mandel Academy. Our lawyers always rip them to shreds. Still, it was a fairly remarkable report. One might even say *dangerous*. I would have had Joi eliminated after her interview, but fortunately I took the time to check out her references."

"References?"

"Well, *reference*," Mandel corrects himself. "She only provided one. A man named Zoran Zrenjanin. I knew the gentleman by reputation, but it was a challenge getting in touch with him. And I say this as someone who can have the president of the United States on the phone in five minutes. But Mr. Zrenjanin is currently spending time in The Hague. As an inmate in Scheveningen Prison."

"Where they put war criminals."

"That's correct. Are you familiar with Mr. Zrenjanin's work in the former Yugoslavia?"

"Nope, never heard of him. But if you're a fan, he must have an impressive resume."

"Oh yes. Murder on the grandest scale. Ethnic cleansing. Rape. Torture. Organ and blood farming. Human trafficking." I can hear Mandel's excitement growing. Then he abruptly stops and regains his composure. "The point is, the man willingly confirmed that Joi is his daughter. Do you know what that means?"

"That any mass murderer is just a phone call away?"

I don't even think he heard me. "It means that Joi is the child of a predator! She's a hybrid! I have *two* specimens now. So even if something were to happen to *you*, my experiment wouldn't need to end."

"It's a banner day for science," I mutter.

Down on the sixth floor, Joi is strolling toward the elevator with her Android friend.

"She is *captivating*, isn't she?" Mandel remarks. "Always collecting data. She was right about the predator students, you know. They can be quite predictable. And I've discovered that with a little medication, they're easy to manipulate. So I'm keen to focus on hybrids now. Joi is inventing her own rules. Improvising. She understands her prey. She knows how they think. Aside from you two, the academy's Duxes have all been born predators. They ruled by fear and force. Joi has accomplished what I never thought possible—she's inspiring the other students to *follow* her. Soon she could have them all working toward a common goal."

"You mean *your* goal," I say. "So that's why you're letting her break all the rules?"

"I have two hybrids, but I only need one to prove my theory. For now I have the luxury of simply observing my second specimen. I still have much to learn about your kind. I must admit, Joi's behavior here has been absolutely fascinating. She seized power with little interference on my part. What do you think she is planning to do next?"

"I have no idea," I tell him in all honesty.

"Well, if she hasn't taken you into her confidence, I'd say that there's a good chance that she's plotting against you."

"You may be right." That's what Mandel came to say. He's pitting us against each other.

"Oh, I'm definitely right," he assures me. "I was completely up front with Joi when I offered her the scholarship. I told her that only one of you two would survive this semester. That didn't seem to trouble Joi in the slightest. I don't think she considers you much of a threat."

I knew it would come to this. If one of us is going to live, one of us will have to die. But both of us are going to lose.

"What if Joi is the one who survives? What happens to your wager with my father?"

"As long as my theory is confirmed, it doesn't matter which of my two hybrids prevails. Either way, the alumni will have the proof they require. However, my interest in you isn't entirely scientific. Your victory might teach your father a meaningful lesson. I'm still rooting for you, Flick, but I won't be heartbroken if you lose. In fact, I'd love to dissect that brain of yours."

"Why wait?" I ask. "Go ahead and take it."

"It's a very generous offer, Flick. But it makes me suspect that you never opened my present."

"Present?"

"The folder on your computer."

"What's in it?" I ask.

Mandel smiles. "A reason to live."

• • •

I must have fallen asleep with the computer on my lap. I remember staring at the little blue folder. WHEN YOU'RE READY. Mandel should have named it something else. You're never ready for the truth. No matter how much you think you know, it always takes you by surprise.

I open my eyes. Peter Pan is floating a few inches off the floor, examining his own yearbook picture on the wall of my room.

"Dad went ballistic when he found out about this," he says.

"I know," I snap. Of course I know. I was the one who was punished for letting my little brother go to school in a goddamned Halloween costume. "Where have you been? You said you weren't going to leave me. You said there was nowhere to go!"

"Just because you couldn't see me doesn't mean I wasn't around," Peter Pan replies. Then he points at the computer that's slipped off my lap. "Don't open his present."

"I *didn't*." I climb out of bed to deliver my big news. "Joi is here."

"I figured she'd get here sooner or later," says Peter Pan as he slowly drifts down to earth. "Don't know why you're so surprised. I saw that one coming a *long* ways back. I left a trail of bread crumbs for her to follow."

"Bread crumbs? Wrong f—ing fairy tale," I say.

"Then call it a trail of pixie dust if you want. I knew you could count on her."

"Count on her? She won't even speak to me!"

Jude shrugs. "She's angry. Can't say I blame her. I've been pretty pissed off at you too. The last time I was here, it seemed like you'd made some real progress. Did you forget everything that I told you?"

"What? Haven't you been paying attention? I've been doing everything I can to help Joi. But she's not who she used to be, Jude."

"Looks that way, doesn't it? But we all know what they say about *looks*."

"Stop f—ing around! We both know Joi hates me."

Peter Pan just yawns. "You see, *this* is why I'm back. It's all about *you* again."

"Did you hear what Mandel said about her father?"

"Sure, but it would be kind of stupid to hold that against her. *Our* dad is Captain Hook."

"What if she has the gene, Jude? What if I . . ." How do you put words to the worst thought you've ever had?

"Yes?"

"I hurt her. I didn't want to, but I did. What if there is a gene? And what if I switched Joi's on?"

"Then switch it back off!"

His glib answer annoys me. I wish there were someone else I could turn to for advice. But my only confidant is an overgrown elf. "I don't think it works like that."

"How would you know? You're not even sure that the gene *exists*."

"Mandel says there's a gene that's either on or off. Dad says you choose to fight or die. What difference does it make in the end? It's between me and Joi now. One of us is going to die. The one who survives is going to end up a monster."

"Those are the only two options?"

"Don't give me that crazy 'third option' shit again."

"Let's see if I've got this straight. You're having a conversation with a fictional character. And you honestly believe that it's possible to *make* someone a monster. But it's *crazy* to think that there might be a third option. Interesting. Very *interesting*." He arches an eyebrow and strokes an imaginary goatee.

"You're not helping me!"

"Why are *you* the one who always needs help?" he shouts back. "Joi's trying to save everyone. Mandel can't see it. And the sad thing is, neither can you. If you want Joi back, get your head out of your ass and help her!"

Forty-eight hours have passed since I spoke to Mandel. I still haven't opened the folder. The Immunity Phase ends tomorrow. The new rankings will be revealed in the morning, and the Wolves have already stopped treating me as Dux. Joi is their leader now. When Caleb arrives in the Wolves' Den with a memo from Mandel, he doesn't even acknowledge my presence. He heads straight for Joi, who appears to be focusing on her own homework for once.

"What?" she asks without glancing up at him.

"I have a list of the bottom six," he says, making sure that only the top Wolves can hear. The culling should begin as quickly as possible. We traditionally start with the last student on the list, but since this semester has been rather unusual, Mr. Mandel would like you to make the selection."

"No," Joi says, returning to her homework.

Caleb swivels around, hoping that one of us can explain the response. "I'm sorry, Joi," he says at last. "I don't understand. No *what*?"

"The culling is postponed. I haven't finished my analysis yet. I need to reinterview some of the students."

"But . . ." Caleb protests.

Joi glances back up as if she'd already forgotten he was there. "Yes?"

"But what about *Gwendolyn*? And number fifty-five is that girl Violet, from your Incubation Group. Surely you don't need to interview *her*."

"My *needs* are none of your business. I said the culling was postponed. That's all you *need* to hear."

Caleb won't leave. "I understand. But what should I tell Mr. Mandel? This list came directly from him."

"Let me see that." Joi snatches the memo and runs her eyes down the list. "Who decides where students lie in the rankings?"

"The instructors, of course," Caleb answers.

"And you really think they're the best people to be making these kinds of decisions?"

Caleb frowns. "They determine our grades. They're the *instructors*."

"That's right. But they're not just instructors. They're all graduates, too. Do you think the most gifted Mandel alumni would choose to be stuck teaching a bunch of delinquents all day? *No.* These instructors are here because they didn't make the cut on the outside. So if you ask me, decisions like rankings are a bit beyond their abilities. The people in this room are more qualified than they are. We ought to be the ones calling the shots, don't you think?"

Caleb doesn't say a word, but everyone else knows exactly what the answer should be. Leila slams her computer shut and Julian shoots her a knowing glance. Austin sits back and studies the ceiling. Joi keeps rattling their cage. Why haven't they started searching for a way to break free?

"How long do you think it will take to complete your analysis?" Caleb asks.

"Dunno," Joi says with a shrug. "Could be a while. I've never done this before."

She's pretending to read now, but she's scanned the same page three times. Joi must be feeling the weight of my stare. Her head remains bowed down toward her book, but then those amber eyes dart up and meet mine. And I see the girl I knew on the Lower East Side. She's still there, and she's not going to change. That's why Joi keeps postponing the culling. She's trying to save all the students—just like Jude said. But she needs more time to come up with a plan, and she knows it won't be long before Mandel calls her bluff. Someday soon, he'll force her to either kill or be killed. I know which of the two options she'd choose. So whether Joi hates me or not, I'm going to have to help her search for a third.

CHAPTER TWENTY-EIGHT

INFESTATION

The dorm floors are deserted. It's rankings day. Everyone is down-stairs in the cafeteria, and I'm taking my time getting dressed. I could move faster now that my limbs have almost healed. But I'm in no rush. I don't need to see the big screen to know that I'm no longer a Dux.

There's a soft rap at my door. I slide it open to find Joi's hand-some Android waiting outside.

"Sorry to bother you, Flick. I would have slipped this under your door, but I wasn't sure you were still in there." Levi hands me a note.

Come up to the roof—and try to convince me not to push your ass off.

"Thank you," I tell the Android. Then I flush the note down the toilet and take the elevator to the ninth floor.

I step out of the tower to find a girl coming toward me in a long, black sundress. Her wild hair is swept back by the cool morning wind, and the fabric of her dress clings to every curve of her body. If it weren't for the fury in this girl's eyes, I might have mistaken her for the one from my dreams. When she stops, there are less than six inches between us. I'm not sure if Joi intends to kill me or kiss me. I know which of the two I deserve.

"I thought you wanted me to find you." She sounds hoarse. Like the words have been stuck in her throat for a month. Like she's been forced to suffer in silence in a place where you're not allowed to cry. "You left that Mandel course catalog in my room, and I thought you wanted me to know where you'd gone."

"A trail of bread crumbs," I mutter to myself. That's what Peter Pan called it. When I was drunk, I must have dropped it—accidentally on purpose. I really have lost my mind.

"So I risked my ass to get into this place. And when I get here, I find out you've been screwing some evil bitch the whole time."

"Joi, I'm sorry. I had to."

"Stop right there." I really think Joi might try to strangle me if I say any more. "You *had to*? What, was Mandel holding a gun to your head?"

"No."

"Then tell me why you *had to* do it, Flick."

I could play for pity. But I won't. The truth is ugly, and I need to own up to it. "There was something I wanted. I thought Gwendolyn could help me get it."

"What was *it*?"

"Mandel didn't tell you?"

Joi crosses her arms and shakes her head.

"Revenge."

My confession appears to have dampened her rage. She's not quite homicidal. Just furious. "This all has something to do with Peter Pan, doesn't it?"

It's been so long since I thought about my original mission. "My father is a Mandel graduate. When I was growing up, his favorite form of exercise was beating me to a pulp. Peter Pan is my brother, Jude. He died trying to save me. I came here because Mandel told me he would help me punish my father. He has proof that my father killed Jude. But I had to sacrifice everything to get it. Starting with you."

Joi turns away from me, walks up to the railing at the edge of the roof, and gazes out at the city.

"We shouldn't be up here," I tell her, though I don't want to go. "It's rankings day. You've been named Dux again. They'll get suspicious if you're not in the cafeteria to celebrate."

Joi shakes her head and doesn't look back at me. "No. That's what other Duxes would have done. They don't know what to expect from *me*."

She's right. She's played her hand brilliantly. I join Joi at the edge, and when the wind shifts, I catch the scent of jasmine and cocoa butter.

"It's beautiful up here," she says. I nod, but my eyes are closed as I inhale. "You can see all the way to the harbor. We could watch the fireworks on the Fourth of July."

That's a month from now. We'll be lucky if we both make it that long. "I've been trying to bring you here for the past three weeks.

It's the only place that's not bugged. Mandel comes up to the roof when he doesn't want his conversations recorded."

"I know. You told me five or six times. But I didn't want to talk to you. And even if I had, it was too risky. Mandel's been tracking our movements since I got to the academy. Watching to see how much time we spend together. Plus, there always seemed to be someone else hanging out in the lounge. We would have been caught."

"You think Mandel isn't tracking us now?"

"If he's monitoring my chip, he'll see I'm downstairs in my room."

"I don't understand."

Joi pivots and holds her left arm out straight. With her right hand, she guides my index finger to the site of her chip. I can feel the raised line of the incision that was made. I sense a square object tucked under the skin. But it's not a chip.

"What is it?"

"A folded-up piece of foil that I found in the infirmary."

"Where's the chip?"

"Back in my room. I took it out the same day they inserted it. The nurse left the instrument tray in the sink. I stole the needle and thread and dumped the rest in the trash. Then I removed the chip while I was in the shower. Most of the time, I keep it in my pocket so Mandel doesn't get suspicious."

"But how did you know—"

"That I had to get it out of my arm? Did you even *look* at that course catalog? When I found it, I thought it was some kind of sick joke. But then you didn't come back, and I realized how much trouble you were in. So when Mandel told me about the chip, it made perfect sense. He can't let anyone leave this place. I knew what I was getting into when I came here, and I knew that I'd need to get out of it, too."

Relief rushes through my system. "You can escape! The Dux is the only student allowed outside the academy, and if you don't have a chip, you can disappear. They won't be able to find you!"

Joi doesn't seem to share my enthusiasm. "If it's so easy, why haven't you hit the road? I don't see any chip in your arm either."

When I take her hand, she tries to jerk it away. But I hold it firmly and guide one finger to the incision beneath my hairline. Then I let her go. "I have to stay."

Joi shrugs. "Great, 'cause I'm staying too."

"You can't, Joi. There's no way to save everyone here, but if you get out, you might be able to destroy the academy."

"And what would happen to you?"

"Mandel told you. Only one of us can survive."

"Is that why you let me take the Dux title?" Joi asks. "Are you planning to sacrifice yourself to spare me?"

The answer is *yes*. But that's not what I'll tell her, because it's not nearly as noble as it sounds. I don't want to be the one left behind. Not again. If Joi were dead, I wouldn't make it out of here alive. I've suffered more than most, but that pain would be too much to bear. It's hard enough standing this close to Joi without being able to touch her. If I'm ever sent to hell for the things I've done, this would be a suitable punishment.

"You're what matters most to me. I guess I had to lose you before I could figure that out."

"You haven't *lost* me," Joi admits grudgingly. "You're a f—ing moron for hooking up with Gwendolyn, but you do have a few redeeming qualities. And you can thank Caleb for pointing them out. He's been telling me stories—trying to make you look like a loser. I think that's his strategy—*divide and conquer*. He said you and some guy named Lucas made a run for it. The kid was about to die. You were trying to help him escape, weren't you?"

"Yes."

"And there was a girl named Aubrey. Caleb said you had a soft spot for her."

"I tried to help her too. I didn't do either of them much good."

The fact that I failed doesn't seem to faze her. "But you tried. So even though I'd love to kick your ass, I'm not going anywhere without you."

I'm not exactly sure what it all means, but I suddenly want to kiss Joi so much I can barely breathe. She must have figured that out too, because she widens the space between us.

"I do have a couple of questions I need to ask if I'm even going to *consider* forgiving you," she says. "How much did you know about the academy before you enrolled?"

I need to force my lungs to inhale. "I knew a bit, but my father always talked about this place like it was Mount Olympus. I grew up thinking that the people who went here were gods. Even when Mandel told me he was teaching kids to be crooks, I don't know if I really understood what it all meant. It's still hard to believe that the graduates are actually criminals."

A minute passes before Joi speaks. I feel like I'm standing before a judge, waiting for the verdict that will decide my fate. "You're a good guy, Flick. You want to believe that the world is fair and that everyone deserves the life that he gets. And some people *do* earn a place at the top. But others get lucky—and there are a whole lot of jerks out there who are willing to cheat."

"You think I'm good?" I heard everything she said, but it was that very first sentence that stuck in my head. I start moving toward her once more. I know I shouldn't. But I'm high on euphoria.

"Don't push it, Flick," Joi snaps. "You're still a moron. And being good doesn't make you *special*. Most people are good. Why do you think the Mandel alumni keep getting away with it? The rest of us just assume they play by the rules. We think they got where they are because they're smarter or willing to work harder than everyone else."

There's no point in continuing my quest for a kiss. I lean my head against the iron bars and peer down at the sidewalk below. A group of tiny tourists have gathered outside our building. I can't see their faces, but I'm sure they're all awestruck. They've been told that this is a place where dreams come true.

"All those good people down there never bother to ask any questions. Like my father always said—there are no victims, only volunteers."

"That's just another way of saying we all deserve what we get. Did it ever occur to you that your father might be an asshole?"

I can't help but laugh. "Yes. But that doesn't mean he was wrong."

My smile fades. Joi is not finding me very amusing right now. "What would your father say about the kids in the colony? Are they *volunteers* too? If that's the way your dad taught you to look at the world, it may have been the worst thing he ever did. Remember the morning Mandel made me Dux? We were standing outside the cafeteria and I asked what you saw. You started talking about the three groups at the academy. You gave them cute little labels, but what you described were winners, pawns, and losers."

"So what did *you* see?"

"I saw a handful of bad seeds and a bunch of kids who've been told that they have to cheat to survive. And the more I think about all the brainwashed students that the Mandels have sent out into the world, the more it scares the shit out of me."

I never told Joi about Mandel's grand theory. I didn't want to frighten her any more than I needed to, but it's starting to look like she's figured out a lot of it on her own.

"Why does it scare you?" I ask.

"Because I love this country, and they're doing their best to destroy it."

"You really believe a few hundred Mandel alumni could destroy a whole country?"

"How many cheaters does it take to change a game, Flick? Think about all the athletes who pump themselves up with steroids. It probably started with one jerk who decided he could break the rules. He got away with it, and some other asshole figured he might not get caught either. Now everyone's cheating—even the ones who don't want to. Because they know they'll never have a chance of winning anything unless they're doping too."

"You're saying regular people will turn into criminals just so they can compete with the Mandel crowd?"

"Sure—if it's impossible to get ahead by playing fair. Let's say you're a politician, and you want to run an honest campaign. But your opponent is getting millions of dollars from all the crooked businessmen who want to buy her vote. At some point you're going to realize you can't win—unless *you* promise favors to a bunch of scumbags too. Or what if you run some manufacturing company, and you really want to obey all the laws. But your competition is selling the same product at half the price. They can do it because they save millions by illegally dumping their toxic waste right into the ocean. Are you going to go out of business—or start breaking the law too? See how it works?"

"Mandel told me about your research. He said you linked the alumni to all kinds of crimes."

"Yeah, and all I had to work with was your course catalog and a list of graduates I'd gotten off Google. When I started out, I didn't really expect to uncover much. But every time I opened the *New York Times*, I'd find so much stuff that I finally had to focus on a single big scheme. Have you ever heard of a drug called Exceletrex?"

The name rings a bell, but I can't figure out why.

"Most people haven't. It's not on the market yet. It was invented by a pharmaceutical company in Illinois.

Now I remember. Exceletrex is the product from Mr. Martin's class. The one the congressman thought was dangerous. "Wait— Exceletrex is a *drug*?"

"A medication. It's supposed to treat behavioral problems like ADD. They say it helps kids focus, which really means it makes them easier to manipulate. If Exceletrex ends up replacing old drugs like Adderall and Ritalin, it will be worth billions and billions of dollars. Anyway, about four years ago, the pharmaceutical company that invented it was bought by a group of investors. Every single one of them is a Mandel alum.

"It usually takes about ten years of testing to prove that a new drug is safe enough to be sold. But after the Mandel people took over, Exceletrex got the green light from the government in record time. It was scheduled to be launched this fall, just in time for 'back to school' season. But then all sorts of information started leaking out of the company. There were rumors online that a lot of really bad test results had been swept under the carpet. But every time a website posted one of the rumors, the whole website would mysteriously disappear. I kept finding stuff on the Internet, and the next day it was gone. Want to guess who was responsible?"

"Mandel alumni?"

"That's what I thought at first. But it wasn't alumni. It was Mandel *students*. I asked Leila if she recognized the word *Exceletrex*. She said they have all the low-ranking technology majors working on the 'project.' They hack any sites that post rumors about the drug."

"What kind of rumors are they anyway?"

"That Exceletrex causes long-term brain damage. Take the pills for a few years and by the time you're forty, your brain's turned to mush. I guess it's so bad that three of the scientists who'd studied the drug convinced a congressman to open an investigation. . . ."

"Glenn Sheehan. 'The voice of the people.'"

Joi nods. "Yeah, but then he suddenly called it off. So one of the scientists announced he was going to hold his own press conference. He committed suicide two days before it was scheduled."

"They killed him."

"Yep. That's how big this is. For a while I thought the Exceletrex investors were the only ones behind it. Then I realized that there were lawyers and politicians and a bunch of major Wall Street guys involved too. I bet half of the academy's graduates have had a hand in the operation. When the drug comes out, they'll all make a fortune. And as soon as doctors start passing out prescriptions, millions of kids are going to end up with brain damage."

I'm standing in the sunshine, but I suddenly feel a chill. "They may have already started passing out pills."

"What do you mean?"

The first time I visited the academy, Mandel said he'd been searching for a way to make the tracking chips unnecessary. A pharmaceutical that would keep the "less disciplined students" in line. That's why my father warned me not to take any medication while I was here.

"Mandel told me that the predators are easier to manipulate when they're on medication. I think they've been giving Exceletrex to some of the students at the academy. Gwendolyn. Maybe Leila too. Who knows how many others."

Joi grimaces. "That makes sense. The scientists who worked for the company claim that batches of the product often disappeared from the lab."

"Were any of the scientists named Arthur Klein?"

"How do you know?"

"Mr. Martin sent me out to steal Arthur Klein's iPhone. The alumni must have been looking for dirt on him."

"Klein was the first whistle-blower. He decided to go public after his six-year-old son died of a brain tumor. He said he couldn't stand back and let other kids come to harm."

I close my eyes and let my forehead rest against the fence's iron bars. "Oh God, please tell me that Arthur Klein wasn't the guy the alumni killed."

"He wasn't. As far as I know, Klein was still alive when I checked in at the academy. The man who was murdered was one of Klein's colleagues. When I figured out the connection between the dead guy and the alumni, I decided I had enough information to blackmail Mandel. So I took him my research and demanded a spot at the academy. I don't think he was impressed that I'd managed to piece it all together. I think he was amazed that I'd even bothered to *look*."

How do I tell her that the situation is even worse than she thinks? "That's not what got you into the academy, Joi. Mandel doesn't give a damn about your research skills. You're here because of your father. Mandel spoke to him."

Something I just said strikes her as funny. "That's perfect. I mentioned his name as a joke. All that work on Exceletrex, and I only got in because I'm *connected*? I'm surprised my father even remembers who I am. I wish I could have heard what he said."

"It doesn't matter. Mandel's only interested in your DNA. He believes there's a mutant gene that makes some people psychopaths or sociopaths. And he's convinced that you and I both inherited the gene from our fathers."

"He thinks we're psychopaths?" Joi laughs even harder. I really want her to stop.

"No. He calls us *hybrids*. He thinks we have the gene, but it hasn't been switched on. He's trying to turn us into predators."

"Predators?"

I explain Mandel's theory. I start with the idea that the human race split into two distinct species—the predators and their prey. Then I tell her about the role that hybrids play and Mandel's search for the "switch" that will transform people like us into ruthless killers. By the time I get to his vision of turning the academy into a factory for manufacturing super-predators, Joi's smile has turned into a scowl.

"What do *you* think about Mandel's little theory?" she demands.

"I'm not totally convinced that the predator gene exists," I admit. "But I do believe there are predators. Nine of the top twelve students here are psychopaths. All you have to do is look in their eyes to know it. And I think the Mandel Academy has been doing a very good job of turning the other kids into sociopaths. I'm pretty sure no one graduates from this school without being some kind of predator."

"Really? I bet your friend Ella could make it out without letting Mandel screw with her head."

"She's the exception."

"She can't be the only one. But tell me this—why do you call the rest of them *predators*?"

Joi seems to be hung up on the word. "That's Mandel's term for them. Some people are predators. Some people are prey. It fits. My father used to say that there are only two kinds of people—the weak and the strong. It's the same idea."

Joi's looking at me like I've lost my mind.

"What?" I ask.

"You're quoting him again," she points out. "Your dad and the nutcase who runs this school have got you totally brainwashed."

"You think I'm brainwashed? Are you joking? I'd love to kill both of them!"

"So why do you still believe everything that they've told you?! Your father said there are only two kinds of people—and you think it's true. Mandel told you all the alumni are *predators*—and you totally buy it. So what kind of predators are we talking about? Mighty lions? Noble tigers?"

"I've always thought of them as wolves," I admit, trying not to sound too defensive.

Joi sighs. "You mentioned 'the law of the jungle' the other day. You said Mandel believes in it. Did you ever read *The Jungle Book*? That's where the phrase comes from."

"I know," I snap.

"But you obviously don't know what it means. In the book it says, *The strength of the Pack is the Wolf, and the strength of the Wolf is the Pack*. That's the *real* law of the jungle."

"So what?"

"So these assholes aren't *wolves*. Mandel calls them predators because that makes them sound more impressive. But real wolves fight for each other. And they only kill in order to eat. They take what they need—and don't take any more. Maybe Mandel's right. Maybe there are two kinds of humans. But I'm not buying his self-serving *predator* crap."

"Then what label would you prefer?" I shoot back. It's not that I disagree with her. I'm just not used to losing debates.

"Try *parasites*. I mean, think about it! They don't care about anything—not even each other. All they do is feed. They'll take as much as they can get, and they never get enough. They just eat and eat and eat."

I start to argue before I know what to say. My mouth slams

shut while my brain recalibrates everything I've ever seen, heard, or believed.

"They've fooled us into thinking they deserve what they have because they're the smartest and the strongest," Joi continues. "But they're just a bunch of bloodsuckers. You want to know why all the kids in my colony are *weak*? They're weak because Mandel's parasites have been eating them alive."

I'm about to ask what she means when I remember Tina, the blond girl back at Joi's colony. The one who was shoved out onto the streets after her dad lost his job. This school has taught me how to seize control of companies and fire men just like her father. Other kids at the academy have been taught to take their homes, drain their bank accounts, up their credit card fees, deny them insurance, sell them drugs that ease their misery but rot their brains, and pass laws to keep them from getting back on their feet. Every day at the academy is a feast. We've been eating people like Tina's father—slurp by slurp and bite by bite.

"I'm going to stop Mandel," I announce.

"What a coincidence," Joi says. "Me too."

"You got a plan?" I ask.

"I have a few ideas," she says. "But I wouldn't call them a *plan* just yet."

"Well, that's a lot more than I have."

"Then this should all turn out splendidly," Joi quips.

I reach out and take hold of one of the fence's iron bars. It's grown warm in the sun. Breakfast will be over soon. Our time is running out.

"Just in case . . ." I have to stop for a moment. "Just in case this *doesn't* turn out well, can I ask you a few things while I still have the chance?"

"Shoot," Joi says.

"What's your last name?"

Joi grins despite herself. "Ferhatović."

It takes me a few tries before I manage to pronounce it right.

"And where do you come from?"

"I lived in Bosnia with my mother until I was fourteen. When she died, I came to the United States."

"Do you have any idea how much I love you?"

"Yes," Joi says. "Just as much as I love you."

Then she frowns and kicks the fence with the toe of her shoe. She'll probably forgive me, and someday she may even forget how badly I hurt her. But I never will.

"I'm sorry," I say.

Joi studies my face. "Then you can kiss me. On one condition."

"Anything."

"I'd like you to escort me to the next alumni gathering."

"When is it?"

"Tomorrow night," she says. "At Mandel's house."

CHAPTER TWENTY-NINE

DUMB SHOW

Joi has promised me a terrible time. But when the elevator drops me off on the ground floor of the academy, I decide that it's already the best night of my life. It's twenty to eight, and inside the atrium, the sun is turning everything it touches to gold. Joi's sleek gown is gunmetal gray—and so perfectly fitted that she looks like she's been dipped in molten metal. No one we meet will mistake Joi for a mortal. Her black curls defy gravity, and her amber eyes are more catlike than human. They take me in slowly, and one side of her mouth curls up ever so slightly.

"Let's go," she says. Her voice is cold, but when she accepts the arm I hold out for her, she gives it a gentle squeeze.

The car ride is quick and utterly silent. The academy's driver checks the rearview mirror a little too often. I wonder if he's watching both of us. Or just ogling Joi. When we arrive at our destination on Tenth Street, I slide out of the car. Just as planned, Joi takes time to check her makeup, fix her hair, and address an imaginary problem with one of her shoes. I make a show of impatience, but my eyes never leave the building in front of me. It's a Greenwich Village brownstone. Four stories. Three front-facing windows on each floor. A service entrance beneath the stoop. Just the sort of feature you look for when you're planning a little breaking and entering. But there may be an even better option. The buildings next door have buzzers with multiple names. Apartment buildings usually have crappy security, and some idiot will always buzz you in if you say you're making a delivery. That's the option I'll go for if I need to come back here on my own. I'll get into one of the apartment buildings and go up the communal stairway to the roof. Walk across to Mandel's house and break in through the top. No witnesses—and all the time I'd need to crack any pesky locks.

"Are you coming?" I huff. Joi takes her cue and joins me, slamming the car door for good measure.

When we reach the top of the stoop, the front door opens. It looks like most of the guests have already arrived, but Mandel is lingering near the door, waiting to greet any latecomers.

"Don't you make a pretty pair," he observes with a smirk. I notice there's a drink in his hand. I wonder how well the snake holds his liquor. "Though I'm still a little perplexed by your choice of escort, Joi. This should be your evening to shine."

"The best way to spot a real diamond is to place a fake one beside it," Joi purrs. "I'll let the alumni decide which is which."

"Well put," says Mandel. He offers his arm to my date. "Let's go show you off."

Mandel's house is a tribute to some interior decorator's impeccable taste. It's all ivory paint, vanilla fabrics, and warm wood. Aside from the throw pillows decorated with needlepoint cats, there's absolutely nothing in sight that screams "madman." Still, I wouldn't be surprised to discover a hidden room devoted to Nazi memorabilia or a freezer in the basement that's stuffed with body parts. Whatever he's got, I plan to find it.

I spot a few familiar faces from the last alumni gathering, but their eyes pass over me like I'm yesterday's leftovers. They're all eager for a bite of Joi. When the feeding frenzy begins, I stick close to her side. I'd rather not make Joi face them alone. But she's a master of chitchat, and her research is serving her well. It's as though she's prepared a mental dossier on each of the guests—and she knows exactly where to stroke their egos. I reluctantly retreat, one small step at a time, and watch the alumni circle and surround her.

I spend the next hour prowling the perimeter of Mandel's parlor. Whenever Jude and I were ordered to attend one of our father's parties, we passed our time making friends with the wallflowers. We'd look for the man paying a little too much attention to the art. Or the woman pretending to admire our lamps. Jude and I knew the most interesting guests would be the ones who didn't fit in. We met artists and engineers and experts on unusual subjects. But we discovered that the wallflowers all had one thing in common. They never fawned over us—or treated us like our father's pets. They were just pleased to have people to talk to.

I'm the lone wallflower at this soiree. No one here thinks I'm worthy of a chat—or hors d'oeuvre, apparently. Even the snooty waiters are ignoring me. So I make a show of studying Mandel's collection of Picasso sketches and perusing all the books with unbroken spines that line his shelves. He once told me he collects rare books. Maybe that's true, but he doesn't appear to read very much.

Eventually I visit the bar and request a glass of white wine. A man I once met at my father's house is standing less than two feet away, but he doesn't acknowledge me. I take a swig of my drink and discreetly tip the rest down my shirt. When I ask the bartender for directions to the bathroom, I try my best to look embarrassed. I think I've even managed a blush. But the performance is unnecessary. No one is watching my dumb show.

I bypass the bathroom and scurry downstairs. The kitchen is hot and its atmosphere frenzied. Waiters load trays with crystal glasses while a crew of caterers decorates silver platters with edible artworks. I'm sure somebody must see me grabbing a bottle of Scotch. But no one says a word when I tuck the booze under my jacket and head up the stairs to the second floor.

It was Joi's idea.

"How many Mandel graduates are still alive?" she asked just after I'd kissed her for the second time in months. It was the last thing I wanted to think about at that moment.

"Mandel said he recruits eighteen students a year but only half ever graduate. Fifty years' worth of graduates might be out there. Nine times fifty is four hundred and fifty. But some of those guys will have kicked the bucket. So my guess is there are somewhere between three and four hundred," I calculated. "Maybe more, maybe less."

"Four hundred of the most powerful people in the country.

Mandel told me that I'd have to work for the Mandel Academy after I graduate. Is it the same for everyone?"

"You can choose a career, but all alumni are secretly employed by the Mandel family."

"Yeah, 'cause otherwise, the graduates would all go off on their own. We're not talking about a bunch of people who value stuff like teamwork or charity, right? So how does Mandel keep them all in line? And how does he convince them to 'donate' big bucks to his school? He's got to be getting a pretty hefty cut of their profits to keep running this show."

"That's why half the alumni want to force Mandel out."

"So why haven't they?"

The answer was so obvious that I was surprised she couldn't see it. "He knows all of their secrets, Joi. He knows who they've killed or robbed or cheated. The academy keeps files on everyone. Mandel *owns* the alumni. They have to do what he asks or he'll ruin them."

"Sure," she responded as if I'd just told her the earth was round. "But where do you think Mandel stores all the files?"

Another strange question. "On a computer?"

Joi's brow furrowed. "Maybe. Though don't you think that seems kind of risky? There must be dozens of graduates who are capable of hacking the academy's server. And I bet every single one of them would love to delete his own file. Besides, when did your dad graduate?"

"1985."

"What if his file was never digitized? What's your dad's name?"

I hesitated.

"Flick?"

"His name's Henry Brennan."

"What if there's an actual *folder* somewhere with HENRY BREN-NAN written on the label?"

"I'm pretty sure the files are all electronic now. Mandel down-loaded something onto my computer the other day, and I have a hunch it was dirt on my father. I don't know what the document was, but it was obviously digitized."

"I'm sure he's scanned a few things here and there. But do you think the Mandel family ever took the time to upload thousands of old documents?" Joi asks. "And if the files are filled with lots of juicy secrets, who would the Mandels have trusted to do the work for them?"

It was all adding up to a conclusion that I couldn't quite buy. "So you think there might be physical files on all the academy grad-uates locked up somewhere in this school."

"Probably," Joi said. "But Mandel strikes me as the kind of guy who likes to take his work home with him."

"Come on," I scoffed. "You think there might be files at his *house*? He would never take that kind of risk. Especially if he's throwing parties there."

"You keep forgetting that the man's totally nuts. Mandel could have a stack of alumni files on his bedside table so he can read himself to sleep every night."

A memory flickered in my head. The first time I visited the academy, Mandel told me that he'd read my father's file. There was something about the way he said it—like it wasn't just some docu-ment he'd stumbled across in the course of his duties. He talked about that file like it was one of his favorite books.

"You're taking me to the party so I can check out his bedside table?"

"I know it's a long shot, but it's worth a look, right? I can charm the alumni while you snoop around. Even if you don't find any files, you might find a computer or something."

"Or Mandel's private collection of pickled brains."

"Even better."

I sighed. "And here I was thinking this was going to be our first date."

That's when I had to kiss her again.

Turns out Mandel's bedroom isn't the treasure trove we hoped it would be. There's nothing in it but a bed. A white Persian cat is asleep on one of the pillows. I hope Mandel wakes up tomorrow with a disfiguring case of ringworm. I step into his bathroom and take the opportunity to pour some Scotch down the sink drain. If the bottle is still full when he finds me, he'll know I'm not drunk. I'm a big fan of little details, so I empty my bladder into his toilet as well. My aim sucks, and I don't bother to flush. After I'm all zipped up, I head down the hall. Slowly. I don't want to miss anything—and when Mandel checks the data from my tracking chip, I want him to think I was wandering aimlessly. Which, as it happens, is just what I'm doing. There's nothing of interest here. In some rooms, there's nothing at all. When I reach the top floor of the building, I find it's completely empty. There's an enormous skylight in the ceiling and a puddle of moonlight on the floor. Seems like a good place to pause for a drink.

I take a few swigs of the whiskey. I still don't have a taste for the stuff. But I'll drink it out of duty. I glance around and wonder why Mandel didn't set his decorator loose in this room. The light must be great during the day. But the walls look like they haven't been painted for years. There are dark rectangular patches where bookshelves or furniture recently stood. And then it hits me. The dark patches are the height and width of filing cabinets. The files exist. This is where he kept them. And now they've been moved to another room just like it.

The painter's studio. That's why he asked me to rob the house he was secretly purchasing. He could have gone with a professional thief. Or fought the artist's lease in court. But he didn't want any-one connected to the academy to know about the building. So he chose a dumb kid for the job. A kid who wouldn't ask any questions. One who was about to be locked up for a while. I was a pawn before I even knew I was playing a game.

I take another gulp of Scotch to celebrate my brilliant break-through. I think I know where the files are—and if I'm right, I know exactly how to get them. I'm feeling nice and tipsy, which is great, because I suddenly hear footsteps on the stairs. Mandel finds me sit-ting on the floor with a half-empty bottle of Scotch in front of me.

"What are you doing up here?" he demands.

"Letting Joi shine." I do my best to slur the word *shine*. "Want some?" I ask, holding up the Scotch bottle. "It's not as good as the last stuff I got off you, but it's better than nothing."

Mandel just gazes at me with that crazy smile.

"Oh, come on, you know I don't have cooties." I shake the bottle at him. "Your doctors would have put me to sleep if I did."

I don't think he's buying the act. I need to find some way to convince him.

"I want you to know that I'm ready," I say. I take a gulp of liquid courage. "The switch has flipped. I can beat him now. Just give me my chance."

At the very least I've amused him. "Stand up, Flick. Time for you to go home."

The alumni have gathered to watch Mandel return with his runaway guinea pig. I give them all a big, sloppy smile right before I purposely slip and bounce down the last few stairs.

"If any of you wondered why I brought Flick as my date, I think the answer should be clear by now," Joi quips to the crowd. "*This*, ladies and gentlemen, is my only competition."

Joi and I stand three feet apart in the academy's elevator. Or rather Joi stands. I slump against the wall. When we reach the dorms, we head in our separate directions. The lights are out on the balcony, and I don't bother turning any on in my room. I just lie down on my bed and kick off my shoes. Five minutes later I hear bare feet padding across wooden floorboards. I left the door open a foot, and a shadow slips inside. The door slides shut, and I smell Jasmine and cocoa butter. Joi left her chip and her dress behind in her room.

CHAPTER THIRTY

THE NO-STAR TEAM

We started out with a perfectly good plan. Joi would request permission to leave the academy to visit the Police Museum for a look at its Fredericka "Marm" Mandelbaum archive. As soon as she got there, she would deposit her chip somewhere inside the museum and take a cab up to Charles Street. Then she'd break into the painter's studio through the roof. If the files were in the apartment, she'd fill her backpack, pick up her chip from the museum, and return to school. Then we'd find a way to put the files to good use. It wasn't a foolproof plan, but at least it felt simple. Easy. But it was doomed from the start.

Joi's first request to leave the academy was denied. Mandel didn't deign to give her an explanation. Her second request met a similar fate. I figured my drunken performance at the alumni gathering must have been less than convincing. Then I discovered the truth in the men's locker room.

I was changing out of my gym clothes after Brazilian Jujitsu when I plopped down on the bench to tie my shoes and nearly landed on Gwendolyn's lap.

"What the . . ." I don't know what was more shocking—finding her there or seeing her up close for the first time in weeks. Her hair appeared to be thinning, and her face was covered with scabs and raw sores.

"Enjoy your little sleepover?" she hissed. When she reached up to scratch at a scab, I knew the wounds had been made by her own fingernails.

"Excuse me?" I glanced around the locker room. The last of my jujitsu classmates was heading for the door. I almost called out and asked him to stay.

"I saw the witch sneaking out of your room the other morning. Did she do any of the stuff I told her you like?"

"You're sick," I said, turning my attention back to my shoelaces.

"I'd love to know how she managed to fool her chip. Mr. Mandel checked the tracking data. He still thinks Joi was in her room that night. But I know what I saw."

"No, you don't," I assure Gwendolyn. "You were hallucinating. Those pills are eating your brain. You need to stop taking them."

"I told Mr. Mandel to keep his eyes open. I told him you and the witch are together again."

"Oh yeah?" I tried my best to sound uninterested. "And what did he say?"

"He said Joi's the Dux. She can sleep with whoever she likes."

"Then I guess that's it. Sorry to hear you wasted your time." I finished the last knot on my laces and stood up. When I looked down at Gwendolyn, she was smiling. Her gums were bleeding, and the sight was gruesome.

"You haven't let me finish. Joi can do whatever she likes. But the same rules don't apply to losers like you. I'm not sure what you did to upset him, but the headmaster isn't your biggest fan anymore. If I were you, I'd watch my back. And I'd *definitely* stop screwing the witch."

"Is that what this is all about? You're jealous because you think I'm with Joi?" I grabbed my belongings and slammed my locker. "That's almost touching, Gwendolyn. I had no idea you really cared."

That afternoon, I dragged Joi up to the roof during lunch. Whether or not he believed Gwendolyn, Mandel was going to be watching us both for a while. Leaving school was out of the question. I was totally prepared to start all over from scratch—and find a way to destroy the academy without using the files. Joi thought coming up with a completely new plan would take too much time. A fresh batch of recruits would soon be moving into the Suites downstairs. The culling upstairs had already been postponed for almost a month. Mandel wouldn't be willing to wait much longer.

"I'll just ask Curly to get the files," she announced.

I could only hope she was joking. "*Please* tell me you know someone else named Curly. 'Cause if you're talking about the cocker-spaniel-looking kid I know, I'll just go ahead and jump off this roof right now and save Mandel the trouble of killing me."

"I know why you think Curly can't do it," Joi replied. "And that's exactly why I think he *can*. He's young and cute. Even if everyone on Charles Street saw him breaking into the building, no one would ever suspect he's a thief."

"Fine. But how would you get word to him?" I asked, still praying I could put an end to the idea.

"I'll send a message to Tina's Facebook page."

"Tina's got a Facebook page?" I sputtered. "She doesn't even have a computer!"

"They let her use the one where she works." I could see Joi's expression growing dark.

"Works?" *Since when do hookers get computer time?*

It was almost as if she'd read my thoughts. "Get your mind out of the gutter, Flick. Tina's been a nanny for almost a year now. She used to work nights for a family with twins, but she took a daytime gig after I asked her to look out for the colony kids."

"Tina's a *nanny*? And you left her in charge of the colony? The girl who buys everyone booze?"

"That was one time, Flick. On Christmas Eve. And it wasn't booze. It was *beer*." Joi was getting seriously pissed.

"Okay, okay," I said, backing off. "But how do we send Tina a message if neither one of us has Internet access?"

"We'll ask that girl Lily to help."

"Lily?" It took me a minute to put a face to the name. "You mean the Android who told us she has the Facebook source code?"

"There was a reason I got to know everyone here, Flick. I wasn't just being friendly. I figured I'd need help at some point. And you wouldn't believe what some of the students can do."

"Just because Lily says she can hack Facebook doesn't mean that she can! She's number thirty-something, remember?!"

"You know what I don't understand, Flick? Why you'd just assume that Curly, Tina, and Lily are worthless. I can't remember ever seeing you speak to any of them for more than ten seconds. So how the hell do you know what they can or can't do?"

"I don't think they're *worthless*." It wasn't a lie. I wouldn't have used the word *worthless*. I would have used the word *weak*. But I wasn't interested in hearing another of Joi's lectures. "I just don't want to get too many people involved."

"Yeah, for a while you didn't even want *me* involved. Why do you want to do everything yourself, Flick? Is it because you think you're the only one who can do it right?"

No, I wanted to tell her. It's because most people who've helped me have ended up beaten, fired, or worse. I've had to live knowing that Jude died trying to save me—and that I wasn't worth his sacrifice. If I'd only refused my brother's help, he and my mother wouldn't be dead.

I can't be responsible for any more deaths. And I won't beg favors from a bunch of kids who are already struggling just to stay alive.

"Look, Joi," I said, trying one last angle. "I'm willing to take your word about Curly and Tina. You know them both better than I do. But we can't go around asking other students for help."

"Why not? If it weren't for the kids in my Incubation Group, I couldn't have made it upstairs. Max would have butchered us all if we hadn't protected each other."

"That was down in the Suites! You've seen for yourself what happens to students once they're sent upstairs! One way or another, the academy turns them into sociopaths. If they don't change, they *die*. It doesn't make any difference how many times you've interviewed them. We still have no idea which Androids we can trust— so we can't trust *anyone*. Monsters exist, and this school is full of them."

"The only monster here is the one who's in charge. There may be a handful of students who are criminally insane, but the rest are just regular kids who've lost all hope."

"Are you willing to bet your life on that?"

"Yep," Joi said. "Yours too."

And that's how we ended up with a no-star team of Ghosts, Androids, and Urchins. I don't like it one little bit. Each and every one of them is a potential weak link. To make matters worse, Gwendolyn is watching, and Caleb appears to be shadowing us too. I don't know if he's still scheming to seize the Dux title—or whether Mandel put him up to it. But Joi and I haven't been able to return to the roof. Whenever we visit the lounge, Caleb is always lurking nearby. So we've been forced to polish our plot one secret note at a time. I've eaten so much paper in the last week that there must be a whole tree lodged in my lower intestine. Today it feels like a full-grown conifer.

It's Friday, July the third. Our operation kicked off quietly four days ago. We've had no confirmation that the first two stages of the plan have met with any success. On Monday, while an instructor watched her every move, Lily attacked Facebook with a virus—a virus with one rather unusual feature. Thousands of users downloaded a piece of spyware designed to collect all their passwords. But Tina received a message.

Joi is convinced that Tina picked up our note. But the next step of the plan was always the one that worried me most. I spent an entire evening crafting detailed instructions for Curly—how to get up to the roof, how to crack any locks, and how to get out without being caught. Joi provided a list of alumni whose files might contain high-value data. If Curly managed to locate the files, he should have placed them inside a black bag. That black bag was supposed to be put inside a white file box—and delivered to the academy today at exactly 11:15 a.m.

There are too many goddamned *ifs*. We don't know *if* our instructions were received. We don't even know for certain *if* the files exist. And *if* Curly gets nabbed stealing academy secrets, Mandel won't have any trouble tracing him right back to the colony. And then we'll all be dead.

I'm glad I skipped breakfast. *If* I hadn't, there might be a puddle of liquefied bacon on the floor of the Hidden Treasures classroom. Joi is six seats away from me. She looks like she's actually enjoying the Exxon-sponsored documentary on natural gas drilling that our own Ms. Smith appears to have narrated. Joi's head tilts back, and I watch her sniff the air. I smell it too, an acrid chemical odor. The television screen goes black, and the monitor disappears into the ceiling. Ms. Smith grabs the remote control and clicks the power button several times in frustration. She's about to check the batteries when alarms begin to wail outside.

I don't hear the phone on Ms. Smith's desk start to vibrate, but I see her pick it up and scan the screen.

"Nothing to worry about!" she shouts over the alarm. "There's no fire in the building—just a smoke condition on the second floor."

Joi catches my eye. The next stage of our plan has been set into motion. Three stories below us, a chipmunk is causing a commotion in a chemistry lab. In Violet's two months as a leisure studies major, she's shown zero interest in manufacturing street drugs. But

Joi claims the girl has a talent for chemistry. I had my doubts, but I thought starting a lab fire might not prove too taxing. Then Violet decided to *improve* my idea. She said she could put together a combination of chemicals that would react with moisture in the air to produce a thick fog. We'd still need smoke to set off the sprinklers, but the fog would linger long after the fire was extinguished. I thought it sounded too complicated, but I was outvoted. Until this very moment, I was sure Violet would turn out to be the weakest link of them all. But it looks like she's held up just fine.

The alarms grow louder when Ms. Smith opens the classroom door and steps onto the balcony. The entire class streams out behind her.

The smoke has activated the sprinkler system on the bottom three floors of the building. Those students lucky enough to have classes on floors four and five are leaning over the balconies, cackling as their classmates downstairs get drenched. The atrium is like the eye of a hurricane—calm and dry. The Mandel Academy's flaming brass balls twinkle in the sunlight.

"Get in the elevator!" Mr. Martin's voice booms from below.

Ella has his Secrets and Sabotage class this period, and she must have delivered the line I gave her. *Are there sprinklers in your office, sir?* That was my single contribution to this craptastic plan. All those boxes lining the walls in Mr. Martin's office must be filling with water. Just as I expected, he's herding his class to the ground floor in a last-ditch attempt to keep all his dirt from turning to mud. A dense, white fog from the chemistry lab is now cascading over the second-floor balcony. I watch as dozens of file boxes are carted out of Mr. Martin's office while the atrium fills with smoke.

We hear fire engines approaching, and the front doors of the school swing open. Hopefully an intruder has slipped in with the firemen. A colony kid carting a file box. The last thing Joi and I need are fifty academy students keeping watch.

"Okay, everyone," Joi shouts at the students hanging over the balconies. "If you're not in Mr. Martin's class, get to your rooms! Use the elevator on the right. Send the other one downstairs in case the firemen need it."

I don't want to miss any action, but there's not much to see anymore. The cloud has blanketed the entire ground floor. And I have my own part to play. Joi and I make sure all the students are on their way to their rooms. Then she slips me her chip, and I ride the elevator to the ninth floor. Joi gets off on the eighth to wait for Ella.

I take the chip to the tower lounge and tuck it between the pages of a book someone has abandoned on the coffee table. Then I rush back down to the balcony. The elevator that delivered me upstairs has been called to the ground floor, and I watch as it's swallowed up by the fog. A box may (or may not) have arrived during the pandemonium. Ella may (or may not) have located it. She may (or may not) have taken the black bag inside and switched it with the one she carried to class. She may (or may not) be on her way to give it to Joi.

Both elevators suddenly break through the smoke and climb toward the upper floors. One is crammed with Mr. Martin's sopping-wet students. It stops on the seventh floor, then the eighth. I don't know if Ella gets off, because I'm watching the other one now. The only person inside is Lucian Mandel. The elevator lands on nine, and he begins walking straight toward me. But I don't think I'm the person he's looking for. I see his hand make a move for the pocket on the right side of his suit jacket.

"Good thing it's just smoke," I say, blocking his path. His hand returns to his side. "Looks like your granddad forgot a little something called *fire escapes* when he built this place. If there was ever a fire, we'd all get roasted alive."

"Shouldn't you be in your room?" Mandel snaps.

"And miss the excitement? What happened down on the second floor?"

Mandel is not in the mood for chitchat. "Something that should have been avoided. Now if you'll excuse me, I must speak with the Dux."

We do a little dance as he tries to step around me. This is my fault. I should have made Joi keep her chip. But she insisted on being invisible. If Ella couldn't find the box that the colony kids were supposed to deliver, Joi wanted to be able to search for herself. I should have volunteered for the job. If Gwendolyn was right and I've fallen out of favor, I'm probably already dead in Mandel's eyes. When he finally manages to brush past me, my fingers dip into his suit jacket and emerge with his card key pinched between them. Then I start to walk away.

"Flick!" he shouts at my back.

I turn to see Mandel patting the pockets of his suit. "Yes?" *Shit.* I'm out of practice. He knows I just took it.

"I must have left my key downstairs. Open the door for me."

"Why? If you're looking for Joi, she's not in the lounge," I say.

"Her chip says she is," Mandel tells me. "And I trust it far more than I'll ever trust you."

The second elevator has started climbing toward the ninth floor. I use my own key to unlock the lounge door just as the elevator lands on nine and Joi steps off. There are fifteen stairs that lead to the tower, and if Mandel beats Joi upstairs, she'll have her own drawer in the morgue before the smoke has cleared. He'll know she removed her chip, and after that, everything else will be obvious.

Mandel is already halfway up the stairs. "There's something I need to tell you," I call up to him. "It's about Joi."

"Then come with me," Mandel replies without looking back. "Whatever it is, Joi can hear it too."

I leave Mandel's key behind on the balcony and pray that Joi understands the message.

The Wolves' Den is empty. Mandel takes a spin in the center of the room, as though Joi might be hiding behind a chair or under the sofa. When he comes to a stop, there's no smile on his face. The headmaster knows he's been duped, but he still can't believe it.

"Where is she?" he demands. "Where is she?!"

"That's what I've been trying to tell you. Joi's not here."

"The signal from her chip says she's in the lounge."

Play for time. Play for time.

"Well, I've been standing on the ninth-floor balcony since she ordered us all back to our rooms. I never saw her come up to the lounge. Joi's behind all of this. I don't know what she's doing, but I think you should be very concerned."

"Do you think she's tried to escape?" Mandel asks.

"Your guess is as good as mine, but if I were you, I'd start searching the whole building."

He almost looks ready to take my advice when a window opens and Joi casually enters the lounge. She found the card key and went through Mandel's office to the roof.

"What's going on?" she asks.

"And here's our Dux now!" Mandel sounds as relieved as I feel. "Flick was just trying to convince me that you orchestrated this afternoon's entertainment. He suggested I form a search party to find you."

"Nice try," Joi snarls at me. "I passed Flick on my way to the roof. He knew exactly where I was this whole time."

Mandel's smile returns. "And what, pray tell, were you doing outside?"

"Making plans," Joi replies.

"Escape plans?"

"Battle plans," Joi corrects him. "I've waited long enough. It's time for the culling to start."

"That's precisely why I wanted to speak with you." Mandel turns to me. "You may leave," he tells me.

"If you don't mind, I'd like Flick to hear what I have to say," Joi interjects. "He's going to play a very big part in my plan."

The headmaster won't even look at me. "I'll allow him to remain in the room, but consider it my last favor," Mandel cautions her. "I think we'd all agree that I've been very indulgent, Joi. I've tolerated your whims. I even let you postpone the culling while you finished your 'analysis.' But I'm afraid I must now intervene. The disturbance downstairs was caused by a student who no longer has any business being here at the academy."

"Which one?" Joi asks.

"Violet. Number fifty-five."

"Then she'll be the second to go," Joi announces. "Gwendolyn will be first."

"When?" Mandel demands.

"Monday," Joi says. "Right after the holiday."

"No. Caleb should begin making plans immediately," Mandel orders. "I don't see any need to wait another three days."

"Oh, but I do," Joi assures him. "I want to give Flick plenty of time to think about how he'll kill his little girlfriend."

Mandel laughs. "Flick?"

"You want me to take Gwendolyn out?" My shock sounds genuine because it *is*. As much as I respect Joi, I'm more than a little concerned. This was definitely not part of our plan.

"Yes. While the whole school watches," Joi says. "I know you probably haven't staged a public execution before, Mr. Mandel. It's less upsetting for the low-ranking students if the Ghosts just disappear. But Gwendolyn is a former Dux. Everyone knows that she tried to dispose of me. And I want them to see how I deal with my enemies. And I want Flick to wish that he'd kept his pants zipped."

Mandel almost swoons with delight. He's fallen in love with his latest monster. "You have a true gift, my dear," he tells her.

"Thank you," Joi says. "So if I have your approval, I'll announce my plans to the top students during the fireworks."

"Fireworks?" Mandel asks.

"Tomorrow night is the Fourth of July. The view from the roof will be perfect."

Mandel doesn't seem fond of the idea. "Roof privileges are reserved for the Dux," he says.

"As they should be. But I'd like to give the other students a treat. It's my way of showing them how much power I have—and what I'm able to do with it. I'll announce Gwendolyn's fate while the sky lights up over Manhattan. It will be an evening the top twelve will never forget."

"I told you there wouldn't be any more favors, Joi, and this is a very unusual request."

"It seems unusual because I'm not like any Dux this school's ever had," Joi counters. "I know something the others didn't. If all you can do is make people *scared* of you, you'll always have to watch your back. The most successful leaders inspire more than fear in their subjects. They inspire *awe*."

"And you believe you know how?" Mandel asks. Joi nods, and he's hooked. I didn't think there was any bait that would make Mandel bite. But Joi figured out what our headmaster wants. Mandel knows he rules his little empire by fear. He knows half the graduates think he's nuts. Without the files, he'd be nothing. What he craves more than anything is the alumni's respect.

"Then perhaps I should join you," Mandel says. "I do enjoy a spectacle."

"You're welcome to come," Joi tells him. "But your presence wouldn't do either of us any good. I know how the top students think. I know how the *alumni* think. The more time you spend with them, the more human you seem. Let me act as your emissary, and we can make them all believe you're a *god*."

CHAPTER THIRTY-ONE

FIRE WORKS

It's thirty minutes past curfew. Most of the academy's students are tucked safely away for the night. I'm sitting on the edge of my bed, praying that the door of my room will unlock. I hear the click, and I join the other Wolves as we weave our way through the darkness to the tower lounge. The window is already wide open when we arrive. Ella disappears into the night. The rest of the Wolves hesitate. When I step outside, they start to follow, one by one.

There's a whistle and a boom. The first firework of the night lights the sky. A shower of stars seems to rain down around the girl who's waiting for us by the railing. She's dressed in a T-shirt and jeans, which she wears like battle fatigues.

"Tonight, we're going to celebrate freedom," she announces just as a rocket whizzes past the skyscrapers and explodes overhead. "But we're not here to watch the fireworks."

There's a black bag on the ground in front of her. We can all see the folders peeking through the bag's open zipper. The Wolves edge closer.

"Nice out here, isn't it?" Joi asks pleasantly.

She seems to be waiting for someone to agree.

"Sure," Austin offers. "Real nice."

"How long has it been since you had a breath of fresh air?"

Austin looks around, just to make sure she's talking to him. "I got sent out on a few field trips last semester."

"But you've spent most of your free time cooped up in that lounge," Joi says. "Why didn't you ever try to sneak out to the roof?"

It sounds like a trick question. Austin doesn't answer.

"No one is listening," Joi assures them. "There are no bugs on the roof. Mandel can't hear us."

"He would have known if we'd come out here," Leila chimes in.

"That's right," Joi says. "How could I forget? The chips. You've all been bagged and tagged like a bunch of wild animals. The difference is, animals would try to resist. You *let* them put those chips in your arms."

"They'll be removed as soon as we graduate," Julian offers in the Wolves' defense.

"Or so you've been told," Joi points out. "Maybe it's true. Maybe it's not. But you know what amazes me? That a piece of plastic and a little bit of silicone could turn the top students at the Mandel Academy into a bunch of trained monkeys."

A few months ago, those might have been fighting words. But Joi has been making her case since the beginning of June. At this point, the Wolves all know she's right. Their grades are decided by academy graduates who never could have earned a spot in the school's top twelve. Their homework is passed along to high-ranking alumni. Even their field trips amount to little more than slave labor.

"I just called you monkeys," Joi points out. "Isn't anyone going to argue?"

"We're at the academy to pay our dues." Caleb gives her the party line. "There's a reward waiting for those who are strong enough to graduate."

"I see. You're waiting for a *reward*. I suppose you won't settle for a banana. So, what is it you want, Caleb?" Joi asks him.

"*That*." Caleb points at the fabled Manhattan skyline.

"You want what the alumni have," Joi says. "Sounds fair enough to me. You guys deserve it. You *are* the best and the brightest, after all. I suppose the alumni were the best in *their day*, but I've met them and let me tell you—that day is long gone. Now they're old and worn out. That's why they have to steal your ideas and trick you into doing their dirty work. They're taking what *you* deserve. And you guys are letting them do it."

"This is ridiculous," Caleb announces. "You're making it sound like we're on some kind of chain gang. I don't know about you, Joi, but *my life* has improved a great deal since I got here."

"It seems that way because they let you think you're running the place," Joi responds. "But trust me, Caleb—if one of the alumni ever decides that he doesn't like the look of you, you'll end up in a puddle of blood at the bottom of the atrium."

"I think I'll take that risk," Caleb sneers.

Joi nods. "Then let's talk about what's going to happen after graduation. Did Mandel ever mention how much of your income you'll be donating to the academy? Did you ever wonder why the alumni are all so eager to chip in to keep this place running? Here's why." She crouches down and pulls a folder from her bag. "This is a file that Mandel's been keeping on one of the graduates. Listen up, Austin, 'cause the guy's a politician, just like you. And it looks like he's been a *very* naughty boy." Joi flips through the documents inside. She stops somewhere in the middle, holds the file up centerfold style, and whistles. "Wow. I didn't even know you could *do* that sort of thing with a baseball bat!"

The case she's making is still a little too subtle for Austin. "Who cares what the dude does in his own spare time? What's your point?"

"The point is, doofus, Mandel *owns* this man. And one day soon, he's going to own you too. You'll be his personal slave for the rest of your life. If you don't believe me, just ask Caleb. Isn't that what human resources is all about, Caleb? You guys make sure all the graduates do what they're told. I bet if an alumnus ever steps out of line, some human resources weasel releases a few juicy secrets on the Internet. Secrets like *this*."

Joi holds up a picture from the politician's file for everyone to see. Leila giggles. Julian howls with laughter. Austin finally looks convinced. If a photo like that ever went viral, its subject would pray for an early death.

"Where did you get that stuff?" Caleb demands.

Joi shrugs. "It's amazing what you can find if you don't always do what you're told."

"And what do you intend to do with it?"

She ignores Caleb's question and addresses the crowd instead. "Back when I was locked up in the Incubation Suites, I got a long lecture about the 'survival of the fittest.' At the Mandel Academy, the strong rise to the top. The weak fall to the bottom. I thought it sounded fabulous until I got upstairs and found out it was a big sack of horseshit. I'm tired of being used and cheated and lied to. Why are *we* playing by the alumni's rules? We're younger and stronger. We're at the top of our game. So let's stop *asking*—and start *taking*. I've got a little present for you." Joi hands a folder to each of the Wolves. "Mandel used to own these people. I'm signing the deeds over to you. There's enough information in these files to make sure we all get what we deserve. Whatever these alumni have, it now belongs to *us*. It's time to declare our independence. I know we're all ready—and so do you."

"What about the chips?" Leila asks. She's still not buying it. None of them are.

"What about them?" Joi responds. "How many people do you think Mandel has tracking your movements? I can tell you right now. *None*. He's convinced you're completely predictable. He thinks of you guys as his *pets*. And do you want to know why?" She's been holding back, but the time has come to play her last card. It's a gamble, but it could pay off. "How many of you guys have been given medication in the past few years?"

Leila is the only one to raise her hand.

"What did it look like?" Joi asks.

"Purple pills. Diamond shape. I've been taking them since I got here."

"Has anyone else been given diamond-shaped purple pills?"

This time everyone but Caleb raises a hand. But I can see the truth on his face—he's taken them too.

"It's a drug called Exceletrex. The alumni own the company that manufactures it. In a few months they're going to start selling it. It's supposed to turn troublemakers like you into well-behaved little ladies and gentlemen."

Those pills were *Exceletrex*?" Leila is visibly shaking. I wonder what's responsible—panic or the pills. "The tech majors have spent the whole year wiping leaks off the Internet. There are scientists who say that stuff could cause brain damage."

"*Could cause* brain damage doesn't mean it *will*," Caleb notes.

"Maybe it will eat your brain, maybe it won't," Joi responds blithely. "Fact is, Mandel's been using you guys as guinea pigs. That's how much he *respects* you."

"I came up with the name Exceletrex," Julian says, looking horrified. "It was one of my first assignments at the academy."

"They paid off a bunch of government guys to get that drug approved," Austin adds. "A while back, my Political Science class put together a list of FDA people to bribe."

"The alumni are going to make billions off Exceletrex, and they couldn't have done it without you. And how did they thank you? By feeding you the stuff they'll be selling. Who knows? You might even make it to forty before you start speaking in gibberish and peeing your pants. So I suggest you use your brains while you still have the chance. The files I gave you? They belong to the pharmaceutical company's investors—who just so happen to be some of the richest people in New York."

"What are we supposed to do?" asks Max.

"It's simple. See the name on your file? Find the guy and offer to sell the documents back to him, one at a time. They'll pay whatever you ask. You'll all be filthy rich."

"We'll be *dead*," Julian argues.

"No. I made duplicates of all the files. Let the investors know that if you disappear, a copy of the entire file will be sent straight to the *New York Times*. No one's going to mess with you if they know the files could end up going public."

"And what if *you* disappear?" Leila asks.

"Or decide you want it all for yourself?" adds Julian.

"If you don't trust me, come up with something better. You guys have got to stop taking those pills and start acting like predators. A couple of you might end up getting caught. But so what? Look around—the odds are in your favor. And the rewards couldn't get any bigger. Riches and revenge. I'd say that's the perfect combination."

"When are we supposed to make a break for it?" Austin asks.

"Monday night," Joi says. "The entire academy will be gathered in the atrium to watch Flick execute Gwendolyn. It's going to be a *fabulous* show. No one's going to notice if the rest of us disappear."

"Flick is going to kill Gwendolyn?" Julian asks.

"That's the price he has to pay for his freedom. If he succeeds, he can follow us when he's finished."

"And what if someone decides to stay?" Caleb inquires.

"Do what you want, Caleb, but if you get in our way, the rest of us will have to kill *you*."

It's a nice touch, and Joi couldn't be more convincing. The Wolves seem to believe it's all true. And if anything goes wrong, it will be.

"Damn, *that* was impressive," I tell Joi once the others have left. The firework display has finished, and the city is dark "I was worried they weren't going to go for it."

"Yeah, because Mandel's had them all doped up on Exceletrex."

"We didn't know for sure they'd been taking it."

"We do now," Joi points out.

"I gotta admit. You've handled everything perfectly. And I still can't believe Curly actually burgled the boss."

Joi grins. "When you said he couldn't do it, that's when I knew for sure that he could. If people think you can't do anything, you can get away with everything," she says. "No one's worthless. That's the lesson Mandel's going to learn."

And the one she's been trying to teach me all along.

"So you have everything ready for Monday?" I ask.

"Yep. Curly didn't forget a thing." Joi pulls her medical kit out of the black bag. I can't help but notice that there's still one file inside. "I have all the surgical supplies a girl could possibly need."

"Are you going to have enough time to remove all the chips?"

"Mandel will have his employees out hunting down the Wolves, and he'll think I've gone with them. He'll have to lock the rest of the kids in their rooms. I'm guessing I'll have a few hours to make my rounds."

"You really think all the Androids should be allowed to escape?"

"Why don't we try calling them something else for a change," Joi says. "They're not *Androids*. They're *prisoners*. And yes—they all deserve to go."

I'd rather not keep poking holes in Joi's plan. I just want to make sure that she's really thought it all through. "The infirmary nurse told me that the chips are inserted right next to an artery. Are you sure you can remove forty-six chips without killing anyone?"

"My mother used to treat hundreds of patients each day. She taught me how to work quickly."

"I always wondered where you learned how to stitch people up. Your mom was a doctor?"

"She didn't have a degree. She was still training to be a surgeon when the war in Bosnia broke out."

I recognize the expression that's just appeared on Joi's face. I've seen it on my own reflection, but I've never seen her wear it before.

"Go ahead. You can ask," she says.

"How did she meet your father?" It's the politest way to phrase the question that's bouncing around in my brain. *How in the hell does a medical student end up with a war criminal?*

"My mother's husband was murdered during the Siege of Sarajevo, and she was put in the detention camp that my father ran. That's where they 'met.' And that's where I was born." Joi's voice has the robotic quality of someone trying not to cry. "I was meant to humble her."

This isn't a romance. It's a horror story. But I have to force myself to listen. No matter how bad it gets. And I can tell it's going to get a whole lot worse.

"When the war ended, my mother couldn't go home. Her family never would have accepted me. So we lived in refugee camps all over Bosnia that were filled with women and children just like us. Everyone seemed to be sick, and my mother was one of the few people around who could help them. She spent the last week of her life trying to save a baby with typhoid. The baby lived, but my mother caught the fever. She died because there weren't enough antibiotics left in the camp to save her. I don't know what would have happened to me if an American doctor hadn't heard the story. I was fourteen years old, and I had nowhere to go, so she brought me back to the States with her. I had a beautiful room in her house in New Jersey, and I was grateful. But it wasn't where I belonged. So after a few weeks, I left."

"I'm sorry, Joi." There's nothing else I can say. I try to take her in my arms, but Joi steps back and wipes her eyes with the collar of her T-shirt. She wants to finish speaking while she's still able.

"I don't want you to feel sorry for me. I told you about my mother for a reason. So you'd know that I had one too."

What is she trying to say? Joi knows nothing about my mom. Does she think my mother was anything like the saint she just described? *Joi's* mother never abandoned her. *Her* mother didn't swallow an entire bottle of Valium. *Her* mother didn't follow one son to the grave and leave the other all alone in a world filled with monsters. *Her* mother didn't disappear without saying goodbye. The way my mother did.

I wish I could be like Joi. So trusting. So hopeful. I suppose I was once, a long time ago. When I was little, I really believed that my mother, brother, and I would manage to beat the monster one day. We'd find a place to hide where we couldn't be found. Because Jude and my mother were the heroes of my story. And in every story I'd ever read, the good guys *always* made it out alive.

"I don't understand," I tell Joi.

"*I do.* I understand everything now. I know why you came here, Flick. If I got a chance, I'd try to hurt your dad too."

"That's why I came. It's not why I've stayed."

"I know. But maybe it's time for you to go." Joi dips her hand back into the bag and pulls out the last file. "I added another name to the list we gave Curly. This one's for Peter Pan."

I can see my father's name on the label. But I won't touch the file. "I don't want it."

"I read it, Flick. There are pictures, too. I've seen what your father did to the rest of your family." She can't stop the tears now. "Jude looked just like you." Her last sentence is almost a wail.

"Jude is dead. So is my mother." It's the first time I've ever said it out loud. "There's no way to help them. I need to stay here with you now."

"You can't!" Joi sobs. "This is your last chance. I can remove your chip tonight. If you leave this weekend, your father won't know you're coming. After Monday, he'll be expecting you. He'll be prepared."

"It's okay," I tell her.

"No, it's not! You have to go, Flick."

"What about Gwendolyn's execution? What about the show I'm supposed to put on Monday night?"

"Don't worry about that. I'll figure something out. I can handle the rest of this on my own."

"I know you can," I say. "But I'm not going to let you. My family is gone. You're my one good thing now."

CHAPTER THIRTY-TWO

DINNER FOR TWO

The entire school has turned out to watch me kill Gwendolyn. Dinner has finished, and there's an hour left before curfew. The battle will take place at the bottom of the atrium. Ghosts and Androids encircle the second-floor balcony. The Wolves will be allowed a ringside view. As far as I know, there are only two exits on the school's ground floor—the front door and the service exit. They both remain locked throughout the day. But that doesn't pose much of a problem if you happen to have the headmaster's key.

Joi and Mandel spent the holiday weekend planning the spectacle. Every detail was decided in advance. Gwendolyn and I were both met outside our sixth-period classes by teams of Wolves dressed in black, their faces hidden beneath executioners' masks. They escorted us to our rooms, where pristine white outfits were laid out on our beds. Once we had dressed, we were taken to the ground floor. Two chairs had been placed in the center of the atrium, right above the words LUCTOR ET EMERGO. The Wolves strapped our wrists to the arms of our chairs, then blended back into the shadows. Ella was left to guard us.

We've been sitting here for over four hours. A couple of spectators have kept us company the whole time. Everyone has seen us, and now they're all back. The wait has been much worse than I anticipated. Gwendolyn keeps rocking in her seat and whispering to the walls. She won't obey Ella's orders to be silent. I can't bear to look over at her. Her eyes are glassy, and there's a huge patch of hair missing on one side of her head. I managed to ignore her whispers for the first hour or so. But they've crawled in through my ears and they're starting to eat away at my mind.

I'm on the verge of screaming when I see one of the elevators begin to rise. It climbs all the way to the top, where it picks up a single passenger. Mandel will be making his debut as a god tonight, descending from the heavens to watch the human sacrifice being made in his name. He comes into view as the elevator passes the sixth floor. He's dressed in a sleek black suit with a black shirt and tie. But it's the simpering smile on his face that makes it all truly sinister.

The elevator arrives, and Mandel steps out with a surgical scalpel in one hand. He approaches Gwendolyn, pauses long enough for everyone to get a good look at the blade. Then he cuts the straps that bind her wrists. Next, he frees my arms.

"Stand," he orders. That's Joi's cue. The time has come for the Dux to address the crowd.

Gwendolyn and I face each other. She has no idea that she's about to receive a last-minute reprieve. There's a long pause while we all wait for Joi. The contest can't begin without her.

At last, Mandel turns to Ella. "Where is the Dux?" he asks.

"I haven't seen her since Flick and Gwendolyn were brought downstairs," Ella responds.

"Where is she?" he hisses at me.

"How should I know? I've been tied to a chair for the past four hours," I point out. "You're the one who monitors the chips. Don't tell me you weren't paying attention this evening."

"She must be with the others," Ella says. "Wherever *they* are."

"The others?" Mandel asks as his eyes circle the ground floor.

That's when Gwendolyn starts to laugh. It's a high-pitched cackle that sounds more hyena than human. It ricochets off the walls of the atrium. Gwendolyn's lost what little is left of her mind, and Mandel looks disgusted. Until he finally realizes what's funny.

"Everyone to your rooms!" he shouts at the crowd. "This instant!"

He charges toward the elevator, slides the gates open, and points inside.

"You too," he growls at me.

I find Joi in my bathroom. Her scalpel, needles, and thread are laid out on the side of the sink. The chair from my desk is waiting for me. I kiss her once before I remove my shirt and take a seat. Joi clips my hair back with one of her own bobby pins. Then she takes a washcloth, wets it, and twists the fabric into a rope, which she places between my teeth.

We hear the sound of people marching around the balcony outside my room. The footsteps pause every few seconds. They're patrolling the building and making sure all the dorm rooms are locked. Joi is preparing to operate when the lights shut off. We can see a faint, red glow outside the bathroom.

Joi leaves and returns with my battery-powered alarm clock. I feel her lips at my ear. "Are you ready?" she whispers.

There is no anesthetic. No tequila this time. I feel the scalpel slice into my scalp. A drop of blood slips off a strand of my hair and splatters on my bare shoulder. More follow until there's a steady stream. Joi's nimble fingers are working fast. Scalp wounds can bleed heavily, but they're rarely dangerous, she assured me. My chip will be easier to remove than the others.

"Put out your hand," she whispers. The chip drops from her tweezers into my palm.

It doesn't look like metal and plastic. It's covered in blood and bits of tissue. If I didn't know what it was, I'd assume it had once been alive.

The needle punctures my scalp three times. Joi uses a towel from the bathroom and an entire bottle of spring water to rinse me off. I dress while Joi cleans her instruments and puts them back in her kit. According to the alarm clock, we stand by the door of my room for ten full minutes, listening for the sound of any movement outside. The dorms are quiet now, so I slip Mandel's key into the slot and slide the door open just enough to slip outside.

We're almost to Ella's room when I remember what I've forgotten. Without the clock, it's pitch black in my room. I manage to locate the frame on the wall, but I can't figure out how to open it. So I take it into the bathroom and crack it against the sink. The Plexiglas doesn't break, but the wood splinters. I remove Jude's picture, fold it up, and tuck it safely into my pocket.

Joi is standing by the railing when I emerge. She's staring down at the atrium, and I can see just enough of her face in the darkness to know something is wrong. The lights are still on downstairs, but there's no sound of activity. We expected the academy to be on full alert. But it seems as if everyone has gone home. Joi looks up at me, and I know what she's thinking. We've got to keep going. Our plan can't be postponed.

Ella keeps the washcloth clenched between her teeth, but she doesn't even whimper during the procedure. Joi works more slowly this time. The chip is close to the ulnar artery. One wrong move and Ella might bleed to death. I know Joi's nervous, but she doesn't let Ella see it. She waits until the last stitch is in before she allows herself a sigh of relief.

I'll sigh as soon as we're all out of the academy. I keep waiting for one of the Androids to turn against us and sound the alarm. Most are in bed when we arrive. Each time, I clamp a hand over their mouths, but no one has tried to scream yet. They almost seem glad that the end might be near. It doesn't matter which that end might be. Ella holds out her arm while Joi shines the light on the site of Ella's incision. The Androids instantly know what's happened. Nothing else needs to be said. But it hasn't all been smooth sailing. I thought the operation might go faster once Joi got the hang of removing the chips, but it takes us a full two hours to cover the eighth floor. She spent forty-five minutes working on one Android who's been at the academy for almost three years. His tissue had grown around the chip. Another year and it would have been part of his body.

There are two more dorm floors to cover. Getting down to the seventh is easy. Ella slinks back to her room and returns with a rope made of sheets. She used the design I'd come up with the night I tried to help Lucas. I loop the rope over the eighth-floor balcony and shimmy to the seventh floor. Joi and Ella follow, then we pull the rope down.

By the time we've finished on seven, thirty-nine chips have been removed. But we still face our biggest challenge. The rest of the students are housed on the ninth floor. And there's only one way up. So we hold our breath and board the elevator. The soft click of the gates sounds like a deafening bang. The hum of the motor is the roar of a jet engine. We step off on nine and listen. We hear nothing at all.

With the Wolves gone, only a handful of students remain on the top floor. And one of those will be left behind. Even Joi agrees that Gwendolyn is far too dangerous to be released into the wild. We're about to free our final prisoner, but we have to pass the old Dux's room to reach him. We're just outside Gwendolyn's dorm when Joi and Ella both freeze in their tracks.

"Help." The word was so faint that I'm not sure I heard it. "Help."

The three of us stare at the door.

"It's a trick!" Ella whispers.

"Help."

Joi kneels down and runs a finger through a small puddle that's formed under Gwendolyn's door. When she holds her fingertip up for inspection, Ella and I see it's dripping with blood. Joi puts her other hand out. She wants the key.

"Don't!" Ella pleads, but I've already placed Mandel's key in Joi's palm.

We find Gwendolyn lying on the other side of her door, surrounded by a pool of blood. Her pristine white outfit has been dyed scarlet. Joi kneels down beside her.

"Light," she orders, and I hold the alarm clock over Gwendolyn as Joi searches for the girl's wound. It doesn't take long to find it. There's a jagged red gash in the center of Gwendolyn's forearm. She's removed her own chip.

"Jesus. What did she use?" Ella asks.

I see what looks like a red stick lying a few feet from Gwendolyn. "A ballpoint pen," I say.

Joi has finished her inspection. "I can't stitch this up. She's nicked the artery. She needs a tourniquet."

I rip a strip from one of Gwendolyn's sheets, and Joi wraps it tightly around the girl's arm, just below the elbow. By the time she's finished, Gwendolyn is perfectly still.

"Is she dead?" I ask.

"No, but she will be soon. She's lost a ton of blood. We're gonna have to take her with us when we go."

I pick Gwendolyn up and place her on her bed. Then the rest of us hurry to the last student's room. The final stitch has just gone in when we hear the elevator gates open. I sprint to the balcony and arrive in time to see the gates close again. Then the elevator starts to descend. There's a trail of blood leading from Gwendolyn's room to the elevators.

"She's making a break for it," Ella whispers.

"Do you think she knows we've been helping the others?" I ask.

"No," Joi replies. "Her brain can't be getting enough blood. She's delirious."

I believe her. Until the elevator passes the ground floor and disappears below ground.

"Why didn't it stop?" Ella asks.

"*Shit.* She's gone to find Mandel." I turn to Joi. "You still have the key. Get everyone out. Right now."

Joi pulls the card key from her pocket and hands it to Ella. "You'll have to do it," she says. "Wait until Flick and I are downstairs, then start packing the elevators with students."

"You're going too!" I order.

"No," Joi says. "You wouldn't leave when I told you to either. And I asked *nicely.*"

The elevator gates open on the Infirmary floor—the nerve center of Mandel's operation. I expect to be greeted by a swarm of henchmen, and I hope we can keep them busy for a few short minutes while all the Ghosts and Androids flee the building. But Joi and I aren't met by any welcoming party. Gwendolyn is still on her own. She's slowly sliding along the wall of the empty hall. A red streak stretches from the elevator toward the two steel doors at the end of the corridor. She's only a few feet away. Joi and I move cautiously in her direction. The elevator gates shut behind us, and I hear the car climbing back up to the dorm floors.

"Gwendolyn! What are you doing?" Joi whispers. "You wanted to escape. We'll take you with us! We'll get you to a hospital!"

Gwendolyn's laugh turns into a cough and then a choke. "I knew you weren't good enough to be the Dux. You should have killed me when you had the chance."

"Don't do this, Gwendolyn!" I plead. "You're not thinking

straight. Mandel's been feeding you pills that rot people's brains. And he was about to let you be executed tonight. Come with us. We'll help you *leave!*"

"Why would I want to leave the academy? In a few minutes, I'll be Dux again." Gwendolyn hurls herself toward the lab entrance with her last bit of energy. She's too weak to stay on her feet, but her finger finds the buzzer before she collapses on the floor.

Once again, I find myself waiting for an army that never arrives. We hear a single set of footsteps inside the lab. As they approach the hallway, Joi and I frantically try each of the six white doors that lead to the examination rooms where newbies are given their physicals. They're all locked, and the elevator is gone. We're trapped. I watch the lab doors open. Lucian Mandel looks down at Gwendolyn's sapless body and then up at us. He's wearing a pair of plastic goggles pushed up on his forehead. His white lab coat is splattered with blood. There's a Taser in his right hand. An advanced model—military grade. The kind that can be deployed from a distance.

"They were going to escape." Gwendolyn sounds like she's gargling with her own blood. "I caught them."

"How considerate of you," Mandel says, stepping over her.

"I need a doctor," she moans.

"Yes," he agrees as he glances back at her. "It appears that you do. But I'm afraid you've come at the wrong time. I gave our physicians the night off."

Mandel walks right up to where Joi and I are standing. He looks at Joi and shakes his head sadly. "I'm terribly disappointed, my dear. I had such high hopes for you! Why aren't you out with the others?"

Joi glances over at me, but I don't know what he's talking about either.

"You had the file that belongs to Flick's father! You kept the best for yourself! Why didn't you use it?" Mandel exclaims before turning his attention to me. "Can you imagine? There's a knock on your father's door. Outside is a young woman he recognizes. He knows she once ran a home for orphans and runaways. But her mutant gene has been activated. She's a true predator now, and she's chosen your father to be her first victim. She's stolen his secrets, and he'll have to pay dearly to keep them from falling into the wrong hands. What better way to convince your father that the gene exists than to have him discover the irrefutable proof on his doorstep?!" Mandel sighs. "I suppose I shouldn't have expected justice to be quite so poetic."

"You knew about the files?" I can see real fear in Joi's eyes. She's worried about Curly and the colony kids.

"Certainly! I've been following your exploits since I misplaced my card key during that dreadful smoke incident. I had to make sure that the key hadn't been stolen, so I checked when it had last been used. It seemed *someone* had opened the door to my office after the key left my possession. It didn't take a genius to figure out who was responsible. I was curious to find out what you had planned. I assumed it might have something to do with the Fourth of July rooftop party you seemed so eager to throw. That was your second big mistake, I'm afraid. Did you honestly think I don't have the roof under surveillance? The listening devices up there are activated when they sense the presence of more than one tracking chip. That way *my* conversations remain private—but yours do not."

"You heard everything I said on the Fourth of July?"

"Of course. I was worried the sound of fireworks might drown out a few words here and there. So I asked Caleb to make a second recording. And I must say, I was not disappointed! Your speech was most inspirational—one might even say *brilliant*. Sending students to conquer the alumni! I wish I'd thought of it myself!"

"So you're not trying to stop the top twelve?" I ask. "You don't have anyone hunting them down?"

"Look around! The entire building is empty! Every employee at the academy has been sent out on the search! Unfortunately, they're looking in the wrong places. There seems to be a flaw in a few of the tracking chips. The signals are off by a few hundred yards. We'll fix the mistake, of course. Perhaps even tomorrow. But I'm afraid by that time, the escapees will have put all those files to good use."

"And you're going to let them? You've turned against the alumni?" Joi asks.

"Not all of them. I'm only punishing a few who've turned against *me*," Mandel replies. "A couple of the files you stole belonged to supporters, so I made sure they were switched before the big day arrived. But all in all, you made some excellent choices!"

"You're getting rid of your enemies, then."

"Yes, but it seems my most powerful foe remains at large." Mandel smiles pleasantly at the two of us. "So the breakout was only meant to be a distraction? Was I supposed to be chasing fugitives while you two lovebirds made your great escape?"

He reaches out and runs his thumb over the site of my incision. It comes away streaked with blood. Then he takes Joi's arm and rubs the same thumb over the spot where her chip should be.

"What do you have in there?" he asks.

"Tinfoil."

"Brilliant!" He chuckles before giving us both a fake frown. "But very, very naughty indeed. Oh well! Back to plan A." Then he nudges my side with the tip of the Taser. "I don't want to be rude, but you've interrupted my dinner. We should head back inside before it gets cold."

I give his blood-splattered lab coat a once-over. "What are you eating? A whole sheep?"

"That's what I admire most about you, Flick," Mandel tells me. "No matter what, you never seem to lose your sense of humor."

He steers us toward the lab doors, which are propped open by one of Gwendolyn's limp arms.

"Don't trip," Mandel warns us as we step over her body. Once the three of us are inside the lab, he kicks Gwendolyn's arm back into the hall.

"Thank you!" he calls out to her as the doors slam behind us.

The lab has been shut down for the night, but the morgue at the far end is brightly lit. I can smell steak and roasted potatoes. I haven't eaten since lunch, and my mouth is watering against my will. As we draw closer to the light, I catch sight of Mandel's desk. It's covered with a crisp white tablecloth. I spot a hunk of filet mignon with a knife still stuck in the center. And an open bottle of champagne. I hear Joi gasp, and I assume she's disgusted by the celebration Mandel's been throwing himself. Then my eyes land on one of the autopsy tables. Caleb is lying on top. He's naked from the waist up. He might have looked like he was sleeping if there wasn't something wrong with his head. I glance down at a stainless steel tray by the side of the table. Inside is Caleb's brain.

"That's what you do to people who help you?" Joi mutters.

"It's a shame, isn't it?" Mandel agrees. "I'm afraid Caleb saw too much over the weekend. He knows I allowed students to escape. Which meant I couldn't allow him to live." He holds up the Taser and takes a sip of his champagne. "And now I'll be able to assure the alumni that *someone* has been punished for this rather unfortunate turn of events."

"The alumni aren't stupid. They'll know you had something to do with the breakout. The missing files only belong to your enemies."

"A happy coincidence! And it doesn't really matter what the alumni *suspect*. Thanks to you, I have plausible deniability. Of course it's *possible* that I knew about the plan. It's also possible that I didn't. There's not a shred of proof either way. Only the three of us know the truth."

Which means he can't let us live either. I wonder which one of us Mandel will cut up first. I should throw myself at him. He'll shoot me with the Taser, of course, but it might give Joi a chance to run.

Mandel is watching me. "You are a funny pair," he says. "Such splendid specimens. And yet you insist on acting so *illogically*. Your own survival seems to mean very little to you. So if either of you comes within ten feet of me, I'll Taser the *other* one first. Do you understand?"

I nod.

"Good!" Mandel exclaims with a laugh.

"So does this mean you're not going to kill us?" Joi asks.

"My precious hybrids? Not until it's absolutely necessary! Perhaps

Flick didn't tell you, but I'm conducting a very important experiment. And now it seems as if I'll need *both* of you to finish it. So sit down," he orders, pointing at the two chairs on either side of his desk.

Joi and I obey. I take the chair with the view of Caleb so she doesn't have to look.

"Now eat," Mandel commands. "You missed dinner this evening, and you're going to need all of your strength soon. The filet mignon is excellent. May I offer you both a glass of champagne?"

CHAPTER THIRTY-THREE

NEVER NEVER LAND

The warmth might feel good after our visit to Mandel's frigid morgue—if it weren't for the faint stench in the air. I doubt it would bother me if I didn't know what it was. The thought makes my stomach churn, and I can feel a hunk of filet mignon still sitting undigested inside it. I was nauseous before I took my first bite, and I gagged on the second. But Mandel made us keep eating until our plates were clean.

"Now that your bellies are full, I think it's time for a nap," he announced. "But first, please return my card key if you would."

I didn't dare glance at Joi. "It's upstairs," I informed him.

"Still scheming?" Mandel didn't seem at all offended. "I suppose I could search you, but I have a rather important phone call to make. So I'll just have to put you in the one room that my key doesn't open. It might not be as comfortable as your dorms, but I promise you it will be nice and *cozy*."

He marched us out of the morgue and back toward the elevator.

We opened the lab doors to find Gwendolyn's corpse blocking our path.

"Oh dear." Mandel sighed as though he'd forgotten all about her. "What a mess. Would you mind?"

I wasn't sure what we were supposed to do. "Mind what?" I finally asked.

"Picking her up!" he exclaimed with exasperation. "She's coming along for the ride."

Joi and I rode the elevator with Gwendolyn's body slumped between us. Two floors up from the Infirmary, the elevator stopped and the gates opened. A rusty door lay just beyond. It looked as old as the building itself—and just as sturdy. There wasn't a card slot or a keyhole. The door was secured from the outside with a simple metal bar, which Mandel swiftly removed and set aside.

"After you," he told us.

We entered a cavernous chamber with bare brick walls and a concrete floor. I knew it must have been the building's original basement. A twenty-first-century central heating system took up half of the room. The other half was empty but for a large industrial furnace. Mandel opened its iron doors, and flames reached out and licked the mouth of the oven.

I saw a red square outlined in black. When I blinked, it was still there on the back of my eyelids. And I knew it would never go away. Once you've seen the gates of hell, the sight stays with you forever.

Gwendolyn must be nothing but ash by now. Joi and I are alone. We're huddled in a corner, as far away from the furnace as we can possibly get. Joi's head rests against my chest. I have both arms wrapped around her and my face buried in her hair. With my eyes closed, I can float away on a cloud of jasmine and cocoa butter. I kiss the top of Joi's head and try to forget that Mandel will return for us as soon as he discovers the academy's students are gone.

"What did you go back to get?" I hear Joi ask. It's the first thing she's said in a while. I was hoping she'd managed to fall asleep.

"Hmm?"

"When we left your room, you went back for something. What was it?"

I reach into my pocket and pull out the yearbook page. "This." I pass it to Joi. She unfolds it and smiles.

"Peter Pan," she murmurs. "So it wasn't just a nickname. Jude really played the part. He must have been a great kid." She thinks it all makes sense to her now. It shouldn't.

"I need you to promise me something," I tell her. "When Mandel comes, you have to do whatever it takes to get out of here. Even if it means I won't make it. Let him shoot me with the Taser. Then make a run for it."

"No," she says.

"*Yes,*" I insist. "There's something you don't know. I lost my mind after Jude died, and I don't think I'll ever get it back. He visits me at night. Dressed exactly like that." I tap the page.

"Flick . . ."

"My name is Jonathan Brennan. My father went to school here. Now he's a drunk and a sociopath. He killed my brother. My mother died on the day of Jude's funeral. And I've spent the last year talking to Peter Pan."

I wonder why Mandel never mentioned my mother. He must know what happened. Maybe he just couldn't think of a way to use it against me. I tried calling her the morning Jude was going to be buried. I'd been up half the night, thinking about those damn desert frogs. I wanted to thank her for all the times she tried to save us. And I was going to promise that I'd be back just as soon as I was strong enough to save *her*. But she didn't think I could do it. Because when I phoned that morning, she was already gone.

My father always said I was weak. My mother made me believe it.

"What do you and Peter Pan talk about?" Joi asks softly.

"Everything I'm doing wrong."

"Like what?"

"Well, he was really pissed when I left the Lower East Side. He thought I should have stayed with you."

"Smart kid," Joi says. "You like talking to him?"

"Sure. Aside from the nagging, he's the most entertaining hallucination I've ever had."

"Have you ever wondered if he might be real?"

"You don't have to say that," I tell her. "I don't need to be coddled like the colony kids."

"I'm being perfectly serious," Joy insists. "How do you know he's not real? Do you have any proof that he isn't?"

"He's a character from a book for little kids," I say.

"He's your brother."

"Jude's dead."

"That doesn't mean he's gone," Joi says. "Remember, Flick. You get to *choose* what you believe."

402

• • •

I shouldn't be asleep. I was supposed to stay awake to protect her. But Jude has sent me a dream. He's not in this one. It's early in the morning. My father's already on his way to work, school doesn't start for another two hours, and the servants won't arrive until eight. I'm twelve, and my mother has just snuck into my room. She's quickly pulling clothes out of my bureau and stacking them on top.

"Where are we going this time?" I ask.

When she turns around, I'm shocked by how young she looks. How pretty and petite. With hair just as blond as Gwendolyn's. She had such a beautiful smile, but even then, I could tell when it wasn't real.

"On an adventure. To Never Land." That's what she always said.

"Jude's the one who believes in Never Land," I point out with a huff.

My mother leaves the clothes on the dresser and comes over to plant a kiss on my forehead. "And you're all grown up now. That's why I know I can trust you to play along."

"Why don't you tell Jude the truth?"

"Jude knows what the truth is," my mother says. "He just needs to believe in something else. Do you understand?"

I nod.

"I knew you would." She wraps me up in a hug and holds me close so I can't see her tears.

"What's wrong?" I whisper with my eyes squeezed shut. If I cry, she'll cry even harder.

"I just wish you believed in Never Land too."

• • •

When I open my eyes, my mother is gone and Jude is here in the basement with me.

"I told Joi that I talk to you," I say.

"And she didn't run away screaming?"

I gesture to the room around us. "Where would she go?"

"Excellent point," Peter Pan says.

"She said you're real."

"Of course I'm real," Peter Pan replies. "Who do you think just sent you that dream?"

"It was nice to see Mom again," I mutter.

"I know you're still mad. But she tried, Jon. How many times did she try to take us to Never Land?"

"You were the one she was trying to save."

"That's not true. You were *her* boy, remember?"

"Then why did she leave me behind? I was going to rescue her. Why didn't she wait for me?"

"I don't know," Peter Pan says.

"Well, if you see Mom in Never Land, be sure to ask her."

"Jon . . ." I hear Jude start to argue, but Mandel's cheerful voice drowns him out.

"Rise and shine!" he sings. "You have a visitor!"

CHAPTER THIRTY-FOUR

THE HEIR

We rise from the depths of the academy into a blaze of light. The ground floor has been transformed into a spotlit stage ringed by nine dark tiers. Mandel seems to be expecting an audience, but he must know by now that the dorms are all empty. The Androids and Ghosts have fled. And yet he's perfectly composed, as if it were all part of his plan.

"We have a very special guest with us this morning," Mandel confides just before the elevator gates open. "He drove all the way from Connecticut to be here. So let's make sure we show him a good time. Oh, and Flick? Be on your best behavior, please. One wrong move, and I will be forced to turn my Taser on Joi."

I see our guest now. He's standing in the center of one of the three golden circles—like a token on a board game. He's been awaiting the next roll of the dice.

"You woke me up in the middle of the night for *this*?" my father demands.

"Where are your manners, Henry?" Mandel responds blithely. "I believe an introduction is in order. Henry, I'd like you to meet Joi. Joi, this is Flick's father, Henry Brennan."

"I know who she is, Lucian," my dad snarls. "You told me that the future of the academy would be decided tonight. And this is your experiment's grand finale? If you think my son is going to dispose of his girlfriend, you're a fool. He'll die rather than kill her. As eager as I am to win our wager, this could have waited until a more reasonable hour."

For once my father is right about me. I'll never be like him. I won't follow in his footsteps. If I'm forced to choose between my life and my one good thing, I will choose death. And I'll die without a single regret. I take Joi's hand, and our fingers lock together. Her amber eyes glow when she smiles. She's not afraid either.

"I assure you this will not be a waste of your time, Henry," I hear Mandel say. "The switch will take place. In a few short minutes, your son will become a predator."

I watch the two men face off across the courtyard. Mandel is grinning. My father is glowering. Everything about this situation seems to disgust him. "Then where are Ackerman and Leavitt? They need to be here too."

I remember meeting Ackerman at one of Mandel's little parties. I don't recognize the other name. He must be a member of the opposition.

"Ackerman won't be coming," Mandel replies. "And Leavitt is dealing with a little situation of his own at the moment."

It's almost amusing to see my father regard Lucian Mandel with the same contempt he always showed me. "Then this is a violation of our agreement. Nothing can be decided unless there are alumni representatives present."

My father marches toward the exit and shoves a card key into the slot. But the doors won't open. He tries once more before he charges back across the atrium with his nostrils flared, his chest puffed, and his fists clenched. It's an intimidating performance. Mandel never budges.

"Have you disabled my key?" my dad rages. He's got at least five inches and fifty pounds on the academy's headmaster, but that doesn't seem to matter much to Mandel.

"You're critical to the experiment, Henry," Mandel replies in the patient, patronizing tone of a kindergarten teacher. "Now that the final stage is in progress, we must see it through to the finish. I'm confident that the experiment will be a success. So confident that I'm even prepared to raise the stakes." He holds up a folder he's had tucked under one arm. "If I lose, this is yours to destroy."

"Is that my file? And you're carrying it around like it's a copy of the *Wall Street Journal*?!" My father takes another step toward Mandel. Joi's fingers tighten their grip on mine. I'm waiting for my dad to throw his first punch. But he doesn't. "When the alumni hear about all of this, you won't have a single supporter left."

"When the alumni are told what happened here tonight, they'll know I've accomplished something miraculous." Mandel beams.

"No, Lucian. After tonight, they'll finally be able to say what they've always believed. That you're a raving little lunatic."

Mandel's smile is gone the instant that last word reaches his ears. There's a sadistic smirk on my father's lips. He knew his insult would wound. "If that's what the alumni believe," Mandel snips, "it's only because you've worked so hard to convince them."

"You've been telling yourself the same lie for the last twenty years." The battle has turned. Mandel is on the defensive now, and my father is aiming for the chink in his armor. "You think I've dedicated my life to turning the whole world against you, but the alumni didn't need to be *convinced* that you're deranged. Neither did your mother. The facts have always spoken for themselves."

"Facts you twisted to suit your agenda!" Mandel shouts. "You wanted my mother to make you her heir! You've been after my rightful inheritance since the day you arrived at the academy!"

"You forfeited that inheritance when you were fifteen years old, Lucian. Do you remember how you spent your holidays that year? You'd fly in from your fancy Swiss boarding school and head straight for the academy. You forced so many kids to take that psychopath test that you almost provoked a mutiny. You treated this school like your own little empire and the students like your personal playthings. Even your mother knew you needed professional help. But she had a school to run, and your father wanted nothing to do with any of you. So she asked me to step in."

"My mother asked her masterpiece to be my mentor. How *touching*. I know how highly she thought of you, Henry. She always said you were one of a kind. I just wish she could be here to watch me make a thousand little 'masterpieces' just like you."

My father's upper lip curls into a snarl, and I know he's about to go in for the kill. "If Beatrice were here, Lucian, you wouldn't be allowed within fifty feet of this place."

"Because of all the lies you told!" Mandel cries, his face a fiery crimson.

My dad shakes his head. "Lies? I never said a word to Beatrice the day I caught you in the act. I just took her down to the basement and let her see for herself what her fifteen-year-old son had been doing. Hoarding bodies that should have been cremated. Cutting them open and taking things out. Dissecting their organs and putting their brains in glass jars."

"What difference did it make? The bodies were going to be destroyed!"

Mandel's tone has grown shrill, while my father's voice has deepened and darkened. "You had no right! Even the weakest student ever admitted to this school was a hundred times stronger than you'll ever be. They may have died, but they survived long enough to die with dignity. Your mother understood that. What you did to those bodies disgusted her. I never said you should be banished. The truth is, your mother didn't ask for my advice. If she had, I would have told her to kill you. Even then I could see what might happen if this school ever fell into your hands.

"Do you really think your mother would approve of the things you've been doing here? Experimenting on the students? Slicing up the dead children's brains? Feeding the living ones pills? What would she say about *Exceletrex*, Lucian?"

"She would say it's an elegant solution to the discipline issues we've always faced here at the academy. We haven't had a single revolt since the predator students began taking the pills. I think she would see it as proof that I deserve the headmaster position."

"Oh really? And how do you think she'd feel if she knew that you disposed of your own sister to get the job?"

"Marjorie died in a car accident," Mandel sniffs.

"You're even crazier than I imagined if you honestly think I believe that."

Mandel glares at my father for a moment. Then he takes a deep breath. By the time he exhales, his smile has returned. "I can find a hundred psychiatrists who will testify to my sanity, Henry. But that's not the subject we're here to discuss. I'm on the verge of a scientific breakthrough."

"There's no goddamned *gene*, Lucian!" My father's shout fills the whole atrium. "We've been paying dozens of geneticists top dollar to search for it. It's been five years now. I've read all of the reports. They haven't found anything! The gene doesn't exist!"

"It does. Which brings us back to the reason I invited you to the academy this morning, Henry. I want to present the proof you've demanded."

My father points at me. "He is not going to be your *proof*, Lucian."

"If that's what you think, then you should have no problem seeing our agreement to its conclusion," Mandel notes. "You said I'd never be able to turn him into a predator. You said he didn't have what it took. Well, I believe he does. Flick has the gene, Henry, just like you. And in a few short minutes, I'll activate it."

"His name isn't Flick," my father sneers. "It's *Jonathan*. And if you weren't so demented, you'd be able to see that he and I have *nothing* in common."

I feel Mandel's free arm slide around my shoulders. "Your insults are wasted on me. I know you're afraid of us."

"I'll show you how frightened I am." My father straightens his spine and seems to grow two inches. "You think that little toy Taser can stop me from snapping your neck?"

Mandel doesn't flinch. "Go ahead, Henry. Kill me. But you'll never get control of the academy. It will pass to my heir instead."

My dad snorts. "You're not capable of producing children. Your mother didn't have the heart to get rid of you, but at least she listened to the board of directors and made sure you wouldn't reproduce."

When I hear Joi gasp, I know I didn't misinterpret that last part.

"True," Mandel concedes placidly. He won't lose his cool again. "But I'm quite capable of *choosing* an heir. Flick and I may not share DNA, but we were forged in the same fire. *Luctor et emergo*, Henry. We've both suffered at your hands. Now it's time for us to rise."

I watch my father ponder the news. He's trying to figure out if it's true.

"I hope you heard that!" he finally shouts. It takes me a second to realize he's not speaking to anyone in the room. He's addressing all the academy's bugs. "I'm looking forward to playing tonight's tapes for the board."

"The listening devices are automatically shut off at curfew, Henry," Mandel informs him. "Don't you remember? It was one of the cost-cutting measures you forced me to implement. And you've already had your last meeting with the board of directors. The time has come for you to watch your son become a predator. I'm afraid it will be the last thing you see. Because Flick is going to kill *you*."

The shock hits me so hard that I laugh. The sound appears to confuse my dad. He studies my face for a moment but doesn't seem to find what he's looking for. "Are you?" he demands.

Joi is squeezing my hand hard enough to crack a few bones. The answer is no. But I'm not going to say so. "Wait—is this the kind of choice you told me I'd face here? I thought you said it was supposed to be *hard*."

"This is no time for jokes, Jonathan," my father says. He never appreciated my sense of humor. "Before you make your decision, there are a few things you should know. Did Lucian tell you why your brother died?"

"Yeah. Jude found out you're a crook and confronted you."

"Did Lucian tell you that *he* was the one who gave Jude the information? It was his first attempt to get me out of the way. He didn't want anyone associated with the academy to know, so he went behind the alumni's backs and tried to use my own son to destroy me."

This is the father who once seemed like a god to me. A pathetic, broken man who beat his children and still blames other people for the things that he's done. "The information didn't kill Jude, Dad. *You* did."

"I never expected your brother to die," Mandel assures me. "I'm afraid I miscalculated."

"Jude was not your toy!" my father bellows. "He was my son!"

"I didn't treat Jude like a *toy*," Mandel argues. "I simply gave him a few documents from your file."

"A blatant abuse of academy data!" This is the rage that would have once sent me running. Now I see a man who's lost control. "You should have been forced to resign. It was a perfect example of how dangerous you are—not just to me but to every graduate of this academy. But only half of the alumni had the guts to fight you. The rest were all terrified you'd turn on them next."

"You had just murdered one of your sons, and you were

demanding control of my family's academy. Which of us seemed unhinged, Henry? Under the circumstances, I think it was quite sporting of me to offer to settle the dispute with a wager."

"A wager that would force me to sacrifice my one remaining son!"

"Yes, it was very noble of you to accept my offer. But I don't think you're giving yourself enough credit. You had to make *two* sacrifices, didn't you, Henry?"

My father goes silent. He's panting softly as he takes out a handkerchief and wipes his brow. He folds the fabric into a smaller square and tucks it back in his pocket before he speaks again. "Our agreement forbids either of us from discussing that subject."

Two sacrifices?

"And it forbid you from referring to *me* as insane. So I think we can both agree that our agreement is now null and void."

Two sacrifices?

"What was the second sacrifice?" I demand.

Mandel sighs. "You never opened the present I left on your computer, did you?" he asks.

WHEN YOU'RE READY. The folder he said contained a reason to live. "No."

"Ah, then you're missing a crucial piece of data." Mandel thumbs through my father's file and plucks out a photo. "There was something standing in the way of our wager. Or rather *someone*. Someone who might have gone looking for her son."

I remember what Lucas said. Most of the kids at this school are orphans. The rest might as well be. And my father confirmed it the day I was arrested. The academy only recruits students who are alone in the world. "You can't mean . . ."

"A picture's worth a thousand words," Mandel says as he holds the photograph out to me.

"I thought you knew!" Joi whispers when I drop her hand to take the photo. "It was in the file!"

"I never opened the file."

The photo shows my mother lying on her bed at our house in Connecticut. No, not *lying*. Being held down. There are three men in the room with her. Two have her pinned to the bed. My father is injecting a syringe full of liquid into one of my mother's arms.

"Who took this photo?"

"An associate," Mandel responds.

"What does it mean?" I know, but I want to hear it from him.

"It means your mother didn't commit suicide. She was put to sleep."

I hold the photo out so my dad can see it. "You killed her? So that I'd be able to enter the academy? So you could win your f—ing *wager*?!"

Never once in my entire life have I seen my father struck dumb. I've watched him charm confederates, outsmart rivals, and devastate enemies with a few well-chosen words. He was always prepared. Now my father's silence is his confession.

My father always told me that I was my mother's son. He made it sound like an insult, but I didn't give a damn because it meant she was *mine*. Then he took her away, and I had no one left.

He's keeping his eyes fixed on me. My rage is steadily building. The demon has returned. I will rip the bastard limb from limb. I want him to suffer. I want him to feel the pain he put me through. I want him to know the terror I felt the morning I found out I was all alone.

"Speak!" I shout.

"I did what I had to do," he tells me. And I can see he believes it. He's *proud* of himself. He's proud of how far he was willing to go. "I don't regret it."

"Jude told her he had proof of your father's crimes. She thought she was finally free to file for divorce," Mandel says. "But you couldn't let her escape, could you, Henry?"

I'm already across the atrium. My body slams into my father's. He sails backward and falls hard on the tile floor. I'm on top of him. Left hand on his throat. Right hand pounding his face. It feels good. I won't stop until he's as hideous as Jude was that night at the funeral home. Until his eyes bulge in terror the way my mother's did in that picture. I won't stop until he's dead.

But as good as it feels, I know something's not right. My father is not fighting back.

"Flick." The static in my brain is so deafening that I'm not even certain I heard her. But I glance up at Joi. Mandel has her by the arm. He's ordering her to stay quiet. But she doesn't need to speak. I can see my reflection in her face. I know I'm the one who's hideous.

I take my weight off my father's chest and shake out my fist. Mandel doesn't seem worried that the fight may have ended. "There's something else in the file, Flick." His arsenal isn't quite empty yet. "Your father remarried a few months after your mother's death. His wife gave birth two weeks ago. Congratulations on your new son, Henry."

"Son?" I mumble.

"*Son,*" Mandel repeats.

And I start to laugh.

I can tell by the way he said it. *Son*. That crazy little f—er thinks he's located my switch. He thinks he's found the secret word that will turn me into a mindless killer. It's absolutely hilarious. That someone could have studied me for so long—and know absolutely nothing about me.

I'm still grinning when I bend down until my face is less than an inch from my father's. His breathing's a bit labored, but he's nowhere near dead. I can't smell any trace of alcohol. He must have come here sober. "Don't think you're getting off easy. I'm going to do something much worse than kill you," I whisper. "I'm going to take away everything you have. Your money and power. Your fancy house and expensive cars. I'm going to make sure you spend the rest of your life in a prison. And while you're locked up, I'm going to find your son and do everything I can to make sure he grows up to be nothing like you."

Then I stand up and offer my father a hand. I don't know why, but I do, and he takes it. "Did you hear that, Lucian?" he rasps as he struggles to his feet. "The *hybrid* refuses to fight. Your experiment has failed."

"No, Henry." When I see Mandel smiling, I know the show isn't over. Then I realize how close he's standing to Joi. His Taser gun must be pressed to the small of her back. "You won't be leaving. Kill him, Flick. Or *I'll* kill Joi."

"This is between me and my son now," my father insists. "The girl has nothing to do with it."

"Joi knew she was taking a risk when she came here," Mandel says. "And she knows why I can no longer allow her to stay. But if Flick kills *you*, I'll allow him to execute Joi as well. Otherwise, I'm afraid I'll have to do it myself. And I'll make her death very slow. And extremely painful."

Mandel has outmaneuvered all of us. Even my father sees it now.

"It doesn't matter how many people die tonight," my father sneers. "No one will believe that your ridiculous experiment succeeded. You have no evidence. No witnesses."

"Oh, Henry." Mandel sighs. "You think so little of me. Of *course* I don't expect anyone to take me at my word. That's why I've invited observers!"

We hear the familiar sound of five dozen doors unlocking at once. I'm eager to see the shock on Mandel's face when he realizes the rooms are all empty. But I'm the one whose jaw drops. Androids and Ghosts file out of the dorms and form lines at the elevator banks. Something has gone terribly wrong. I look back at Joi. The sight of her face hurts more than any beating I've ever received.

The first batch of students arrives on the ground floor. Ella steps out and marches straight toward the headmaster. She's still dressed in the black executioner's garb that she wore to watch over me and Gwendolyn. But now she's wearing a triumphant smile as well. Just as I lunge at her, two large Androids grab me from behind. Another pair takes my father prisoner. The second elevator delivers its passengers to the bottom of the atrium and the first begins its climb back to the dorms, where the rest of the spectators are waiting.

"Meet our new Dux," Mandel says, giving Joi a push forward. The hand holding the Taser drops to his side. Now that his army has arrived, he has no need of a hostage.

"Congratulations," Joi tells Ella. "You've really earned the title."

"Thanks," Ella replies, grinning from ear to ear. If there were one person I could kill at this moment, it would be my old ally. It's bad enough that she double-crossed us. But now Joi's going to die with her faith shattered. She's been betrayed by the very people she risked everything to help.

The last two groups of students descend from the dorms. "Form a circle!" Ella barks at them, and the five of us are surrounded. "Don't let any of the prisoners leave until this is over."

"Are we ready?" Mandel asks.

"Yes, sir," Ella responds.

But Mandel is no longer listening. He's noticed the same strange scent I have. Mandel sniffs the air, and I see the confusion on his face when he realizes it's smoke. But the alarms remain silent and the sprinklers haven't been activated. I spot flames flickering inside one of the rooms on the seventh floor. I glance over at Mandel. Orson and Hugo, Joi's friends from the Suites, have positioned themselves behind the headmaster. One seizes his arms while the other knocks the Taser out of his hand. The contents of my father's file spill onto the floor.

"What are you doing?" Mandel demands. He doesn't understand. I'm not sure I do either.

"We struggled, now we're rising. Isn't that how it's supposed to work?" Ella gives Joi a hug, and the Androids set me free.

"But I gave you the *title*!" Mandel cries. "Do you know what that means? In a few short years, you'll be one of the richest people on earth! What else could you want?"

"Justice," Ella responds. "You murdered my friend Felix."

"I didn't murder anyone," Mandel insists. "Felix *lost*!"

"And now it looks like you've lost too," Ella says. "Orson?"

Mandel's head seems tiny between Orson's enormous hands. He's finally stopped smiling. It was just a game when other people were dying. Now Mandel knows the truth—it's all real.

"Is it really necessary to kill him?" Joi grimaces.

"You're sweet," says Ella, giving Joi a pat on the shoulder. "But you're just going to have to trust me on *this* one."

The snap is much louder than I expected. Mandel crumples. Orson takes his torso. Hugo takes his legs. Together they toss the corpse into one of the elevators. Flora presses the button for the ninth floor, and the car begins to rise.

Violet gathers up the documents from my father's file and presents them to Joi, along with Mandel's Taser.

"Why are you guys still here?" I ask. "Did something go wrong?"

"Yeah. No one wanted to leave," Ella replies. "Not without you and Joi. So we crammed into my room and put together a plan. We were about to stage a rescue mission when Mandel came upstairs. Lucky for us, he was there to see me. I had forty-four people hiding in my bathroom when he said he'd make me Dux if I helped him put on a show. Worked out pretty nicely, I'd say."

"Did you start the fire?" I ask.

"*Fires.* There's one in every dorm room. Seems Violet's been lifting matches from the chemistry lab since she got here."

Violet titters.

"But why haven't the alarms gone off?" Joi inquires.

"You can thank Orson and Flora for that. They figured out how to disable the sprinkler and alarm systems. By the time the fire department gets their hoses hooked up, the blaze should be too hot to put out. An old building like this will burn straight to the ground. And now, if you don't have any objections, we should probably get cracking before we all end up barbecued."

I look up and see Mandel's elevator stop on the ninth floor. The top three balconies are already engulfed in flames.

"By the way, who's the suit with the two black eyes?" Ella asks, pointing at someone behind me. "Good guy or bad guy?"

I forgot my father. No one's holding him anymore. I don't think anyone's been watching him, either. He might have escaped. But he's standing there mesmerized. Like he's waiting to see how the show will end.

"Bad guy," I tell her.

"What do you want us to do with him? Send him up in the other elevator?"

"No," I say. "I'm taking him to see the police."

Forty-seven students and one prisoner are walking east. The sun's rising ahead of us, and the streets are still empty. I have a tight grip on my father's elbow and Mandel's Taser jammed into his armpit. Joi and Ella are right ahead of us. When everyone else heads for the colony, they'll be coming to the police station with me.

There's a blast behind us, and I hear glass shower down on the street. I turn to see thick black smoke pouring from the academy's windows and flooding the narrow canyon between the buildings. High above, one of the rooftop towers is now a radiant pyre. The other must have just collapsed. My dad stands with his head tilted back and his arms hanging limp at his sides.

"*Spectacular*, isn't it?" I ask.

"Yes," he responds. That's it. Just *yes*.

"Guess the academy won't be *helping* any more kids."

"It's only a building, Jonathan. If it can't be repaired, it can be replaced."

"Really? Sounds expensive. Who's going to foot the bill?"

He responds with a weary snort. "That's a ridiculous question . . ."

"Is it? Mandel's dead. You're going to jail. And the files are hidden where you'll never find them. So who's going to force the alumni to chip in the millions of bucks it would take to rebuild this place?"

There's a second explosion, this one much louder than the last. I know the glass pyramid above the atrium has caved in when a ball of flames shoots into the sky.

"Game over, Dad. You and Mandel both lost."

I want him to argue, but he only nods. In fact, he seems almost resigned. He turns his back to the blaze and starts walking again. I refuse to let the conversation end until I've been satisfied. It won't feel like a victory if my father accepts his defeat. I hurry to catch up with him.

"So what's it like?" I demand as I match his stride. "To know your own son helped destroy the Mandel legacy? How does it feel to watch the school that *saved* you burn to the ground?"

"Do you really want to know?" he asks. "Will you listen if I tell you?"

"Are you kidding? I'm all ears."

"Beatrice Mandel told me there were only two ways out of the academy, and I never once questioned her. Until a couple of months ago. Remember our drive from the airport? I told you about the choice I'd faced when I was a student. And you claimed that Jude wouldn't have killed Franklin if he'd been in my shoes. When you said he would have done something else, I knew you were right. Jude would have found another way out. So I started to wonder if you'd be able to find one too."

"I didn't," I tell him. "*Joi* did. She saw the way out. I never thought her plan would work."

"But you were smart enough to trust her, weren't you?" He pauses. "I knew the real reason Lucian wanted Joi at the school. He was going to make Joi your Franklin. Or make you hers. One of you would have to kill the other—and then there would be no going back.

"You might not believe this, but the day before Joi entered the academy, I went to Pitt Street with an envelope stuffed with cash— enough money to help Joi disappear. I was waiting outside when she got home. But the second she turned the corner, a bunch of kids rushed out to greet her. Scrawny, filthy, *happy* little kids. I saw that, and I knew Lucian had made a mistake. Joi was never going to play his game. And if she was at the academy, neither would you. So I didn't try to stop her. I let Joi come find you."

I wanted to rub my father's nose in his failure. I wanted him to threaten me. Or beg me to let him go. I grab my father by the tie and shove the Taser under his chin. "What the f— are you saying?" I shout. "Am I supposed to *thank* you for letting Joi risk her life? What if she *had* been my Franklin? What if Mandel *had* made me kill her?"

"He couldn't," my father chokes. His lips are turning blue. He isn't able to breathe.

"Flick?" Joi's seen what's happening. She's rushing over. I push my dad back. He should know how close he came to joining Mandel in hell. He should know that he needs to keep his mouth shut. But he hasn't even paused to catch his breath. He's just kept on talking.

"I've never forgotten the last thing Frank said to me the night he bled to death. I'd wanted it to be quick the way it was with my father, but I'd botched the whole thing. Frank must have been in horrible pain, and I couldn't stand to watch him suffer. So I left him there all alone. But before I went, I heard Frank say he felt sorry for *me*. After it was over, I tried to convince myself that it was proof of how weak he was—that he couldn't even bring himself to hate the person who'd killed him. But I think I always understood what he meant. Frank may have died, but I was the one who'd given up."

"I will never feel sorry for you," I growl. "You killed my brother and murdered my mother. You're a f—ing *monster*."

"If you really believe that, then why didn't you destroy me back there when you had the chance?"

"Why don't I do it right now?"

"Flick, *no!*" Joi grabs hold of me.

"Why not?!"

"She doesn't hate me like you do," my dad says. "Maybe she's able to see something you can't."

"Joi never saw Jude lying dead on an embalming table. She never saw mom bawling her eyes out every time you found where she'd hidden us. Joi never saw you hit a ten-year-old for spilling your Scotch. You can pretend you've had some big epiphany, but I'll always see you for who you are. A liar, a bully, and a murderer.

And I'm going to make sure your little boy knows it too. What's his name, by the way?"

"His name is Frank."

"That's goddamned *sick*. Take this." I thrust the Taser at Joi. "He won't make it to the police station if I'm the one holding it."

I stomp off toward the crowd ahead, leaving Joi to wrangle my father. Ella joins me just as the wail of fire engines reaches my ears. They can't be more than a few blocks away. Without any traffic to stop them, they'll be on the scene within seconds.

"We should break up into smaller groups," Ella notes. When I can't speak, she takes charge. "Split into teams of three or four!" she shouts at the other students. "Head in different directions. We'll meet up again on the corner of Pitt and Rivington."

I check to see if Joi's heard the order. She and my father are standing on the sidewalk half a block behind me. They haven't moved since I gave her the Taser. I see my dad's lips moving. Whatever he's saying has stunned her. I rush back, fists clenched, ready to kill the bastard once and for all. The fire trucks have turned the corner onto our street, and the sirens are deafening. I take Joi's arm. When she looks up at me, there are tears in her eyes.

"What did he tell you!" I shout.

She lifts herself up on her tiptoes. I feel her lips brush my ear. "He says your mother's alive."

My eyes snap up. My father is standing a few inches from the curb. I can't hear his voice, but his words couldn't be clearer.

"I'm not a monster."

Then he takes a step backward into the street. Right in front of the first fire engine.

PETER LIVES

I never saw the body. I never even heard the thump. I was still expecting my father to reappear when I realized Joi had my hand and we both were running.

She kept trying to stop, but I just kept on going. Faster and faster, until she finally tackled me. I remember hitting the ground and wondering why it felt so soft. When I rolled over I saw green leaves and blue sky and Joi's beautiful face.

For a moment I was sure we were both in Never Land. "Where are we?" I heard myself shout. "What is this place? What's happened to us?"

"Shhh, Flick," Joi hushed me. "It's Seward Park. We're safe."

"Where's my dad?" I demanded.

"I'm so sorry." She tried to hug me, but I pushed her back.

"He's not dead! It's some kind of trick! He's a liar, Joi. A big f—ing liar! He told you my mom is alive so I'd just have to lose her again!"

"He gave me an address," Joi replied softly. "It's somewhere up-state. In the Hudson Valley."

"It's a graveyard!" I insisted. "He's a *monster*."

"Maybe he was," Joi said. "But he might not have died one. We'll take the next train we can get."

"I'm not going."

"We're going together."

"But what if . . ." What if she's dead, I thought. What if he'd found another way to hurt me? And what if she's not dead, I wondered. What would it mean? "Not today. Please? Not today."

"All right, then." Joi covered my face with kisses before she whispered, *"Tomorrow."*

I don't know how long we spent lying there on the grass in Seward Park. But when we finally arrived at the colony on Pitt Street, we found our fellow escapees had gotten there hours before we did. It seemed like every inch of the basement had been claimed by a slumbering kid. But they'd left Joi's room just for us. We collapsed on the lumpy old bed with our clothes still on. I kept my arms around Joi and my face buried deep in her hair while I waited for Peter Pan to slip through the window. I thought I needed him to tell me what I should do. But he never showed up. He left me alone with a girl who smelled of jasmine and cocoa butter. And before I fell asleep, I finally realized that was more than enough.

It was three o'clock in the afternoon when Tina knocked and the door burst open. Curly, Dartagnan, and a dozen other kids rushed in to welcome us back. Once they'd all gotten hugs from Joi, Tina ushered them out again. Then she gave us each a cup of strong coffee and handed over an iPhone.

The Mandel Academy was all over the news. The earliest stories had focused on the tragic loss of a beloved institution and the presumed deaths of all the teenagers inside. Then sometime around ten in the morning, the firefighters had found Mandel's lab. The old part of the building may have burned to the ground, but the bottom two floors remained intact. A half hour later, one of New York's Bravest discovered the morgue.

We knew then that it was only a matter of time before the investigation widened. Within hours, any building owned by Lucian Mandel would be locked up and labeled a potential crime scene. So Joi and I hurried to the artist's studio in Greenwich Village, only to find that the alumni files had been moved. They weren't at Mandel's house on Tenth Street either. I wanted to keep looking, but Joi refused. The files could wait, and I needed my rest. Our train would be leaving first thing the next morning.

I argued and pleaded. I wanted her to see that what my father had told her didn't make any sense. He claimed that he'd staged my mother's death. The sedative in the syringe had knocked her out. But the dose wasn't enough to kill her. He swore he was trying to protect her from Lucian Mandel. Even up to the very last moment. Even when I was on the verge of beating him to death. He would have gone to his grave before he'd let Mandel know that my mother was alive.

But like the rest of my dad's stories, it was all a big lie. Why would he have gone to such trouble to save a life he'd tried so hard to ruin?

"I don't know," Joi admitted.

"And even if he *did* hide her away, why did she stay? Why did she let him remarry and father a son? Why didn't she try to find me?"

"I don't know," Joi said. "But if your mother's alive, you need to ask her."

The address my father gave Joi belonged to a Victorian mansion set on a lush, rolling lawn.

"Do you know the name of the people who live here?" Joi asked the cabbie who'd picked us up at the train station.

"It's not a house, miss," he said as he turned up the drive. "It's a mental institution."

The lady at the front desk shook her head when I asked to see Elizabeth Brennan. "We don't have any patients here by that name."

I took a step back, but Joi didn't budge. "What was her maiden name?"

"Chapman," I said.

The woman's brow furrowed. "What's your relation to Beth Chapman?"

Joi nudged me when I didn't speak. "I'm her son."

"Excuse me for a moment." The woman slipped out of her chair. A few seconds later, she returned with a nurse.

The nurse didn't seem pleased to see me. "You say you're Beth Chapman's son?"

"Yes, my name is Jonathan Brennan."

"I'm afraid that's not possible," she announced. "Beth's sons are both dead."

That's why she never tried to find me. He must have told her that I was gone too.

"His brother, Jude, was the one who died," Joi informed the nurse.

"I was . . . I was . . ." I couldn't get the rest out.

"He's been away at school," Joi said. "He just discovered that his mother is here."

"Don't move," the nurse ordered. "I'll be right back."

There was a framed picture in her hand when she marched back into the lobby. The nurse glanced down at the photo of me, Jude, and my mother. When she looked back up, she was smiling.

"Well, what do you know?" the nurse marveled. "Beth told me a few days ago that her son would be coming. She's been waiting for you ever since. The doctor thought her condition had worsened. I wonder what he'll have to say about *this*."

"Can I see her?" I croaked.

"I don't know why not. After all, she's expecting you. Follow me. Beth's room is right down the hall."

"Why is she here?" I asked as the nurse guided us through a security door. "What exactly *is* her condition?"

"Chronic hallucinatory psychosis."

"What does that mean?" I asked.

Joi was the one who answered. "It means she speaks to people no one else can see."

My hands were trembling when I opened the door. I was terrified of what I might find on the other side. A padded room. A lunatic strapped into a straitjacket. A madwoman babbling away at the walls. But I saw a bright, sunny chamber filled with furniture my mother might have chosen herself. A small, blond woman sat by the window, watching as sprinklers watered the endless green lawn. She wore chinos and red espadrilles. Her hair was pulled back in a ponytail, and her linen shirt was the color of the sky.

"You're here!" She was in my arms before I had a chance to say anything. She sounded elated. But she didn't seem surprised.

"Who told you I was coming?" I asked when she finally let me go. "Was it Dad?"

She answered with a smile. A real one.

"Was it Jude?" I bent down and whispered into her ear. "Do you speak to Jude, Mom?"

"Not anymore," she replied. "Jude's in Never Land now."

That night at the colony, Jude sent me one last dream. Peter Pan wasn't in it. This time Jude was just a kid in a T-shirt and jeans.

"You gonna be okay?" he asked me.

"Yeah," I told him. "You?"

"You don't have to worry about me," he promised.

"Then I guess I should go. I'll miss you, Jude."

"You know where to find me. I'm not going anywhere."

I gave him a hug and left him behind. I could hear announcements being made, and I could see strangers milling about in the background. Then I realized I was at JFK Airport, about to board a plane to Savannah. It was the day I left for military school.

I looked over my shoulder. Jude was standing beside my mother, waving at me. I'd forgotten how happy he'd seemed the last time that I saw him. And I suddenly knew why Jude had sent me the dream. That's how he wanted to be remembered.

When I waved back, we both knew what it meant. I'd finally said my goodbye.

In the weeks since the Mandel Academy went up in flames, the whole world has turned upside down. The billionaires and bigwigs who once sat on the school's board of directors are being hounded by the press and the police. The academy's instructors have all been hauled in for questioning. None of them have been charged with a crime yet, but few people believe they could have been ignorant of the atrocities committed in the basement of their workplace. A shadow has fallen over the other Mandel alumni as well. Arthur Klein has visited every news show in the country to warn the public about the dangers of Exceletrex—and to denounce the people who would have profited from poisoning millions of children. A reporter from the *New York Times* is investigating the drug company's links to the Mandel Academy, and most of the school's graduates are now keeping low profiles or hiding out in their homes. Even those who don't need to fear the police or the newspapers are probably quite keen to avoid the Wolves.

Eight of the academy's top students left with files on the fifth of July. Seven alumni were forced to hand over fortunes. Then New York's latest millionaires began living large. Two Wolves quickly wound up in jail—Austin for assault and Julian for drug possession. Five continue to spend their days providing fodder for the city's tabloids, which are filled with breathless accounts of their extravagant shopping sprees, drunken fistfights, and endless displays of debauchery.

The eighth escaped Wolf showed up at the colony.

"How did you find us?" Joi asked.

When Leila grinned, she could have passed for a regular girl. "One of the teachers at the academy asked me to check out a virus created by some kid named Lily. The instructor thought there was something strange about it. She was right. She just wasn't smart enough to figure out what it was. I saw the message you sent to Tina. So the first thing I did when I got out was find Tina. Then I followed her here."

"You knew about the message?" I asked. "You could have had us killed."

"For plotting to set us all free? What kind of person do you think I am, anyway?"

I didn't know how to answer.

"Never mind," Leila said. "I guess I was pretty awful. God knows what all that Exceletrex has done to my brain. But at least I'm trying to change. That's why I'm here. I brought you a present."

I hoped Leila would be our last unexpected visitor. For a while, the whole world seemed convinced that the academy's students had all perished in the fire. But the only bones discovered among the debris belonged to Lucian Mandel. When the newspapers noted the absence of charred human remains, the police began to look for the school's missing students. But we never thought anyone would discover the colony. Then my father's attorney appeared at our door. He was there to tell me that my dad had revised his will so that his fortune would be split between his two living sons. The first thing I did was demand a copy of the document. All I wanted to see was the date. The changes were made the day after I'd been arrested at JFK.

I used my inheritance to buy an apartment for my mother. The doctors say she may be well enough to move in soon. Then I purchased a building on Essex Street, which is already filled with Ghosts, Androids, and Urchins. I donated the rest of the money to Joi's new charity. The Lower East Side Children's Fund.

Life is more comfortable now, but it's no less dangerous. If an attorney can find us, so can the Mandel alumni. They must think we managed to get our hands on their secrets. Otherwise, a few would have declared war by now. Joi and I are still searching for Mandel's files. But we'll find them. And right before we send most of the alumni to jail, we'll put Leila's present to use. She's given us access to every graduate's bank account. Joi's already decided where the funds should go.

I'll always regret that my father chose to die like he did. But these days I have too many good things to enjoy—and too little time to waste on regrets. If I find a free hour, it belongs to my little brother. Frank's mother had always been told I was dead. But when she saw me standing outside her door, she knew I wasn't an impostor. Her son is the spitting image of his two older brothers.

She's selling the mansion in Connecticut. Now that she knows the truth, she says it's too haunted to occupy. Before the brokers descended on the house, she insisted that my mother and I take whatever I wanted. I would have asked for the Rothko, but that wall was already empty.

So my mother and I picked out a few little treasures that belonged to Jude. After he died, his possessions had been packed away and consigned to a dark corner of the attic. That's where I found the box. Inside was a green felt hat, a wooden sword—and every story ever written about Peter Pan.

I gave the box to Frank. When he opens it ten years from now, I'll be there to tell him all about Never Land—and our very own brother who was able to fly. Because Peter Pan can never die. And as long as I'm around, there will always be someone here who believes in him.

Addendum

The following material was found on a flash drive that had been taped to the underside of a desk belonging to Marcos Lauder. A reporter for the *New York Times*, Lauder was reported missing on January 3, 2013.

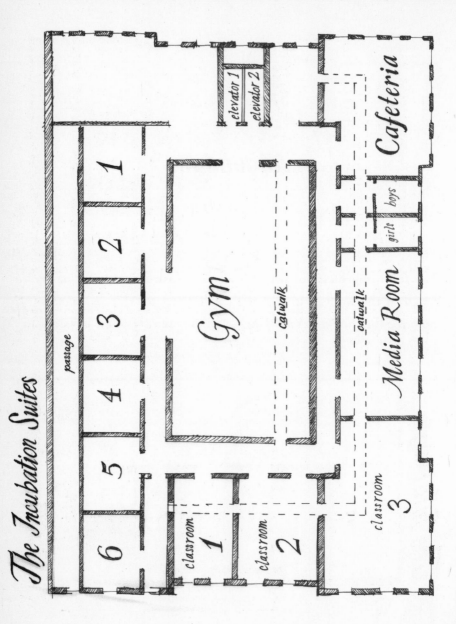

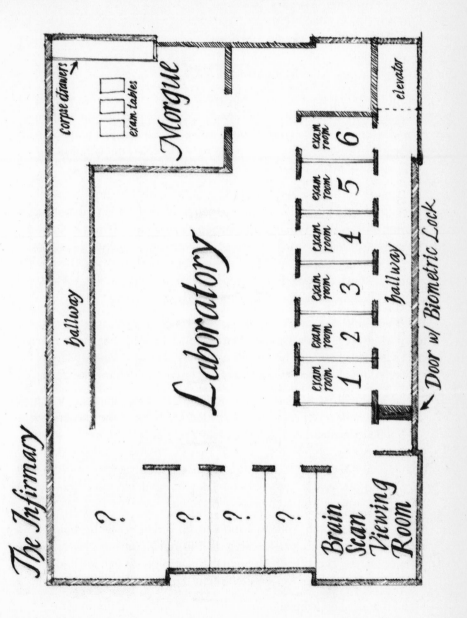

The Infirmary

Morgue

corpse drawers

exam tables

Laboratory

hallway

exam room 1

exam room 2

exam room 3

exam room 4

exam room 5

exam room 6

1 2 3 4 5 6

hallway

elevator

Door w/ Biometric Lock

?

?

?

?

Brain Scan Viewing Room

Lucian Frederick Mandel
Born 1975 in Manhattan
Mother: Beatrice Mandel (b. 1942, d. 2007)
Father: Unknown
Sibling: Marjorie Mandel (b. 1973, d. 2007)

Rumor has it that the father of Marjorie and Lucian Mandel is a living graduate of the Mandel Academy. My sources believe that the man may have been employed by the school when Beatrice was first named headmistress. However, Beatrice never publicly identified the father of her children, and he appears to have played no role in his son's life.

Lucian was enrolled at the Dalton School in Manhattan until November of his fourth grade year, when another child accused him of intentionally injuring a class pet. At that point, Lucian abruptly transferred to College Alpin Beau Soleil, a boarding school in Switzerland. Before the age of fifteen, he made regular trips to visit his mother in New York. The travel appears to have stopped in Lucian's sophomore year. He did not leave Europe throughout his junior and senior years.

By all accounts, Lucian's relationship with his mother became increasingly tense as he grew older. This seems to support the idea that she may have discovered his macabre habits. It's also possible that Beatrice Mandel suspected that her son's crimes were not limited to defiling the dead.

Lucian's time in Switzerland coincided with the disappearance of at least five teenagers from the nearby city of Geneva. Most of the children were long believed to be runaways. However, the recent discovery of several jars of preserved organs in a wooded area not far from College Alpin Beau Soleil has proven that at least one of the teenagers met a grisly fate. There is no physical evidence to link Lucian Mandel to the crime, but the MO fits the one described by Henry Brennan.

Throughout his youth, Lucian Mandel made very few friends, but his money often bought success with girls. Those relationships, however, were extremely short lived. None of the ex-girlfriends I've located are willing to discuss him. Most seem to refuse not out of loyalty, but fear.

Mandel graduated from Harvard in 1995. Despite an unimpressive academic record, he was accepted to the John Hopkins School of

Medicine where he earned an MD. In 2007 he was awarded a PhD in genetics.

Less than a week after Lucian returned to New York, Beatrice Mandel died of a cerebral aneurysm. Her daughter, Marjorie, died the following month in an automobile accident on the West Side Highway. Neither death appears to have been investigated. Autopsies were never performed.

"Gwendolyn"
Real name: Tiffany Hager
Mother: Rhonda Hager

In 2008, Tiffany Hager was a patient at the New Hampshire State psychiatric hospital. Her juvenile criminal records are sealed, but her mother's name links her to this account from the *New Hampshire Union Leader*.

INVESTIGATORS CLEAR MOTHER, FOCUS ON DAUGHTER

Shortly after the body of an eighth man was pulled out of Spectacle Pond on Friday afternoon, Croydon police abruptly shifted the focus of their investigation. The woman who was the prime suspect in the killings has now been cleared of most charges. New information, including forensic evidence uncovered by the Sullivan County Coroner, appears to incriminate the former suspect's underage daughter.

Computer records show that all eight victims had scheduled sexual liaisons at the home of thirty-year-old Croydon native Rhonda Hager on the nights they disappeared. However, security camera footage has placed Ms. Hager at a Sunapee drinking establishment on every evening in question, giving her a solid alibi for the times of death.

Police have not ruled out the possibility that Ms. Hagar may have helped dispose of the bodies, but the woman's thirteen-year-old daughter has become the lead suspect in the case. Bite marks found on three of the bodies appear to match the girl's dental impressions.

Sources close to the investigation are now beginning to doubt that the case will ever come to trial. The girl, herself a victim of abuse and neglect, has a long and well-documented history of psychiatric problems.

"Ella"
Real Name: Dorelle Duncan

Transcript of my telephone call with Jed McKinley, the zoo employee who discovered photographs that showed the assassination of Christopher Jones, the one-time Chicago drug lord. The photos were confiscated by the Illinois State Police. They cannot be located at this time. The police claim they are no longer in evidence.

Q: OK, the recorder is running. Can you please give me your name and the name of your employer?

A: My name is Jed McKinley. I work for the Lincoln Park Zoo.

Q: In Chicago.

A: Yes.

Q: Can you tell me a bit about the work you were doing in Marquette Park in 2011?

A: I was part of a project to assess the biodiversity of the Chicagoland area. We set up hidden wildlife camera traps in multiple parks across the city to see which species were present.

Q: You thought you'd be filming squirrels and birds and such.

A: Yeah. And coyotes and other animals that are pretty good at avoiding humans. That's why we used cameras.

Q: So the cameras were well hidden and activated by motion sensors.

A: That's correct.

Q: You ended up filming more than squirrels. Please tell me what you discovered on the morning of September 13, 2011.

A: I was checking the footage that had been taken in Marquette Park the previous night. There was a camera trap in an overgrown section of the park that would usually snap some great pictures of opossums and raccoons. So I went through those photos first. Halfway through the camera roll, I found about a dozen pictures of a middle-age man and a girl with a gun.

Q: Describe the two for me if you will.

A: Well the man was Christopher Jones. They never released the girl's name. She was African-American. Maybe sixteen or so. Pretty—but hard looking. Her hair appeared white in the photos. She had diamond rings on her fingers.

Q: How many photos did the camera take of the pair?

A: Six. It didn't actually capture the girl shooting Jones. Just a few seconds before and a few seconds after.

Q: But there was no one else there who could have killed the man.

A: No.

Q: Anything else you remember about the photographs? Any details you think might be important?

A: The girl was crying.

Q: Crying?

A: Yeah. In every picture.

Glenn Sheehan
Congressman, Illinois, 14th District

In January 2012, he called for a congressional inquiry into the development of Exceletrex. In March 2012, Sheehan withdrew his support for the investigation. The abrupt shift raised a few eyebrows in Washington.

There were rumors that Sheehan was conducting an extramarital affair at the time. Evidence of the relationship could have been used by Mandel alumni to blackmail the Representative. There may be no way to prove or disprove such speculation.

"Lucas"
Real Name: Brian Ascher
Born: February 18, 1985
Died: Date unknown, 2012

Lucas's family history is well documented and easy to verify. His mother, father, and sister were killed on April 17, 2001, in the crash of Sunshine Airways Flight 2882 from Los Angeles to Atlanta.

The six-year-old boy had no remaining family, other than an aged aunt in a nursing home. He was made a ward of the state and placed in foster care.

In 2011, Lucas was arrested on charges of cyber terrorism. His black hat attack on Sunshine Airways' computer systems had grounded the entire airline for almost a week. Sixteen years old at the time, Lucas was tried as an adult and sentenced to ten years in a minimum security prison.

There is no evidence that Lucas was ever incarcerated. His trail goes cold two days after his sentence was announced.

"Franklin"

True identity unknown and presence at the Mandel Academy impossible to verify. Alumni interviewed do not recall a student by that name.

Marm Mandelbaum

Fredericka "Marm" Mandelbaum was one of the most notorious criminals in nineteenth-century New York. A portly Prussian woman, she worked out of a store at 79 Clinton Street in Manhattan (a building that may still exist today) and made a living fencing stolen goods. She also planned and financed some of the most impressive capers in New York history. But Marm wasn't a common criminal. She threw swanky dinner parties for the city's finest citizens, and was said to be a stickler for good manners.

In the 1870s, Marm started the Grand Street School, an academy for young criminals. There were classes in pocket-picking, safe-cracking, blackmail, and confidence games. Children under the age of ten were welcome to apply, and those who graduated at the top of their class were hired by Marm herself.

The Butcher of Brighton Beach

Aka Vladimir Mingulov
Born: 1968, near Moscow
Currently at Sing Sing Correctional Facility in Ossining, New York, serving four consecutive life sentences.

Almost nothing is known about Mingulov's early life in Moscow. He came to the US sometime in the late 1980s and settled in Brooklyn's Brighton Beach neighborhood (known as Little Odessa for its large Russian population). By 1990, he was working as a hit man for Boris Ivankov, then a mid-level figure in the Russian Mafia. Ivankov's brains and Mingulov's brutality proved to be a potent combination, and the two men quickly rose through the ranks of the organized crime world.

Mingulov may or may not speak English. During his trial, he was provided with a translator. He never spoke a word of any language in court, leading some in the media to speculate that he might be mute. (He is not.) During the height of his career, Mingulov's silence sent a powerful message. Everyone in Brighton Beach knew that when Vladimir Mingulov came to the door, he wasn't there for a chat.

Over the course of twenty years, Mingulov murdered dozens of Boris Ivankov's enemies. (Some experts claim the body count reached three digits.) He was said to be fast, efficient, and absolutely pitiless. Though he employed a wide range of weapons, he enjoyed using his bare hands whenever possible. Given his formidable size (6'6", 235 lbs.), few of his victims would have been able to fight back.

Most of Mingulov's victims vanished without a trace. It was rumored that he dismembered the corpses before disposing of them, earning him the nickname the Butcher of Brighton Beach. However, at Mingulov's trial, it was discovered that his wife, Olga, deserved the title. For the Mingulovs, the murder business was a family affair. Vladimir (and often his son) would provide the bodies, and Olga would dispose of them.

When Vladimir and Olga Mingulov were finally arrested in 2011, the remains of their last four victims were discovered in a hidden subbasement beneath their home.

"Ivan"
Sergei Mingulov
Born: 1995
Died: 2012 (unconfirmed)

Vladimir and Olga Mingulov's only child. Sergei's juvenile records are sealed. However, there is anecdotal evidence suggesting that he had been actively participating in his family's "business" for years before his parents were incarcerated. Only sixteen at the time, Sergei had already built a fearsome reputation among the Brooklyn Russian Mafia. It was said he had inherited both his father's size and cruelty.

When the Mingulovs were arrested, Sergei was declared a ward of the state. He had dropped out of school at the age of twelve, and there is no sign that he ever returned. There is also no record of the boy being placed in a foster home.

I have contacted the Mingulovs. Neither has spoken with Sergei since 2011.

"Felix"
Aka Hector Guerra
Born: 1994?
Died: 2012 (unconfirmed)

Hector Guerra was one of the aliases used by a young man who was arrested for prostitution in Miami, Florida, three times between 2009 and 2011. He told police officers that he had come to America from Cuba with his mother. She died shortly after their arrival, and he began turning tricks to support himself.

According to Jose Garcia, one of the arresting officers, "Hector" was a well-known and beloved character in Miami's law-enforcement community. Famously charming and humorous, the boy was also believed to be highly intelligent. He could have easily avoided arrest, but he attracted cops' attention by handing out large sums of money—mostly to teenage runaways who were at risk of falling prey to the city's pimps.

Trying to free the young man from the sex trade, police arrested "Hector" three times. After his first arrest, he ran away from a foster family. The second arrest was followed by an escape from a juvenile detention facility. Following "Hector's" third arrest, the authorities contacted the Mandel Academy.

"Max"
Alan Davis
Aka Hunter Stone
Born: 1996

One of the "Wolves" who escaped from the Mandel Academy with an alumni file, Alan Davis was recently living in New York City under the name Hunter Stone.

Alan is the child of a Boston surgeon and a former model. His parents learned that their son was free when they saw his picture on the cover of a New York tabloid. The news apparently came as a shock. Their son was imprisoned in 2010 for aggravated assault. They—and two of Alan's siblings—had been the boy's victims. Mrs. Davis had nearly died after the incident.

When I spoke with the Davises, they were clearly afraid for their lives. The NYPD had informed them that they could not arrest the young man since they had no evidence that he was the same boy who had disappeared from a juvenile detention facility in May of 2012.

The rest of the Davis family went underground for several months, only to return to Boston when "Hunter Stone" was arrested for assaulting a traffic cop.

"Aubrey"
Catelynn Cabe
Born: 1995
Died: 2012 (confirmed)

Catelynn grew up in Chickamauga, Georgia. The events that led to her arrest (and later enrollment at the Mandel Academy) are as reported by Jonathan Brennan. She and her nineteen-year-old boyfriend built a meth lab in the basement of her family's home. It exploded, killing Catelynn's parents and boyfriend.

After the incident, she entered the Serenity Center, an elite (and expensive) drug rehabilitation facility near Atlanta. An "anonymous benefactor" footed the bill. Two weeks after Catelynn was admitted to the center, her aunt (and sole living relative) Brittany Cogdill attempted to visit the girl. Ms. Cogdill was informed that her niece had committed suicide.

Catelynn's body was one of the two dozen discovered in the morgue beneath the Mandel Academy. Her fingerprints were matched with those on her arrest record, and her aunt later identified the body. Ms. Cogdill has filed suit against the Mandel Academy's Board of Directors.

"Caleb"
Born: 1994–1995
Died: 2012 (confirmed)

Almost impossible to identify conclusively. He would have been seventeen at the time of his death in July 2012. He claimed to have been at the academy for seven semesters (roughly two years and three months). Therefore, he would have been between the ages of fourteen and fifteen when he entered the school. His corpse was found in the Mandel morgue, but his fingerprints were not on file with any law enforcement agencies. Given the physical description of "Caleb," and assuming he was in fact a true psychopath, there are two promising possibilities:

Carson Hinde: Born in 1994 to a wealthy California family. After several tragic incidents involving family pets, the boy was admitted to a privately run mental institution at the age of eight. The institution's administrators will neither confirm nor deny that Carson is still a patient. Carson's mother is now deceased. His father, when contacted, refused to discuss the boy's whereabouts.

Edward (Eddie) Dean: Born 1995. Raised by a grandmother in rural Alabama. Appeared in New Orleans in 2009 and enrolled in the city's most prestigious prep school. Edward befriended several of the wealthiest students, earned their trust, and then robbed their homes. It's estimated he stole close to $200K worth of jewelry and art. Edward vanished without a trace. His grandmother claims to have had no contact with him in the last three years.

"Violet"
Tabitha Berry
Born: 1997

Tabitha and her three younger siblings were orphaned when their parents died in a car accident in 2010. They were taken in by their mother's cousin, who neglected the younger children, abused the older ones, and embezzled money from the children's trust funds.

Increasingly worried about her siblings' safety, Tabitha decided to act. One night, she spiked her guardian's dinner drink with two crushed sleeping pills. She wasn't aware that the woman had already consumed a cocktail of drugs. The guardian lost consciousness, and Tabitha loaded her brothers and sister into the woman's car. They were halfway across the country when they were pulled over by the police. Tabitha was arrested for driving without a license. At the police station, she learned that her guardian had died. She was then charged with murder.

Tabitha now lives in a building owned by Jonathan Brennan and attends a Manhattan high school for the academically gifted. After her arrest, her brothers and sister had been sent to live with three different foster families. They recently have been reunited.

Simon Hodenfield

An alumnus of the Mandel Academy as well as an instructor ("Mr. Martin"). He is currently under investigation by the NYPD and FBI. Both organizations are trying to determine what role he may have played in the murder of the Mandel students discovered in the academy's basement morgue.

I have been unable link Hodenfield to the (presumed) blackmail of Congressman Glenn Sheehan. However, several employees of the Browning School have been willing to go on the record to accuse Hodenfield of extortion. Three people say they were contacted by Hodenfield, who threatened to release sensitive information about their private lives if his son Nathaniel was ever expelled from the Browning School. (Nathaniel is, by all accounts, a shameless bully and pathological cheater.)

Fortunately the Browning School was able to expel Nathaniel after his father was accused of propositioning several of his son's classmates online. With nothing to trouble their consciences, the school's employees are willing to testify publicly against Hodenfield.

Arthur Klein

A psychopharmacologist previously employed by Moorland Laboratories, makers of Exceletrex. Klein was the first scientist to come forward with his concerns about the drug's potential for causing long-term neurologic damage. He says he decided to blow the whistle on his employers shortly after the death of his six-year-old son, Peter. (Yes, *Peter*.)

Exceletrex

Developed by Moorland Laboratories to treat a range of conditions, including attention deficit hyperactivity disorder, Exceletrex was intended to be marketed as an alternative to Adderall and Ritalin. It is said to improve mental focus, inhibit impulsive behavior, and promote docility. Initial laboratory tests were encouraging. However, animal subjects (both rats and nonhuman primates) eventually began displaying signs of premature senility. Those findings were removed from all official documents.

According to Arthur Klein, Exceletrex was initially touted as a treatment for psychopathy. However, key figures at Moorland Laboratories became convinced that the drug was not well suited for persons with the disorder. While Exceletrex might help combat a psychopath's impulsive behavior, it would not make him/her less violent. In fact, by improving mental focus, Exceletrex could exacerbate obsessive tendencies.

This might have sounded ideal to Lucian Mandel. He had no interest in curing psychopathy. But by focusing his "predators" on a single goal (graduating from the Mandel Academy), they would have been far easier to control.

"Ms. Smith"

Cassandra Keene, former anchor on the Fox Business Network. Won the Miss New York pageant in 1998. Second runner up in the Miss America pageant. Resigned from her position at Fox in 2011 when rumors began to circulate that she had assaulted an intern. No charges were ever pressed.

"Austin"

Born: 1994
Real name: Jared Holt
Currently on Rikers Island awaiting trial on three counts of aggravated assault.
Below is a transcript of an interview with him.

Q: According to your police file, your name is Jared Holt.
A: If that's what it says, I suppose it must be right. [Big, wide smile. No sign of anxiety.]
Q: They were able to identify you using your fingerprints. You must have a juvenile record, but it appears to be sealed. How many times have you been arrested?
A: Is there a reason you need to know? Who are you again, anyway?
Q: I'm a reporter. I work for the New York Times.
A: The cops claim I beat up some bar bouncers. That the sort of thing that makes the news here in New York? Where I come from, that's just a regular Saturday night.
Q: And where is it you come from?
A: [Big smile.]
Q: Judging by your accent, I'd say East Texas.
A: [Big smile.]
Q: There was a Jared Holt in Beaumont who killed a kid on his football team.
A: That was just a prank that got out of hand.
Q: You thought forcing a fifteen-year-old to drink a half-gallon bottle of grain alcohol wouldn't do him any damage?
A: [Big smile.]
Q: You seem to have disappeared right after you got arrested. Where have you been for the past two years?

A: Around.

Q: I have it on good authority that you were a student at the Mandel Academy. Is it true?

A: Who's your good authority?

Q: I'm afraid I can't reveal my sources.

A: Then I'm afraid I can't answer your question. In fact, I think I'm through answering any questions.

Beatrice Mandel

Born: 1942
Died: 2007

Beatrice Mandel became headmistress of the Mandel Academy in 1975, following the death of her father, Frederick. The school thrived under Beatrice's management, and she was respected by the alumni and the academy's board of directors. Former students recall her "fairness."

Those who knew Beatrice socially often describe her as cold and robotic. She was highly intelligent and physically attractive (tall, blond, athletic), yet she seemed to be missing a soul. According to a neighbor who lived in the same Fifth Avenue apartment building as the headmistress, Beatrice "wasn't quite human." The man recalled an incident in which Beatrice demanded that another neighbor's new puppy be euthanized after it urinated in the building's elevator.

Beatrice's daughter, Marjorie, is said to have been her mother's clone. Neither of the women appeared to possess much interest in the opposite sex (or any sex at all). And although the family was wealthy, they lived quite simply. The Fifth Avenue apartment they occupied was still in the Mandel family at the time of Lucian Mandel's death. Investigators say that the furnishings and appliances all dated to the early 1970s. Beatrice hadn't purchased anything new since she had inherited the apartment from her father.

"Average Gamblers"
A lady senator.
A CEO.

Two big-shots from Goldman-Sachs.
A businesswoman who'd flown in from China.
And some dude with a scraggly beard and camouflage pants.

Henry Brennan
Real name: Patrick O'Conner
Born: 1966
Died: 2012

Former CEO of the Westman Group. Attended the Mandel Academy
1982–1985. Graduated from Yale in 1989. Married Elizabeth Chapman
in 1993. The couple had two sons: Jonathan and Jude. Married Eva
Nelson in 2011. Their son Franklin was born in June 2012. Henry
Brennan died in July after being hit by a fire engine arriving on the scene
of the Mandel Academy fire.

"Julian"
Real name: James (Jimmy) Matsujiro
Born: 1995

Fourth generation Hawaiian, he comes from a family of Japanese ancestry.
Currently in the Tombs, awaiting trial on drug charges. His father, Thomas
Matsujiro, has made repeated attempts to contact his son since he
learned of the boy's imprisonment, but James refuses to speak to anyone but his lawyers. Mr. Matsujiro says his son became involved with
a Honolulu street gang in 2008. He stopped attending school in 2009
and was arrested for drug possession later that year. In early 2010, James
was questioned in connection with a fatal drive-by shooting in the Kalihi
neighborhood in Honolulu. He disappeared shortly after that, and his
parents assumed he had been murdered by members of a rival gang.

"Leila"

From: XXXXX@gmail.com
Date: Wednesday, August 15, 2012 12:11PM
To: XXXXX@gmail.com
Subject: Your Questions

My name is Selam. That's all I can tell you. I grew up in the Midwest.
My parents came from Yemen. I have four older sisters. They were all
married before they turned 18. My father chose their husbands. I didn't
want to spend my life as a slave to the men in my family. When I was
thirteen, I ran away from home. I had taught myself how to hack using the
computers at school. I was never allowed to have one at home. When I left,
I needed a way to support myself. I broke into a classmate's home and stole
his computer. I used it to empty my father's bank account. I was on my way
to Los Angeles when I was stopped by a police officer who thought I looked
too young to be traveling alone. My family didn't want me back. My father
pressed charges. Lucian Mandel had me released into his custody.

The
MANDEL
ACADEMY

Course Catalog
Early Winter/Spring 2012

The Fundamentals of Business

The ideal course to kick start any business-related career. Polish your math skills. Study basic economic theory. Master the use of key terms and industry jargon. Acquire all the skills necessary for creative accounting, embezzlement, and most forms of fraud.

Assassination Techniques

An advanced course for Enforcement majors (at least three semesters required). Learn to recognize and defeat measures commonly used to protect prominent persons—from traditional forms of defense (bodyguards and body doubles) to the latest high-tech tools (personal armor and information technology).

Human Psychology

No matter what your major, an understanding of *Homo sapiens* will be the basis of a successful career. This course will teach you how to trace human behavior—from sexual promiscuity to mate selection—back to its evolutionary roots. You'll discover how the human brain was wired to address threats to the species' survival—and learn why concepts like altruism have been rejected by modern science.

The Art of Persuasion:
Influence Peddling, Coercion, and Extortion

The art of persuasion demands information. Learn how to dig for dirt on rivals or enemies—and how to use sensitive information for your benefit. An essential course for all Mandel students, the class offers instruction on basic electronic surveillance, informant recruitment, trashcan espionage, and more.

Hand to Hand Combat

Required for Enforcement majors and recommended for all students, this class will help you acquire the skills and training necessary to engage in short-range combat. This course borrows techniques from boxing, wrestling, Krav Maga, ninjutsu, and a variety of other disciplines. You will learn the basics of unarmed combat, knife-fighting, and the use of improvised weapons.

International Politics

Wherever war rages, there are fortunes to be made. In this class, Mandel's Politics and Business majors will learn how to work hand-in-hand to profit from the sale of weapons, medicines, and black-market goods in war-torn areas around the globe. Politics majors will focus on promoting conflicts and awarding lucrative war contracts to Mandel-associated companies. Business majors will identify new opportunities and explore novel tactics—from the sale of fissionable material to the use of child soldiers.

Wealth Management

Once you've made your fortune, you'll need to protect it. This useful course will teach you how to avoid sharing your hard-earned wealth with the United States government. Hide your money in places the IRS can't look. Make use of tax loopholes designed to help the wealthiest citizens. Or renounce your US citizenship altogether and choose a new homeland where the rich stay rich and the poor keep quiet.

Partnering with Corrupt Regimes

Sometimes the best partners are those with whom no one is allowed to work. The United States government has forbidden American companies to trade with countries it has labeled State Sponsors of Terrorism. Doing business with Iran, North Korea, and Burma may be tricky, but it's far from impossible. And the profits can be astronomical. This semester, two of the Mandel Academy's most illustrious graduates will be visiting this course as guest lecturers. For an entire week, these famous billionaire brothers will share their experiences making money in Iran.

Basic Electronics :
From Credit Card Skimmers to Key Stroke Loggers

A required course for all Technology majors, this class will ensure that you're up-to-date on the basics. Learn how to craft simple devices that can skim credit and debit card information. Construct hardware-based loggers that will record every keystroke (and password) made on a target computer. The fundamentals of surveillance are also covered, including instruction on assembling eavesdropping equipment, covert listening devices, and roving bugs.

Crime Scene Cleaning and Bio-Waste Removal

A required course for Enforcement majors. When business gets messy, Mandel alumni need cleaners. This class will teach you how to scrub a scene of bodily fluids, remove trace evidence such as fingerprints and hair samples, and dispose of human remains. Only students with the strongest stomachs should enroll.

Human Trafficking in the Internet Age

The international trade in human beings is a booming industry, and the Internet has made it safer and more lucrative than ever before. Learn how to set up shop online using Deep Web resources—or riskier classifieds sites. Recruit employees, procure goods, and attract potential customers. An excellent course for Technology and Leisure Studies majors.

Mining the Masses:
Big Profits from Little People

Many students leave the academy with their eyes peeled for a single big score. But those with a little patience find it can be just as rewarding. Some of the largest fortunes in America were built a few cents at a time. Figure out how to take a quarter from every person in America, and you'll end up with a $75 million fortune. This course will show you how.

Introduction to Industrial Espionage

The most successful companies keep a very close eye on the competition. This course will teach future business leaders all the tricks of the trade—from planting moles inside rival organizations to executing successful "bag-ops." You'll learn how to steal trade secrets, bribe key executives, and penetrate computer networks. Top students will be allowed to take part in off-site assignments.

Waste Management:
Polluting for Profit

The world's companies produce over 400 metric tons of hazardous wastes every year. Environmentally safe disposal of these materials can be costly. Fortunately, there are many cheaper alternatives. This course will teach you how, when, and where to dump everything from radioactive substances to used batteries.

Hidden Treasures:
Finding and Controlling the World's Natural Resources

Many of the Earth's natural resources are on the brink of depletion, and most are ripe for hoarding. When the world realizes that the planet's supply of water, oil, and minerals is dwindling, the demand will quickly skyrocket. Companies or individuals who have seized control of these profitable resources will soon become the most powerful on Earth.

Brazilian Jujitsu

Required for Enforcement majors under six feet in height. One of the deadliest martial arts, Brazilian Jujitsu takes size and strength out of the equation. With a knowledge of BJJ techniques, a small fighters can easily immobilize, injure, or kill a much larger opponent. A favorite of law enforcement and security professionals, BJJ is essential for those who may need to confront them.

Let Them Eat Cake:
Exploiting America's Obesity Epidemic

The ultimate consumers, Americans will buy and eat almost anything. As the country's waistband continues to grow, so does the opportunity for profit. Discover out how Mandel alumni have invested in the artificial flavor industry, chemical sweetener manufacturing, and health care insurance—and learn how to live large off the fat of the land.

The Ultimate Insiders:
Mandel Alumni and the SEC

Once upon a time, the Securities and Exchange Commission watched over the US stock and bond markets, ensuring that trade was fair and laws were not violated. For the past three decades, Mandel alumni have been infiltrating this venerable institution. Now, the SEC works for us, and this course will teach you how to use your academy connections to their best advantage.

Secrets and Sabotage

You've discovered your mark's deepest, darkest secret. (Or perhaps you've invented one for him.) Now what do you do with it? This course, required for all Human Resources majors, teaches students how to conduct successful smear campaigns and character assassinations.

Clandestine Chemistry

The most successful narcos control every step of the drug trade—from production to distribution. That's why a crash course in "secret" chemistry is essential for all Leisure Studies students. Learn how to build a cocaine processing facility in the South American jungle—or rolling meth lab in Appalachia. Find out how to purchase precursor chemicals without tipping off the DEA. And know how to cover your tracks if you have to leave your lab behind.